NEBRASKA HAVEN

ANDREW ROTH

COPYRIGHT NOTICE

Nebraska Haven
First edition. Copyright © 2023 by Andrew Roth. The information contained in this book is the intellectual property of Andrew Roth and is governed by United States and International copyright laws. All rights reserved. No part of this publication, either text or image, may be used for any purpose other than personal use. Therefore, reproduction, modification, storage in a retrieval system, or retransmission, in any form or by any means, electronic, mechanical, or otherwise, for reasons other than personal use, except for brief quotations for reviews or articles and promotions, is strictly prohibited without prior written permission by the publisher.

This is a work of fiction. Names, characters, businesses, places, events, locales, and incidents are either the products of the author's imagination or used in a fictitious manner. Any resemblance to actual persons, living or dead, or actual events is purely coincidental.

Cover and Interior Design: Derinda Babcock, Deb Haggerty
Editor(s): Cristel Phelps, Deb Haggerty

PUBLISHED BY: Elk Lake Publishing, Inc., 35 Dogwood Drive, Plymouth, MA 02360, 2023

Library Cataloging Data

Names: Roth, Andrew (Andrew Roth)
Nebraska Haven / Andrew Roth
368 p. 23cm × 15cm (9in × 6 in.)

ISBN-13: 978-1-64949-878-6 (paperback) | 978-1-64949-879-3 (trade hardcover) | 978-1-64949-880-9 (trade paperback) | 978-1-64949-881-6 (e-book)

Key Words: Christian Westerns; Oregon Trail; Civil War; spiritual growth; faith; historical romance; Old West

Library of Congress Control Number: 2023xxxxxx Fiction

DEDICATION

To the brave men and women who settled the American Great Plains, enduring untold hardship with a steadfast faith.

"Be strong and courageous, do not be afraid or discouraged, for the Lord your God will be with you, wherever you go."

—Joshua 1:9

PROLOGUE

"Where's that go?" Murphy growled to no one in particular, gesturing to the dim path that snaked through the hills to the south. He knew few of the troopers in the patrol would reply, having cheated most of them on more than one occasion. However, he didn't recognize this trail, and it was always important to gather information. Information was power.

The twin columns of Union troopers cantered along the Oregon Trail, the wide and dusty road leading through the Nebraska hills in the afternoon sun west of Fort Kearny. Yet the unfamiliar path that led toward the river irritated Murphy, and he sighed, knowing he'd have to speak with Thornton if he truly wanted answers.

He glanced to the Christian who rode beside him, the only soldier in the regiment willing to ride this close to him. Thornton seemed amiable, despite Murphy's endless jibes. Thornton never gambled his pay and always sent his earnings home to his family in Ohio.

Murphy rubbed a gloved hand across his whiskered chin, then scratched his arm through the heavy woolen regulation jacket. He scowled as he scanned the silent troopers around him once more, searching for any other soldier who might answer him. Up ahead, Lieutenant Alcott slowed the column and indicated the patrol turn into the faint trail Murphy had noticed. The horses' heads hung weary, but their hooves moved forward eagerly into the narrow track, sensing nearby water.

Murphy squinted at Thornton. "All right, where are we?"

At first, the Christian didn't reply, and Murphy sighed again, louder this time. "Thornton, I don't remember this trail," he said, gesturing to the narrow track the patrol now followed.

"No reason you should," Thornton finally replied. "This road is fairly new. Hazlett the hunter built himself a stone house along Peach Tree Creek, and he's widened this path to the spring, trying to get the stage contract."

At the head of the troopers, Lieutenant Alcott sagged in his saddle. The officer seemed at ease, as if he knew where he were headed. Murphy glanced over his shoulder to the well-defined emigrant trail that now slipped from view as the soldiers rode deeper into the hills bordering the north bank of the Platte River.

Murphy studied the unfamiliar track, barely wide enough for a wagon. Bare earth revealed recent work, as if someone had toiled to widen the new road. A shallow stream broke from a deep ravine, and Murphy stared at the clear water as dust sifted through the slanting rays of the westering sun. Shadows stretched across the path, a welcome relief from the open prairie and heat of the early summer plains they left behind.

With a grunt, Murphy spit into the road, his hatred of the Great Plains roiling in his guts. He wouldn't miss this forsaken land when his enlistment ended in a couple of weeks. He hoped the eruption of the new war back east wouldn't prolong his time in the army.

He glanced over his shoulder again, but the Oregon Trail had vanished. He'd never traveled this shortcut, and unlike the other troopers of the patrol who slumped listlessly in their saddles, Murphy felt alert as he gazed everywhere, scanning the new route, searching for ... He scratched the graying whiskers along his jaw. Searching for what? Why should he care about this new path to the river or a stage contract to the hunter from the fort?

Murphy frowned and relaxed, imitating the other soldiers as they made their way through the short knolls. He would be leaving Nebraska Territory soon, and whatever he saw today would be forgotten in a month when he returned to the east. A grin tugged at his weathered features as he thought of the night life of Philadelphia and the dives along the waterfront there. He wanted so badly for his enlistment to end and to return to normal life. No more patrols in the blistering heat or bone-chilling cold, no more helping pioneers as they navigated the cursed trail along the Platte. No, he shouldn't care about any stone house or stage contract or anything else around Fort Kearny. With less than a month left of his enlistment time, he'd already cleaned the regiment out of everything of value.

Murphy sneered at the soldier beside him out of the corner of his eye. All except Thornton. Only the Christian hadn't played dice or cards or made bets on shooting practice.

He pressed his lips into a thin line as he scanned his blue-jacketed companions. They all hated him, but perhaps with good reason.

Beside the trail, the steep walls of the ravine dropped away as the shallow stream gurgled merrily. The track broadened, and the patrol rode into a clearing—almost a small valley—with some level ground and a pair of structures at one end. A trio of deer grazed along the ridge. Murphy's bushy eyebrows bunched as he surveyed the large stone building ahead, six glass windows staring back at him. The other squat structure was also of native limestone, cut into the side of a hill. Probably a barn, he mused, noticing the stream that wound behind the barn and disappeared into the distant line of trees marking the river.

The lieutenant held up a hand, and the sergeant called a halt as the column approached the big house. A tall man in buckskin pants, his shirt sleeves rolled up, stepped from the smaller building—the one Murphy believed to be the barn—a pitchfork in one hand. He grinned when he saw the army patrol.

"Howdy, Lieutenant. Welcome," he called, striding forward to shake the officer's hand.

"Who's that?" Murphy demanded as the troopers were permitted to dismount. He arched his back and stretched his legs, keeping his gaze fixed on the stranger.

"Hazlett," Thornton said, leading his horse to the creek.

"The hunter?" Murphy couldn't recall the lean man from the fort.

"Yep. He hunts meat for the garrison. They say he found some gold in California and came back here to set up shop."

No one else spoke as the tired men allowed their mounts to drink from the small stream. Murphy knelt and scooped water, drinking enough to slake his thirst. A cavalryman always drinks what's available and holds his canteen water in reserve. Murphy tried to hide his surprise as he tasted the fresh, cool water.

"I'm pleased to know about this water," he mumbled, glancing upstream. But it irked him he'd been unaware of this hidden oasis on the prairie, tucked in the hills between the river and the emigrant trail.

Thornton nodded. "Well, no reason why you should know about Peach Tree Creek. Only Hazlett's new trail allows access to the big trail. This water flows from a limestone cave." He turned to greet the approaching hunter. "Well, Hazlett, you did what you set out to do. The place is coming along fine."

NEBRASKA HAVEN

Hazlett and the Christian shook hands, and Murphy frowned again, annoyed that he should care when he'd told himself to not get involved. He'd be leaving soon. Philadelphia beckoned. But then he shrugged, accepting the inner drive to take advantage of those around him. He was, after all, a pirate at heart. He couldn't deny it. And a pirate must seek treasure.

He led his horse back to the center of the yard, leaned his forearms across his saddle, and studied the stone house once more. Out here on the plains, treasure came in various packages. Beggars couldn't afford to be choosy.

Hazlett stepped forward and helped a trooper scrape a rock from his horse's hoof. Murphy leaned close to Thornton.

"How'd he build this place? Where'd he get the stone?"

Thornton ignored Murphy's question for a moment while they watched the lieutenant stride to the shade of a cottonwood, indicating an extended break at the hunter's homestead. Then Thornton nodded, his eyes brightening, obviously pleased to be asked about the new construction.

"He works on this place when he isn't hunting meat for the fort. A couple of soldiers helped him in their spare time. Men from York who used to cut stone in the quarry. He figures to build this stone house as protection from the Indians if they try to burn him out and to let rooms to travelers on the stage."

Murphy scoffed. "Stage? Why would the stage come here?"

Thornton deliberated, shaking his head as he gestured to the northern hills. "Why, the Oregon Trail lies yonder, barely a stone's throw. The location couldn't be better."

Murphy winced when Thornton shot a friendly grin his way. Usually, the older Irishman would have nothing to do with this religious farmer. But something drove him on, pushed him to learn more.

"But what about the soddy at Fort Kearny? I thought that was the stage stop for this region." He glanced from the two-storied stone structure to the stone barn, half dug from a nearby hillside, as he stroked his bristled chin.

Thornton laughed and rolled his eyes. "Have you been inside that soddy? Dirt floor and dark walls. Mice everywhere, filthy—the man who runs it is always drunk. I've heard folks complain about that place more than once. Hazlett built this to get the stage contract. He's even widening the trail through the woods along the river to accommodate wagons. It's already a better ford than the one closer to the fort."

Murphy stared, watching the hunter speak with the lieutenant as the troopers milled, enjoying the break. He chewed his lip, feeling the familiar sensation build within him as his mental wheels turned. The location was ideal. The buildings were of better construction than any others he'd seen on the prairie. The road through the hills was wide enough for wagons and led to the emigrant trail. Thornton said there was a good ford across the river. Good water and rooms to let upstairs.

"Welcome, men," Hazlett boomed as he approached the resting troopers and reached for the pitchfork leaning against the barn. "Welcome to Peach Tree Creek." He forked a bundle of hay to the lieutenant's horse. "I'm working on putting up prairie hay for travelers, and I hope to one day build a water trough, but all in good time." He pointed back into the hills. "There's a limestone bluff back yonder where the spring originates. An old peach tree is there, planted who knows when."

The hunter indicated the building. "What do you think of the house?"

Murphy said nothing but listened attentively.

"Hazlett, you've done well," Thornton said. "Any news on the stage contract?" He looked to the south, and Murphy followed his gaze, seeing the telltale fringe of woods that bordered the Platte River and the hacked limbs revealing a dim trail through the brush.

"Not yet," the hunter answered, resting the fork against the wall of the barn. "Let me show you around." He took off with a quick step, eager to show off his construction.

Hazlett led a few of the interested soldiers toward the tall stone building, Murphy tagged along with a deepening curiosity. A trooper with a thick beard spoke up.

"Hazlett? It gets mighty cold out here in Nebraska come winter. How do you suppose you'll keep that big house warm?"

"These hills to the north help block the wind. I have a rock fireplace at the east side of the sitting room and the kitchen stove on the west side. That big room is half the downstairs. Plenty of fuel at hand with the trees of the river so close. For the sleeping rooms, folks will have to use bed warmers. A brick in a burlap sack works mighty well, I'm figuring. Besides," the hunter added with a grin, "it's sure better than the station at Kearny. With the war on now, I expect more travel across the plains. Come," he invited, gesturing to the front door. "Take a look."

Murphy wanted to take the lead as the pack of soldiers moved toward the house, but he hung back, watching everything carefully. The long, two-storied structure had a front door in the middle of a wide porch that ran the entire length of the building. As Murphy stepped into the entry, he saw a side door opened to the left, revealing the large sitting room and kitchen Hazlett had described. A pair of doors on the right revealed two small bedrooms. A staircase directly ahead led to the four additional bedrooms upstairs. A pantry cleverly built beneath this staircase could be accessed from the kitchen. No basement.

Murphy interrupted Hazlett's tour, unable to contain his interest. "Why is there no basement?"

"I'm no digger," Hazlett explained. "I had enough of that in the California mines."

Murphy considered as he surveyed the layout. A fine house, to be sure. Anyone could see the advantages of this station over the one in town.

"Prepare to mount!" the sergeant shouted from outside, and the troopers hastened to move into position. Murphy peered longingly over his shoulder at the stone house as he found his horse.

"Mount!"

With one fluid movement, the soldiers threw a leg over their horses, and the twin columns moved toward the river. With a final glance over his shoulder, Murphy watched Hazlett wave to them as the house and barn slipped from view behind a screen of trees. Looking around, he saw recent evidence of saw and axe. The trail seemed wide through the stunted undergrowth that bordered the river.

A dip over the low bank and the troop forded the shallow river with ease. The Platte River was not deep here. Thornton was right. This ford seemed much better than the one the current stage route followed.

A quick four miles took the weary patrol back to Fort Kearny. The short trek was not nearly enough time for Murphy to ponder on this sudden turn of events. He could feel his pirate heart tingling with anticipation. Murphy immediately recognized the advantages of the new stage station. Better built, better ford, better water, warmer in winter, the place held so many advantages over the dilapidated building in Kearny. A stage contract would ensure a modest income. If he learned in time that he did not like the stage station business, he could always sell and leave. Murphy saw no reason why he shouldn't own this fledgling venture. He must have time to think, to plan. How would he acquire Hazlett's station?

NEBRASKA HAVEN

The city lights of Philadelphia could wait while Murphy capitalized on one last deal on the Great Plains. Back east, the newly elected lawyer from Illinois had stirred a hornet's nest of controversy. War soon followed, and Murphy had no desire to find himself in combat. But perhaps none of that would concern him. He could temporarily shelf his hatred of Nebraska. The country was nothing special compared to the woods of Pennsylvania, but the allurement of easy money was difficult for him to ignore. The stage station appeared a sure thing.

Murphy grinned. Like taking candy from a baby.

CHAPTER I

Jill Foster drummed her fingertips on the windowsill, closed one eye, and squinted. If you simply looked at the nearby trees, not allowing the eye to drift to the far reaches of the busy riverfront beyond, you would never know a war was going on. She opened her eye and studied the trees of the park sprawling below her gaze, focusing on the beautiful, stately oaks and bright emerald lawns.

Green leaves shimmered and swayed in the early summer breeze. Jill stood at her dormitory room window and watched the people pass on the sidewalk below. Paducah was quiet this time of day, but nicely dressed shoppers mingled with businessmen in frock coats. An occasional woman walked with a child, or a shopkeeper talked to a customer.

The scene reminded her of days gone by, simple and carefree. She frowned, wishing things could be as before when there was no war. She wrapped her arms around her waist, hugging herself tightly, trying to retain former ways. Why did things have to change? She grimaced, remembering only a month ago this very park had been covered with the wounded from the Battle of Shiloh.

A shiver snaked down her back, recalling the gruesome sight of bloody men strewn haphazardly on the manicured green lawn below. Today, however, the park lay serene and disclosed no signs of that upsetting tragedy.

Suddenly a blue-clad soldier strode intrusively into view. Jill huffed as she hastily turned from the window, hating to be reminded of alterations that had come unbidden to her tiny corner of the world.

A blast from the distant riverboat interrupted her reverie, its smokestacks barely visible through the dense foliage of the park. Jill pursed her lips, reluctant to leave but knowing she must hurry to catch the awaiting steamer. She glanced a final time from her window, straining to see the gleaming ripples of the Tennessee River bordering the park. Her vision blurred as she recalled fond memories the room had provided. Then her gaze detected more soldiers in dark blue uniforms moving along the docks, and she bit her lip and turned away.

Yankees were such an inconvenience, she supposed as she stuffed her last dress into her valise. Though Jill was opposed to slavery in theory, she felt irritated to see blue uniforms all around her. Whether here in Kentucky where she taught or at home in her native Missouri, it seemed the blue devils were like a swarm of invading ants, destroying the Southern way of life. The only life she'd ever known.

Slavery was an abomination, to be sure. But to push into the South and wreak havoc was deplorable too. Jill knew many people who'd lost everything to the destructive invasion of the Yankees.

She placed the last of her personal belongings in her brightly colored satchel and closed the bag, again wishing the war were not happening.

With a final survey around her now bare room, she hoisted the heavy luggage and walked to the door.

"Oh, Jill, I didn't know anyone was still here," a kind voice surprised her in the hallway.

NEBRASKA HAVEN

Jill recognized the nasal tone of the Northern girl before she turned to greet her. "Hello, Mary," Jill replied, a muscle twitching along her jaw. "Yes, I'm still here. Just finished packing," she added, unable to conceal the genuine sadness in her voice.

Mary frowned. "I know. It's hard to believe it's true. I've been here two years, and I know you were here before me. I worked so hard to get hired as a teacher. Now it's over, and I'll be lucky to find work elsewhere."

Jill nodded, not wanting to think about the improbability of future prospects. Moving toward the stairs, hoping the other girl would not follow, Jill walked past her and descended to the ground floor. Despite her wishes, she heard Mary clumping on her heels.

"Ladies," a gruff voice accosted the two young women as they halted on the final step. Mr. Hopkins stood by the foot of the wide stairs, his threadbare suit looking more rumpled than usual.

Jill felt relieved for the opportunity to lower her heavy carpetbag. "Good afternoon, Mr. Hopkins. I guess this is goodbye for real." She took the outstretched hand of the older man.

He shook his head. "I'm afraid it is, Miss Foster. We tried valiantly to keep our doors open, but enrollment has declined rapidly during the past year—and even before."

The schoolmaster scowled and glanced out the open front door at the park across the street. "Ever since Lincoln's election," he mumbled. He looked back at the young ladies and sighed, a wounded look in his eyes. "Perhaps when this wicked war is over, we can return and continue our work."

Mary stretched a gloved hand forward to shake the headmaster's hand. "Well, Mr. Hopkins, it has been a privilege working here. Thank you for the opportunity, and

I hope to hear from you when that chance arises. I have given my contact information to the clerk." Mary bent to retrieve her solitary suitcase and then brushed a loose strand of hair from her face. "Will you be walking to the docks, Jill?"

Jill nodded. "I will join you in a moment, Mary."

Understanding Jill's veiled implication, Mary's eyebrows bunched as her lips puckered. She nodded curtly to Mr. Hopkins before marching from the great lobby, her back rigid as she descended another flight of stairs to the sidewalk.

Mr. Hopkins and Jill watched her go, neither speaking for a moment. As Mary crossed the street and entered the park, Mr. Hopkins cleared his throat.

"She was a good teacher, though often ignorant of our ways."

Jill glanced sharply at the headmaster, surprised at his candor. Then she thought of the Northern girl and her extremely tolerant views, both politically and socially. "Yes, she struggled with understanding Southern patterns of conduct and reserve." Bending to fetch her own bag, Jill looked at the schoolmaster. "Thank you, Mr. Hopkins, and I look forward to hearing from you as soon as the ladies' college is reopened. Or should you locate another post, please keep me in mind."

"You will be my first consideration, Miss Foster," Mr. Hopkins promised. "You're a fine teacher."

"Thank you. Have a good day, sir."

Jill joined Mary where the other teacher waited under the shady branches of a huge oak tree. Together, they made their way across the soft turf as Jill remembered the uniformed men lying here in pain only a few short weeks ago. She had walked among them, serving water. Occasionally, she'd even found a gray clad soldier whom she tried to encourage and comfort.

Surveying the green acres around her, Jill winced. Manicured hedge rows indicated shaded walking paths, cool and discreet where couples took romantic strolls. Yet Jill couldn't erase the memory of the bloody bodies scattered under the spreading branches of the grand trees, many of the stately old oaks over a hundred years old.

Quiet as a graveyard, the park seemed eerily peaceful now, its somber silence seeping into Jill's soul. She shuddered and picked up her pace, eager to reach the distant docks.

A shrill whistle split the air, and Jill peered through the trees, sighting the waiting steamboat. Workmen bustled about the waterfront, the dirty laborers moving incessantly from the piles of goods on shore to the open decks, piling the materials slated for distant ports.

The pair of teachers slowed and then halted under the protection of the final shade tree of the park, as if reluctant to leave the lives they'd known behind. For a moment, they stared, watching the hullabaloo before them. Jill glanced over her shoulder, wondering if she'd ever see Paducah again—the little Kentucky city perched on the banks of the Tennessee River where it joined the larger Ohio River. Jill's heart felt heavy in her chest as she thought of the past three years, her coveted position at the ladies' college, where the finest Southern families sent their daughters to be educated in the ways of social graces. Finally, the war could no longer be ignored or overlooked. As the conflict ensued, student enrollment had dwindled.

Her gaze returned to the river, waves rippling in the afternoon sun as Jill noticed the waiting steamboat and lifted a hand to shield her eyes. Scanning the crowd, Jill searched for a place to wait while dock workers rushed up and down the gangplank, loading materials and supplies. Mary moved to a nearby awning and seated herself on a crate, fanning herself as she watched the activity about her.

Jill sighed, not really wanting to join this other teacher from her school but considering it far too impolite to simply ignore her. Jill liked her own company and preferred to be alone. Especially today as she thought of her return home.

Moving carefully through the crowd, she found an empty crate under the same awning as Mary but chose a box that allowed a little distance between her and the Northern girl. Placing the heavy bag near her feet, Jill swatted at the wooden crate with a linen handkerchief before seating herself, her back toward Mary. She wiped a gloved hand across her brow, feeling dejected.

What was God doing? Why did this have to happen to her? Since her initial escape from St. Louis four years previous, Jill had always tried to be a good Christian and serve God when convenient, attending services on Sundays when they didn't conflict with her social calendar.

The Foster family were regular church attendees, a habit Jill continued when she left home.

Left home? She wrinkled her nose. Hastily sent away was more like it.

Sundays were God's day. At least the morning was. The Bible was for the pastor to read and interpret to his congregation. If one tried hard to be good, good things should follow, right?

What was God doing with her? Jill remembered leaving her home in St. Louis amid some type of social catastrophe, swiftly packed off to a girl's college after her father made an unwise political comment. In the middle of his store, for God's sake, where everyone could hear him.

Jill squeezed her hands together and glanced up. She'd worked hard to become a teacher. Why did she have to lose her position and return home? What could St. Louis hold for her after all these years?

Jill sighed again, eyeing the dingy steamer with a skeptical eye. The dual smokestacks bellowed rhythmically, a stream of gray smoke venting from the tall tubes, threatening to shower soot and sparks on her clean dress. Jill huffed and looked away as her thoughts returned to herself.

She'd not gone home after graduating but had immediately reported to her new posting in Paducah. Letters from home told of mundane matters and routine life, stories of her father's store—boring to Jill. Her self-absorbed life was so much more interesting and glamorous than her parents' life in Missouri. They were, after all, mere shopkeepers.

She let her shoulders slump. Here she sat—on a common wooden crate in a dirty boat dock—made to wait for her steamer with a Northerner. Having lost her job, possibly her career, Jill was now forced to return home to wait for further employment. How embarrassing.

Mary said something behind her, but the actual words were lost to Jill. "What was that, Mary?" she inquired over her shoulder, unable to conceal the tone of annoyance in her voice. She shifted, looking at the former teacher.

"I said I'm thirsty. How long do we have to wait before we can board and retire to our quarters?" Mary pulled a ticket from her pocket and peered at the paper, searching for details.

"I believe we are to board as soon as some of this cargo is loaded. I'm sure if we requested, we could be taken to our stateroom immediately," Jill said, wanting to show Mary how Southern hospitality worked. Or was *supposed* to work. Surely it had operated correctly before this ghastly war. "Sir?" she called to a deck hand, swiftly moving large boxes with a hand truck. "Sir, can you help us?"

The roughly clad laborer eyed Jill and then lazily tipped his hat. "Yes, miss, what can I do for you?"

Ignoring the workman's brazen appraisal, Jill drew a breath. "We would like to board immediately and be shown to our quarters. Can you arrange this?" Jill grew impatient with the necessity of making her own decisions. In the old days, a gentleman would hurry to her side to help in any way. Not anymore, she realized wistfully.

Again, the man with the dirty overalls eyed Jill up and down before responding. "The captain is over there, miss." The worker hooked a thumb over his shoulder as he moved his hand truck to another crate. "He's the one tallying the cargo."

Jill scowled as he strode away, and her irritation pricked at his unwillingness to help. Heat crept up her neck at his rude scrutiny and abrupt departure. Southern hospitality, indeed. Jill tensed as she felt Mary's eyes upon her. Turning away, she motioned swiftly to a nearby black man.

"Boy? What is your name?"

The young man straightened slowly and then glanced behind him, looking for another person this lady must be addressing.

Jill continued. "Yes, I am talking to you. Come here."

He wiped his sweaty palms on his soiled shirt and hesitantly approached the two ladies, walking with a pronounced limp.

"Yes, miss? Did you call me?"

Jill pulled a glove from her hand. "Yes, I did. I asked your name."

He straightened, but looked away, not meeting her gaze—like a soldier awaiting inspection. "Samuel, miss."

"Samuel, run over to the captain and find out when we can board."

Samuel glanced at Mary, and she smiled encouragingly. His jaw muscles worked, and he glanced again at Jill. She nodded and he turned, limping toward the steamer's captain.

"Look, Jill, he limps," Mary noticed.

Jill saw but said nothing. It was warm sitting here near the waterfront. Perhaps she should've stayed under the protection of the trees in the park. What would this sun do to her complexion?

Both girls watched as Samuel spoke to the captain, and then, the older man glanced at them. Turning back, he said a few gruff words to the young man. Slowly, the hobbling servant made his way back toward their place under the awning.

"The captain says it won't be long now, and you're to sit patiently. He will get to you presently," Samuel reported, his white teeth flashing.

Jill barely noticed but Mary was quick to respond. "Thank you, Samuel. May I inquire as to the cause of your handicap?" She gestured to his leg.

His eyes clouded as he looked down at his foot, but then he grinned, understanding spreading across his sweaty face. "My foot? Sure, miss. I was born this way. I limp and can't run. That's why Master Carter lets me work on the docks. He knows I can't run away. I'm strong and can work hard, but I can't move fast."

"Well, I guess that means you'll have to discover an alternate method of escape," Mary giggled, her hand covering her mouth.

"Thank you, Samuel," Jill interjected, glaring at the Northern girl.

The young man stared at Mary for a moment, a look of wonder shining in his dark eyes. He blinked, as if coming to a decision. Lowering his gaze, he hobbled to the crate. Despite his impaired foot, he wrestled the wooden box with strength and agility. Piercing the two girls with a final backward glance, he carried the heavy load onto the waiting steamer.

CHAPTER 2

Jill turned on her companion, her eyes narrowing. "That was not right. I know you do not agree with things you've observed here in the South, but it's wrong of you to interfere. That man has a job to do, and you shouldn't be putting ideas into his head. He might be punished just for hearing you suggest such a thing."

Mary faced Jill squarely, glaring as she put her hands on her hips. "Well, you're right, I don't understand. But I think this war is going to fix that. It'll spell the end of slavery. Even in the Border States, like in England."

Jill glanced around, seeing no one listening. Thankfully. She lowered her voice anyway. "You should be ashamed of yourself, Mary. You are a guest here, an outsider, and your political views are not welcome. We believe in the Constitution, what is legal. The states can decide for themselves. We don't need the president to tell us how to think."

She paused and drew a deep breath. "Secession is wrong, but slavery will continue. Why, the South is winning the war, and the president has promised the Border States will keep their slaves for remaining in the Union."

Mary turned away, her chin lifted as her brown curls bounced defiantly at Jill's rebuttal. "Well," she added, her back toward Jill. "I hope the North wins and the Union is more like my Minnesota, where everyone is free."

Jill replaced her white glove, resigning herself to act more than ever like the Southern lady she was. Mary was not Southern and should be excused for her ignorance. Everyone knew the Border States only stayed with the Union because of Mr. Lincoln's promise. Maryland, Delaware, Kentucky, and Missouri were slave states that decided to remain in the Union even after the other eleven Southern slave states seceded.

As a Christian, Jill did not hold with slavery. However, as a Southerner, it was not in her to object to tradition, a social system that worked well for farming families, many of whom were the aristocrats of the South.

She frowned when she considered her own father's backward political views and glanced at Mary from the corner of her eye. Father's loose tongue had informed everyone in St. Louis of his Union-supporting beliefs.

The two ladies sat in silence for a short while longer, each refusing to apologize for their opinions. Finally, Samuel approached slowly, hobbling.

"Excuse me, miss. The captain says I'm to show you to your room. The cargo is taking more space than expected, and you ladies will have to share."

Jill bristled at the news, but this was wartime and all had to make concessions. She leaped to her feet. "Good. Mary and I are teachers from the same school. It will be fine to share a room. Come, Mary, let's find our quarters," Jill called, attempting to be a good example.

Mary looked askance at her, then pursed her lips at Jill's apparent sincerity and reached for her luggage.

"Oh, I got that, miss," Samuel spoke—too quickly. He bent, hefting the bag easily and then took Jill's carpetbag under his other arm. Leading the two young ladies toward the gangplank, he maneuvered around piles of cargo and various boxes. Jill noted how furtively the slave kept surveying the crowd, as if searching for someone. The huge steamer bellowed giant puffs of steam and smoke in a rhythmic pulse, the noise increasing as they approached. Other passengers were boarding as well. Jill felt her chest tighten as she passed a quartet of blue-clad Yankees. They always made her feel uneasy, like they were unwelcome guests who wouldn't go away.

Following Samuel up one flight of stairs to a row of staterooms, the two teachers were led through a narrow passageway. Halting before a door, Samuel pulled a key from his pocket. Jill could not help but notice the anxious look in his eyes as he fumbled with the lock. "This is where you ladies will stay."

He opened the small door and placed the two bags inside, then held the door open for them.

"I hope your journey is an easy one, and if you need anything, I'll be close at hand." He looked sharply over his shoulder before backing into the hallway.

Mary, seeming not to notice the black man's cautious movements, moved eagerly into the little room, but Jill eyed Samuel thoughtfully as he lumbered back down the passage.

Before Jill could ponder further the intent of the young man's words, Mary had claimed a bunk and stretched out with a groan. "I'm so tired."

Jill felt stunned at the girl's thoughtlessness. Why, her dress would surely wrinkle.

"I've slept terribly since we were told the news. I'm not looking forward to returning home unemployed, but Father will help me find another job. He wasn't keen on me coming to Kentucky, anyway."

Jill's own father had not been excited when she announced she would be teaching in Kentucky, either. At first, her parents had argued it was too close to political unrest, then the location was too close to the fighting. After Shiloh, Jill had to agree, but she knew only too well how much her father had paid for her education. A job had been desperately needed. Jobs—any jobs—had been scarce since the beginning of the war.

She exhaled slowly, unhappy to be returning home unemployed. Still, three years of experience would look good on any application. She would try immediately to find work elsewhere. Perhaps Mr. Hopkins would locate work for her.

Sitting on the edge of her bunk, Jill felt glad to get out of the dust and heat of the waterfront. Too many men had leered openly at her, making her uncomfortable. The war had also changed proper decorum, Jill thought grimly. Men would never have taken such liberties with young ladies before.

With the advent of the blue tide from the north, Jill could see that the formality, the courtesy, the proper respect of Southern ways, was on the decline.

She leaned back, relaxing, careful not to muss her dress. The steamer would not be untying from the dock for another hour, and she had time to think. Only a week had passed since the faculty learned about the school closing. The news had not come as a total surprise. Even the teachers could not ignore the ever-increasing number of empty chairs in their classrooms.

Writing her parents a quick note of explanation, she had purchased passage on an upstream steamer. From Paducah, the ship would travel the short distance down the Ohio and make the turn into the Mississippi, working upstream to St. Louis.

Jill glanced at the silent Mary and wondered if she was asleep. Her thoughts returned to home. Father had done well with his store in St. Louis, or so it seemed. He and Mother always lived well, and when Father experienced the social rebuff from customers for his brash sympathies, Jill had been quickly whisked away to the yearlong school for teacher training. And Father continued to send money. She never went without, often enjoying luxuries others struggled to obtain or simply did without. But Jill's parents made sure she maintained a standard to which she was accustomed, although not extravagantly. That would come later, when she married, after catching the eye of a dashing gentleman.

With a yawn, she listened to the even breathing of her temporary roommate. Mary had gone right to sleep. Jill frowned at the Northern girl's inappropriate talk before the common dock slave. She hoped Samuel would not get into any trouble because of Mary's indiscretion.

Awakening with a start, Jill realized she must've dozed off. A quick glance showed Mary still asleep in her bunk. Amazingly, she was not snoring, shaking Jill's assumption of all Northern girls. Loud shouts from outside drew her to the small porthole that looked out over the docks. Footfalls thumped along the narrow passageway outside her door. The ship readied for departure.

She looked out the small window and scanned the wharf, searching for sign of Samuel, but the slave was nowhere in sight. Then she smiled, chiding herself for even giving the young man a second thought. Certainly her father's upside-down ideas were not affecting her.

Moving quietly to not awaken Mary, Jill checked her reflection in the small mirror tacked to the wall, tucking a loose strand of chestnut hair into place. She shook her hair, watching the locks shimmer as the light caught the golden-brown tresses. Men had complimented her hair color, and she thought of it as one of her best traits, along with her perfect manners. Opening the door without a sound, she stepped into the hallway.

Jill pulled her gloves on again as she walked forward to a place at the railing, hoping to observe the casting of the ropes. Her heart felt heavy as she watched the large steamship glide gracefully into the current. Her last view of Paducah was of the dirty waterfront with the lovely green park stretching behind the crowded docks. She leaned forward, straining to catch a final glimpse of the ladies' college, hidden from view by the trees. She sighed as the park slid from view.

Again, Jill wondered if she would ever return to Paducah. It was a good town to work in, an old Southern town. She mused that a person always remembered their first job fondly.

Leaning on the railing, listening to the chug, chug, chug of the steam engine working the paddles, Jill wondered again what God was doing with her. On the banks, deep forests had replaced the sights of the small Kentucky city, and she felt suddenly lost and without direction. Of course, she planned on returning home to submit applications to other schools, but where was she truly going?

After her abrupt flight from St. Louis, she'd outlined a plan for her life which included becoming a teacher, moving in grand social circles, and locating a wealthy husband. To marry a gentleman was always her aim, then to settle and have children. What else was there? And now Christ had thrown a stumbling block into her path. Certainly, this was bad timing, losing her job—she'd never anticipated disruptions to her goal.

"Why, God?" She scanned the distant shore, but her whispered inquiry received no reply. Surely the Lord wanted her to be happy, and her plan felt like a good idea.

"I love you, Jesus, and want to do the right thing. Well, I mean, as long as it works into my strategy. I have such a wonderful goal. If I'm married to a gentleman and rich, I can help at church socials and give money for dangerous mission trips to foreign lands full of heathens. Guide me, Father. Help me achieve your will, which I'm certain is part of my plan."

She glanced down at the water where waves rippled upon the river's surface. Sunlight gleamed across the river, the final rays of the long day spearing through the trees on the bank. She remembered how disappointed she'd felt when she heard the school was closing. As if God hadn't heard her prayers, as if the Lord wasn't listening to her. Was he listening now?

With a sigh, she moved into the narrow passageway. Something caught her eye as she turned, and she paused, searching for the culprit. Her gaze narrowed as she found Samuel, surprised to find him aboard. The young man stood very near the boiler, handing wood to the fireman. She stared at him for a moment, not knowing why his presence there drew her attention.

Shaking her head, annoyed with herself, she returned to her cabin.

CHAPTER 3

Returning to her cabin, Jill found Mary awake and standing in front of the small mirror. "I wondered where you'd gotten to," Mary mumbled, hair pins in her mouth as her nimble fingers worked her hair into a bun above the nape of her neck.

Jill watched for a minute, arms crossed as she leaned against the closed door. "Didn't that slave Samuel tell us his master was in Paducah?"

Mary continued to wrestle with the stubborn hair. Frowning at the results, she plucked the pins to make another attempt. "Samuel? You mean the man who loaded our luggage? I don't remember him saying he was from Paducah. Why?"

Jill pushed away from the door, the thin mattress barely compressing as she sat on the bed. "I just saw him on the deck as we left the waterfront."

Mary held her loose hair up in the back, watching in the glass as she turned first one way then another, scowling at each angle. Finally, she pulled the locks tightly and tied the bundle with a ribbon. Letting the long hair bounce, she bobbed a little to watch the effect of the dancing ponytail. Satisfied, she turned back to Jill.

"What? You saw him on deck? Maybe he belongs to a person on board. Or perhaps his master is traveling." Mary bent to open her valise, removing clothing for later.

Jill watched the young woman unpack as a scowl creased her face. "I don't know. I had the impression he belonged in Paducah."

"What do you think of this?" Mary pulled a long evening gown from the carpetbag. Holding the dress against herself, she twirled in front of the small mirror.

"I think it's lovely, but I hardly believe you will have occasion to wear it on this ship," Jill remarked, her eyebrows rising. These Northern girls had no decorum. What was appropriate or not seemed to matter little to them.

"No, silly. Not on board. I was thinking of my welcome home party. I'm sure Father will have one."

Mary suddenly frowned and, dropping the gown back into the bag, sat heavily on the bed, her face somber. "Of course, there will be no young men to dance with. They are all at the war." Mary tensed and looked at Jill. "Mother's letter said the only young men in town are the wounded returning from battle. Most are missing a limb." She paled and bit her lip before turning away.

Jill chewed the inside of her cheek. She hadn't even considered a welcome home party. She was not happy to be coming home even if it was only to be a short visit and planned on writing letters immediately to other ladies educational institutions. She would find something soon, Jill felt certain.

Before she could respond to Mary, a knock interrupted them. Jill shot a curious look at Mary and went to the door. "Who is it?"

"It's me, miss. Samuel. I have your dinner." With another confused look at Mary, Jill opened the door. There stood Samuel, a tray balanced in his arms.

He entered the room, his limp pronounced and dragging in the close quarters. "I fetched you something to eat from the kitchen. They call it a galley. There's not much choice."

He placed the tray on a small table. Bowing, he backed from the room, pulling the door closed behind him.

"Well, I'll be," Mary breathed, a slow smile spreading across her face.

Watching her, Jill tilted her head. "What?"

"I think he's running away. I should never have suggested it." Mary giggled, her eyes brightening.

"That's not funny," Jill snapped. "Running away is a crime. Often slaves are beaten severely or even maimed for making the attempt. I hope you are mistaken."

Suddenly, Mary changed the subject. "I am sure I am. What do you think we're having for dinner? I'm simply famished."

Jill watched as Mary lifted lids, surveying the meager portions.

The two former teachers ate the slices of cheese, enjoying the hard bread and apple that accompanied the sparse meal. Jill lifted the small kettle of tea and Mary nodded, her mouth full of apple.

"I didn't expect anything to eat aboard ship. I thought we'd be stuck having crackers and water until tomorrow when we stopped at St. Louis." Mary brushed at her lips with a napkin, searching for crumbs. Disgusted, Jill turned away, wondering how this woman had ever been hired to teach young ladies proper behaviors. Then she remembered Mary's job had been to teach cooking, not actual dinner manners. Jill smiled to herself. The Northern girl had no sense of conduct.

She glanced at the tray of food. Jill hadn't anticipated food on the trip either. She wondered again about Samuel. Why had he served them? He was certainly not attached to their travels.

Jill bit her lip as the ugly topic of slavery crossed her mind again. Once, a customer who owed Father money offered to give a small boy to pay the debt. Father had refused. "Slavery is wrong," Father had insisted, a hint of accusation in his tone. "I am a Christian."

Jill remembered a small crowd had formed, listening intently to the exchange. "Are you questioning my faith?" the man had demanded, flushing crimson. "It's allowed in the Bible, Foster. Are you saying I'm not a good Christian?"

Jill recalled how the crowd had pressed in to hear her father's reply.

"I will not judge. Only I will not own slaves."

The crowd whispered hotly among themselves, and for a while, Father's business had suffered. It suffered more when the Supreme Court determined slaves were their master's property. But with the coming of the Yankees into Missouri, his business had picked back up as the blue devils shopped at her family's store. At least, that was Jill's understanding.

Jill smarted from some social fallout, the incident marking her family among the populace of the city. Old friends snubbed her on the street, and shortly after that, she'd been quickly sent away to a girl's college in Louisiana.

Missouri was a besieged state now, the army protecting it from Confederate guerillas who plagued the Union occupation. St. Louis was a large city, and the guerillas mostly stayed far to the west, along the Kansas border. Though officially a Union state, Missouri had strong ties to the South.

Not that Father was a Union man, not properly speaking. Jill and her family loved the South and its social ways, but slavery had created a stink that could no longer be ignored, although Jill tried her best.

The two teachers finished their meal and then walked a little on deck before retiring for the evening. No more was seen of Samuel, but Jill noted with repugnance that several Yankee soldiers were on board.

NEBRASKA HAVEN

Jill had a fitful night on board the steamer. The constant slapping of the giant paddle wheel made her lie awake and stare into the gloom of her little cabin. Mary slept like a log, snoring contentedly.

Jill frowned, not pleased that, in the end, she'd been right about Northern girls.

She was neither eager nor excited the next afternoon when she stood at the railing watching the steamer approach St. Louis. Her packed bag at her feet, she watched as the large ship moved slowly through the dense river traffic preceding the docking of the huge craft. Several smaller ships scrambled from their path and Jill even saw a young boy in a skiff stand and wave his straw hat to her. She returned the wave, smiling at the boy's loud whoop at sight of her.

Having said her goodbye to Mary, promising to write if she landed another job, she stood at the railing beside the mounds of cargo to be offloaded. A loud blast from the steamer alerted the watching crowd that the ship prepared to dock.

As men bustled about the deck to secure ropes, someone moved beside her, jostling her elbow. Turning, she stared, startled to see Samuel.

CHAPTER 4

"Hello, miss. Let me carry this for you." Samuel took up her carpetbag, his eyes darting nervously over the crowded deck. A sudden shout interrupted the question on her lips.

"Jill! Jill!" A slender, white-haired man waved excitedly from shore. At first, Jill didn't recognize him. Father was always silver above his temples, but when did he go totally white? He looked like an old man.

"Father!" Jill yelled, waving in return. The gangplank dropped into position, and Jill strode across the boards hurriedly, rushing into the awaiting arms of her father.

"Oh, Father, it is so good to see you." She embraced the older man.

"Let me get a look at you, Jilly." He stepped back, his hands still on her shoulders, appraising her. "You are beautiful. I can't believe you're actually here. Mother and I received your telegram only a few days ago. She will be so happy to see you," he said, letting his arms drop from her.

As the shopkeeper stood back and closely scrutinized her, Jill made her own assessment. This was not the same man she remembered. Father's clothes hung on him like a scarecrow, loose and ill fitting. His thinning hair had lost all its original color and his eyes held a look of acute sadness. Or was it defeat? Even his suit seemed old and worn, hanging on his slim frame. Shoulders sagging, he resembled a broken-down horse she'd seen once, almost too weary to pull a wagon. Hadn't he been much more robust when she saw him last?

"How is Mother? I haven't heard from her lately. Is everything well?"

A worried furrow creased her father's forehead. "Well, things have been better." He smiled suddenly, and the worry lines disappeared. "Not to bother you with all that now. Let's get you to Mother. Let me fetch a buggy."

He moved toward a row of buggies and began haggling with a hack. Suddenly, Samuel appeared beside her.

"You," she snarled with an apprehensive glance all around. "What are you doing in St. Louis? Is Mr. Carter with you?" She peered over his shoulder, searching for someone connected with Samuel. He turned, scanning the crowd, as if he searched for someone too.

"No, miss. Master Carter isn't here. I took your friend's advice and found a different way to escape. I just walked on that boat, and here I am. I told folks I belonged to you, and that's why I served you last evening. It made them believe my story."

He paused, looking around again. Jill blanched and stepped back. What was she to do? Samuel was a runaway slave. The authorities would be looking for him. She glanced quickly to where her father talked to a plump man he obviously recognized. They seemed to be quarreling.

Grabbing Samuel's arm, she led him behind a corner of a nearby warehouse, Samuel hobbling hurriedly to keep up. "Listen, you are not my servant. If you had any sense, you would've stayed on board with Mary. She's going to Minnesota, a free state. This is Missouri, another slave state. You have escaped nowhere, you fool."

His eyes widened with understanding and then clouded with panic. As if drawn by a magnetic force, Jill and Samuel turned together toward the steamboat. Two men with belt guns and badges were milling about the crowd, obviously searching for someone. Jill recognized their intent at once.

Samuel straightened, dropping her bag as he crossed his arms over his chest. "I don't care. I am free of Master Carter. He'll never catch me now." Samuel's eyes held a fierce determination.

Jill glowered at him. "Those two men there. They're searching for you, I'll wager. You couldn't get back on that steamer now if you wanted to. They'll search it next." She surveyed the crowd, thinking. "Out of the frying pan into the fire," she hissed bitterly, grinding her teeth.

"Good thing I got off the boat, huh?" he said as they studied the throng around them, watching the law officers as they searched.

Suddenly, Samuel went on, his voice trembling. "What am I gonna do? I thought the boat would take me to a free place. I can't outrun 'em. Now I'm as good as caught," he whispered, his eyes abnormally large.

"Hush," Jill snapped, scowling. "Let me think." She looked around quickly, watching her father finally conclude his business with his plump companion. Should she do anything? Samuel was no concern of hers. Surely, he'd gotten himself into this mess. Jill bit her lip, considering. But her father disapproved of slavery. "All right. Stay right here," she commanded.

She rushed to a farm wagon where a man had just unloaded baskets of fruit. "Hello, sir. I need you to take my servant with us. Follow that hack there. We're going to Sutton Street. Let him out behind our buggy, please."

The farmer looked at Samuel and then turned back to Jill. "He'll have to ride in back, and the ride ain't free." Motioning for Samuel to climb in, Jill paid the farmer from her meager funds. She moved swiftly forward to intercept her approaching father.

Smiling, she reached for his elbow, turning him around and steering him toward the buggies. "Father, have you gotten us a ride? Who was that man you were talking to? He seemed angry." Jill hoped to draw his attention away from the limping man climbing into the farm wagon behind them.

"A business associate, nothing more, I assure you. Rogers is all about business," her father grumbled, helping her into the buggy.

Drawing away from the waterfront, Jill glanced over her shoulder, her heart in her throat as she watched the two men with badges surveying the crowd again. Squinting, she peered at the farm wagon behind her, hoping they hadn't seen Samuel.

Jill's father prattled on about war talk and different military leaders whose names Jill had made it a point to ignore. She asked him simple questions about the store, vaguely aware of his evasive answers. Was something wrong? He would not say, but she wondered.

As they turned the corner onto Sutton Street, she glanced covertly behind them. The vehicle that followed was indeed carrying Samuel and, she was horrified to realize, her satchel. She had left her luggage with the young man when they quickly fled the waterfront.

Passing her father's store, he pointed out new paint and minor repairs to the roof and porch. "I must keep it up or customers will not want to shop here. Appearances are very important," he explained, his head bobbing with the words.

Jill glanced at the familiar Foster's Market emblem above the boardwalk before her sharp eye caught the closed sign in the window. "Father? How can the store be closed during business hours? Don't you have a clerk to work the counter when you're absent?"

NEBRASKA HAVEN

He shifted beside her. "There is little business during the afternoon hours," he said, dismissing Jill's concern with a casual wave of his thin hand.

A block past the store, the buggy halted. Her father stepped stiffly down, turning to help Jill. She looked back and saw Samuel scrambling from the farm wagon.

"Father, that man has my satchel. I must've forgotten it on the dock. I'll fetch it and be right in." Not waiting for a response, she moved swiftly toward the other vehicle while her father paid their driver.

Jill retrieved her valise, hissing at Samuel in a low voice. "Go around back and hide in the storage shed. I'll come out later."

Both buggy and wagon moved away, and Jill was impressed how quickly Samuel disappeared.

Before following her father into the house, Jill noticed the peeling house paint and rotted wooden porch stairs. Boards creaked under their weight, sagging as they crossed to the front door. A musky, stale odor greeted Jill as Father pushed the door open, allowing her to enter first. She narrowed her eyes as she walked into the darkened living room, the windows screened by full length heavy drapes. Dim light revealed the silver candlesticks that normally stood on the mantel were now gone. A thick layer of dust covered the elegant furniture and Jill frowned, recalling how much her mother enjoyed a clean, well-lit house full of fresh air. What had happened in Jill's absence? She hadn't visited since Christmas a year and a half ago, right after the new president had been elected. The house had been immaculate then.

Jill recalled that time in Paducah when Lincoln's election had caused such a stir. The war had soon followed.

Leaving her bag by the front door, Jill followed her father through the gloomy house to the dark hallway.

Father stopped before his bedroom door, pausing with his hand on the knob. He looked at Jill, a sorrow in his eyes she didn't recognize. Jill tensed, sensing something wrong, some calamity. She searched his somber gaze, an unspoken question in her scrutiny.

Father said nothing, gulping the lump in his throat as he slowly pushed the door open. Jill peered around the door frame, her heart beating loudly in her ears as she wiped her damp palms on her dress. She hesitated, then stepped in, unsure if she wanted to enter, to discover what she feared lurked in the silent room. A tall, four poster bed filled the small chamber. A pale, thin figure lie there, propped by pillows.

"Mother! What's wrong? Why was I not told?" Jill rushed to her mother's bedside. The woman looked twenty years older than Jill last remembered. Gray, stringy hair had replaced the light brown that Jill knew so well. Deep wrinkles lined her mother's formerly smooth skin.

"Oh, Jilly, is it you? It is good to have you home," Mother croaked. "I have missed you terribly." Her trembling hand reached for Jill's own. Jill took it, noticing the blood vessels straining through the thin, translucent skin. With a questioning glance at her father, she sat on the edge of the bed. He stared back at her, only his sunken eyes revealed his deep emotion. She turned back to her mother.

"Mother? What's happened? Why are you in bed?"

Her mother coughed, and her thin shoulders quaked. The fit brought a little color to her ashen face. Jill put a supportive hand under her mother's back, holding her. As the coughing subsided, Jill laid her mother gently upon her pillows.

"This is not the time, Margaret," her father warned, leaning over his wife.

"Oh, it's never the time with you, but we have to tell her," Jill's mother whispered, her eyes closed.

"Tell me what?" Jill demanded, glancing from one parent to the other.

Her father sighed as he rubbed the back of his neck, a resigned look on his tired face.

"Father has ruined us. The store is doing poorly, and now he has gone deep into debt to fix it up and restock. We have nothing but the store left. All has been sacrificed for that worthless business. We barely eat," her mother complained. Her eyes opened briefly and then closed again with the effort of her speech.

"Now, Margaret, you shouldn't get yourself all excited. It's not good for you," Jill's father cautioned, leaning forward to smooth his wife's hair.

Her mother did not respond, but simply lay motionless for a minute, long enough that Jill grew alarmed. "Mother? Are you alright?" She squeezed her mother's limp hand.

"She is resting, Jilly. It's best for her." Father drew Jill from the bed and out of the room. With a final glance at the still form in bed, the door closed. She followed the retreating figure of her father through the dark hallway into the kitchen where she sank into a chair. He busied himself at the hand pump, filling a kettle. Stoking the low fire, he encouraged the stove to warm, rested the kettle on a grate, and finally seated himself across the table from Jill, holding his head with both hands.

She stared at him, not knowing what to think. How had this happened so fast? Why did she not know? How long had her parents suffered?

"Father? What is going on? Why have you kept this from me?"

The old man she barely recognized looked up, the strain etched into his face. "People say I'm a Union man. I'm not, but it has destroyed my business. Some Union soldiers shop at the store, but not enough. I've gone deep into debt, trying to keep the store open. Even this house is not ours anymore."

"And Mother's silver candlesticks?"

He ran a shaky hand through his diminishing hair before he nodded. "I had to sell them, along with everything else of value."

Jill listened, her lips parted in amazement. Her father had always been so confident, acting like money came easily. Her parents had spoiled Jill, allowing numerous dresses and fine things. Even college had been encouraged, Jill's accomplishments a source of family pride. Their life had all looked right, and the family had been prosperous, hadn't it? Now she was not so sure.

"Father, have you gone into debt for the store alone or ..." She hesitated, not wanting to say it aloud, not wanting to know the truth. "Or for me too?"

Jill felt her chest squeeze as she waited for his reply. Had her selfish, thoughtless desires forced her family into ruin? Why hadn't she been more interested in them? She could've written, asked how they truly were. Instead, she had avoided them, not even wondering if Father's pro-Union comments had affected the family business, their financial situation, or even their health.

Her father didn't respond at first, simply running his hands through his lessening hair, combing the strands as if trying to recapture their former luster, to make them grow and thicken once more. Eventually, he looked up, his eyes dim and tired. "You are our only child. We wanted you to have everything. It was a challenge to keep up with your purchases, but what else were we going to do with our money anyway? We love you, Jilly. It made us so proud to see you looking like a fancy lady. Your education demanded a certain style, but it cost more than we anticipated." He paused, standing to fetch two cups from the sideboard.

"Besides, it was not all on account of you. The store started to do poorly. A couple of men offered to buy it from me, but I refused to sell. Now it's too late to sell. That man at the waterfront today ... Rogers. I owe him a considerable amount of money. I can't even afford to pay my debts."

Her father retrieved the whistling kettle and poured, steam rising.

"When you got that job at the ladies' college, we thought it would put us back on our feet. It didn't. Things went from bad to worse when Mr. Lincoln got elected. The stress was too much for Mother, and in her weakened state, she caught pneumonia. The last doctor said she was too weak to fight the illness."

Replacing the kettle on the stove, he returned to his seat, dropping heavily into a chair. Sipping the hot drink, he eyed Jill over the rim of his cup. "I really don't know what to do, Jilly. I have prayed for God's help, but I have to admit I've been a poor steward—my pride dictated my spending. I've been foolish. There is no one to blame but myself."

Jill sat dumbfounded, listening to her father's tale of woe. She had no idea. All those years, she'd gone to parties, bought nice things. All without any thought of how it impacted her family. She believed they were prosperous. Now she knew the bitter truth. Her self-absorption shamed her.

She straightened, squaring her shoulders. Jill needed information. She was good at problem solving when she had all the facts. "What can be done now, Father? What plan do you have? Do you not have any working capital?"

He sighed. "All I own is some petty cash and a deed to a piece of land in Nebraska I took in trade a few months ago. No one will give me money for the property. I should never have accepted it in exchange for goods. But I've done that for years. Many shopkeepers take things in trade. I'm no different than other store owners, but my business has not flourished." He looked at Jill, a grim smile touching his thin lips. "Except you. We're so proud of you. Look at you. You're a fine lady. And you can play piano. But it's all over now. If the store doesn't turn around, we're lost. There's nothing else." He grew silent, his eyes staring hollowly across the room.

Jill felt the dread envelope her like a wet blanket, draping her in doubt and anxiety. Nothing else? Her father had no idea how true those words were. She had written to her parents that she was coming home for a short visit. She didn't want to worry them with the news the school had closed, that she was unemployed. She didn't even have any real money to offer her father.

Later that evening, Jill made soup. She was surprised how little food she found in the kitchen. Feeding her mother had felt like an ordeal—the older woman did not really want to eat. Her father ate his meal in the kitchen. After his long speech of the afternoon, he now proved quiet and distant.

After everyone ate, Jill cleaned the few dishes, her hands swishing the soapy water in the sink, her thoughts wandering hopelessly. She glanced out the back window, seeing the squat storage shed behind the house, and her chest tightened, suddenly remembering Samuel. She had totally forgotten the runaway.

Taking a pot of soup and a bucket of water, Jill tucked a blanket under one arm and slipped outside under cover of darkness. She scanned the unfenced yards, peering at each of the neighbor's houses as she made her way to the small shed. She found Samuel there, his eyes glowing in the dark, his teeth flashing as he grinned at the sight of her.

"I knew you'd come, miss," he said, eager hands reaching for the soup.

Jill watched him hobble to a wooden box and sit down, the nearby kitchen light filtering through cracks in the wall. She leaned her head against the door frame and studied him as he ate, trying unsuccessfully to order her problems in her mind. Jill eyed Samuel, wondering if there was anyone she could trust. She wanted to talk, needed to talk, but she eyed him skeptically. He was, after all, a runaway. Yet something about his plight appealed to her, and she pursed her lips tight before she spoke.

"How did you know you could trust me?"

He plunged his spoon into the soup, his attention on the meal. "I felt the good Lord tell me you would help. I know I can always trust Jesus. He guides me. Didn't he guide me to you?"

She crossed her arms over her chest, her nose wrinkling as she ignored his confusing reply. "What will you do now?"

The spoon froze in midair, and his gaze lifted to hers. "Why, miss, that's easy. Whatever you want me to."

Jill blinked. Her head came off the door post, her back rigid. "What? What do you mean by that? You are of no concern to me."

He stared at her, and his eyes gleamed in the darkness, reflecting the kitchen's dim lantern light. "Miss, I'm with you now. Whatever you want me to do, or wherever you go, I'm with you. I trust you."

Jill could feel the knot in her gut tighten. The ache had been there all day, getting tighter as the hours dragged by. Now the knot burned, threatening to explode. She knew she needed a plan, but this was not it. Whatever her solution, it would not, could not, include another person, let alone a runaway slave. The authorities would be searching for him, bringing unwanted attention upon her family. She couldn't afford any more inconveniences. Her plate was full, heaping, over full.

She dropped her arms by her side and then clasped her hands together, intertwining her fingers, wringing them tightly. She had too much to worry about. Her parents' difficulties overwhelmed her. Why, she didn't even have a job. How could she take on Samuel's problems too?

Her voice trembled as she spoke, her words coming in curt, clipped tones. "Samuel, I have more than I can handle without tying up with the likes of you. You must be leaving and go about your own affairs. My family needs me, and I must figure out how to help them." Her words sounded harsh in her ears, but she didn't care. She needed to be rid of him.

Samuel looked at Jill, a soft glow settling on his features. "Miss, can't you see? The Lord has brought us together for a purpose. We're a team now. I'm to help you, and you're to help me. God will guide us, don't worry."

Jill stared at him, unable to speak. Turning on her heel, she fled to the house, slamming the kitchen door behind her.

CHAPTER 5

Jill fumed as she thought of Samuel. The simpleton. She pressed her lips tightly together, busying herself around the kitchen. She must keep her hands busy, or she'd go mad.

The hand pump creaked as she worked water into a steel pot. Once full, Jill placed the heavy container on the stove. She opened the grate of the blackened, iron stove and tossed in a handful of sticks before slamming the metal grate shut.

A sigh escaped her as she dragged a wet rag over all the counters, again and again. Then she took cooking skillets and pots from their hooks on the wall and scoured each of them. A loose strand of brown-gold hair danced across her cheek, and she angrily pushed the hair aside with the back of her hand.

Jill had to think. To find another teaching position now would be very difficult, if not impossible. Her school was not the only one that closed because of the war. There seemed to be an abundance of female teachers on the market, although any male educators would probably join the army. Even the potential suitors she waited for had vanished since the Confederates fired upon Fort Sumter over a year ago. Although a gentleman-husband would solve many of her problems, perhaps her family's problems as well, there'd be little chance of finding one now.

Hating the war even more, Jill cleaned. What of other work? Besides working in her father's store, she had no skills. What else was available? She'd look into possibilities tomorrow.

What if her father's poor standing in the community influenced Jill finding employment? She nibbled her lips roughly, ignoring the painful bite. St. Louis was a big city, yet everyone would know about the businesses that supported the Union and those loyal to the Confederacy.

Out on the western border, near Kansas, the fighting continued between Yankees and Confederate guerillas. But here in St. Louis, the fighting was less visible, more subtle, as Southern sympathizers frequented similar thinking businesses and shunned pro-Union ones. Or worse, Jill heard some Union men had even been targeted by mobs, their homes and farms destroyed.

She considered the nagging thought, knowing her concern had merit. Perhaps she could not find work in St. Louis.

Starting in the kitchen, she vowed she would clean the entire house. She was home now, and she would soon put things right.

Abruptly, her hand stilled. The wet rag rested on the table, her eyes staring at the wall. What were they going to do? Her life had seemed so well planned and orchestrated. Everything was going right. A college education, a very good job, even some of the young men of Paducah knew of her and had called. Her future seemed bright. Very bright.

Now, all had crumbled, the pins knocked out from under her. On top of all this, a runaway hid in their storage shed. What had she been thinking? She'd helped him escape. Why? Could she be in trouble too?

She shook her head. No, Samuel was not her fault. Jill would not think of him. He was on his own.

She felt the heat stir in her gut again as she thought of his ridiculous words. A team he had called them. She whacked the edge of the table with the wet rag. They were a team? Well, her team was losing, and if he knew what was good for him, he'd not tie up with her. Jill focused again on the wet dish rag. What was God doing with her? She shook her head. *Keep moving.* She wiped the already clean table and moved to the sink to rinse the cloth.

Her eyes narrowed as she recalled Samuel's remark about God. A plan, a purpose? Nonsense. That plan seemed bad, and she would not think on his suggestion again. God was obviously busy elsewhere, avoiding her. Perhaps God had no time for her. Surely the war occupied much of his attention.

Jill slowed, feeling suddenly tired as a wave of exhaustion washed over her. She leaned against the counter. It'd been a trying week, to be sure. First, she'd lost her job and then her homecoming had revealed a mess. Not to mention she'd helped a slave escape.

She smiled wryly, remembering Mary's hope of a homecoming party. Well, perhaps Mary's return would be better than hers.

Finally, she lifted her gaze and looked around the clean kitchen before her knees buckled and she slumped into a chair. She leaned her head against her palm, elbow on the table, and drew in a ragged breath. What was she going to do? Afraid if she stayed seated longer, it would not be possible to take herself to bed, she banked the fire in the old black stove. After dousing the lantern and lighting a candle, Jill shuffled down the hallway.

Hinges creaked as she pushed her old bedroom door open. She held the candle aloft, inspecting the familiar room. Nothing had changed, as if she'd not left long ago.

She ran a finger over the small table beside the bed, a path in the dust revealing the room had not been disturbed since her last visit. She didn't care. Tonight, the uncleaned bedroom would do.

Removing her dark blue traveling dress, Jill pulled the covers back and climbed into bed. The sheets smelled like dust, musty and dry. She snuggled deeper into her blankets, wishing to find a measure of comfort. When she was younger, she used to pray before sleep claimed her. Tonight, she huffed at the memory, not wanting to talk to the Lord.

Jill usually slept soundly. This night, however, dreams haunted her. She remembered the dreams vividly as she climbed from bed the next morning.

A wide-open space, grass fluttering in the breeze. A flat, ugly river, thick stands of trees along each low bank. Soldiers.

The images made no sense, she decided, dismissing the thoughts as another interruption to her desires. Dreams held no significance, she decided. They meant nothing. She would get no sleep here, she mused, as her fingers deftly shaped her chestnut hair into the style she desired. She glanced at the closet. A simple cotton dress would do for this day.

Jill's worry came back when she found her mother still sleeping when she checked in on her. Closing the door quietly behind her, she hurried to the store.

Jill marched the single block to her father's business, intent on gathering details, perhaps finding some answers. She stepped onto the boardwalk, spying her father through the large front window. For a moment, she watched him as he stood in the middle of the jam-packed structure, the aisles crowded with supplies, as he fussed with a stack of blankets, folding them and then folding them again.

He looked up sharply when the doorbell announced her entrance. Jill caught the gleam of eagerness in his eyes fade when he recognized her.

"Well, don't look so glum when you see me," Jill remarked as she strode toward him. The familiar smells of leather, coffee, and tobacco wafted around her, reminding her of her youth. "I've come to see what I can do."

She scanned the big store, noting the room was indeed crowded, but not with customers. The shelves and aisles teemed with merchandise.

Her father hugged her. "I'm sorry, Jilly. I have so few customers these days." He walked behind the counter, then turned to face her, spreading his arms wide. "Doesn't the store look grand? I've put everything I have into sprucing it up. I hope it helps."

Jill tried to smile, not wanting to crush his hopes. "I'm sure it'll do the trick," she said in an encouraging tone she didn't truly feel. She moved behind the counter to stand with her father, looking at everything around her. Was there anything she could improve? Anything she could really do to help their situation?

A ring of the doorbell startled both her and her father. Jill watched as a tall man in a blue uniform entered the store.

"Good morning, Mr. Foster," he called, approaching the counter.

"Good morning, Captain Needham. How are you today?"

Her father beamed at the other man, and Jill marveled at the sudden change in him, pleased to see the old salesman in him step forward. Just like the old days.

The captain wended a path around stacks of merchandise and halted in front of Jill and her father.

He eyed Jill curiously but only tipped his hat to her. She bristled, annoyed the blue devil stood in her father's store. It was, after all, the Yankees fault his store did poorly.

"Mr. Foster, some rebel guerillas are making mischief in St. Louis. Last night, they looted and burned a business downtown. I wanted to warn you to be alert for any strange men hanging around."

Jill glanced wide-eyed at her father, but he only smiled at the captain, his face relaxed. "Not to worry, Captain. I'm sure they were common thieves and not targeting particular businesses. Nonetheless, I will keep an eye out. I thank you, sir."

Coming from behind the counter, he laid a reassuring hand on the soldier's shoulder and steered him toward the door, making small talk of the weather. After the officer left, her father turned, and Jill saw the anxious lines etched into his face once more.

"I was afraid of this," he muttered as he walked back to Jill. "I will stay in the store tonight. I must keep it safe. This"—he gestured at the goods about him—"is all I have left."

Jill patted his arm, trying to reassure him. But who would reassure her?

She puttered about the store a few hours but discovered nothing to fix or mend. Everything seemed in perfect order, plenty of stock, all in its place.

At noon, she wandered slowly homeward, her thoughts heavy with concern. Her father seemed somehow lost, overwhelmed. He'd always been the strong one, giving all his energies to the store. That space was his kingdom, his domain, where he felt very sure of himself and confident. Now, he appeared small, unsure of himself. He was nothing like the man Jill remembered.

In the kitchen, she located a loaf of stale bread. She couldn't find butter. She cut a thick slice for lunch and, hoping her mother might eat some, visited the gloomy bedroom.

Her mother would eat nothing. Jill worried at her slender arms and neck, yet Mother refused to allow any morsel of the bread between her thin, blue lips.

Slowly, Jill washed the few dishes, taking her time, wondering what she could do. Her hands stilled in the soapy water, and she glanced toward the celling. Where was God? Had he abandoned her like she felt? Her heavy heart felt empty, as if she stood alone against the world. Why were all these things happening to her?

Her eyes narrowed. She usually didn't think much about God, only considering him when things weren't going smoothly. Would he listen to her and help in these trying times?

Pouring the dish water on the rose bushes, Jill watched as the water seeped into the soil, disappearing from view like her career, her dreams, and her future. She gritted her teeth, trying not to allow panic a foothold.

A hiss from the storage shed made her jump, and Jill whirled, almost dropping the dish pan as she saw Samuel gesturing to her. She'd forgotten him again. He glanced warily around before motioning to her.

Peering about to make sure she was unobserved by neighbors, Jill stole to the shed.

"Miss, I'm glad to see you. I ate all the soup, even though it was cold. The bucket of water is holding out, but I'm wishful to know how long I'll be here."

She pursed her lips as she studied him, tilting her head at his casual manner. His dark eyes shone, and she frowned, realizing he seemed happy. Her gaze darted behind him where she saw an unrolled canvas tarp had formed a comfortable bed. Clearly, their conversation of the previous evening had not bothered him.

Jill glared, hands on her hips. "Listen, Samuel. You must be going. I want you gone before tomorrow morning. Tonight, you'll have to make a run for it. Lord only knows how far you'll get with that limp. And we know from the men at the docks that the authorities are aware of your escape and are searching for you. But you're no concern of mine. Get out of my life."

Jill watched Samuel's face fall as she spoke. She could tell her harsh words hurt him, but so be it. She had bigger fish to fry.

"But miss," he began patiently. "I'm to be with you. There's a reason we're together. I feel it. God wants us to work together."

"Well, that may be what the Lord wants, but it's not what I want," Jill snapped, turning her back on him. "Be gone by morning."

Her father came home in the afternoon for a small dinner. "I must get back to the store. A sheriff stopped by today and informed me of the looters, repeating what the captain told me. He said to keep an eye out for a runaway from Kentucky too. The sheriff laughed and said it wouldn't be hard to catch the slave, he limps terribly. He thought it was the work of the Underground Railway and said that whoever was aiding the runaway would likely be jailed if not worse. Folks are getting mighty upset about the Northerners coming down here and stealing their property."

Jill stared at him as she leaned against the counter. He had always been such a strong supporter of people's rights. She wondered what had made him change. Or had he? Were his comments just a broken response to their current situation? His spirit had seemed so strong once, even in the face of public opinion. Was he losing his resolve? Sadness filled her anew as she studied him, her once-solid father now reduced to such shaky ground.

He chewed his bread thoughtfully for a moment, sighed, then looked at Jill, his eyes softening. "All my ideas have come to nothing. My pride and selfish wish to be successful have driven this family to the brink of ruination. If that one slave escapes, it would make me happy to know some good came from my stupid beliefs."

Jill straightened. "Father, they're not stupid beliefs." She lay a hand on his arm. "I hope he gets away too."

He shook his head. "It won't be easy for the fellow, what with a limp."

Jill smiled wryly to herself. If only her father knew how close that runaway slave truly was, hiding in his very own storage shed.

Father hurried back to his store, informing Jill he would sleep there to ensure its safety. Jill continued cleaning the house, her mind awhirl. Was nothing going to work out right for her? Now she feared the law was looking for her as well as Samuel.

She supposed no one would hire a woman who'd been in jail. Her thoughts stewed, pestering her as she pondered her dire circumstances. Would she ever work again?

When Jill quizzed her father about Mother at dinner, he confessed the doctor refused to come to their house anymore, believing she acted sick for attention.

"Besides, he knows I can't pay my bill anymore," he admitted. "Maybe in the beginning she acted sick, but not now. He doesn't believe she's really ill, but the pneumonia has worsened." He looked at Jill, apprehension and exhaustion mingling in his sunken eyes. "Thank God you're here now to help. I've been alone for a long time, trying to figure out how to keep things afloat."

Jill felt her eyebrows bunch as she shot a quizzical glance toward the ceiling. Thank God? She wasn't so sure.

After sunset, Jill walked slowly to the storage shed. Glancing all around, she determined the situation seemed safe enough. Samuel waited for her inside, seeming content although a little wary.

She relayed her father's information about the sheriff and the supposed work of the Underground Railway and how they believed the slave had help in his escape. Samuel seemed delighted.

She scowled at him. "How is this good news?"

"Well, miss, they're not just looking for me now. They're looking for you too. Our fortunes are connected. We're a team, see?"

Her mouth puckered as she contemplated his twisted logic. But there was some truth to what he said. If they caught him, he might lead them to her. She needed to know more if she was going to get the two of them out of this pickle. To order Samuel to leave the shed was to condemn him to immediate recapture and possibly, her to jail. The St. Louis authorities were already searching for him. It would be safer for him to stay put a day or so longer.

Moving to a wooden crate, she sat down. She smoothed her dress before resting her elbows on her knees and leaned forward. "Samuel, I've noticed you speak very well. How is that? Certainly, all slaves cannot speak as you do. Can you read?"

He smiled, nodding. "Yes, miss. Even though it's forbidden, Master Carter taught me to read. I needed to know what the crates and barrels said on the docks. When folks told him it was illegal, he told them I needed to read to work on the docks and not to worry, I could never escape with my limp." He chuckled, his eyes flashing. "I sure showed them, didn't I, miss?" He stopped, tilting his head. "Miss? I don't know your right name."

Jill drew a deep breath. "Jill Foster. Why do you talk a lot about God? Are you a Christian?"

His dark eyes brightened. "Oh, yes, miss. I even read the Bible when I clean the church. I've been going to Sunday meetings all my life. I've been washed clean by the blood of Jesus. My sins are forgiven, and now I live by the Spirit."

Jill frowned and shifted on the crate. She was in no mood to have Samuel explain this. Besides, she didn't care.

"All right now. Stay here tonight until I can figure out what to do with you. Stay quiet and I'll bring more food."

That night, Jill tossed and turned, images of wide open, empty grasslands filled her mind once more. A flat, slow river swept through her dreams, bringing feelings of anxiety and dread.

A shot rang out in the night. Jill opened her eyes, lying in the darkness, not quite sure what she'd heard. She gripped the musty blankets and drew them to her chin, her body tensing as another pistol shot shattered the still night.

CHAPTER 6

Jill stared at the unseen ceiling of her bedroom when another shot and then a fourth resounded. She thought she could hear shouts. A shiver raced down her back and a sense of panic and foreboding paralyzed her for a moment.

Then, she leaped from her bed and flung open her door, wrestling into a robe as she hurried to the living room. She leaned against the front window, peering through the thick curtains, but saw nothing.

She wanted to light the lantern but feared the glow would draw attention. Instead, she made her way to the kitchen and put wood in the stove. Placing a kettle on to boil, she returned to her post at the front window and waited for ... she knew not what.

Through the darkness, she made out several figures at the end of the block, near her father's market. Fearing the worst, Jill contemplated leaving the house and going to the store.

No, she decided, it would do no good if something happened to her and made her father upset that she'd left the protection of the house. Besides, what could she do? She would wait and see what happened.

Her anxiety grew as she paced, her thoughts whirling. Gently opening her mother's door, Jill could clearly hear the older woman's labored breathing, laced with a distinct rattle. She crept closer, lifted her mother's cold hand, and shivered.

Nervous and worried, Jill wandered the house until a dull gray hovered in the sky outside. Dawn threatened, yet Jill felt no excitement at a new day.

Jill sipped her tea, probably her fourth or fifth cup, as she stole furtive glances from the front window. She cringed at sight of a cluster of dark faced men coming down the street. Her teacup rattled in the saucer, and she placed the porcelain on the end table before wrapping her robe tighter around her.

Watching their approach, dread stealing into her bones, Jill was not surprised when the trio entered their gate. She jumped at the anticipated knock.

A sense of calamity descended upon her like a funeral shroud. She knew their arrival heralded bad news. Jill gripped the doorknob and drew a deep breath, forcing herself to do this. She had to know.

Opening the door, the men quickly removed their hats. One was the plump man her father had argued with at the docks, and another wore a badge on his vest. Jill wondered if this man was one of the sheriffs she'd seen on the waterfront. Were they here for Samuel?

The lawman stepped forward. "Miss, I hate to bother you like this. Can we come in?"

"No," Jill shook her head. They did not need to come in. She needed to know. "What is this about?"

They shuffled their feet, glancing at one another before the fat man spoke. "Miss, if we could come in ... I'm afraid we have bad news for you."

Jill shook her head again. They did not need to come in. They could tell her right there on the porch. Besides, the news was probably what she figured, and after telling her, she would want them gone immediately. Rejecting entry to the house would make it easier to get rid of them.

Jill thought it best to hurry things along. "Is this about my father?" If they were here for Samuel, wouldn't they have said so by now?

The sheriff cleared his throat. "Yes, miss. I'm afraid to tell you there's been an altercation. It seems some men were trying to rob his store, and your pa tried to frighten them off with a gun. But they weren't much frightened, and one of those men shoved your pa. He fell, miss ... hit his head. I hate to be the one to tell you, but ... he's dead."

Jill nodded woodenly. Somehow, she'd already known. The words were merely a formality. Nodding again to show she'd heard his words, Jill closed the door. She leaned against the hard wood for a long time, hearing their retreating boots on the porch. She could hear the fat man's voice as they walked away. They seemed to be arguing about something. Then the sheriff's voice raised, cutting off the protests of the bigger man.

Jill stared at the silent room. There was nothing to do. Nothing she could do. Her heart pounded like a slow drum, and she focused on the somber rhythm.

After a while, shadows changed in the room as the sun rose, and she moved to the couch. Jill knew things would have to be done but didn't want to start doing them yet. Things were becoming too ugly, too fast.

Well, this is a fine kettle of fish. I'll bet Mother won't last long either. She pondered on that a while and then realized she was not simply being morose, but it possibly could be true. In fact, it probably was true.

She narrowed her eyes and gazed down the hallway. Again, she had to know. Pushing herself off the couch, she made a slow path toward her mother's bedroom. The door was closed, and momentarily Jill halted. Should she go on? Did she really want to know?

Gently pushing the door, Jill peered through the vibrant light streaming in from the eastern window. Her mother looked to be sleeping, the room bathed in brightness and silence. Forcing herself on, Jill sat on the edge of the mattress like she'd done the day before, her eyes fixed on the still, small form in the bed. Maybe she would take her mother's hand, and the old woman would open her eyes.

Jill picked up the cold, lifeless hand, gently stroking the wrinkled skin. "Mother? Mother? It's Jilly. Wake up, Mother."

The thin face appeared relaxed, motionless. Jill saw how thin Mother's hand had become, the transparent skin as frail as onion skin.

The tears came then, rolling slowly down her cheeks. Her heart ached, and a weight rested heavily on her shoulders. First Father and now Mother? Things were moving too quickly for Jill. She stretched out on the bed, lying beside the dead woman as she cried, still gripping the cold hand.

What would happen to her? She felt so alone, so lost. Everything was falling apart. This horrible war, she thought, this horrible, terrible war.

Why, God? Why?

Who could she blame? President Lincoln, the Yankee horde that had invaded the South, or the anti-slavery remarks her father had made? Or could she blame God? Suddenly, she didn't want to be alone.

Her lips pressed into a thin line. Where to turn? Jill thought of Mary as merely a colleague, no one she would call a friend.

Her eyes widened. She had no friends. Jill's friends had slipped away when the trouble started with her father and the store some years ago. Jill had no close friends now, only society acquaintances. She had purposefully avoided such relationships—such entanglements—not trusting people anymore.

NEBRASKA HAVEN

Loneliness swept over her, and she shivered. *This is too much for me to endure*, she thought, glancing up at the ceiling.

Her sluggish, pained mind suddenly thought of Samuel. He could come in now. He could sit and have tea with her. She would not be alone.

Laying her mother's hand on the blankets, Jill reached for the gray hair, smoothing the stiff tresses with a caressing hand. Jill looked at the restful figure, thankful she was finally at peace and would not have to hear about Father. Then Jill rose, moving toward the kitchen. She felt like she should hurry, before too many people were up and moving about, but she felt weighted down, as if her legs were too heavy. She pushed on, not wanting the neighbors to see Samuel coming in her back door.

Jerking the kitchen door open, her robe falling open, she stumbled to the storage shed. Her eyes scanned the nearby houses, searching for movement.

He was there, watching her with anxious eyes. "Miss Jill, what is it? What's wrong?"

It was the first time he'd used her name. "Samuel, I need you to come inside. Come in right now." She wrapped her robe tightly around her and held the shed door open, gesturing for him to follow her.

He peered suspiciously around. "Now, Miss Jill? But it's light and someone might see," he protested, continuing to cast searching glances behind her.

"Samuel," her voice rose shrilly. "You need to come inside right now. I don't want to be alone."

He peered at her, his eyes softening. "All right, Miss Jill. I trust you."

With another glance toward the nearby houses, they scampered back to the house, Samuel's limp hardly slowing him. When the kitchen door closed safely behind them, they stood, letting their quickened breathing slow. Then Jill turned to Samuel. "The tea kettle is probably empty. Let me put some more on. Sit down."

Samuel eased himself into a seat at the table, perching on the edge of a chair. Jill filled the kettle and replaced the teapot on the stove. Opening the grate, she tossed in more wood.

Taking the last of the cheese and bread from the cupboard, they ate a quiet meal. Jill decided she had nothing to lose by telling Samuel everything. First, about losing her job. Then, meeting him on the docks. Now, about Father and Mother.

Jill walked through the events, remembering their particulars as she explained each of them to Samuel. It felt good to go over the details of the past few days. She liked having someone to tell her story to. It helped to list the facts. She was glad she had thought of bringing him inside.

Samuel listened closely, not interrupting. After hearing about the sheriff's visit, he nodded his head, a sage look on his face.

"What does that mean?" Jill asked, mimicking his head movements.

"It means we must tell the right people. They send someone to pick up the body. Also, you'll have to go to the store and make inquiries. If your pa owed people money, it won't take them long to come sniffing around. Miss Jill, we need to conclude your family business and get moving."

"Moving?" Jill squeaked, her eyes widening as she squirmed on her chair. This wasn't what she expected from Samuel. She thought she simply wanted a little company. Perhaps his presence held deeper purpose.

"I know you have to grieve," he went on hurriedly. "That's normal. But you need to be moving. For now, you need to be strong. The Lord wants us to get out of here fast. It sounds like you don't have much choice, anyway."

Jill frowned, suddenly questioning her decision to have him join her. She needed help, companionship, not crazy ideas. "Samuel, I cannot simply leave when there is so much to do. I need to settle my father's affairs, possibly sell the house, and evaluate our assets."

"Well, I don't know what that means, but you need to be quick about it. The Lord wants us going soon." He leaned back in his chair and stared at the ceiling while he stroked his chin. "Do not fear, for the Lord is with us. He will guide and protect us. His ways are righteous and true. He will comfort us."

Jill rolled her eyes in exasperation. She wondered at his simplicity but ignored his suggestions, instead choosing to make some obvious decisions, ones she knew she must do. She cleared her throat and held up a hand. "All right. Let me go to the store and make an appearance. I suspect this Mr. Rogers will be knocking at my door soon enough. While I'm out, I will make arrangements with the undertaker. Meanwhile, you stay hidden. Don't go by any window where someone might see you. Don't answer the door for anyone. I'll be back soon."

CHAPTER 7

Hurrying down the street, Jill felt the conflicting emotions swirl within her. Sadness, fear, and intense worry pervaded her mind, permeating her very soul. What was she going to do? Father and Mother were gone, the family business in shambles and debt. Her own future seemed to be of little importance now, but she could not forget she was newly unemployed. Any ideas of her life's objective were shoved aside as she considered the many responsibilities she now faced.

Anxiety simmered to a boil, and she slowed, coming to a stop near a tall elm tree. She leaned on the rough bark, gathering her topsy-turvy thoughts. Samuel told her to stay focused, not to let her mind wander. He said to do one thing at a time, the rest would sort itself out.

A scowl creased her face as she recalled he'd also mentioned some things about keeping her eyes on Jesus. And being strong and courageous.

Jill drew a deep breath and shoved from the tree, pushing these other thoughts from her mind as she continued her mission, nearing her father's store. As she feared, a throng of strange men filled the mercantile. Her step faltered as she read the large "Closed" sign hanging in the window.

She veered suddenly, taking the street to her right. Perhaps the undertaker first.

It took only a matter of a few minutes to explain the situation to the hawk-eyed man in black. The incredibly thin man rubbed his chin as he listened to Jill describe the two deaths, his beady eyes darting to and fro.

"I must confess," he began, speaking slowly and clearly. "I have already been informed of your poor father's demise. Your mother, however, I did not expect for some time. The doctor had hinted, though, that she was not well, God rest her soul."

Jill could not help but think of the man as a buzzard, waiting for people to die so he could profit. She thought it odd the man seemed so aware of the dead and sick throughout the community.

After making the necessary arrangements, Jill set off again for the store. She could not put it off further.

Approaching the market, Jill slowed, heavy weights dragging at her steps as she climbed the stairs to the boardwalk. She paused outside the door, her hand on the handle. Again, Samuel's words came to her, bolstering her resolve. This deed, this errand, must be attended to or it could never be put behind her.

And behind her it must soon be. She must move on with her own plans. Something had to be done for her. She had nowhere to go, nothing to do. Any direction would be a help, but currently there was none. Maybe Samuel would have ideas when she returned to the house. He seemed to have some notions anyway, more than she did.

Jill peered through the large front window. The sheriff who'd brought the news of Father's untimely death stood beside the counter. Jill also recognized Mr. Rogers, the man from the waterfront who'd argued with her father and accompanied the sheriff early this morning. Filling her lungs, she squared her shoulders and opened the door.

Heads turned as the bell announced her arrival. Jill flinched at the cheerful sound on such a somber morning.

NEBRASKA HAVEN

The sheriff stepped forward first, if a little hesitant. "Well, hello, Miss Foster. I am sorry to see you again under such circumstances. I'm sure you're anxious to know the details of the break-in."

Jill took the proffered hand. "Actually, sheriff, I am anxious to hear all details of my father's business. My understanding is that his store was not doing well." It surprised her how controlled her voice sounded in her ears. The false confidence seemed to give her strength.

The burly man from the waterfront cleared his throat and stepped forward. "Miss Foster, I am sorry for your loss, but as for the business you inquired about, I am afraid it now belongs to me."

Jill wanted to turn and run. She wanted to fall to her knees and cry but steeled herself as she faced the big man. "Mr. Rogers, I presume."

She stared at him a moment, unable to say more. Things seemed too harsh and overwhelming. With a real effort, she pushed the thoughts of her parents' deaths from her mind. Later, she promised herself. Later she would think on these things.

"Mr. Rogers," Jill repeated, not even trying to sound cordial to this man with the pink face. His chubby cheeks obscured his chin.

He mopped his sweaty face with a handkerchief, then thrust the linen back into his chest pocket. "Yes, I am Mr. Rogers. Mr. Foster owed me a great deal of money and had signed his store and merchandise over to me as collateral."

His story seemed to agree with the one her father had relayed to her. Jill did not think this man would try to cheat her, just that he was rude and unfeeling. Not even a day had passed, and the wicked man stood in the store with the sheriff, demanding his due.

"Please bring your copy of the contract to my parents' house tomorrow afternoon at two o'clock. Also, bring a sheriff or a lawyer, someone who can arbitrate the meeting, and we will resolve this matter swiftly. Thank you, sir."

Jill turned on her heel, leaving Mr. Rogers' mouth hanging open. Placing one foot in front of the other, she soon gained the boardwalk. Each step seemed a victory. Striding rapidly, she passed the elm tree that had lent her support earlier. Her thoughts whirling again, she could feel control slipping away, fading fast as panic swelled. Jill knew she must get home.

At the end of the block, as her parents' house loomed, she picked up her pace. Nearly running, she rushed for the comfort of familiar surroundings. Jill bounded up the sagging porch steps, pulled the door open, and fell into the sanctuary of her own home.

Samuel closed the door behind her as Jill stumbled to the couch. "Oh, Samuel, you were right. Whether I'm up for it or not, decisions must be made."

Jill told him of the undertaker and his plan to retrieve Mother's body that very afternoon. Also, the arrangement of the meeting at the house for tomorrow afternoon.

Samuel sat beside her as she cried, her tears falling unchecked. "I did it, Samuel. Just like you said I could. I don't know how, but I talked to them."

"I'll tell you how," Samuel said, nodding. "It was the Spirit. He carried you, Miss Jill. And he will continue to carry you, don't you worry. God is with you. He knows our every tear."

Ignoring his words, Jill continued to sob. Life seemed too demanding and difficult in this very moment. She wanted only to crawl into bed and not get up. Ever.

A knock at the door interrupted her thoughts. Samuel rose quickly to limp away, disappearing down the hallway. Jill wiped the tears from her cheeks and watched him go before she peeked through the curtains, recognizing the mortician, his black frock neatly brushed. In his stove pipe hat, he appeared unusually tall.

Dabbing at her eyes with her pocket hanky, Jill opened the door. The very slender man removed his hat, making his apologies for disturbing her on such a day. He motioned to an assistant, and they moved to retrieve the form of Jill's mother. She had only a brief moment to say goodbye before the two men wrapped her mother gently in a black sheet and carried her from the house to the waiting wagon.

"The funeral for the deceased will be tomorrow at ten o'clock," he declared with importance. Then he cleared his throat, and his eyes darted as he lowered his voice. "The dual ceremony will include a discount," he informed Jill and then was gone.

Returning unsteadily to her place on the couch, Jill collapsed once more. Samuel appeared, bringing tea and bread with cheese slices. Setting the tray down, he served Jill.

She sniffled and sat up as she accepted the offered cup and saucer. "Samuel, thank you," she murmured. "I don't know how I would manage without you."

"The Lord provides in surprising ways, miss," he replied, taking a seat opposite her on a chair.

They ate in silence. Jill noticed the shadows grow long across the wooden floor. Was this dreadful day almost over?

She only nibbled at her sandwich, but the tea seemed to help settle her nerves.

What now?

Jill glanced at the quiet Samuel. He seemed so calm and controlled. "Samuel?" She placed her empty teacup on the small table. "What am I going to do? Please help me. You've been a tremendous help so far."

Samuel tilted his head. "Do you know where your father banked? There must be some clue in the house to show you which direction to go. I am sure your father would've left a diary or a bank book or some business papers. Where would they be?"

Jill considered, grateful for his suggestion. Of course. Surely Father kept a journal or a list of accounts. She glanced at the oak roll top desk in the corner and waved a hand in that direction.

"If there are such papers, they would be there," she replied, not wanting to get up and begin a search. Not yet. Jill felt impressed with what she'd already accomplished today. She didn't know if she could do more.

Samuel studied her, as if guessing her thoughts. "Miss Jill? I know you've pushed hard to get a few things done today, but believe me, it'll help you in the long run. Grief takes time. Getting a few things taken care of now will give you a time to rest later, and then you can wrestle with your sorrow." He shrugged as he gathered the empty cups. "There's a time to live and a time to die, a time to mourn and a time to laugh."

Jill had no idea what he rambled about. She just wanted to be left alone. Then she felt her eyebrows arch at her selfish thought. She wanted to be left alone, but not *be* alone. She was surprised how Samuel's presence comforted her.

Forcing one last effort of the day, she rose. "Samuel, I am going to my room."

CHAPTER 8

With sagging shoulders and a heavy step, Jill retreated from the room. She could feel Samuel's eyes upon her as she navigated the dark hallway.

She tumbled into bed, fully dressed, numb, and exhausted. She stretched out on the mattress as her gaze searched the shadowed ceiling, her hands laced behind her head. Where would she start tomorrow? Her thoughts turned to Samuel, and she almost smiled. He'd been so helpful today. How would she have gotten through this day without him?

Her sleep was filled with images of rolling, grassy hills and that long, flat river that flowed on forever. Jill refused to think about the haunting image, wanting to not think of anything. To just sleep, to rest, to have no problems. But her dreams were disturbed by the tree-bordered waterway, drifting endlessly.

A gentle knock awakened her. Dim light hovered behind her drawn drapes. "Good morning, Miss Jill. I have tea on and some bread and jam. Come when you're ready."

Samuel's shuffling gait retreated down the hall. For a moment, Jill refused to consider what the day might bring.

Then, she remembered the impending funerals and the afternoon meeting. She groaned, wishing to just go back to sleep and think of that stupid river that wouldn't leave her alone.

Sighing, she rolled over, recalling yesterday's progress, and she clenched her teeth. It would do no good to stay in bed. Things had to be done. *Better to just get up and have tea. Maybe Samuel will have ideas.*

She threw back the covers, startled she still wore the previous day's dress. Ignoring the rumpled garment, she padded barefoot down the hall to the kitchen. Samuel gestured to a chair at the table where a steaming cup rested beside a plate.

Eyes half closed, she wrapped her fingers around the hot cup. "Samuel, is there any reason why I need to get out of bed so early? The funerals aren't until ten. I don't feel like getting up this morning." She yawned and then lifted the cup to her lips.

Samuel replaced the kettle on the stove and glanced at Jill over his shoulder. She was surprised by his serious tone as he spoke. "Yes, miss. There are lots of reasons why you need to get out of bed. Trust me. We need to search this house for traveling things and look for important papers. Get dressed now, Miss Jill. We have a busy day ahead of us." He finished with a smile, and Jill marveled at his ability to encourage her.

But she did not smile in return. She wanted to do the right thing, but as she entered her room, the unmade bed called to her. Closing the door, she went back to her bed's inviting covers. A few moments later, a firm knock sounded at her door.

"Miss Jill, get up now. Come on. Time to get up." Through the door, she heard him clap his hands, as if reprimanding a disobedient child.

Eyes wide, she stared at the ceiling. How did he know? Persistent, she thought to herself as she dragged herself from bed once more. Oh, well, she would try hard to get through this day as she'd done yesterday.

After dressing, she let Samuel lead her around the house in search of belongings that would help in their leaving.

"We need to find gear we can carry. Your family has no buggy and team, so we cannot take heavy trunks. Only bags we can easily carry," Samuel told her.

Jill was reminded of her heavy traveling valise she'd brought from school. Of course, the carrier held her books and extra winter clothes. Would this bag she packed not contain winter things? The thought worried her, but only a little, as she considered the other, more pressing business at hand. Winter clothes could wait. Surely they would not need to leave the house for weeks, perhaps months.

They searched every corner of the house, bringing possible travel gear to the sitting room. It was Samuel who discovered the wooden box under her parents' bed.

With trembling fingers, Jill pushed the lid open. Inside lay bundles of papers and a small stack of money. She quickly counted the bills.

"Forty-three dollars. Well, this will be a help," Jill commented, putting the money aside and reaching for the papers.

"Wait, Miss Jill."

Jill looked up, startled at Samuel's interruption.

He tilted his head. "Don't you need to get ready for the funerals?"

Jill suddenly remembered. "Yes," she nodded, pursing her lips. Fear swept over her like a wave. Then, looking at Samuel again, she studied him closely. "I wish you could come with me. I'd greatly appreciate the company." Jill hung her head, staring gloomily at the floor.

She shook her head. "I know it's not possible. I'm sure the town is full of men looking for a limping runaway," Jill whispered as she eyed him critically. How had she so quickly come to rely on this complete stranger?

Samuel nodded, a smile curving the corners of his mouth. "Well, Miss Jill, then let's not give them one to find. If I wore one of your father's outfits, I could pass as your personal servant. No one would suspect me of being a runaway."

Jill's head snapped up and she stared at him, hope mingling with concern. "Samuel, no, it's far too dangerous." She hoped he couldn't hear the disappointment in her voice.

"If the Good Lord can close the mouths of lions and protect Daniel, he can certainly protect me while I go to a funeral," Samuel stated matter-of-factly.

Jill felt her eyes widen as she peered at him.

"Best place to hide a tree is in the forest," he added with a grin.

The day had begun with a bright sun, but by ten o'clock, clouds had gathered, and a fine drizzle fell. At the cemetery, Samuel stood a discreet pace behind Jill, shielding her with an umbrella. She felt grateful for the rain. It hid her tears. Only the undertaker and the preacher joined Jill and Samuel for the funeral.

The rain continued all day and even strengthened. Mr. Rogers and the sheriff arrived at the Foster home promptly at two o'clock, accompanied by a man Jill didn't recognize. The sheriff introduced him as Mr. Stanton, the banker.

As the men and Jill seated themselves in the sitting room, Samuel stayed well hidden in a room down the hallway. Jill did not serve tea.

"As I was saying," Mr. Rogers explained to Jill. "The contract clearly shows your father signed his store and goods over to me in the event he was ever unable to repay his debt."

Jill found Mr. Rogers's manners lacking. And him a Southerner too.

She said nothing, letting the silence hang like the dark clouds outside. Soon, the three men glanced at one another and shifted in their seats.

"Miss Foster," Mr. Stanton finally broke in. "I would not lend your father more money after he mortgaged this house. Mr. Rogers was kind enough to attempt to help your father."

"Help?" Jill growled. "Rob is more like it." The trio of men arched their eyebrows, and Jill dropped her gaze, reproach filling her at her social indiscretion. Again the men shifted, no longer looking at each other.

"Call it what you will, miss," the sheriff put in. "But the paperwork seems to be in order. Your father has lost this house to the bank, and his store must go to Mr. Rogers." He paused, letting these hard facts sink in. "Now, the question is, how long will Mr. Stanton give you before he needs you to vacate the premises?"

All eyes turned upon the banker. He seemed to squirm slightly and then squared his shoulders. "I am afraid I must take possession the day after tomorrow. Mr. Foster has not made a payment in months. The bank has obligations. All the furniture goes with the house as well. There is little you need take with you."

Jill sat silent once more, feeling empty and stunned. The day after tomorrow? She thought she might have months before she would be forced out. Everything was being taken from her so quickly. She must leave the house in two days? How? Where would she go? She understood his words but couldn't grasp the meaning. Was he serious?

Mr. Rogers wiped his hands on his pants. "I'm eager to open the store under my own name, if there are no legal objections." He glanced quickly at the sheriff.

The sheriff stroked his chin. "Well, I see no reason why this transfer of property need be dragged out. It's obvious these men are in their legal right to take possession. Nothing suspicious or fishy here."

Like when Jill saw the men bringing the news of her father's death, here also she knew there was nothing she could say. As if a tidal wave approached, she couldn't stop this change or hold the men back. Bad news seemed to surround her.

The three men rose together. "I am sorry for your loss, Miss Foster," Mr. Rogers acknowledged before hurrying to the door. Mr. Stanton glanced an appraising eye around the room and then quickly followed.

The sheriff had a pitying look in his eyes as he spoke, turning his hat round and round in his hands. "Miss, I'm sorry there's nothing more I can do for you. With the war on, folks are more apt to take care of themselves. It's not like it used to be."

He paused, letting his eyes roam around the room like he hadn't seen the room clearly before. Jill bristled as she watched his mental wheels turn.

"I see you are preparing to leave." He gestured to the pile of empty luggage in the corner. "Any idea where you're heading?"

Jill surveyed the mounds of clothing, blankets, and gear heaped beside the wall. "No, I have no idea what I'm going to do."

She read the anxiety in his eyes, clearly worried if she'd be out in time. A muscle twitched in his jaw, and he nodded once before moving to join the two men on the porch.

Jill touched his arm, halting him. "Sheriff, if I wanted to study a map, get ideas, where would you suggest I look?"

NEBRASKA HAVEN

He tilted his head. "Well, there's the library on Second Street. Or there's the big map on the wall at the train depot. It's not detailed, but it helps orient a person."

Jill nodded, grateful for any suggestions. She trailed him to the door and braced herself against the frame as the three men gathered on the porch, shrugging into their raincoats.

She studied the dreary day, watching the rain fall as the men stepped to the railing and looked out. One by one, they glanced back at her as if they sensed the gloomy events of her day, the heavy weights that rested on her shoulders.

Nothing more seemed to be said as the trio trudged down the street, the rain and steel sky helping them fade from view. Jill leaned against the open door, somehow reluctant to retreat into the dark, drab house, to face what must come next.

She sighed and then shivered, the day's chill finally driving her indoors. "Samuel," she called.

He appeared, his eyes darting around the room. Jill pursed her lips at sight of Samuel in her father's suit.

"They've finally left? Good." He rubbed his hands together as he hobbled into the room. "We need to pray and plan."

Jill blinked. "Pray? That's not necessary," she protested.

Samuel peeked through the curtains. "Now, Miss Jill. We need to make plans, and the first and best thing to do is to seek the Lord's guidance. Anything we do from now on must be his doing. Let's pray and ask him for direction. That way, we can't fail. Without God, we can't succeed."

Not wanting to fight, Jill clenched her teeth as she followed Samuel to the couch. He bowed his head, relaxing his shoulders. Jill smirked at his submissive posture but then closed her eyes.

Samuel cleared his throat. "Lord, we come before you with humble hearts, asking for your blessing and guidance," he began in reverent tones. "We need to know which way to turn. Show us your path and how we're to follow it. You are mighty, Father, and we trust in your hand. We know you will provide for your people. Speak to us in a way we can understand. May your Spirit lead us wherever you want."

Jill tilted her head, peeking through one narrowed eye as the runaway slave prayed. She'd never heard prayers like this. Samuel spoke to God as if he was a friend, someone sitting right here in the room with them. She'd never thought of God as someone that close, near at hand. She'd always pictured him up in the clouds, distant.

The silence grew until Samuel opened his eyes and peered at Jill. "Don't you want to say anything to the Almighty?"

She laughed, startled that the awkward silence was because of her. "Oh, yes. I have a few things to say."

Samuel closed his eyes and lowered his head once more.

Jill shifted, wondering how honest she could be with the Lord. "Well, God, I'm not used to talking to you like this, but I'll give it a try." She squeezed her hands together and drew a deep breath. "I'm not happy with how you're handling things. I lost my job and both parents and I have nothing. What am I going to do now? No direction, no opportunities, no help. Thanks a lot," she concluded, the sarcasm dripping from her final words.

Expecting a rebuke from Samuel or at least a lesson on proper prayer, Jill looked at him, prepared for battle. Instead, Samuel chuckled. "Good job. God knows your heart. He knows you're hurting. It's good to pour your pain and fears out to the Lord. If you can't be honest with God, who can you be honest with?"

Jill scowled, disappointed the expected spiritual clash hadn't materialized. Samuel had been kind and encouraging instead. Jill sighed, angry with God for all the wrongs in her life. Did he really know how he'd messed things up for her? Why had God allowed this to happen? What purpose could there be in her life turning upside down?

Jill stood, eager to escape this faithful man's presence. Clearly, Samuel loved the Lord and reflected his closeness to God. Jill thought she loved God, but why was he so silent now when she needed him most?

She hurried to the kitchen. "I'll fetch tea," she called over her shoulder. Her hands shook as she placed cups in saucers and reached for the kettle. She bit her lip, steam shrouding her with damp heat as her thoughts raced.

Questions. All she had were questions. What now? Where to go? How to get there? Where was God?

She glanced out the window, watching the rain fall, the gray, gloomy day mirroring her mood. She had no answers. She hoped Samuel might come up with something.

They drank tea as they analyzed the bundle of papers in her father's box. Most were old receipts or outdated documents, easily understood and cast aside—unimportant or unhelpful. Among them, Jill found the notes from Mr. Rogers and Mr. Stanton. Everything appeared in order.

"Look at this." Samuel waved a stained, rumpled document. Jill studied the paper and then frowned, recognizing the worthless deed to land her father had taken in exchange for goods. The property was located somewhere in Nebraska Territory on the Oregon Trail, just west of Fort Kearny. The paper contained a full description of the buildings and land holdings, even explicit directions from Fort Kearny. Jill put the land title aside, remembering Father had said it had no financial value. Weary, depressed, her heart full of grief, Jill dragged herself early to bed.

Tossing and turning, peace eluded her for many long hours. Finally, sleep claimed Jill only to distress her further with images of wide-open pieces of prairie and an ugly, tree-lined, flat river that wound on and on.

A dismal gray light streamed through her window, falling across her face. Jill blinked, turning from the dull gleam. She'd slept longer than intended. She hugged herself tightly and stared at the ceiling. So what? She didn't have to get up for anything special, she reminded herself. At least there were no funerals or meetings today.

Jill heard Samuel rustling about in the kitchen. He'd proven himself useful, she thought with appreciation. More than that, he was good company, helping her cope with the struggles around her. She felt assailed on all sides, with difficulty and pain, but Samuel stood right there with her.

She rolled over and propped herself on one elbow. Who was he? She'd only met him a few days ago, and now she couldn't think of being without him. He seemed suddenly indispensable.

She shook her head, remembering he was a fugitive from the law. A runaway slave from Kentucky, sought by authorities all over St. Louis. If Master Carter offered a big enough reward, soon bounty hunters would pick up his trail and be searching for him. Jill frowned and lay back, stiffening as she tugged the covers higher.

Suddenly, she clenched her teeth and kicked the covers away. If they came looking for him, Samuel's trail would lead to her.

CHAPTER 9

Jill's thoughts kept returning to the Nebraska property. It seemed to be her only possible solution right now, but she hated the idea of fleeing farther from the South. Perhaps she could sell the land. Did anyone want property in Nebraska, and how much could she get for the property? She wasn't quite sure even where the land was located.

She peeked through the drawn curtains, watching the rain. "Samuel? Have you ever heard of Nebraska?" Jill let the curtains fall into place as she turned, glancing at the runaway. How odd, she thought, asking an escaped slave about geographic locations even she didn't know. But he had been educated to a point, and these were desperate times.

He shook his head. "Master Carter didn't like to talk about different places in front of me. I was never allowed to see maps." He shrugged. "Supposed to keep me from getting ideas." A moment later, he added with a grin, "I guess that didn't work."

Samuel sat on the couch, Jill's mother's Bible open on his lap. She turned back to the window but studied him from the corner of her eye. He'd been reading now for over an hour. She'd never seen her mother open the thick book. In fact, Mother only carried the heavy volume to church when they occasionally attended services. How could anyone look at the Bible for this length of time? All that *thee* and *thou* would drive her crazy.

Church attendance was expected of good folks of proper upbringing—even if her own family hadn't gone much. At the girl's college in Paducah, going to church had been encouraged as part of proper social customs. You didn't question it—you simply obeyed. And a thick Bible tucked under one arm appeared a good prop.

Jill arched an eyebrow, recalling what her father had said about the importance of keeping up appearances.

Samuel, however, acted like he actually *enjoyed* church things. Praying, reading the Bible, seeking God's guidance. Doing all those things without being told seemed foreign to Jill.

"Where is Nebraska?" he asked, looking up from his reading.

Jill hesitated, wondering how to explain. "We were in Kentucky. We came west to Missouri. If you continue farther west, you come to Kansas. Above Kansas is Nebraska." Jill puckered her brow and then added, "I think."

"Is it a slave state, like Missouri and Kentucky?"

Jill's frown deepened. "Well, properly, it's not a state at all. It's a territory. They don't have the population yet to become a state."

"Are there slaves in territories?" Samuel persisted, interest shining in his eyes.

Jill wrapped her arms across her middle as she considered how to answer. "Well, in the old days, no. But after the war with Mexico, some of the western territories were allowed to have slaves, like New Mexico Territory. But I believe Nebraska is a free territory," Jill said, not completely confident of her information. Suddenly, she wished she'd paid more attention to this sort of thing. Who could've guessed how important it might become?

NEBRASKA HAVEN

Politics surrounding slavery seemed to always be changing and shifting. Jill remembered when slaves who escaped north of the Ohio River were considered free. Then, in 1850, slaves who had escaped north of the Ohio had to be returned to their masters in the South. She rubbed her forehead. This was all more than she needed to be considering right now.

Samuel sat forward in his seat and smiled. "Miss Jill, you say Nebraska is a free territory, and you own land in Nebraska, right? Well, there's our answer. Go to Nebraska."

Jill smiled at his simple logic. "No, Samuel, I am not going to Nebraska. It's far from here, and I have no desire to go there. I like the South. I was raised here. I would like to stay here. Besides, I'm waiting for word about another teaching position. I think I should stay."

He scowled and slumped back on the couch before closing the Bible and setting the big book aside. "But you have nowhere else to go. You must leave this house tomorrow. Where will you go?"

Jill fidgeted and turned away, not knowing how to respond. What could she say? She'd been wrestling with that very question. Jill chewed her lip as she peered past the dark drapes again, letting her mind work.

Going to Mary in Minnesota was not an option. Mary wasn't really a friend, anyway. The towns or residences of other school faculty were unknown to Jill. She'd purposefully avoided such personal connections. She was not aware of any family connections, had no local friends, and no other real options. But she wanted to stay in a place where she felt comfortable with the culture. Besides, her life goals specifically called on her to marry a gentleman one day. She'd never heard of gentleman outside of the South.

Nebraska? Jill smiled to herself, disregarding the preposterous notion. No, it was too far away. Besides, she didn't know if the title to the land was legitimate. What if it had been fabricated? It would be just her luck to travel all that way to discover the place didn't even exist.

But the thought niggled at her, teasing her with its refusal to be ignored. What would Nebraska be like? Wasn't that area what people called the frontier and full of wild Indians? She'd even heard of the vast herds of buffalo that roamed the Great Plains, that endless expanse somewhere to the west of Missouri. Were there houses or buildings out there? Were there schools or towns ... other people of refinement?

She shook her head, almost laughing at herself. It didn't matter what Nebraska was like, she had no intention of going there.

She narrowed her eyes, her nose wrinkling. But where, then? There was no time to write letters of inquiry to other colleges for teaching positions. They would be inundated with applications, no doubt. The war had taken its toll on educational institutions everywhere. Jill remembered the report of some Southern military institutes allowing their cadets to join the war. The schools had closed. There were few ladies' schools, anyway.

"Miss Jill," Samuel spoke again, his voice breaking into her thoughts. She glanced at him over her shoulder. He wore a serious look, and his eyes gleamed in the dim light. "I'm going to pray about Nebraska. I have a good feeling about this." Then, as his face relaxed, he closed his eyes.

She scowled as she watched his lips begin to silently move. Why did he not feel the anxiety Jill felt so acutely? He was a runaway slave, for God's sake, hunted by the authorities all over. If he was recaptured, he was sure to be severely punished. Yet, the young man seemed confident of God's protection.

Jill shook her head, irritated by his self-assurance. "Samuel, you don't know what you're talking about," she snapped. "Nebraska is far from here. We don't have a buggy, we can't pay for stage travel, and you have a bad limp. We probably couldn't even walk there if we wanted to. Besides, I'm not entirely convinced this piece of land really exists. Father took the deed from a desperate man in exchange for goods. The man might've fooled Father. On top of all that, you're wanted by the law. Perhaps I am too. We're criminals, you and I." Jill chortled at their ridiculous situation.

Teasing or not, she felt concerned. The house would have to be vacated tomorrow. They had nowhere to strike out for, no destination.

Her desperate idea from last night returned and she glanced sharply at the slave. What if she ditched Samuel? She wasn't truly responsible for him. He couldn't walk very fast and would slow her down. Traveling without him would certainly be safer. Or would it? She thought about traveling as a woman alone.

Jill's chest tightened, and she clasped her hands together, squeezing her fingers. She could get away, go ... go ... where?

She drew in a deep breath and then let it out slowly. No, Jill concluded, looking at the young man on the couch. He'd been such a help when help was needed. She was lonely, and he was now her friend. Her only friend. For better or for worse, she would help him. Maybe it was foolhardy to tie up with a runaway, but Jill felt she owed him. He certainly had helped her. Besides, an easy companionship had arisen between them that surprised her. She felt compelled.

She inhaled sharply. And Father had hated slavery.

Samuel opened the Bible again. "I'm going to pray more about Nebraska. There must be some way to get there we can afford. Besides, I like the sound of the name."

Jill crossed the room and sat on the chair facing Samuel. "You enjoy reading the Bible?" She gestured to the thick book he held.

"Oh, yes, Miss Jill," he said in a soft voice. "The Word of God speaks to me."

"Is that how the Lord will guide us? I mean, through a verse in the Bible?" Jill wondered how God communicated with people. Certainly the Almighty had never said anything aloud to her. She marveled at her unexpected interest as her circumstances worsened.

Samuel shrugged. "Sometimes, he leads me to a Scripture that speaks to my particular concern. Other times, the Spirit fills my heart with a thought or idea. Other times, the Lord speaks to me through the wisdom of other Christians I respect."

Jill huffed. "Why doesn't he just speak plainly, out loud, so I can hear him? Perhaps a booming command from the clouds or a giant finger pointing in a certain direction."

Samuel laughed. "When God revealed himself to Elijah, it was not through a mighty wind, fire, or an earthquake. God whispered."

"Whispered?" Jill leaned forward, her gaze locked on Samuel. "Does God whisper to you?"

He nodded. "The Spirit works in different ways. Sometimes whispering to my soul. Other times not saying a thing, allowing me to pray and make decisions that will develop my faith. You know, live and learn."

Jill wrinkled her nose. "Learn what? If God doesn't speak, doesn't guide me, what am I to learn? Sounds like he forgot me."

Samuel chuckled. "That's foolish. God never forgets us. He guides us, allowing us to learn from every situation we face. To build our faith, to develop our trust. He is faithful to use our struggles, our frustrations, our sorrows to shape us into the people he wants us to become."

As Samuel finished speaking, Jill scowled. She held up a hand, palm out, as if trying to stop his meaning from reaching her. "Well, I don't like it. And I'm going to do what seems best to me. Of course, the Lord is welcome to join us, if he is so inclined, but I must make a decision quickly. And I am not going to Nebraska."

Samuel laughed loudly as he slapped his knee.

"What's so funny?" Jill demanded as she clenched her teeth. She grew tired of this spiritual banter that seemed to be of little help. She needed assistance, not veiled suggestions.

"You sound like Jonah. When God told him where to go, he turned and ran t'other way." Samuel quieted, becoming serious once more. "I think the Lord is speaking to you. I think you should pray about Nebraska."

"Nebraska," Jill whispered, rolling the word on her tongue. Was God guiding her? She shook her head, unsure. "But I don't want to go to Nebraska."

Samuel grinned. "Maybe that's the point." He gestured about with a hand, indicating everything. "Maybe this isn't about what you want. Let's see what God wants."

CHAPTER 10

The gentle rain persisted all day. Jill spent the time putting clothes into her valise, taking them out in favor of others, and restlessly going through all her parents' things. It felt hard to believe she would be leaving her childhood home behind.

Jill frowned as her hands stilled, remembering the way her friends had turned their backs on her one by one. The political climate of Missouri was not friendly to people who spoke out against slavery. Missouri had stayed in the Union for the simple reason that it benefited politically from this decision. Where the other Southern states had vacated their seats in Congress, Missouri remained, keeping its political voice in government.

A slave state Missouri might be, but they were not a part of the Confederacy or involved in the Southerners attempt to withdraw from a more powerful nation. Consequently, Jill's father had been punished in his business for his anti-slavery attitude, and Jill had been punished socially.

She'd looked forward to going away to school, leaving no real ties in St. Louis other than her parents. Now she was here once more—facing all these unfamiliar and unappealing events.

Silently, she finished packing, resolving to leave St. Louis far behind.

The day they needed to vacate her childhood home dawned clear and blue. Outside, birds whistled merrily, and Jill took the fine weather as a good sign, an omen that something positive would present itself this day. She needed hope, a direction, a decision. Desperately, she wanted to know what to do.

Samuel studied the azure sky and hailed this as an answer to his prayer. "See, Miss Jill, this is the Lord's will. We're going to Nebraska."

Her hopeful spirit waned at his confident tone. Last night's sleep had been fraught with disturbing images of open prairie that stretched in every direction, along with that dirty, slow river. Jill felt weary, as if she hadn't slept at all. She was in no mood for teasing this day. Fear filled her as she realized the time to depart had come, and a cloud of despair surrounded her. She felt a sense of desperation to make a decision, any decision. Only the unknown land in Nebraska kept coming to the forefront of her mind, seemingly her only option, and she hated it.

She crossed her arms over her chest and glared at him. "And how do you propose to get there, I would like to know?" Her tone held an icy sharpness she regretted. Their predicament wasn't Samuel's fault. Jill suddenly felt sorry for him. He would've done much better tying up with someone else, someone who had ideas and options. Jill hoped she would not hold him back from getting away. He deserved what he searched for, whatever that may be.

"I've been thinking on that," he explained, ignoring her frigid inquiry. "I believe God will guide us as we begin. We just need to trust and strike out, like Abraham struck out, not knowing exactly where the Lord would lead. Just strike out in faith. The Lord will provide the means."

Jill smirked. "That's a stupid plan. It's like having no plan at all." She kicked her travel valise.

"No, Miss Jill. It's the perfect plan. We trust in the Lord. Let him provide a way. Our thinking will just get in the way. Let the Almighty do his thing. He loves his people. He wants to do good things for us. We just have to believe he will. If God is for us, who can stand against us?"

Fatigue, grief, anxiety, and a desire to let someone else make the decisions forced Jill to abdicate. Resigned, she shrugged. "Samuel, we have no other option. I'm willing to give it a try. I want to spend some time writing letters today, informing Mary and headmaster Hopkins of my intention to settle in Nebraska. They can send letters to Fort Kearny. I hope this is only temporary, until I can find something better. In the meantime, we will go there and see if Father was hoodwinked."

A sudden knock interrupted them. Samuel scurried from the room, his limp forcing him to sway like a ship in a storm. Jill rose and smoothed her dress before opening the door. Her eyes widened as she recognized the banker standing on the porch.

"Mr. Stanton, good afternoon. What can I do for you?"

He removed his hat. "Miss Foster, I wanted to make sure there were no complications with the plan to vacate the house today."

"No, Mr. Stanton. No complications. We—uh, I mean I, will be leaving tonight, have no fear. The house will be empty in the morning, I assure you."

"Fine, fine," he muttered. "Well, I'll leave you to your packing. Good day, Miss Foster."

Mr. Stanton turned to leave but stopped with a word from Jill. "Mr. Stanton, I will be leaving a few trunks with personal effects. Please see they are delivered to the train station in the morning. I will leave some money for the shipping cost and a note of their destination."

The man nodded and continued down the porch steps. Jill watched him depart, glad to see him go. Perhaps it would be better to start fresh somewhere else. Missouri certainly had not been kind to her.

The day passed too quickly. Jill wrote her few letters and went over her packing again and again. They would have to carry all they needed for now. The trunks would meet them at Fort Kearny, taken upriver on a steamboat. She felt eager to study the map at the train depot to get her bearings.

After the sun set, Jill closed the door firmly behind her, saying a final goodbye to the only home she'd ever known. Glancing at the house, Jill could feel the tears threatening. A lump rose in her throat and she bit her lip. Her heart swelled with sadness, and she fought the emotion, sensing now was the time for strength, not weakness. "This is where I was raised. I will never see this house or my parents again," she whispered, caressing the handrail to the back door.

Samuel shifted beside her, adjusting the strap of the heavy carpetbag on his shoulder. "Now, Miss Jill, don't be afraid. God says to be strong and courageous. Don't worry, he will guide us. Remember what the angel told the Virgin Mary?"

Jill shook her head as she glanced at the few stars that dotted the night sky, grateful for the darkness that would conceal their departure.

"Gabriel said to not be afraid, that God had something important for her to do. That's for me and you too, Miss Jill. Don't be afraid. God is with us. He has something for us to do."

She sighed, not encouraged by his confidence. But she nodded and swallowed hard, following him into the dark street. Together, they started toward the train depot.

NEBRASKA HAVEN

Jill saw the familiar bulk of her father's store loom in the darkness. With the aid of light from a nearby tavern, Jill read the unfamiliar words over the old building. "Roger's Emporium." Jill felt her throat tighten, and she squeezed her eyes shut for a moment. This was not the time for tears. Later, she promised herself.

Samuel's limp forced him to move slowly, and Jill looked up at the night sky as they meandered. Only a few clouds played peek-a-boo with the growing number of stars. The moon would be up soon. She hoped they would be far on their way before morning.

"Samuel? Does your foot hurt when you walk?"

"No, miss. It doesn't hurt at all. It just doesn't let me move fast." He chuckled. "It's all I've ever known. I limp because of the shape of my foot, but it doesn't hurt."

"Was it hard being a slave with a bad foot?" Jill shivered a little, not sure if it was from the night's chill or from being nervous.

"It's hard being a slave, no matter what. My foot made it difficult to work in the fields, so master made me learn to read and put me on the docks. I'm very strong and can work hard, but I cannot move quickly."

"Yes, I see." Jill glanced around, searching for observers.

"Don't you worry about that, Miss Jill. God will get us where we're supposed to be." Again, his confidence did not touch her. Perhaps her doubts were too great, but Jill feared so much. Would they be caught by the sheriff? Would Samuel's limp prohibit him from travel? Was the land in Nebraska a farce? There were too many variables.

She remembered Samuel's words. *Do not fear.* The phrase appeared in the Bible, he'd said. Jill noticed he'd packed her mother's Bible as a possession for the road. Foolish, she thought. Books are heavy. She'd packed her own books in the large trunks along with her winter clothes and house items, which Mr. Stanton assured he would send to Fort Kearny.

Samuel carried a satchel in one hand, her heavy bag slung from one shoulder, and a bundle of blankets strapped to his back. Jill carried only a small valise. They had so little. But, she mused, plenty of folks nowadays had little else. Not a week went by in Paducah she hadn't seen refugees fleeing the war, carrying only what they could of their possessions. Lots of people had suffered from the war. Her story seemed nothing special.

The walking took the chill from her. Starting out at night had been her idea—to avoid prying eyes. Besides, there would be less traffic on the road this time of night ... she hoped.

They turned a corner and Jill sighted the train depot, the long, low building looming in the darkness. A single gas lamp draped a halo of light on the wooden landing. No one was in sight as Jill rested her valise on a bench and moved to the map painted on the wall.

Samuel hobbled up the steps and dropped his load, joining Jill in studying the dim outline and colored lines that indicated borders, rivers, and roads.

"Where are we?" he asked, squinting at the drawing.

"Here's St. Louis." Jill placed a finger below the junction of the Missouri and Mississippi Rivers.

"Where's Nebraska?" Samuel slowly scanned the map of Missouri and its neighbors.

"Over here, I think." Jill pointed to an empty place above Kansas, just to the left of Iowa. She traced a finger up the Missouri River to Omaha.

"It's not even marked on the map," Samuel muttered, a hint of worry creeping into his tone.

She turned on him, glowering in the dim light of the gas lamp. "I thought God would help us. I thought he would guide us there," she accused, unable to keep the scorn from her words.

Samuel nodded slowly, his face setting in stern lines. "You're right, Miss Jill. Thanks for reminding me." He glanced at her and smiled. "See? We're good for each other. You encourage me."

Jill scowled as she turned back to the map, frustrated he hadn't perceived her sarcasm. "We can cross the Missouri here above St. Louis," she said, tracing a route across the river. "Then turn west."

"Why not go west now and avoid crossing the river? The Missouri River looks big."

Jill's finger moved farther west, indicating other rivers and labels. "The Ozarks are there. Rough land. We need to keep to flat land if we can." She glanced at his crooked leg for significance.

Samuel nodded and then took a step backward. "I've been thinking. You would do better without me. Maybe you should go on alone."

Jill blanched, wondering if he'd guessed her earlier feelings. Then she snorted. "Forget it. You wouldn't make it a mile without me, and I need your help as well. Just look at the way I've got you loaded down like a mule. You're stuck with me now, Samuel, so help me figure out which way to go. We're a team, right?"

He grinned at her as he reached for the luggage. "Right. Let's go."

They trudged on, passing block after block of darkened streets as they walked north toward the Missouri River. Occasionally, dogs barked, making them quicken as they passed. The city pressed around them, and Jill tried to concentrate, worried she'd lose her nerve if she thought too much of the enormity of their journey. She asked Samuel about his life as they hesitated behind buildings, peering around corners to study the road ahead.

Samuel told tales of serving in the big house on the plantation, learning how to read and speak better. Once, he even worked with a wood carver, learning the trade.

"I didn't have to move around quick when I worked with the lumber. I liked it, the smell of the wood chips and the feel of the smooth timber. The wood carver didn't like me, though. Said I bothered him with my talk of Jesus. I think he had an evil spirit in him." He paused and then added, "Jesus was the son of a carpenter, you know."

Jill explained how to properly eat soup at a ball.

Samuel chuckled in the darkness during her story, his white teeth flashing.

"What's so funny?" Jill demanded, sensing his lack of appreciation for the finer social graces.

"Is that important to know? How to eat soup at a ball?"

"Absolutely," Jill snapped, irritated at his question. "A mistake like that could destroy your social standing in the community. Proper etiquette, on the other hand, could play an important part in your social position, helping you climb the social ladder. Lacking proper manners could affect even who you married, who your social contacts were, even your husband's position in the community."

"I guess I never thought about my social standing," Samuel grumbled with a snort.

Even in the dark, Jill could tell he laughed at her.

"Have you thought of your future? What kind of legacy you hope to pass on to your children?" His unexpected query startled her.

"Children?" Jill felt her eyebrows arch. "Yes, family is important."

"And the type of man you will marry? Will his social standing be significant in your choice?" Now his persistence felt too intrusive, as if he'd crossed a line. What right did he have to ask her about whom she'd marry?

Jill shifted the valise and puckered her lips. "Of course. I mean, I guess I always figured I'd marry a gentleman."

"Because you love him or because of his social standing?"

She shot him a sharp glance from the corner of her eye. "I don't think that's any of your business."

"What I'm getting at," Samuel explained hurriedly, "is I don't hear God figures into your reckoning."

"God?" Jill frowned, confused. She watched Samuel shrug.

"Does the Lord have a say? Do you seek God's guidance in such important matters?"

Samuel said nothing more as the pair tramped on, but Jill wondered at his inquiry. She didn't plan on being in Nebraska long enough to find a husband, although she would gladly give up her struggles and allow a wealthy man to assist her, help lug the heavy load she now found herself carrying. But she was young and had plenty of time before marriage. Besides, the gentlemen were currently preoccupied, off fighting the war. She would have to wait regardless. In time, she expected to return east with a posting. Teaching was her career, and she loved the South. The land of gentlemen.

As for God, Jill's frown deepened. She had to confess she thought little of the Lord, unless when drowning in calamity, like now. It'd never occurred to her to include Jesus in her future plans.

Slowly, the buildings and houses thinned. All the next day, they hid in an orchard, nibbling on bread and ham slices they'd brought with them.

"We'll have to stop and buy more food." Jill yawned as Samuel spread a blanket under a tree for her.

"You get some rest, Miss Jill. We have plenty of food for a day or two. First, we need to put distance between us and the city."

The next night, they came to the river.

CHAPTER II

"See anything?" Jill pressed against the fence, scanning the riverbank, searching for a way across. Maybe a boat or a ferry. No ... a ferry might attract unwanted attention. She reminded herself she traveled with a runaway, one who noticeably limped and was easy to identify.

Samuel nodded in the gloom, the dull moonlight casting a beckoning ribbon across the rippling water. Waves lapped the distant banks while crickets chirped musically around them. An owl hooted. All seemed peaceful, and Jill wondered if they should find a place to sleep. Perhaps they should wait to try and cross tomorrow night.

"I see a man in a boat. His pipe glows every time he puffs," Samuel reported in a whisper. Jill's gaze followed his pointing arm.

"All right. Let's see if he'll take us across. I don't see any other choice."

Samuel hefted Jill's heavy bag and marched toward the little boat, his gait slowing as he shuffled in the loose dirt. Jill stepped forward, remembering to take the lead. She was supposed to be the one in charge.

The lone man's head turned at their approach. "Who's there?" he challenged. Jill saw him reach toward his belt.

"Sir? We need to get across the river tonight. Important business demands it. Would you allow us to rent your boat, or do you ferry passengers?" She drew up next to the boat, surveying its length. Plenty of room for the two of them. This should do nicely.

The man grinned in the moonlight, revealing missing teeth. White whiskers shadowed his face, and Jill could tell he was old, but the sharp glint in his eye told her he was not to be trusted.

"Ah? A lady with her slave? Well, I don't need to be fishing tonight," he said as he pulled in his line. He dropped the pole into the bottom of the boat and took his pipe from his mouth as he turned back to Jill. "Of course, I'll take you across ... for a price." He rubbed his whiskers with a gnarled hand and arched his brows, eyeing Jill from top to bottom. "Say eight bits?"

Jill chuckled. "Ridiculous. I'll pay four bits, a quarter apiece." She stepped to the boat and gripped the side, preparing to board. Her heart pounded and she wondered where the strength to bluff came from. She felt terrified. What if this man refused and guessed they were escaping? Would he alert the authorities?

The old man laughed and reached for the oars. "All right, miss. Boy, untie me."

Jill glanced at Samuel and then scrambled into the boat, making room for him after he shoved off from the bank. The man allowed the boat to drift and point upstream while he drew deeply on his pipe. "A beautiful night for a boat ride," he said as he pulled at the oars. Moonlight shimmered brightly, and when the man's coat shifted, Jill saw the butt of a pistol in his belt.

Samuel and Jill sat quiet. She wondered if Samuel felt the same fear that stifled her.

"Well, the war couldn't be going better," the old man commented, his arms pumping as he watched Samuel and Jill in the stern of the boat. Behind him, the bow pointed diagonally across the river.

Jill shifted, wishing the ride were over. "I was in Paducah when the wounded came in from Shiloh," she offered, hoping to put his searching comment to rest.

The pipe glowed as the man nodded. "I read about that in the paper. That Yankee Grant is a bad one. I think Jeff Davis will have to look out for him."

Jill said nothing as the boat neared midway, the currents swirling, forcing the old man to maneuver around a submerged tree stuck near a sandbar. A trickle of sweat slipped down the back of her neck and Jill shuddered as a chill pierced her heart. She felt the panic swell and fought the sensation down, trying to stay in control and not allow her fear to overtake her. Samuel's words rang in her ears. *Do not fear.*

"I don't see how the war can go on much longer," the old man continued as the boat rounded another snag. "Boy, push off there. Don't let us get caught up." He bobbed his head at a third oar in the bottom of the boat.

Samuel lifted the pole and pushed off from the snag. The boat skimmed past the obstacle and continued toward the northern bank. Jill tensed, preparing to leap from the boat when they neared shore.

"I mean, I was with Lee in Mexico, and I know he can't be whipped," the man went on, straining against the oars. Jill frowned as she studied the man, his pipe glowing from the work. He noticed her scrutiny and released an oar, pointing to his leg. The bow swung downstream as her gaze dropped. Jill gasped, realizing he had only one leg, a wooden stump protruding from his torn pants.

"That's where I lost my leg," he said as he grabbed for the oars and righted the boat.

Jill gripped the sides of the craft, wishing they were closer to shore. She considered jumping into the river and taking her chances.

No one spoke for a few minutes, and the boat completed the crossing, the bow pushing into the soft mud of the opposite bank. Jill leaped onto shore and scrambled to hold the rope until Samuel climbed out.

"I will be taking my pay now, miss. But before I do, I wonder what side yer for? Are you a Yankee, helping this boy escape? Do you work for that Underground Railway I've read about?"

Jill stared at him, her eyes widening, knowing she was caught. Her blood seemed to freeze along with her tongue, not protesting, not arguing. Guilt hovered around her, and she couldn't move, couldn't reply.

The boatman nodded and took the pipe from his lips. "Uh-huh, I thought so," he mumbled as he replaced his pipe and reached for his belt gun.

Jill wanted to scream, but her heart leaped to her throat. She watched in horror as the old man grasped the gun and brought the pistol level, but Samuel's oar knocked the weapon from his hand. A splash sounded as the pistol disappeared, the river swallowing the weapon.

Samuel moved beside her, the oar outstretched toward the one-legged man. "Miss, grab our bags," he ordered. Jill moved, her hands trembling as she hurried to comply. She tossed the luggage onto shore.

"Well, you got the drop on me," the old man said as he leaned back, lifting the oars. "You see I can't chase you. But unless you kill me, I will surely tell the sheriff about you. I seem to remember a reward for a runaway with a limp."

Jill laughed as she gathered the baggage, handing some of them to Samuel. The boat drifted from the bank, and she shook her head, suddenly free and excited. They'd crossed the river. They would go on. "I don't care what you tell the sheriff. It's a big country between here and Minnesota. I doubt if he can find us."

They stepped into the brush as the boat turned, the man making for the other side of the river. Jill tripped and heard her dress rip as she shoved the bag she carried ahead of her, using the colorful valise as a shield to push branches from her path.

Blindly, she wrestled through the dense undergrowth, plowing a way among the trees and bushes. Limbs reached for her, and Jill felt them scratch her skin, but she fought on, suddenly aware of her strength, her ability to keep moving forward. She'd done it. With God's words in her ears, she'd been strong. Exhilarated with their success, she almost fell as she stumbled onto a moonlit road.

"What was that about Minnesota?" Samuel asked as he emerged from the woods and joined her on the road.

Jill paused, ignoring the cut on her palm and the tear in her dress as she doubled over, hands on her knees. She looked down the road. The moon was high now and they could walk for hours before dawn. "I just said that to lead them astray. Come on, Samuel. We've got a long way to go."

CHAPTER 12

Their routine fell quickly into place. They always walked at night, always moving west, always toward Kansas, the free state. By day, they rested in the woods or in a farmer's orchard.

Three days after their departure, Jill had slipped into a sleepy village for supplies right before the store closed for the night. They would need to ration any supplies, never knowing when they might be able to enter a store again.

During their travel, they talked. Jill noticed Samuel's limp had become more pronounced the farther they traveled. He kept moving, despite the hobble, but she knew his deformity kept them from covering ground quickly.

"What are you truly looking for?" she asked him. "What do you want out of life?"

"A place to call home," he replied after a pause.

"Any place?" she prodded.

He chuckled softly, glancing at the moon through the overhead branches. "No, not just any place. A farm would be best. I love working with my hands. A place I can do some good, help folks." He glanced sideways at Jill. "I'm open to whatever the Lord brings me. Who knows? Anything is possible in Nebraska."

Jill smiled into the gloom, wishing good things for her new friend. Friend? She tensed, not liking the term. Friends had betrayed her, turned from her. But Samuel seemed different.

She was about to reply when he stopped and then hissed, gesturing for her to follow him as he plunged into the ditch. They scrambled under the overhanging foliage as Samuel lifted a finger to his lips.

She strained to hear something but heard only the crickets chirping. An owl soared quietly through the avenue between the trees, but there was no other sound. She opened her mouth to ask Samuel what he'd heard when her ears caught the sound of pounding horse hooves.

Samuel leaned further into the deepest shadows and Jill followed. There they crouched, hearing the riders approach. The hair on the back of Jill's neck prickled, and her palms moistened as she stared at the road. Samuel stiffened beside her, frozen into a motionless shadow. Her heart beat loudly in her ears, and Jill hoped the riders couldn't hear the noise.

A band of seven men, dressed all in black and wearing wide hats that hid their faces, approached. When they had come almost to the spot where Jill and Samuel hid, the men pulled their mounts to a walk and passed unhurriedly, the winded animals blowing steam, small clouds forming as the horses breathed. Slowly, slowly, the riders made their way down the dark road.

The pair waited in silence until the group vanished from view.

Samuel rose hesitantly, looking both ways up and down the trail. "Patrollers," he hissed, leading Jill back onto the road. "They ride at night looking for runaways."

They plodded on, taking only a couple of short breaks, their conversation now stifled. They passed the outskirts of a village tucked into a curve of the river, just to the south of them. Soon, wooded lanes and small clearings lined the road.

Velvet blue replaced pitch black in the eastern sky, and Jill knew dawn approached. Weary and footsore, she was about to signal the halt for the day when she saw a dim glow farther along the road. As they neared, she recognized a campfire.

"Samuel, let me do the talking. We'll act as if you are my servant. Look sharp now. I don't want to get in anything we can't get ourselves out of," Jill warned.

They slowed, peering at the three wagons with wary eyes. Two of the vehicles sat a short distance away while a fire crackled beside the third, the canvas covering soiled and ripped. Jill studied the dirty wagon closer and watched as an old woman moved about, an iron kettle simmering on the campfire.

As the woman bent to the blaze, Samuel stepped on a stick. She looked up, her eyes narrowing as she considered the travelers.

"Who's there? Come out with you and let me have a look."

Jill and Samuel glanced at one another before walking into the firelight.

"Well now, refugees, I'll wager," the woman said, straightening beside the fire. Her hand went to the small of her back and she winced. Jill read the pain in her lined features. "I'm not young like I used to be. Missy, tell your boy to gather more firewood."

With a cautious glance at Samuel, Jill nodded. Samuel dropped the carpetbag and moved into the deeper shadows of the nearby woods.

Jill gratefully laid her own bag down. It had been a long night. She felt tired and anxious, not sure if she could trust this situation, but needing a rest.

"Why don't you mind that stew, missy? I don't like to bend over. My back gives me fits something fierce." The old woman didn't wait for a response but sat down on a camp bench. Jill squatted by the fire, fussing with the soup and a skillet of sliced potatoes. Her mouth watered at the delicious aroma and hunger pangs twitched inside her. She hadn't realized how hungry she was.

Samuel returned with a load of wood.

"Say, boy, you're strong," the woman announced, studying Samuel as he dropped the firewood beside Jill. "I could use someone like you around my camp. I only got Earl, and he's in worse shape than me." The woman eyed Jill for a moment, scrutinizing her ability at the fire. Then, she glanced again at Samuel. "Where you two headed?"

Jill hesitated. How much should she tell this stranger? Was there any way this woman had heard about a limping runaway from Kentucky? Jill quickly scanned the nearby woods and decided they could get away if they needed to.

"We're going west," Jill replied honestly enough, yet purposefully vague.

The older woman pursed her lips and stared at Jill, making her feel uneasy as she fiddled with the frying potatoes, the intoxicating smell wafting around her.

"You and your slave running away?"

Icy fingers of fear gripped her heart, and Jill laughed, trying to cover her panic. "Oh, yes, we are. We can't go back now. All we have is what we carry. We ran before the Yankees burned our farm down around our ears." Did this woman suspect? Jill glanced at Samuel. Should they make a break for it? How far could they get with his limp before being captured? Dawn was already breaking in the east.

The old woman cackled, her gray hair bobbing in the firelight. "I know what you mean, missy. Me and Earl lost everything in Louisiana. Nobody cares what the soldiers do. They were even Johnny Rebs, our own boys in gray. We tried to tell them we were loyal Confederates, but they cleaned us out anyway. Thank the Lord they never found the root cellar."

Jill stood and faced the woman. "I barely escaped with the clothes on my back. I lost everything too. I grabbed Samuel here, and we headed west. I figure to get a new start out there." She pointed away from the rising sun, eager to match the woman's story of loss with her own and form some kind of connection. She desperately hoped the woman would recognize a kindred spirit and not someone they might turn in to the authorities for possible bounty money.

A jostling of the wagon canvas drew Jill's attention. An old man clambered from the wagon and then straightened, pulling his suspenders over his shoulders. He stared at Jill and then glanced at Samuel before letting his gaze rest on Jill again. She could feel his penetrating scrutiny and she stiffened, feeling even more uneasy.

"Nan, I heard you talking to someone. Who is this?" He gestured toward Jill.

"Just some refugees, Earl. They're moving west like us."

"They are?" Earl squinted even harder at Jill. Her flesh crawled at the way the man's eyes devoured her.

"Are you thinking what I'm thinking, Earl?" Nan called to her husband.

Earl stroked his chin, still gawking at Jill. "Maybe. Are you thinking of allowing these two strong helpers to travel with us?"

Nan slapped her knee. "That's exactly what I'm thinking. I declare, Earl, sometimes you can read my mind. These two will eat food, but we have plenty of that. We need help with the chores and such." The old woman rose and approached Jill.

Nan gestured to the distant pair of wagons. "We joined up with these other folks bound west, but we had no idea how hard camping out would be," Nan declared. She glanced again from Earl to Jill, pondering something, her eyes narrowing. Jill could see the thought made the old woman hesitate. Making up her mind, she spoke again.

"What do you say, missy? How about you and your boy come with us? We aim to join a wagon train at Westport and go to our daughter in Oregon. You two can sleep under the wagon. It's better than walking."

Jill peered at Samuel and then realized she should not be looking to him for decisions or confirmation. Jill looked at Earl as he continued to openly leer at her. Desperate, she gripped her hands together, wishing for help in making a decision. She wished she could talk to Samuel. Was this the answer to their prayers? Was this their travel plan for moving west? Beggars can't be choosy, she determined, squaring her shoulders. She would take the plunge and hope this opportunity was from the Lord.

"Well, now, Nan, we're only going as far as Fort Kearny, Nebraska. But I'm right pleased to accept your invitation. We will travel west with you."

CHAPTER 13

Each day, Jill and Samuel moved farther from St. Louis, feeling safer as the miles slipped behind them. Perhaps they could escape the range of the bounty hunters or sheriffs searching for the runaway from Kentucky.

With only a few days' journey to Westport, Jill and Samuel had little time to get accustomed to Earl and Nan. The other two wagons of the party kept their distance from the cantankerous older couple.

Earl complained ceaselessly about Samuel riding on the wagon, arguing wagons were for his kind of folks. Jill's repeated assertion that they traveled faster by not forcing Samuel to walk seemed to have little effect on the angry old man. He even suggested leaving Samuel behind, promising to take good care of Jill if she came along without the slave. Jill refused to abandon Samuel, and tension grew between them until Jill offered to make meals and fetch water. Grumbling, the old man finally relented.

Today, she walked behind the slow wagon, her head bowed to the dust swirling around her. Samuel sat on the tailgate and Jill glanced at him, wondering what would happen to her. Her life had been so simple, pleasant even, despite the war. Parties, evenings with other young people, dances. Her life seemed so right, so carefree, as if poised on the brink of success. If her plans had continued unhindered, she soon expected to be married to a wealthy gentleman, her position in society cemented, her financial concerns nonexistent. But once again she was reminded of her predicament. Her parents were gone, she was unemployed, and the authorities searched for her.

She squinted and pursed her lips. All of this had happened so quickly, so unexpectedly. Who could've guessed her family had nothing? Living in a mound of debt, they had struggled to provide for her and their livelihood. Like a ship hulled by a strafing broadside, they had sunk in the sea of life's challenges. She didn't think of God or spiritual matters when things were going well, but now that she felt in the depths of despair, she couldn't help but wonder what the Lord was doing with her. Didn't he care about her plight?

Jill drew in a deep breath and gagged on the dust. Things could hardly be worse. She urgently hoped to leave Nan and Earl at Westport and join another wagon. Earl's hungry gaze sought her constantly, making her uncomfortable. Last night, in hushed whispers, Samuel had relayed the possibility of an evil spirit inhabiting Earl. Jill smiled into the darkness, discounting his spiritual sensitivity. Then she scowled, unable to shake the idea that Samuel could be right about the cross-grained man.

Samuel prayed continuously for the Lord's protection, though, and Jill felt some relief that nothing had transpired between her and Earl.

Soon it became apparent to Jill and Samuel they were little better than slaves to the older couple. Called on repeatedly to fetch this and do that, the older people barked orders like battlefield commanders.

Still, Jill didn't feel in any position to complain about her station. As each mile passed, she felt grateful they didn't have to walk. Besides, they ate well and slept each night beneath the safety of the wagon.

NEBRASKA HAVEN

Samuel had confessed with some reluctance that he felt pleased they did not have to walk as well. However, he, too, hated traveling with the demanding pair.

"It's like being with an old Master Carter," Samuel muttered one night before they settled to sleep beneath the wagon.

Nevertheless, the distance to Westport was covered in good order. Soon, the trio of wagons pulled into a grove of cottonwoods, the distant river in sight, and Jill and Samuel pitched camp while Earl lumbered toward town in search of news of a west-bound wagon train.

Jill went for water while Samuel gathered firewood. The quiet, early summer day felt warm and pleasant, puffy clouds like overstuffed sheep floated overhead. A column of blue clad soldiers passed her, and Jill frowned—the war still with her, not allowing her to forget.

She glanced toward town, observing great activity in that direction. Westport was a noted "jumping off" place for the Oregon Trail. One of many beginning points, Earl had informed her last night around the campfire. He had leaned closer as he explained how the various routes all converged in central Nebraska, along the Platte River, before heading toward the summit of the Rocky Mountains.

Jill glanced around as she made her way to water, the bucket swinging easily beside her. Wagons of varying size and outfit nestled in clumps amid the groves of trees. People of all ages and nationalities seemed to be represented. Nearing a small stream, Jill overheard both German and French.

Bending to scoop a bucket of water, Jill tensed at the unexpected reflection of someone across the stream, watching her. She gasped and looked up, relaxing when she saw a young girl. Sighing, she felt grateful the figure wasn't Earl. Traveling with the old man had made her jumpy and nervous.

"Hello." The young girl smiled, tilting her head as she returned Jill's scrutiny. Jill guessed her age at about fourteen, possibly too old for the pigtails that draped her pixie-like face.

Jill nodded. "Hello." She glanced toward camp, then smiled. She relished the chance to talk to someone other than her traveling companions. She knew Nan would be calling soon, demanding her evening coffee.

"My name is Reyna Maguire. Are ye waiting for a wagon train west?"

Jill immediately liked the girl's lilting voice, an Irish accent making her words sound like song. Her clear, innocent look drew Jill to her, and something about her connected them, almost as if they'd already met.

"Do I know you?" she asked, ignoring the girl's question.

Reyna laughed, a musical sound. "Now how would you be knowing me, us only just met?" The laughter twinkled in her blue eyes, and her twin red-brown braids bobbed.

"I don't know. You seem to remind me of someone," Jill mused, dragging the heavy bucket from the stream. Little rivulets spilled over the full pail, sparkling like jewels in the afternoon sunlight.

"We're waiting for a wagon train, though they say it's too late in the season. We been waiting nearly ten days. Me uncle is impatient and anxious to get going. He's looking for a plot of land to call his own. He says every day tis wasted that we're not on the trail. I tell him, 'Uncle Tim' says I, 'you must have faith'." Reyna concluded her story with a warm, kind smile.

The youngster's words reminded Jill of Samuel's persistent talk of faith. She frowned, wondering how Reyna's uncle responded to the constant preaching of God's will and the Lord's plans. Jill shifted the heavy bucket as her interest in Reyna waned.

"Well, nice to meet you, Reyna. Maybe we'll be on the same train." Jill nodded once and then moved toward camp. As she suspected, she heard Nan calling her name.

Jill continued to think about the girl she had met at the stream when Earl returned to camp. He breathed hard from the short walk and needed several minutes to catch his breath before he could speak. He welcomed a bowl of stew from Jill and ate half of his supper before reporting his findings.

"There's been no wagon master willing to tackle the trip across the plains this late in the season until now. Captain Bridgett has completed this same trip three times before. He's willing to lead if the train leaves in two days. After that, he says it's too dangerous. It'll be too late to build shelters in Oregon before winter is upon us. He demands absolute authority." Earl paused to eat more stew, chewing slowly with his mouth open as he watched Jill.

"Earl," Nan whined, "tell us more. You have me on pins and needles. Is this the train we're to join?"

Jill cringed as Earl dragged his sleeve across his lips. "That's up to us. This Captain Bridgett is a no-nonsense kind of man. He said if a wagon falls behind, it'll be left. The safety of the whole train is more important than a single family. He'll leave anyone who cannot keep up."

He paused again to let his words sink in. All the travelers seemed to be thinking the same thing. Nan and Earl were old. Samuel limped. If anything slowed them down, the wagon train would go on without them, leaving them alone and defenseless on the prairie.

"Not only that," Earl continued, "the captain said we would have to make Independence Rock by Fourth of July, or we'd be moving too slow. Which means, the season already being late, he would push harder than regular trains. A few extra miles a day, he said, to make sure we stayed on schedule."

Nan nodded slowly, her eyes narrowing as she digested his words. "Are there not any other trains this year? We have to get to Oregon by fall." Jill noticed the pleading in her voice. Without the help of their daughter in Oregon, the old couple would be hard pressed to survive anywhere.

Earl rubbed the back of his neck. "I know, Nan. Don't push me," he growled. "I don't know what else to do. If we go on this train, we'll have to move fast."

Silence lay heavily over the little campsite until Earl added, "We could always stay here for a year and go next spring with another wagon train."

"What good will that do?" Nan snapped, her eyes flashing. "We don't have any way of making a living here for a year. We'd starve or freeze, come winter. That's stupid. We must go on this train. You'll have to man up and work hard."

Earl glowered in return but said nothing. Nan often bullied Earl and talked down to him. He was lazy and slovenly, Jill agreed, but no one should be spoken to in such a way. Their predicament and the wearisome travel from Louisiana had made them short tempered and rude with one another.

Jill knew little of relationships. Except for her own parents, she never knew other married folks or how other couples communicated. But the way Nan and Earl treated each other seemed wrong, she was sure. She vowed to never emulate them.

Samuel watched Earl from the corner of his eye. Nan was mean to the old man, no doubt. He scowled when he saw Earl turn his gaze from his wife to where Jill bent over the fire. The old man stroked his chin, watching Jill, thinking he was unobserved. Samuel tensed, feeling the desire to protect his companion. Jill had helped him escape, was continuing to help him escape. He vowed to guard her at any cost.

CHAPTER 14

The next morning at breakfast, Earl announced they would join the wagon train that intended to leave on the morrow. He reminded his small party they'd need to move quickly each day. Then he squinted at Samuel, his eyes gleaming with malice. "That means you, boy. If you can't keep up your chores, we'll leave you on the side of the trail."

"We will do no such thing," Jill interjected, rising to stand beside her friend. "Samuel will stay with me. If he is put off, I go with him."

Earl's bushy eyebrows arched and then he scowled, pursing his thick lips. Jill ignored his sullen look and returned to her chores.

Although Jill felt certain the Oregon Trail passed near Fort Kearny, she wanted confirmation. That night, as Captain Bridgett made his rounds to the twenty-six wagons going with him the next day, Jill decided to inquire of the intended route.

"Captain Bridgett, will the wagon train go through Fort Kearny? It's my destination, and I'll be leaving the train there."

Bridgett nodded, his broad-brimmed hat bobbing. He glanced around the campfire where a number of the travelers had gathered to hear his final instructions. "Yes, Miss Foster. There are many beginning points to the trail. St. Joseph, Independence, Westport, even Omaha. But they all join around Fort Kearny. The trail follows the Platte west from there. From here, we'll go along the Kansas River to the Blue River and swing north. We'll join the Platte near Fort Kearny."

"And the border?" she persisted. "Kansas is close, correct?"

He gestured to the west. "Just across the Missouri River. We're less than a mile from it now."

"Why not follow the Missouri to where the Platte River joins it? Wouldn't that way be better marked?"

The wagon master nodded again. "Of course. They meet at Omaha. But we need to make up time, so we'll go west before turning north to follow the Oregon Trail. This way is faster. We'll move into Kansas immediately."

The big man paused and looked over the emigrants that agreed to go with him. He shifted his feet, scuffing his boot at a tuft of grass. "I don't mean to frighten any of you. Well, maybe I do. We're starting late and will need to make up time. This will be a hard trip. We'll not be able to wait for slow wagons. If you're not prepared to move fast, don't go with us. If you are willing, then lighten your loads now. Throw everything heavy off your wagon."

"But those are our belongings," a thin woman protested, looking to her husband with a pinched brow. She cradled a baby against her chest, and Jill could read the anxiety on her pale face.

"I know," Captain Bridgett agreed. "But we must move fast. One day, steam-powered trains will cross these plains, and they can carry endless weight. But until then, we must make the tough decisions about what we can and cannot carry. The mules and oxen will have to pull your belongings all the way to Oregon, up and over the Rocky Mountains. Think long and hard about what you intend to take with you." He paused a moment before continuing. "Now, get some rest. We leave early tomorrow."

Jill shot a knowing glance at Samuel sitting just outside the ring of firelight. Kansas was a free state. If they could only reach it.

Samuel nodded once, his eyes shining in the darkness.

Jill felt pleased at Bridgett's information. She and Samuel had only to journey with Earl and Nan a short distance, and then they'd be free of the crabby couple. She pondered Captain Bridgett's far-reaching words about a future train. Why would a train come out here? Men say things to scare women, she figured, knowing many of the families on the small wagon train were reluctant to leave cherished family heirlooms behind.

Jill wondered again about the house she owned in Nebraska. Whether it really existed or not or was even habitable, she could not know. So many ideas swirled in her mind. She hoped this venture did not prove to be a wild goose chase.

Jill pushed the troublesome thoughts from her mind. She would not even allow herself to think of her parents' passing for now. Recalling the last few days still felt too painful. Soon, she told herself, she would take time and really give herself over to these memories. For now, she must remain focused. A small measure of peace lingered as she appreciated having a direction to go. *Keep moving*, she told herself doggedly.

A frown teased her lips as she wondered if this was truly God's will. Was the Lord guiding her, as Samuel suggested?

Her gaze traveled down her soiled dress, noticing the rent in one sleeve. Then she studied a small cut on her hand she'd received this morning while cutting kindling for the fire. Dirt smudged her hands, and she felt the stiff, dried sweat along her neck under the collar of her dirty dress. She lifted a hand to her hair, wondering what a fright it must be. When was the last time she'd seen herself in a mirror? Her muscles ached from all the work she'd performed, muscles she didn't even know she possessed.

A hint of a smile tugged at her mouth, turning her frown around, and Jill lifted her chin, aware of the change within her. The fine Southern lady was becoming tough, resourceful, capable.

The wagon train had already been on the trail for two hours. Jill knew now what Captain Bridgett had said was true. The big wagon master had awakened everyone at three o'clock that morning and hurried them to pack and move. Now, the eastern sky glowed pink and gray behind them, and the meadowlarks were calling.

Watching the steel gray morning change colors, Jill realized she didn't mind the predawn start. The glorious sunrise made the early hour worthwhile. She found herself eager to see this land where she would temporarily live. According to Captain Bridgett, she and Samuel would be with the wagon train for only a short while.

The two dozen wagons had crossed the Missouri River without mishap, and Jill couldn't help but recall the one-legged boatman that had helped them cross it first, near St. Louis.

She drew in the rich smell of fresh prairie hay, her lungs expanding in the morning sun. Kansas! Jill remembered hearing about the tension the anti-slavery groups had caused Southerners here. They were called Jayhawkers, and folks in Missouri considered them busybodies, interfering in other people's business. However, Jill's father had liked how they'd championed the cause to end slavery. She winced, recalling how his unpopular political views had destroyed his business. And his life.

There was little time to talk with Samuel now, and Jill missed their interesting conversations. She walked every day, being the only one in their small group able to do so. She did not want to ride in the crowded wagon and listen to Nan complain or endure Earl's crude glances. This day, however, Jill saw both Nan and Earl riding the high front seat, and she allowed the wagon to roll past her. Resuming her pace, she walked alongside the runaway slave where he sat on the tailgate, his legs swinging.

"Good morning, Miss Jill," Samuel greeted her warmly. "Isn't this a wonderful day the Lord has made?" He gestured at the sunrise behind her.

"Indeed, it is, Samuel. But I wanted to tell you something important."

Alarm rose in his eyes. "What's wrong, Miss Jill? Has that dirty man done anything to you?"

Jill smiled, thankful she did not have that to report. "No, thank God. I wanted to let you know some significant information." Here, Jill moved a step closer to the large wagon wheel. With a quick glance forward to where Nan and Earl still sat, she lowered her voice.

"We are now in Kansas, a free state. There is no slavery allowed here."

Instead of the expected exuberance, Jill was surprised to observe deep lines of worry etched Samuel's features.

"Samuel, didn't you hear me? This is free land. No slavery," Jill repeated.

"I heard you, miss. It just gives me a lot to think about. As a slave, I don't have to take responsibility for anything I do. It is the master who is responsible. All blame for slavery is on someone else. But as a free man, I am now responsible to God for my choices, my behavior. What I become is because of my efforts, not the wishes of the master. If I fail in life here, it is my fault. I will not be able to blame someone else. It is a heavy responsibility."

"So? Are you ready for it?" Jill challenged, her chin rising. She sensed they'd both embarked on an adventure they weren't sure how to navigate, yet here they were, ready or not. She wondered if there was more to this journey than merely locating a place to live.

He grinned. "Yes, miss. The good Lord has brought me out of bondage, just like the Israelites out of Egypt, and I will make a go of it. I promise to work hard. You will be proud of me."

"I am already proud of you, Samuel. You have real courage to do what you have done. You have also helped me find courage within myself. I am honored to be your friend."

He gaped at her, eyes round. "Friend?"

Jill laughed. "Of course, friends. We've helped each other, like friends do. We're a team, right? And now you're free or at least on the way to freedom. You certainly deserve it."

Samuel shook his head. "Don't you believe it, Miss Jill. I don't deserve anything. I'm a sinful man like anyone else. I've harbored hatred in my heart and wished men dead. I've coveted what others have. Only by God's grace do I find hope for my life. Not in freedom, not in my strength, not in anything but Jesus."

Jill's smile faltered and she looked away. Samuel certainly knew how to destroy a happy moment. While congratulating him on his escape from Missouri, he'd only been able to see his debt to the Lord. As he entered an exciting adventure of immense possibilities, he could only see the huge responsibility that now faced him. Must everything be a spiritual reckoning?

Scowling, she blinked, and her glance fell to the dusty trail they followed. Irritation stewed in her guts at his response to her kindly meant comment. She'd left everything to come west. Her career, her home, all the social events she so cherished. Her entire life's goals had crumbled in a matter of days. All she could think of was herself while Samuel wanted a life of impact, a life where he could serve the Lord. The depth of his thoughts frightened her.

Jill looked up to find Samuel still staring at her. "I've never had a friend like you," he whispered, his eyes darting to the front of the wagon.

"Well, you have one now." She gave him a parting smile and moved away from the rolling wagon.

Jill stopped to pick a few late spring flowers from the roadside. They would not last the day, but she couldn't resist the desire to hold a colorful bouquet.

Samuel had told her, prepared her, there would be time to grieve for the loss of her parents. But the death of her dreams plagued her as well. Each day, Jill purposefully took walks from the wagon as it rolled along on the rutted trail. Each day, she allowed herself to think a little more on the last days of her father's and mother's time on earth. Jill loved her family, distant as they were from her own life in Kentucky.

Her quest for flowers took her farther from the trail, and she halted on a rise to survey the open land around her. A shiver raced down her spine, alerting her and making her senses tingle with anticipation. An unexpected excitement surged, startling her. She surveyed the boundless grasslands stretching to the horizon. Something familiar about her surroundings called to her, telling her she'd seen the barren plains somewhere before. A memory haunted her, as if concealed behind a curtain, just out of reach.

The emerald slopes were covered in short grasses that blew in unison, like waves before a gentle wind. Few trees were visible, except along the waterways that wound between the low hills. When had she seen this land before? Everything seemed so different from her previous homes in either Missouri or Kentucky. Those places had been covered in trees.

Jill frowned and lifted the vibrant bouquet to her nose, smelling the fragrant flowers. What was God doing with her? The sudden loss of her entire family seemed at first to paralyze her. She could hardly think or function. Jill glanced down at Earl's wagon, passing on the road below. Samuel was reading her mother's Bible, legs dangling from the rear of the wagon.

She narrowed her eyes as she studied the silent figure. He seemed to be mysteriously placed in her life for the sole purpose of helping and supporting her in the dark days after her parents' death. Had God truly placed him there for that purpose, as Samuel claimed? Jill was not used to seeing God work in specific situations, although she had to admit, she'd never looked.

The large wheels turned and groaned as each wagon passed her. Jill watched the wooden vehicles roll along as she continued walking, picking more flowers. The sky was incredibly blue, she thought suddenly. When was the last time she noticed the color of the sky?

Her grief was lessening, Jill guessed, if she was able to notice the sky. She would always miss her parents. She loved them. But now it seemed she was on an adventure of her own. Ever since losing her job in Paducah, it was as if events were being orchestrated to move her toward Nebraska. Was that her destiny?

She shook her head, unwilling to give in to the unexpected pull. She smiled at Samuel's influence in such a short span of time, seeing spiritual meaning where none existed. Or so she thought. Soon, she would return east, to her career, to the life she loved. Dances and fine gowns and gentlemen of culture. This necessary trip to Nebraska was for a brief time only.

Halting again, Jill regarded her surroundings. All around, rolling hills stretched as far as the eye could see, to the endless horizon. Bright green grass with a tinge of blue carpeted the plains, reminding her of a gentle breeze across a lake as the stems bent and swayed before the ceaseless wind. Maybe this was where she belonged, at least until she received a letter from the east. She couldn't deny her eagerness to hear about a job.

Jill hastened to catch up with the retreating wagons, her mind still processing grief and God's role in her future. What challenges lay ahead for her in Nebraska?

CHAPTER 15

Occasionally, Samuel would burst forth in song, singing praises to God. His loud, bass voice sounded deep and spirit-filled, and the words made Jill wonder. If God knew her like Samuel said, what was God doing with her? Was it his plan she come to Nebraska? It certainly wasn't her first choice.

Soon the wagon train made the little anti-slavery village of Lawrence, a Jayhawker stronghold. Captain Bridgett discouraged people from his caravan visiting the town before preparing for the next day's departure, reiterating he would not wait or slow down for those who could not keep up. Winter would be on them too soon in Oregon, and shelters must be constructed before the snow fell. Speed was paramount.

After Lawrence, they soon reached the Jesuit mission in St. Mary's, far out on the prairie from Westport. The wagon master pointed out the Pottawatomie Indians to Jill, many of the men with short hair. "The Jesuit priests work with the natives, teaching them Christianity and a trade," Captain Bridgett explained from horseback as Jill trudged beside him through the tiny hamlet. "Assimilation into the white man's culture is not easy for the Indians."

She recalled Samuel's comment about change. God is constant, but change is inevitable.

Jill's steps faltered as the small wagon train passed through the mission, throngs of children waving to the travelers. Was God changing her? She strode quicker, keeping pace with the moving wagons as Captain Bridgett spurred his horse away. Far to the west, the sun leaned above the valley, yet she knew the wagon master would not stop for camp at this likely spot. Many miles lay ahead before they would halt for the night.

Earl snickered and Captain Bridgett only waved when a wagon with a broken hub stopped before the blacksmith shop at the mission, a casualty to the arduous trip and quick pace set by the wagon master. Jill pressed her lips tightly, grateful she wasn't among those unable to continue west. She had to get to Nebraska, to her land near Fort Kearney if it truly existed.

Following the Kansas River, the trail dipped among swales and curved around hills, the track clearly cut into the prairie turf from many wagons.

Day after day, Jill walked beside the wagon, thankful to escape Earl's brazen and overt glances. He was a foul man behind Nan's back, and Jill wondered about her safety. He hadn't made any overture toward her, but a dark and ominous cloud permeated Earl's presence. Jill was willing to endure his coarse behavior for the duration of the journey if it took them to her land in Nebraska.

Jill made it a point to leave camp whenever the opportunity afforded, quick to volunteer to fetch water or collect firewood. One evening, Nan searched the wagon for a change of clothes while Earl hovered uncomfortably near Jill as she knelt to start the evening fire. His familiar presence did nothing to calm Jill, the opposite effect filling her as she piled kindling and reached for a match. She felt him brush against her shoulder, the contact sending chills across her back.

NEBRASKA HAVEN

Samuel, having observed the intentional touch, moved forward, anger bristling in his dark eyes. Jill leaped to her feet, stepping between the old man and her friend.

"Samuel, will you begin dinner while I gather more fuel?" she asked as she fled camp, not waiting for a reply. She needed to get away from the lecherous Earl. She strode into the gathering shadows as dusk descended, her steps taking her toward the trees lining the nearby stream where the sound of water tinkled musically.

She gritted her teeth. Was she never to know peace around Earl? The grandeur of the prairies amazed her and lifted her spirits, but the wagon she traveled with always depressed her, robbing her of an unexpected growing sense of joy.

Jill slowed her pace as she left the vicinity of the wagons. The sun had already set, and the evening sky glowed with the reflection of the final rays on the gray clouds, a deep velvet blue splashing across the eastern sky where the first star peeked. Paintbrush strokes of pink, orange, and yellow swirled overhead.

Wending a path over the prairie, Jill reflected on her journey thus far. Home seemed a long way behind her. Would she ever see Missouri again? She would not be heartbroken if she didn't, she mused. St. Louis had not been a happy place for her. But perhaps deeper into the South was where she should return if fortune smiled upon her. Perhaps Mr. Hopkins would write soon of a job opportunity. She longed for quiet evenings on wide verandas and dinner parties where the gentlemen walked out under the magnolia trees to smoke cigars while ladies discussed the latest Paris fashion.

Yet her memories faded as she scanned the darkening horizon, the sun hiding behind the distant hills. She breathed deeply of the fresh air, fascinated by the endless prairie in ways she never anticipated.

She bent to retrieve a stick. Better make it look like she'd left the wagon to fetch firewood as she'd said. Another stick lay just ahead.

Jill continued, loading her arms with the sticks they would need for cooking. She allowed her thoughts to trip over the recent events that brought her west and felt surprised at the growing sense of eagerness assailing her. Surely she longed to return to the bustle and clamor of her teaching and the many socials that filled her off duty time. Yet something unexpected tingled along her nerves as she considered the unforeseen difficulties that had pelted her, like a deluge in a summer rainstorm. Despite her frustration and fears, she enjoyed the prairies they crossed.

Startled by this realization, Jill slowed, tentatively bending to pick up another stick while keeping her load balanced. Although greatly worried she was trekking to a place that might not exist, she'd been wholly surprised by the adventure of her travels. With a sigh, Jill agreed with Samuel that God had provided in very astonishing ways.

She'd crossed the Missouri River at night with a Confederate sympathizer who tried to take her captive. She'd bargained for a ride with the most disagreeable couple she'd ever known. And now she journeyed across the most beautiful land she'd ever seen, full of colorful flowers, multitudes of animals, and a sky that changed in an instant. Already they'd seen violent hailstorms, and once, a tornado that swayed across the horizon while the sky darkened as if night had fallen. And all of this with Samuel, a devout Christian who fled from Kentucky.

Jill shook her head, not wanting to consider all she'd endured recently. She glanced to the clouds that lingered just above the western skyline. Crickets called while bats swooped to catch mosquitos. Peace filled her, and Jill wondered if the Lord were truly active. She'd never searched for God before, always understanding he was at church if she ever wanted to talk with him. Now, after watching Samuel speak with the Almighty everywhere, she realized how silly that sounded. Whenever Samuel wanted to share thoughts with the Creator ... he did.

Samuel. What could she say about this unlikely companion? Comforting, encouraging, helpful, he had quickly established himself as a true friend. Her only friend, Jill reminded herself with a frown. Her childhood had taught her to keep her distance from people, never allowing anyone too close. She always felt afraid they would abandon her when they found out about her father's political views and her family's low social standing ... as so many had abandoned her father.

Not Samuel. He accepted her as she was. Flawed and imperfect.

Jill gripped her large bundle of sticks as she neared the creek bottom. Vaguely, through the deepening gloom under the trees, she heard the faint sounds of someone digging. Curious, she moved in that direction, still deep in her own thoughts.

She hesitated when she saw a man with a shovel, watching as he dropped to one knee and removed dirt from around a small tree.

Her gaze shifted to a sudden movement from under a nearby bush. A black and white creature scurried across the trail ahead of her. Jill screamed and tossed the bundle of sticks, the firewood flying toward the retreating skunk as she backpedaled, her legs churning madly.

The man grunted and fled his hole, dragging his spade with him. He scrambled away from the skunk's onslaught, stopping only when he straightened beside Jill, his chest heaving with the exertion. Together they watched the skunk waddle around the sapling, its tail hoisted like a flag as it investigated the newly dug hole.

The creature turned to look at the pair in the deepening darkness, and they backed another few steps, placing more distance between themselves and the odor that suddenly permeated the place they vacated. Jill stumbled and reached for the stranger's arm, righting herself as they watched the skunk.

The man turned on her, glancing first at her hand on his arm and then staring intently into her face, his eyes narrowing. He scowled before thrusting his spade into the earth at his feet. "Well, that was brilliant. The first black walnut sapling I've found on this trip and now it's lost. There's no way I can get near it now. I almost had it out too."

Jill released his arm, taking another step backward. She bristled at his accusing tone, stunned that he blamed her for the skunk's unexpected assault. Her irritation grew as she remembered why she'd left camp in the first place.

Jill squared her shoulders. Defensive now, she rested her hands on her waist as she glared at him. "I had nothing to do with that ... that skunk ruining your tree. I was merely picking up firewood when it startled me as well as you," Jill stammered, heat rising to her face and settling on her cheeks.

"You as much as *herded* it toward me." He jerked the spade from the ground. "I was almost done," he lamented as he turned to walk away.

Annoyed at his remark, she stomped her foot. "Wait," she called to his retreating form. "You insult me and blame me for this accident? And now you're leaving without an apology? Are you no gentleman?"

The young man paused and slowly turned to face her, one hand scratching his bearded jaw as he shook his head. "Probably not."

He walked away, leaving Jill standing alone in the dark.

CHAPTER 16

Jill clomped back to camp, her fists clenched. How dare the young ruffian be so rude? She was only gathering wood, minding her own business, when that skunk surprised her. She hadn't intended to scream, but the animal startled her. Throwing the armload of firewood at the creature had merely been a kneejerk response. An accident.

She marched through the darkness, heedless of any obstacle that might stand in her path. As she neared camp, she halted just outside the ring of light from the small blaze to regain her composure. Samuel caught her eye and she read the concern there. She smiled at him, not wanting him to worry.

"Where's the wood you went for?" Earl demanded, scowling at her from his seat near the fire.

Jill shifted. "I saw a skunk and dropped it."

Earl laughed, a look of disgust on his lined face. "That'll happen in the dark."

Nan did not think it so funny. "What are we going to use for fuel?"

"I'll go," Samuel volunteered, hobbling toward the darkness. Jill detected evident fatigue in his sluggish movements.

"No," Jill interjected, hating the thought of being near Earl. "I'll go this side of camp." Jill pointed in the opposite direction the skunk had traveled and slipped once more into the gloom.

She strode into the darkness, the sounds of a harmonica drifting from a nearby campsite. Earl and Nan didn't encourage friendliness with the other wagons, and Jill didn't try, either, still too consumed with her own issues. What if someone learned Samuel was a runaway slave? Besides, she would be leaving the wagon train soon. No need to make short-term acquaintances.

Slowing her pace and allowing her eyes to adjust to the dimness, she scanned the ground for any sticks. She limited her search to only the empty places, avoiding thick foliage or bushes that might harbor animals.

Her mind turned to the young stranger who had accused her of ruining his tree uprooting. How ridiculous that he would be digging a black walnut sapling from the ground at this time of day. What was he going to do with the tree, anyway?

Jill fumed as she walked, searching for sticks. He'd acted like she'd intentionally chased the black and white creature upon him. She halted on a low rise, the prairie spreading around her with the line of wagons behind her. She chewed her lip. Who was the man anyway? Jill had never seen him before, although that was not unusual. With Captain Bridgett's plan of waking early and traveling late, there was little time for socializing among the people of the wagon train.

She thought of the skunk forcing the man from the hole—the way he'd raced away—and she chuckled. She doubted if she'd ever see him again, certainly never to speak to him again.

As she continued to hunt wood, Jill's heated emotions began to cool. She giggled to herself, remembering how angry the man had been with her. Served him right he could not finish retrieving his dumb old tree, she thought with a touch of glee.

Returning to camp with a handful of sticks, Jill deposited the tiny bundle by the fire and accepted the bowl of soup Samuel handed her.

"That won't be enough fuel for coffee in the morning," Earl grumbled.

"Feel free to fetch more, Earl," Jill retorted, her chin lifting.

"Hey, now, missy," Nan butt in. "Don't be sassy. Earl's right. That's not enough fuel. No need to be cross with him. He's done nothing wrong."

Jill glowered at the older man and gritted her teeth to bite back the fiery retort on the tip of her tongue.

Earl gave her a lopsided grin before turning to the coffeepot steaming alongside the coals.

Samuel caught Jill's eye and motioned for her to walk away. She joined Samuel at the rear of the wagon where he busied himself throwing their few blankets into the deep shadows between the wheels. Together, they stole glances toward the older couple.

"There is no sense in talking to Earl. He's bad, Miss Jill. The Spirit is not in him. He's dark. You need to keep your distance. It won't be long now until we're in Nebraska. I heard Captain Bridgett say so. Then we can leave these folks and be on your own land."

Jill nodded, seeing the wisdom in his words. Patience was the best course for now. Still, the looks and the occasional nearness of Earl bothered her. Jill longed for the day when she would not have to tolerate this man's disgusting presence.

The showdown occurred only three days later. As Jill unloaded gear from the wagon to begin the evening meal, Earl placed a familiar hand on her waist, pretending to reach past her into the wagon. Jill felt her heart leap to her throat as she jumped away from him. She trembled, fear and revulsion welling within her as she faced him.

"Keep your hands off me, Earl," she hissed between clenched teeth. "I don't like the way you're always pestering me when you think Nan's not looking. I'm sick of your looks and touches." She could feel the heat rise to her face, shame and embarrassment mingling in the flush on her cheeks. His touch had both infuriated and frightened her.

"What's your problem? I was just getting cook things from the wagon," he soothed, but Jill saw the nervous look he gave Nan.

Samuel stepped past Jill and faced Earl. "Don't you ever lay another hand on Miss Jill."

Nan marched forward, frowning at Samuel's threatening words.

"Who are you to talk to my man that way? You'd best be remembering your place, boy. This isn't New York or New Hampshire where they allow folks like you to talk that way to folks like us."

"Earl put his hand on me," Jill cut in, trying to draw Nan's fierce attack away from Samuel.

"Now don't be listening to her, Nan. This girl is just trying to protect her uppity slave, that's all," Earl protested, but Jill heard the fear in his voice.

Slowly, Nan turned on him. Jill read the hurt and sadness in the old woman's eyes as she glared at her husband, her mouth twitching while she gripped her apron with both hands. "So? You went and touched another young girl, Earl? Will you always be getting us in trouble?"

"She's lying, Nan. Don't believe her," the older man protested, his hands outstretched.

Nan turned back to Jill and Samuel. "All right. You're on your own. I don't know who to believe, but it doesn't really matter. You two were going to leave us in Nebraska anyway. Fetch your gear and get out. You'll have to find another wagon to ride with."

For a moment, complete silence fell on the foursome. Then, Samuel reached past Earl and grabbed their luggage. Hauling all three bundles of clothes and blankets, he led the way from the wagon.

Jill stared at Earl and Nan a moment longer, anger burning. Earl stood sheepish now beside Nan and wouldn't look her way. The older woman gazed at Jill, hands resting on her hips. She did not seem angry at Jill, only resolved to have the young girl from her wagon. Jill wondered if Nan had experienced something similar before.

Turning on her heel, Jill followed Samuel into the gloom. They would have to sleep on the prairie without the benefit of the wagon to protect them, but she didn't care. She felt suddenly grateful to be rid of the older couple. Earl had haunted her steps long enough.

Samuel halted beside an outcropping of limestone, bulging from the prairie like a welt. He dropped the bags at his feet and studied Jill.

"Miss, it was the right time to be away from them. The Lord has told me we're better off without them. The foul old man had evil in his heart."

The tension of the moment drained from her, and Jill's shoulders slumped. He meant well, but Samuel's odd words were no comfort. Jill sighed. "I know, Samuel. I just couldn't take any more. He disgusts me."

She sank to her knees, one elbow resting on the valise, her back against a ragged stone.

"Now what are we going to do?" Jill looked up at the first stars appearing in the evening sky. Would God provide some avenue for them to take? Fort Kearny couldn't be far now, but any distance was too great for two people walking alone on the prairie.

"Patience and faith, Miss Jill. That's what my mama always told me. Patience and faith." Samuel looked around, his gaze straying to the tree-lined watercourse farther along. "I'll gather wood. A little dinner will go well right about now."

Jill watched him hobble away, not saying anything. She shifted against the luggage, a sharp point of rock jabbing into her back. She sighed again, not caring about the pain. Too discouraged to move, she pondered their predicament and wondered what their next step should be.

Captain Bridgett would not allow any delay, even time for her and Samuel to find another wagon. They would simply have to walk the remaining distance to Fort Kearny. How far was it, anyway?

Jill surveyed the stars above. While darkness descended, they twinkled and multiplied as she studied the heavens. She thought again of Samuel's faith. It seemed so real, so alive, yet her own spiritual ideas paled in comparison. Did she not have enough faith in God?

Footfalls rustled nearby, grass swishing as someone approached, and she lowered her gaze, expecting Samuel. A small figure emerged from the dark, and Jill started, recognizing the young girl she'd met at Westport. Jill chewed the inside of her cheek, remembering. What was her name?

Jill shifted against the limestone rocks, and the girl halted, then chuckled as she came on.

"Why, hello, there. I have not seen you since Westport Landing. And how are you doing, miss?" The slight brogue of the young girl reminded Jill how much she'd enjoyed hearing the girl speak.

But then she stiffened at the girl's innocent inquiry. Should she say anything of their trouble? Something about the confident young girl reassured Jill, and she found herself wanting to release her burdens to the young redhead.

"Well, I've been better. I've just been kicked out of my wagon. My friend and I will be looking for another wagon, I suppose." Jill hoped the hint was received. Could this girl help provide aid?

"Kicked out of your wagon? Out here? That can't be good," the girl said, clucking her tongue as she stopped near Jill, studying her in the twilight, one hand resting on a small hip.

"But it is good. The man we traveled with was inappropriate ... if you get my meaning. I'm happy to be away from him." Jill remembered now. Her name was Reyna.

"Oh, a dark one, was he? Mother warned me of men such as that."

Jill sat up. "Where is your mother, Reyna?"

In the dim light of the stars, Jill saw the girl frown. "The good Lord has called both her and me pa home to heaven. They are at the feet of Jesus now. It's me uncle I travel with." Jill liked how the girl gestured and swayed as she spoke, her two braids dancing. *Like what a sprite must look like.*

"I am sorry to hear that," Jill said, sympathizing with this young girl as she recalled her own loss.

"What will you be doing now?" Reyna asked, peering closer at Jill.

Jill shrugged. "I don't know. Samuel has gone for wood, and we'll have a fire for now." She paused and glanced down the slope toward the darker shadows of the streambed. She frowned, wondering what they would do and how Samuel would handle the situation. "I suppose he'll want to pray and ask God for direction," Jill muttered under her breath.

She turned to Reyna, startled to find the girl staring hard at her.

"Is your friend a Christian then?"

Jill nodded. "Oh, yes. Samuel knows the Holy Spirit by name and is often communing with the Almighty." Jill grinned, hoping Reyna wouldn't notice the ring of sarcasm in her words. Samuel always talked about the Lord and his plan. Sometimes it annoyed her. How could any of this nightmare be God's plan for her?

"I'll not be leaving my brother in the Lord alone on the prairie," Reyna declared, tossing her braids. "You must join our wagon. I am sure me uncle would approve."

Jill blinked. Join their wagon? She rose to her knees, hope rising within her. "Do you mean it? We can join your wagon? It won't be for long. We are only going as far as Fort Kearny."

Reyna nodded. "Me uncle owns the wagon, and small room there is for anyone else, but when the Lord speaks, 'tis best to obey," Reyna explained, holding up a finger. "Not to worry. Me uncle is all blow and bluster, but has a heart of gold, he has."

When Samuel approached, both girls turned, and Jill informed him of Reyna's invitation. Samuel beamed, his face shining in the starlight. "See, Miss Jill? I knew the Lord would answer my prayer."

Retrieving their belongings and the little fuel Samuel and Reyna had gathered, they followed the young Irish girl through the dark.

Soon a wagon loomed in the blackness, and Jill noticed the absence of a canvas cover. Her eyebrows arched at the entire wagon box filled with small trees, each leafed and pointed skyward.

Beside the wagon, a small fire glowed and a man knelt, poking the flames with a stick, sparks fluttering aloft. Jill followed Samuel, allowing his limping gait to set the pace, but her eyes were fixed on the campsite and the man who glanced up to observe their approach.

When she recognized his bearded face, her steps faltered, and disappointment washed over her. Her stomach tightened, as if she were marching into battle, steeling herself for war. Their eyes locked, and Jill gasped as the tree hunter rose to his feet.

CHAPTER 17

"You," he hissed, his eyes narrowing.

Reyna turned to look back at Jill, head tilted, her blue eyes full of surprise. "Do you know me uncle then?"

"Your uncle?" Jill whispered, her shoulders slumping. She wiped her damp palms on her dress.

"Sure. This is me uncle, Tim Hunter." Reyna introduced the young man and moved forward. "Uncle Tim, these good Christian folk need a lift, and I've offered our wagon. They're not going far but need help. The good Lord would have us lend them a kindly hand."

Eyes blazing, the man glared at his niece. "Reyna, what are you talking about? We are not going to give these people a lift, and I don't care what the Lord says. This is the woman I told you about who attacked me with a skunk."

Reyna giggled. "Oh, so it is you, miss? Uncle Tim has told me that tale more than once, I'm afraid. He had his heart set on that black walnut sapling, and he claims you ruined his digging."

Jill glowered at the man by the fire, her anger rising with memory of that fateful meeting some days before. She crossed her arms over her chest.

"I did not attack you with that skunk. The foul animal scared me as much as you. It was an accident the thing sprayed the area where you were digging. It was not my fault," Jill explained.

Samuel moved alongside Reyna, dropping the fuel for the fire near the little blaze.

"Wait a minute." Tim lifted a hand. "You're not staying with us. You'd better keep your firewood. Now, off with you, and make your own camp."

"Uncle Tim," Reyna interposed, head held high. "I have offered our wagon to these folks. They are in need, and we will not be turning them away from our fire. It's not what the Lord would have us do." She acted older than her years, and Jill could sense Tim Hunter was used to a saucy tongue from his young niece.

Tim rolled his eyes. "Reyna, I've told you before that I care very little for what your God wants me to do. You're lucky to be with me at all. It was not my idea to take on my sister's kid, but I've done so, with great reluctance, I might add. But you cannot tell me what I must do with my own wagon," Tim snapped, shifting his glare from Jill to the Irish girl.

Jill didn't much care for Mr. Tim Hunter, but they needed a ride. What could she say to sway this man's opinion or to allow her and Samuel to travel with them? Didn't Reyna mention something about farmland when they'd met back in Westport? Perhaps this man sought a place to settle.

"I have land," Jill blurted, her words halting Tim's tirade and any retort Reyna may have.

Silence descended on the little group, only the crackling blaze making a sound. Slowly, Tim turned to face Jill, his eyes conveying his doubts at her declaration. "What did you say? Land? What kind of land?"

Jill had his attention now. She smiled to herself, realizing the land might be a bargaining chip. She moved forward, her arms dropping to her sides as she nudged the coffeepot closer to the coals with the toe of her shoe. *Act smooth, confident,* she instructed herself. *Don't let him see your panic.*

Looking up, she eyed him casually. "Do you have enough cups, or should we fetch our things?" Her voice sounded calm, with no trace of the anxiety that threatened to bubble out of her at any moment.

Tim shifted and crossed his arms over his chest but didn't reply.

Jill glanced at Samuel, giving him a subtle nod. He rummaged through their baggage until he located the tin coffee mugs. Kneeling beside Jill, he poured four cups of coffee and distributed them.

Tim accepted a cup, scowling his impatience. Reyna moved next to Samuel and began helping him prepare a meal.

Jill seated herself on her valise. "My friend Samuel and I are going to a piece of land I own in Nebraska, near Fort Kearny. Six hundred and forty acres of prime farmland. It was abandoned only a few months ago, and I'm heading there to claim it."

She lifted the cup to her lips, observing Tim over the rim. Whether the land was prime farmland she didn't know. Or if it even actually existed. But she knew she needed this man's help.

Tim dropped to a knee close to the fire, staring into the flames. He sipped his drink, steam swirling above his mug as he pondered Jill's words.

"What's in it for me? Why should I care if you have farmland?"

Jill shifted again, suddenly sure of herself. As a young girl in St. Louis, she'd heard men at her father's store discuss fishing techniques, and she smiled as she studied Tim. The fish was inspecting the bait, circling the hook.

"Reyna told me you were seeking a farm. I need a place to wait while I search for a school in need of teachers. I will live on the land and write letters seeking a teaching position back east. In the meantime, you can farm the land. I have no need of it. I will require only the house."

"And what of this house? Where will Reyna and I live? Is there room for the two of us? Summer is half over, and I need time to get my trees in the ground. I won't be able to build a home for us before winter. Nor do I have the money to do so."

Jill hesitated, gripping her mug. She wished now she'd taken the time to review the particulars of the property near Fort Kearny. Only the living arrangement had concerned her, and she hadn't paid any attention to the description of the land. She promised herself to review the deed she carried at the earliest opportunity.

"I can assure you that if the house is big enough for us all, you are welcome to join us. I believe the deed spoke of a large house on the property, but I would not assume what large means in Nebraska. I think it's worth your time and effort to take us there. It's on your way." Jill shrugged, feigning indifference. If this man suspected the fear and terror hiding just beneath the surface of Jill's calm exterior, he would not trust her in the least.

"Fort Kearny, huh?" Tim said, taking another sip of coffee. Jill nodded, pensive as she watched the farmer casually enjoy his drink. "What happens to the land or us if you get this teaching job you're waiting for?"

Jill shrugged again. "I don't want it. You can stay and rent it from me. Or perhaps buy it from me one day."

He nodded but remained silent. Jill shifted on her seat, impatient to know, one way or the other. "Look, you need the land, I need a ride," she snapped, prodding him. Tim scowled at her and pursed his lips, clearly pondering her proposal. Finally, he nodded again.

"What did you say your name is?" Tim asked.

"Jill Foster. This is my friend, Samuel."

Tim glanced again at Reyna. He sighed loudly, and then faced Jill. "Well, Fort Kearny is on our way." He paused, making Jill irked even more at his slow deliberation. Finally, he stuck out his hand. "All right, Jill Foster, you have yourself a ride."

CHAPTER 18

Jill cringed when Samuel was nearly poked in the eye as he settled behind the high wooden seat where Tim and Reyna rode. Because of his limp, he was allowed to ride in the back of the wagon. There was little room between the numerous trees Tim was taking west, yet Samuel threw a grin her way as he nestled among the branches, not one to complain.

She looked at the line of wagons stretching before them. She'd spotted Earl and Nan once but had not exchanged words with the couple. She felt relieved to be done with them.

Occasionally, when Reyna wished to walk, Samuel would ride up front with Tim. It turned out Samuel knew quite a bit about farming, and he and Tim found lots to talk about. In the evenings, Jill felt pleased when Samuel kept Tim's attention on farming rather than allowing him to sense the fears that assailed Jill. The land might be merely a wish.

"I worked on a plantation for many years," the runaway slave explained around the campfire, his dark face gleaming in the ruddy glow of the blaze. "It's no wonder I learned about making things grow."

Sowing, harvesting, irrigating, weeding, fertilizers, and even grafting were some of Samuel's talents. Tim plied the young man with questions regarding all kinds of planting techniques and preservation of trees through extreme conditions. Samuel reported he knew only a very little about this topic, being from Kentucky. Bitter winters were not his specialty.

Jill noticed the most exciting conversations developed between Reyna and Samuel. They discussed Scripture for hours, even reading the Bible to each other while they rode on the high wagon seat. Sometimes they sang the old hymns.

On one of these occasions, Reyna quizzed Samuel about his life as a slave. Jill walked beside the wheel, leaning to hear her friend's explanation. Samuel shared many details, but the story he enjoyed telling the most was about his escape. His eyes glowed as he highlighted Jill's participation, how she was instrumental in helping him flee captivity. "Like Moses out of Egypt," he would say. Then, a wide smile creasing his face, he would add, "We're friends, you know."

During these times, Tim would relinquish his position on the wagon with some reluctance. Mumbling loudly while descending the tall wagon, he would allow Samuel to take his place, muttering how he didn't need another Bible lesson. Since Tim refused to ride in back like common cargo, he walked beside the wagon.

Jill never rode the wagon. She enjoyed the brisk walk that the prairie allowed. As she explored little groves of trees or the occasional spring, Jill found the exercise invigorating. And new, at least to her. She'd never had to walk everywhere before as a lady in the South. Or use wild land facilities behind clumps of bushes or concealing hills.

Although the land impressed Jill, its low hills and endless sky calling to her soul, the temporary peace she'd enjoyed when first out of Missouri quickly dissipated. As

NEBRASKA HAVEN

they neared their destination, Jill grew more anxious. She couldn't dispel the doubts that niggled at her constantly. What if there was no land for her in Nebraska? Would Nebraska be like Kansas, rolling plains in every direction? Could they live in the house on the property, or would they be homeless? What would she do for a living if she couldn't get another teaching position? She needed a job. What would she do if nothing awaited her? And what about Samuel? Somehow, she now felt responsible for him too.

Jill reached into her pocket and fingered her small wad of money, disappointment and concern wrinkling her brow. They could not be far from Fort Kearny now, and she felt her tension mount.

The wagon train had already turned north along the Blue River, leaving the Old Military Trail that led to Forty Riley on the Kansas River. She wondered how long it would take to reach the Platte River of Nebraska.

She glanced up, shielding her eyes from the brilliant sun as the prairie hay waved in the constant breeze. Meadowlarks sang from the tall grasses, accompanying the rolling wagons along their way. Prairie chickens scurried from their path, and a small herd of buffalo had been sighted on the horizon, quietly grazing.

A horse pounded the turf behind her, and Jill glanced over her shoulder. Captain Bridgett tugged on the reins, slowing his horse to match her pace. The wagon master's animal heaved, breathing deeply, and she reached a hand to stroke the sweating neck of the beast.

Bridgett pointed to the north where a line of gray clouds lingered. "Might be rain, but I can't complain. We've been unusually lucky with fine weather so far."

Jill remembered the day dark clouds had lowered low while wind whipped wildly. In the distance a tornado careened and skittered across the prairie as the animals were quickly herded into the safety of the circled wagons. She chose not to remind the captain of this memory.

"You're pleased with our progress?" Jill stepped from the walking horse, her attention shifting to her path through the tall grass.

"Indeed I am," he nodded, studying the line of wagons as they rolled. "You can never tell what these old plains will throw at you. Tornado, blizzards, heat, or Indians." He looked at Jill. "Watch for prairie rattlers," he warned casually, as if the dangers around them were all a natural part of the journey. "Our progress is adequate. As long as we arrive at Independence Rock by Fourth of July, we'll be all right."

He paused and peered sharply at Jill. She felt his scrutiny, used to the attention of men, but ignored his interest.

"I can't quite figure you out, Miss Foster," he said abruptly.

She glanced up at Captain Bridgett and smiled. "What's to figure out? I'm certain you've seen countless people moving west, searching for new opportunities, as I am now."

"But you're a lady," he protested with a chuckle. "Surely you could find a place to weather the storms of this infernal war. A pretty lass like you could easily catch herself a husband."

Jill stiffened, not wanting to explain she would not marry just any man. Her training, her talents, and her position in society allowed her to be selective. "Many of the gentlemen are fighting, occupied with the war. Until I can locate a teaching position, I am regulated to a piece of land my family owns near Fort Kearny." She shrugged. "The war cannot go on forever, and then I will return east and settle."

"But Nebraska," he said with an evident note of skepticism. "There's nothing to recommend this empty land to women, let alone a lady of quality like yourself. You will find little in the way of comforts you are accustomed to."

Jill frowned, worried she'd already come to the same conclusion. Her gaze swept the bleak landscape, and she wondered again at God's guidance to these plains. Was she right in coming here? Samuel had assured her the Spirit had opened this door, but was she a fool to listen to someone she'd barely known?

She inhaled and reminded herself she had no other choice, the land her father had taken in trade her only option for now.

Lifting her chin, Jill eyed Captain Bridgett. "I'm eager to see the land I own. Whatever happens out here, I hope and pray the Lord is with me."

Bridgett chuckled again and gripped his reins. "One day, there will be families and towns out here, settling these endless grasslands. But not yet. I fear you will be very much alone out here, surrounded by rough men. I'm not sure God has come to the prairies yet."

His laughter pealed as he spurred his horse ahead, and Jill gritted her teeth, feeling more alone than before the wagon master's conversation.

Jill heard the creak of wagon axles and the groan of wheels, but the monotonous sounds were unable to lull her heightened anxiety. Her chestnut hair was pulled back and tied with a ribbon, her bonnet hanging loosely down her back as she walked, sunshine bathing her face. She enjoyed the sun on her face now, her pale skin drinking the warm rays as Jill studied the prairie flowers and the azure sky, wishing the beautiful day could make her problems go away. At least the war was far away. She hadn't seen a blue uniform in weeks.

The land is so different than anything I've known, she thought as she surveyed her surroundings. The thick forests and big rivers of Kentucky and Missouri were gone now, replaced by these ever-extending grassy hills in all directions. Few trees decorated the plains, and Jill felt as if she could see for miles.

Small, darting birds called from the thickets, and Jill tried hard to not think of her challenging and daunting situation, wanting to enjoy the unexpected beauty around her. She smiled to herself. It was true, the beauty of the plains had surprised her. Despite her apprehension, she had to admit she liked the prairie. She breathed in the fresh air, filling her lungs with the intoxicating scent of prairie hay and wildflowers.

The nagging itch at the back of her neck pestered her, reminding her she had real problems. For today, however, she soaked in the sunlight, like crops drinking the summer rains. For the first time in a long time, she battled between comforting surroundings and the difficulties of her life. Before, there had been only negative feelings, worries, troubles. Yet the serene prairie seemed to calm her, and for today, she caught a glimmer of hope in the plains around her. They were so big, she so small.

She frowned, barely hearing the wagons rolling by as she plucked a few stalks of long grass. She really felt out of her element. This peaceful prairie was not a college for young ladies. It was wide, open, and too vast for her to comprehend. What was she doing out here, anyway? What had compelled her to think she could find a home on the Great Plains, even a temporary one?

She knew the answer, of course. A lack of options, she reminded herself as she lifted the fragrant blades to her nose and then tossed them aside. It was not like she had other opportunities or choices. This piece of property her father had taken in trade was all there was left to her. It was this or nothing.

NEBRASKA HAVEN

Not that she'd be the only war refugee in America. She'd seen plenty of dispossessed people, folks who'd lost everything and fled battlefields or destroyed homes.

Jill peered at the line of wagons, searching for Tim's wagon. A smile crossed her face when she saw Samuel in Tim's seat. When had he and Tim exchanged places? He and Reyna had become good friends, kindred spirits in God's service, Samuel told Jill last night over dinner. Tim must've given up his seat once again in an attempt to escape the tiresome dialogue between the two Christians.

Her smile vanished and her heart lurched. Was she a Christian? She loved God, but rarely thought of him. Samuel had petitioned her to read the Bible each day, but life was too busy, too demanding. Yet Samuel turned everything into a spiritual lesson, always looking for God's intervention and provision.

Jill shrugged. She would add that to her list of things to work on. She wanted to read Scripture more. Faith was important, she decided, but she had really big things to worry about right now.

She peered behind the wagon, searching for Tim, locating him striding beside the heavy vehicle. She pursed her lips when she saw him looking at her. She picked up her pace, not allowing him to catch up. Why was he looking at her?

Jill glanced over her shoulder. Tim looked away when he caught her eye and stretched his back. Then he walked on, quicker now, as if he intended on joining her. She watched him from the corner of her eye as he passed the lumbering wagon. Perhaps he intended a walk of his own, she surmised. Perhaps he, too, was impressed with the picturesque scenery.

Despite her faster gait, he gained on her. Her heart thudded in her chest and a sense of panic filled her. Tim and she usually kept their distance from one another, both wanting to stay out of the other's way. At least, that's how Jill felt. Now, here he was, hurrying to catch her as she walked along the trail.

"Jill," he called. Her frown deepened as she slowed her pace.

CHAPTER 19

"Good afternoon, Miss Jill," Tim greeted, falling in step beside her. He'd taken up using the name Samuel called her, and for some reason, the familiar title rankled her.

"Good afternoon, Mr. Hunter," she replied stiffly, not wanting to start conversation. She cringed as she noticed a brown patch of tanned skin through a tear in her sleeve. They walked along in silence, and Jill tried once again to enjoy the afternoon sunshine, but felt nervous, like a bug under a microscope.

"I was wondering if you could tell me anything about yourself," he said. "I'm interested in learning where you're from. I believe Reyna said your pa owned and operated a store in St. Louis."

The memory of her father flooded over her at Tim's inquiry. Jill had spent hours recalling the demise of her family and her descent in social standing. All of it could be traced back to their failure in business. How little she'd understood a person's standing in a community could affect their success—her success.

She glanced at Tim and wrinkled her nose. "Why?"

He hesitated and then blinked. "Well, I figure we're to be neighbors of sorts. Better get acquainted."

Jill didn't trust his answer, but there was some truth to what he said. Besides, it'd been a long time since anyone had asked about her. She sighed. Maybe she could scare him off with too much information.

"Yes, Father owned a store. A rather humble affair, I would call it. He made people uncomfortable with his anti-slavery views, and it cost him his livelihood. Mother was sickly for as long as I can remember. As the business declined, so did her health. They kept it all from me, providing what a spoiled, only child could wish for. I had no friends in St. Louis, and I tried not to make any when I went away to school. I guess I always thought they would desert me."

"And yet you rescued a runaway slave."

Jill looked at him sharply.

Tim smiled and turned to look forward. "Reyna told me. Samuel said you helped him run away. Don't worry, your secret is safe with us, but it makes no sense to me. I mean, isn't that what got your family in trouble in the first place?" Tim turned, glancing at her before looking at the wagons behind them. Forty yards stretched between his wagon and the one behind.

The sudden tension Jill felt at Tim's presence put her on guard. She didn't like how much he knew about Samuel. Or her. Sure, she'd freely shared, but she wanted to frighten him away, to leave her alone. Then she frowned. Or perhaps she wanted to test him.

"Yes, I guess you're right. It's just that I felt it was a way I could support my father and his views. Right before he died, my father told me he hoped this slave would get away. I guess helping Samuel was a way to strike a blow at those who ruined my family. Of course, I didn't realize that at the time. Only now am I starting to figure out why I helped him."

Jill paused, glancing up to see Samuel perched on the wagon seat, talking with Reyna. She smiled to herself, recalling how he'd given direction in those first days after the deaths of her parents.

"I still don't get it," Tim persisted. "Why risk your neck? I mean, what do you get out of it?"

She tensed even more at Tim's selfish query, angry she could identify the motivation for what it was. She shrugged. "He has become a dear friend."

Tim snorted. "A dangerous friend. You could have been captured, placed in jail, because of him."

Jill stared at the tree farmer, unimpressed with his untrimmed beard and strong features. She wanted to launch a fiery retort when she froze, suddenly recognizing his selfish response for something she used to consider. She nodded as she bit her lip.

Jill's silence made him scrutinize her profile. "What? You look like you want to say something."

"I was like you, God forgive me," she whispered.

"Like me?" Tim chuckled. "In what way?"

He seemed pleased with her description, as if she'd complimented him. But Jill shook her head, suddenly seeing things clearly. "I was selfish, only thinking of myself. Now I realize the Lord brought Samuel to me for help. He has been a tremendous support."

"Selfish?" Tim chuckled again, this time without humor. He removed his hat and dragged a hand through his unruly hair before shoving the hat back down. "I guess I am selfish, if you call someone wise and cautious being selfish. I need to look out for myself, do what helps me. No one's going to help me except myself."

Jill stared at Tim, seeing a glimpse of the person she'd become, and hating what she saw. "Oh, God, forgive me," she whispered again.

She blinked a few times, staving off the tears that threatened. Was this why God brought Samuel into her life?

Was this part of her purpose for coming west? To see herself in the reflection of this tree farmer stabbed her heart like a knife. Had her self-absorbed life become more important than the life the Lord wanted for her?

Tim cleared his throat, drawing Jill from her musings. "Will he go with you when you return east?"

Jill glanced again at Samuel where he chatted with Reyna on the wagon seat. "Samuel is free to go where he wishes. I have no hold on him. From what I gather, he is like me, without family. I hope he will always be with me, I have a lot to learn from him, but the choice is his." Jill looked down at her feet swishing through the grass. "Although," she added, "It won't be safe for him to return east." She turned her gaze back to the plains, stretching in every direction. "Perhaps this wide-open land will become his home."

Tim said nothing to this, and Jill felt grateful, allowing her guard to drop as she scanned the plains.

She'd not known what to expect on the prairie. The plains had not been discussed among the crowd she frequented, except to refer to them as "frontier" or "beyond civilization." Jill felt surprised how much the wide-open space affected her, filling her with delight and a feeling of vulnerability—and an unexpected sense of adventure.

Before, she'd struggled to maintain control. Out here, she had no choice—there was no control. The prairie was too big and powerful.

Abruptly, Tim's silent presence made her feel uneasy. He'd made it no secret that he blamed her for losing the single black walnut sapling he'd found that night in the creek bottom. Why was he now trying to befriend her, to get to know her better?

He made no sense, she decided. Rude and discourteous to begin with, now wanting to talk to her. Well, Jill knew what good manners were, and despite Tim Hunter's lack of them, she would always extend courtesy toward him, she resolved. She was, after all, a lady.

"Am I to assume from your sudden interest in me that you have forgiven me for the skunk incident?" Jill inquired, padding her words with formality.

Tim shook his head. "Certainly not. I'm not the Christian. That's Reyna's department. Forgiving one another, praying for people, and pleading with God for certain outcomes. No, I'm not kind like she is." He turned to her with a glint in his steely eyes. Jill shivered.

"My older sister, Reyna's mother, was like her. Kathleen married an Irish missionary and then went off and died in Africa, helping people. I don't see how that's fair of God, to take a loving soul like hers from earth. It would make more sense to take an unbeliever like me. I don't care about God and what he does. He seems mean."

Jill almost smiled at his words. They reflected her own thoughts exactly. What was God doing? Jill decided the Almighty truly moved in mysterious ways, like Samuel claimed. Yet God had revealed her selfish desires, making her consider another way. Surely she didn't want to be as selfish as Tim Hunter.

"I will say this, though," Tim went on. "Reyna has a spiritual peace and understanding that scares me. She is much older in maturity than many adults I know. She seems to have a connection with spiritual matters, a depth, far beyond her years."

He glanced suddenly at Jill, a smile creasing his worry-lined face. "She told me that God wanted you to join our wagon. She said doing so would have eternal consequences."

Jill laughed.

Tim grinned. "That's the first time I've heard you laugh. I like it."

She stifled her outburst and pressed her lips tightly together. "Well, I don't think there is any eternal consequences that guided me to your wagon. Merely mutual benefits. I needed a ride. You need land to plant. We are simply helping one another get what each requires."

"Still, I'm glad we've met. Reyna and Samuel enjoy each other's conversations." Tim gestured to the wagon rolling nearby. "No doubt, Samuel has saved me from hours of tortuous recitation of endless Scripture."

Jill looked away, not wanting him to see her smile of understanding. Tim could be witty and clever ... when he wasn't being rude.

"Besides," Tim added, "Reyna has assured me she is praying I find another walnut tree before we get to the farm. She says there was a reason why I didn't get that last one. I told her it was because of you and your magical power over skunks."

Jill's smile broadened in spite of herself, surprised at how she enjoyed his gentle teasing. She speculated why he didn't trim his unruly beard and wild, unkempt hair.

A shout from ahead disturbed her appraisal of Tim, and Jill blushed, wondering why she had taken the time to study him. She peered ahead to where Captain Bridgett stood, waving his flat brimmed hat. He cupped his mouth and shouted something. Those ahead passed the words down the line of wagons. The Platte. He'd seen the Platte River.

CHAPTER 20

Jill waded through the knee-high grass, her dress dragging her down as she hurried to the low rise, eager to see for herself. When had the wagon train left Kansas and entered Nebraska Territory? Her chest heaved, and she giggled as Tim raced her. Jill squealed with delight when he passed her and then glanced over his shoulder, as if to challenge her to keep up. She smiled at him and then looked away, embarrassed, amazed how he made her feel surprisingly relaxed where she'd felt so uneasy only moments before. When was the last time she'd felt relaxed?

She joined him on the summit and bent, hands on knees as she panted. On the other side of the hill, far out in the middle of a wide valley, a long line of dark trees indicated the path of the river. Straightening, she shielded her eyes and studied the shining ribbon stretching far to the west. Many sandbars and islands, some quite large, diverted various threads of the watercourse. Yet these wandering threads always reunited, forming the wide Platte River once more, flowing east to the Missouri River. She frowned, disappointed, finding the river unpretentious.

"There she flows. Too thick to drink, too thin to plow," Captain Bridgett announced as he stood beside Jill.

"Yes, but the land is beautiful," Tim breathed. Jill looked at him, startled his gaze did not follow the wending river, but analyzed the surrounding land instead. Her gaze followed his, and she tilted her head, pondering the fertile plains. This famous river of the west, the one the Oregon Trail followed, seemed so unassuming, flat, drab. There was nothing majestic or marvelous about it. Yet, Jill realized, the muddy water gave life and life abundant to the surrounding region. Jill pursed her lips. Perhaps she shouldn't judge things by their appearances.

As she looked at the river, something tugged at the edges of her mind. Recollections of her dreams back in St. Louis washed over her, and a shiver snaked down her back. This slow, level, dark river seemed like the one in her dreams, she felt certain.

She studied the murky water as the wagons continued to roll toward Fort Kearny. She felt the river had a draw on her, a pull. Like this was where she was supposed to be. But why? She'd seen the Missouri, and the Ohio, and even the mighty Mississippi. Yet this shallow, muddy river somehow touched something deep inside her.

Jill shook her head, clearing her muddled thoughts, and walked down the grassy hill. Finally, the wagon train reached Fort Kearny, which was as unimpressive as the river that lay nearby. A couple of blockhouses built of graying, weathered logs, made up the central part of the little outpost. Also, a blacksmith shop, a dirty tavern catering to a rough lot built of sod that doubled as a stage station, and a general store. Behind the general store, Jill sighted a low roofed, open-air shelter, like a barn without sides. Stacked furniture filled the spacious structure. A graveyard of broken wagons and discarded things lay scattered beside the open-air barn.

"They went bankrupt last year," Tim said from his high perch atop the wagon as Jill walked alongside. She followed his pointing arm, noting the little shack and abandoned corrals near the ramshackle stage station. A sign with faded letters tacked to the empty structure could still be made out. "Pony Express Office."

Jill turned back to the small military post while the wagons rumbled past her, destined to stop on the western edge of this frontier town. Barracks and a few houses filled the spaces behind the shops which lined the large parade ground of the fort. A red, white, and blue flag fluttered from a tall pole.

Tim pulled his wagon far to one side and allowed the remainder of the caravan to pass. Captain Bridgett rode back to shake hands with Tim and then waved at Jill as he galloped back to the head of the column.

Jill stared as Nan and Earl passed. The old woman lifted her chin and peered ahead, ignoring Jill. Earl merely scowled at her, like the small boy in class reprimanded for making a disturbance. She hoped never to see them again.

As she stood there, feeling relief flood over her in a wave, she knew her travels were soon to be over. They'd made it. Almost. Her land was close by. Yet a shudder quaked her shoulders, reminding her she hadn't actually seen the property.

Jill looked around. Gone were the busy streets of St. Louis or even the grace and charm of Paducah. Now, she saw the dust and the stunted trees that bordered the river to the north. Things were certainly different, but she would need to live here for a while at least.

The walk from Missouri had changed her in many ways. She felt stronger and her skin was tanned from the sun and wind. Her gaze dropped to her dirty dress and then to her hands, marveling at the chapped skin and calloused palms. Before, her hands had been so white, so soft. Now, her dresses all looked worn and travel stained. No longer was she the pampered Southern girl. With a little pride, Jill realized she'd become a pioneer.

Gathering firewood, fetching heavy buckets of water, helping feed the stock, and even helping unhitch the wagon, all these things she could now do on her own. Although she'd never camped outside before, she could start fires and make meals over a blaze. With satisfaction, Jill realized she had grown and developed as a person.

But the changes were not all merely physical. Her constant discussions with Samuel and Reyna had helped a spiritual interest blossom within her. She vowed to study the Bible when time allowed. She wanted to know God. No longer did she want to sit by and wonder how God worked or interacted with his people, she wanted to experience his presence and look for the Lord's hand in her life, in all things, like Samuel and Reyna did.

She drew in a deep breath, feeling God rebuilding her, shaping her into the woman he wanted her to be. She recalled the verse Samuel liked to quote ... we are the clay, God is the potter. A smile tugged at her lips as her heart swelled. Yes, she could live here. She was anxious to see all that Nebraska—and God—had in store for her.

Tim gestured to the army outpost and Jill squinted at the Yankee soldiers, her chest tightening. But then, eyes shining, Tim pointed to the elm and cottonwood trees the soldiers had transplanted from the river and now ringed the parade ground.

"We'll spend a day here, gathering supplies, before we head for the farm," Tim advised.

They made camp quickly. Samuel went in search of wood while Jill wandered down to the river's edge for water. A well-trodden trail led her through the thick underbrush to the grassy bank of the slow-moving water. Piles of driftwood and debris lined the low banks. She knew Samuel would have no trouble collecting an abundance of firewood here.

A pair of deer lifted their heads at her approach, water dripping from their chins, before they bounded into the deeper undergrowth. A crow called a warning as a hawk soared too close, its wide wings flapping as the red-tailed hawk sailed farther downstream.

Bending to dip her bucket, Jill stared at the dirty water. She glanced upstream to see if anything could be blamed for the murk. Nothing. She frowned and walked from the river, her empty bucket swinging as she gripped the rope handle.

Tim grinned and pointed to the well in front of the general store when she returned to camp. "A soldier told me you can drink the river water, if you allow it to settle for, at least, an hour. The silt will drift to the bottom of a bucket. I guess we'll not have the clean water of Tennessee anymore, hey, Reyna?"

Samuel delivered an enormous load of firewood and then took the bucket to the well for water as Jill helped Reyna start a fire. Soon, dinner simmered.

The aroma of frying bacon and baking biscuits filled the air, and a feeling of satisfaction and real anticipation permeated their little campsite. They'd made it to Nebraska, and they reveled in their success.

With ample time allowed for cleaning and comforts, Tim searched for a third stone to balance the Dutch oven over the fire. Samuel dragged a sun-bleached log beside camp, creating a perfect bench, while the girls cleaned laundry and hung clothes out to dry.

Tim wiped his hands on his pants and glanced at Jill. "I'll go to the store and see what I can learn. This place of yours must be close." He eyed her, waiting for a response, but Jill only shrugged, not wanting to admit she didn't know where the farm was located.

She watched as Tim stalked from the campsite, all her hopes riding on what he discovered.

CHAPTER 21

Tim returned at supper time, a grimace creasing his bearded face, worry lines pulling at the corners of his eyes.

"What be bothering you now, Uncle Tim?" Reyna asked, observing the worrisome look on her uncle's face. "I can tell something is giving you trouble."

Tim accepted a cup and a plate from the young girl and sat on the log near Jill. He glanced at her, his scowl deepening.

Jill squirmed as he ate his dinner. She could tell he was trying to figure out the best way to tell her something. Bad news? However, she didn't press while he ate his stew. After he tossed his empty bowl beside the fire, she drew a deep breath.

"Mr. Hunter, if you have news for us, please spit it out. We would all like to hear what you've learned," Jill demanded, annoyed with his brooding silence.

Tim shifted on the blanket covered log. "Well, I heard at the store that the Federalist Navy has captured New Orleans. The Yanks have closed the Mississippi River to Confederate travel, all the way to Vicksburg. I guess it's cut off Texas, Louisiana, and Arkansas from the rest of the South."

He paused and sipped coffee, his eyes still somber. Jill knew his moody behavior concealed something more.

"I can tell you are not finished, Uncle Tim," Reyna accused, mirroring Jill's own suspicions.

Tim frowned at his niece and then glanced at Jill before staring into the fire. "It might amount to nothing. I asked a few soldiers about the land you own. A couple of the newer men knew nothing of the place. That worried me some. Finally, I met a sergeant near the old Pony Express office who laughed when I said we were going to farm that land."

Jill narrowed her eyes and stared into the fire, waiting. She'd been afraid of this. Her heart pounded slowly, thudding like a mournful drum at a funeral procession.

Tim sipped coffee before he spoke again. "'Farm it,' he says to me, and then laughed outright. 'That land is not worth the time the man put into it. It was old Murphy who retired from the army who owned it. But he wasn't the first. A hunter built it, paying men to quarry stone for the house and barn. A big, grand house he built, with no flat land of any size to plant his fields. No farmer would buy it from Murphy when he decided to sell and move after the first winter on the place. Said it was too hard to live there alone all winter.'"

Jill's heart sank. What was her father thinking when he took this worthless land title from a former Yankee soldier? She wondered if he had felt sorry for the veteran. Jill was sure Murphy was still laughing for the way he'd tricked her father.

Jill sighed, an act she caught herself doing more frequently these days. Life was hard on her, getting tougher all the time. Would things never go her way? She thought of Samuel's God. Samuel always said God made his people promises about how he would provide for them. If this was part of the package of becoming a Christian, she wanted none of it. Silently, she reconsidered her desire to pursue the Lord. Would life always be difficult, even with God's presence within her?

Only a few short months ago, Jill would've said she was a Christian. She believed in God and the importance of attending church, although if services interfered with her social calendar, she couldn't really be expected to attend, right? Certainly, Bible reading was not important, but she felt grateful the pastor read his Bible. That way, he could share with his flock what he'd discovered in the mysterious pages of Holy Scripture.

But after meeting Samuel, the name Christian had taken on a whole new meaning. Not a title of convenience, but a call to action. According to Samuel, Christians were filled with the Holy Spirit, guiding them through life and its many challenges while surrendering your desires for God's plan.

Jill scowled into the flames. She did not want to give up her life. She wanted a God who would give her what she wanted ... when she wanted it. She did not like God's method of building patience and faith through trials. It seemed like too much work, she decided.

Then she tilted her head. Who was she trying to fool? She had no control over the difficulties that had overwhelmed her. Perhaps she should submit to God's plan and hang on, look for his hand in her life. Could things get worse?

Jill sighed. *Let the adventure begin*, she thought bitterly. Besides, she was getting used to hard times. Perhaps this was her lot.

"Well, things go wrong for me all the time now," Jill complained, letting her head hang. "I've had nothing but bad luck since the school in Paducah closed. I thought that was bad enough, then my parents died, the family business was lost to me, and now I'm out on this empty prairie with a worthless farm. What else could go wrong?"

Silence met Jill's words. Then, Reyna spoke. "It is in the darkness that a lamp shines brightest."

Jill's head came up. "What does that mean?"

"It means you are in the darkness, Miss Jill," Samuel explained. "And a light will shine for you, show you the way. God wants to show you something in this dark time."

"It means you are walking through the shadow of death," Reyna said softly. "But God is with you, guiding you. Be patient and watch for his hand. He is growing your faith and drawing you to himself." She rested her hand on Jill's. The young Irish girl smiled, and Jill felt encouraged, as if something truly was going to happen.

"It means nothing," Tim muttered, tossing a stick on the fire. "Your luck has played out. That's all it means. God doesn't care about you, Jill Foster. He's busy with other things. The War Between the States has probably gotten his full attention. You are simply out of luck, and I think we should be going on with this wagon train."

Tim leaned forward as he spoke, looking around Jill to his niece. "There's still a chance to find land farther west for us to plant the trees. No offense meant, Miss Jill, but I can't afford your bad luck thrown on top of our own. Reyna, we'll be moving on at first light."

Jill peered at Reyna, expecting to hear a heated debate about why they couldn't go on. She was surprised when the young girl merely nodded, not saying anything.

Placing her dishes on the ground, Reyna turned to Samuel. "Will you be willing to spend some time in prayer with me? I feel the Lord is wanting to let his will be known."

The former slave rose quietly and hobbled after Reyna, stepping just past the edge of the firelight. They huddled near the wagon, and Jill heard them pray and recite Scripture verses as she studied the dancing flames at her feet, wondering what she should do. Tim leaped to his feet and stalked into the night, his shoulders sagging.

Alone by the fire, Jill sat, chewing the inside of her cheek. She didn't feel like praying. That was for religious people. She simply felt lost and forlorn. For the hundredth time, she asked herself, what was she going to do?

If Tim and Reyna went on without her, how would she get to the farm? How would she and Samuel make it through the coming winter?

I can't keep worrying, she told herself, biting her lip until it hurt. She pushed herself up and gathered the dirty dishes, then carried them down to the river.

A bright moon lighted her way, revealing the path through the foliage to the river's edge. She halted on the bank, studying the shaft of moonlight shimmering on the slow water. Tiny ripples revealed snags just below the surface, and Jill arched an eyebrow, wishing someone would reveal the snags in life to her.

She knelt and thrust the dishes into the water, scrubbing them violently, her mind refusing to calm. She wrestled her predicament, mulling it over, searching for solutions. She would be left alone on the prairie with an escaped slave.

When Jill returned to camp, she slowed and then paused when she heard heated voices. Tim and Reyna stood beside the wagon, no sign of Samuel.

"You must have faith," Reyna argued, her voice firm and resolute. "You cannot expect everything to go your way. We are serving others. They need us."

"I am not serving anyone. I need to get these trees in the ground soon or lose the lot of them. I don't care what happens to these strangers," Tim snapped, his face red in the firelight.

"That's just it, Uncle Tim. You only worry about yourself. Think of these good people. They need our help and"—her hand gestured to the wagon full of trees—"you'll be getting your precious trees in the ground. We need to go to Jill's farm."

"You heard her, Reyna." Tim flung his arm above the fire, gesturing impatiently. "She's bad luck. We should cut and run while we can."

"If events surrounding a person make bad luck, then I'm bad luck. Your sister died with her husband while treating sick people who had malaria. I survived. Was I their bad luck?"

Tim hesitated, then shook his head. "No, Reyna. I don't think you're bad luck. Things happen, that's all."

"That's ridiculous." The young girl waved a dismissive hand, her voice lowering. "Things do not just happen. God uses everything, every event for his glory. It is no accident I stand here with you. The Lord has brought me to you to share his good news. That has been clear from the beginning."

Tim shook his head again, the deep scowl on his face vivid in the firelight. "Reyna, don't start on me with your preaching." He ran a hand through his dark hair and then peered once more at his niece. "I want what is best for you. I think we should go on with the wagon train. The farm is not what we hoped it would be."

"And I want what is best for you, and that is to go to the farm and watch the Lord work. He is not done with Jill, and he certainly is not through with you, Uncle Tim."

Jill moved forward, stomping noisily to sound her presence. Tim glanced at Jill and his eyes softened. He dropped to the fallen log as if his knees had buckled beneath him.

"Is everything all right?" Jill asked, fearing the answer. They would desert her in the morning, she was sure of it. And why not? She had risked everything to come to Nebraska. What right did she have to ask others to risk with her?

Tim stared at the ground and rubbed the back of his neck, his broad shoulders sagging. Jill could see him grapple with his options, neither of them good. Then he raised his face to peer at Jill.

"It seems Reyna and I will be going with you to your farm." He paused, glancing from Jill to Reyna and then back to Jill. "But if things don't work out, we'll hurry to catch the caravan."

He looked to Reyna for confirmation, but the girl only glowered at her uncle.

Jill could not believe her ears. Did he tease? An inner joy warmed her as hope raced through her veins. Tears brimmed her eyes. She would not be alone. Tim and Reyna would join her and Samuel. And God? Was God with her?

The next day, Reyna discovered two black walnut saplings in the trees bordering the river.

CHAPTER 22

The farm on Peach Tree Creek lay four miles west of town, across the river. When Jill told Tim the name of the creek, his eyes shone with excitement. A good omen, he called it. They followed the blacksmith's directions and drove to the farm, everyone anxious and eager but none more than Jill.

"There's two ways to get to Hazlett's old place," the burly smithy had informed Tim as Jill stood beside him. "You can ford the river here," he said as he gestured to the nearby road cut through the underbrush toward the river. "Then turn west along the emigrant trail that cuts through the pass in the hills. That way will take you to Fort Laramie and over the Rockies. Or you can go west out of town and turn north at the better ford. Can't miss it. With your loaded wagon, I suggest the better ford. Besides, when you cross, you'll be on your land. It borders the north side of the river. The crossing above town is wide, but soft mud, and not as solid as the one Hazlett developed."

Jill pursed her lips but didn't correct the smithy when he'd referred to the land as Tim's.

"I thought the man's name was Murphy who used to own it," Tim said.

The blacksmith grinned. "Hazlett built the place, wanted the stage contract. He lost the place to Murphy in a card game."

Well supplied, Tim drove the wagon along the narrow trail west of Fort Kearny, the thick undergrowth of the river on their right. They covered the short distance in an hour. Jill walked with Reyna part of the way, but they were implored by the impatient Tim to climb aboard when they forded the river.

The girls sat on the tailgate, squealing as they lifted their dangling legs above the muddy water. At first, Jill cast only a hurried glance downstream, unimpressed with the shallow Platte River. Then her eyes narrowed, and she studied the wide watercourse, mostly full of sandbars and stands of isolated thickets on low islands. A sense of belonging, of returning to familiar surroundings filled her as she stared, surprised at the unexpected sensation. She'd never been here before, yet the river and the golden-brown hills beyond seemed so familiar. Of course, she'd seen them in her dreams, but she wrinkled her brow, wondering why.

The wagon jostled and pitched, but the team of horses pulled the heavily laden wagon without mishap. With a lurch, the horses heaved, dragging them onto the opposite bank. Thick shrubs and even a few larger trees screened the side of the avenue cut through the woods, a canopy of branches shielding them overhead as they drew away from the river. Water dripped from the wet wagon, and Jill's heart pounded in her chest when Tim drove the wagon into a clearing. Reyna squeezed Jill's arm, her eyes glowing, as Tim slowed the horses and halted.

Fear gripped Jill, and her heart leaped to her throat, unable to speak. She wiped her sweaty palms on her dress, keeping her gaze fixed on the shrubbery fringing the river. Reyna dropped to the ground and raced around the wagon, but Jill stared behind her, refusing to look at the stone house that belonged to her. This was the moment she'd been waiting for, fearing and hopeful. She'd traveled so far.

NEBRASKA HAVEN

Could she live here? Did she have a choice? Was this land as worthless as she dreaded? She was not sure she could handle another setback or defeat. Things had already been too difficult.

In an instant, she remembered the school closing, the passing of her parents, the loss of everything that connected her to Missouri, but she also remembered she'd come to know hope. A spiritual interest she didn't know had been discovered and grew within her, wanting to blossom. She'd discovered a new friendship too. Samuel had helped her.

Despite the challenges of the arduous trip, Jill had willingly given up her self-absorbed and pampered life. Samuel said she was on an adventure—one she'd always been on but only now come to understand. God's plan for her was unfurling, and she trembled, gripping the wooden side of the wagon. She glanced up at the passing clouds and then nodded. Abruptly, anticipation flowed through her veins, reminding her she was here, in Nebraska, and she might as well look around. Now, she would learn about her inheritance.

Jill drew a deep breath and let it out slowly before jumping to the ground. Warily, she turned, peering to her left, away from the house. A squat, stone barn nestled among tall weeds, the turf roof appearing like an extension of the hill it'd been carved from. She would investigate the barn later, she promised herself.

Jill drew in another deep breath, steeling herself. She could hear Tim, Samuel, and Reyna jabbering away behind her, but she felt afraid to turn and see what the hullabaloo was all about. This could be the beginning of good things, or simply an addition to the nightmare she had experienced these last weeks.

Finally, clenching her fists by her side, she turned and looked across the yard. More tall weeds and grass filled the clearing, stretching all the way to the covered porch running the length of the huge stone house.

Peering past the overgrown yard, she studied the structure. They'd been informed that native limestone had been discovered and removed from nearby, cleverly cut and fitted snugly together by soldiers from England with quarry experience.

One of the front windows lay shattered, shards of glass scattered across the porch and among the weeds. The other windows stared blankly back at her. The house was empty, draped in loneliness and silence. For an instant, Jill considered climbing back into the wagon and leaving, but then remembered she had nowhere else to go.

Samuel waded through the thigh high weeds and opened the door, vanishing within, Reyna on his heels. Tim turned and smiled as he stretched a hand toward her, inviting her on.

"It looks worse than it is, Jill," he encouraged softly. "Come on, let's look 'er over."

She hesitated and glanced up at the tall building, noting the three windows across the second floor. Her gaze dropped to Tim's, and he gestured again, a warm and welcoming look about him. Tentatively, she reached for his hand, grateful to have someone with her as she surveyed the property. A thrill raced through her as their fingertips touched, but Jill lowered her gaze before Tim could see her surprise. For a moment, she scanned the exterior before following Tim across the porch and inside the stone house.

The entry lay thick in shadows. Before them, a staircase led to the second floor. Through the wide door on her left, Jill could make out a large stone fireplace, a pair of buffalo hide-covered couches facing the hearth, and the broken window. Two doors faced the entry on her right. Samuel came from the farthest one, a wide smile on his face.

"Looks good, Miss Jill."

She tugged free of Tim's grip as heat stole up her neck, concerned Samuel had seen them holding hands. She stepped forward, scanning her house, hoping the moment had gone unnoticed.

Jill faltered, afraid to hope this new life might work out. She glanced at the stairwell, noting the layer of dust that would have to be removed. Reyna called from the sitting room, and Tim followed Jill from the entry into the spacious room. A kitchen filled the far corner, a long table against the wall.

Jill stared, unable to believe it might be real. Except for the broken front window, the house appeared solid.

Tim stepped close behind her, and she glanced over her shoulder at him, a smile trembling on her lips. His nearness seemed so comforting somehow, reminding her she was not alone.

Reyna stepped from the kitchen, brushing her hands and speaking aloud what they all were thinking. "It is good. The house will need some repairs and cleaning, but all in all, it will do very nicely. It's almost too big, though, probably difficult to warm in winter."

The young girl strode to the entry and then they heard her steps on the stairs. "Wait, Reyna," Tim called, a note of worry in his voice as he shot Jill a meaningful glance and turned to chase his niece.

Jill watched him go, surprised how his absence struck her.

Samuel hobbled up beside her. He nodded, a grin on his cheerful face. "You gambled and won, Miss Jill. But it's not really a gamble when you bet on the Lord. He led us here."

Jill tilted her head, wondering at Samuel's words as the pair retraced their steps to the front porch. They leaned against the railing, peering down the length of the veranda, appreciating the craftsmanship. The house seemed truly well built. Someone had gone to great expense for this fine building.

She would have liked to explore the second level, but it could wait. Her knees felt weak.

Tim and Reyna emerged, joining them on the front porch. "This house is grand, miss, no doubt about that." Reyna grinned. "There are four rooms upstairs. Two bedrooms downstairs. One looks like it might've been an office, there being shelves built along one wall. A big kitchen with a pantry, a bigger sitting room, and a long dining table."

Tim stroked his chin, his gaze shifting to the surrounding land. He narrowed his eyes, and Jill could see he considered the possibilities. Would the land suit his needs? Would he take Reyna and leave, hurry to catch up with Captain Bridgett's wagon train? She wrinkled her nose, a little annoyed that she cared whether he would like the farm.

"This house will be grand to live in, Miss Jill," Reyna reported, crossing her arms over her chest. "Indeed, the biggest I've ever lived in."

Jill nodded. It would be the biggest house she'd lived in as well, not counting the college dormitory.

Tim turned back to the trio. "The floors are solid, as are the stairs. There are six rooms for sleeping. I wonder what this man Murphy was thinking when he built such a big place?"

"It was not Murphy," Reyna corrected. "He only took it from Hazlett, the hunter for the post."

Tim chuckled. "The hunter? Now another Hunter has arrived at Peach Tree Farm."

CHAPTER 23

Reyna took charge of cleanup, which took the rest of the day to mop and scrub the floors and move their scant bedding and gear inside. Tim and Samuel would share one of the downstairs rooms, Reyna and Jill another. The girls chose the room with the shelves. Jill hoped to use the space for an office as well as bedroom. The upstairs would not be utilized since it would be harder to heat in the winter.

"I can start cleaning that tomorrow," Reyna announced, waving a hand at the upstairs.

Rusty water spilled from the pump out the back door, quickly followed by a clear stream. Tim tasted the gushing cascade, his eyes glowing. "Good water," he mumbled, his eyes straying again to the distant hills.

Samuel found firewood, and soon water boiled on the kitchen stove, which seemed far superior to any Jill had used. The large stone fireplace in the sitting room was left alone at present. Samuel would check the chimney first thing in the morning to make sure it was not obstructed by bird's nests or leaves.

They worked for hours, boiling water for cleaning and another pot for coffee. For lunch, they munched on bread and cheese purchased from the store at Fort Kearny. In the late afternoon, the trio realized Tim had disappeared.

Jill glanced out the window, searching for the farmer. She knew where he'd gone.

Jill stepped to the porch and scanned the nearby hills, feeling uneasy. Not a level piece of land in sight except for the small clearing before the house. If Tim didn't like the land .... She returned indoors, grabbed another rag, and kept cleaning, refusing to permit her mind to go down that path.

Samuel unhitched the team from the wagon and picketed them next to the barn. "Tim will choose where the horses should go." He gestured to the silent, squat stone structure. "Maybe the barn isn't suitable for them after such a long emptiness."

Reyna cleared the broken glass away at the window. A replacement would have to be ordered soon. A blanket covered the hole temporarily.

They served the evening meal on the large plank table in the dining room. A few items of furniture had been found and moved to better locations after a thorough cleaning. Soon the sun began to drop in the west, and shadows stretched across the wide, wooden floors, heralding the end of the first day on Jill's land. Locusts whirred in the trees down by the river as Jill and Reyna stood before the sink, washing dishes. The sound of the axe on wood drifted through the open back door, revealing Samuel at work. Just then, Tim returned, his boots thudding on the porch. He'd been gone all afternoon and Jill's nerves felt stretched when he finally appeared in the doorway.

She pursed her lips and squared her shoulders as Tim approached. She knew this moment was coming and had dreaded it. All day, Jill had watched Reyna and Samuel work to make the house livable, but she had known they were simply wasting their efforts. Once Tim returned from his survey of the hilly land, they would be packing up and leaving. There was no way Tim would find this deserted farm worth investing his efforts. Jill's blood chilled when she saw the dour look on his face. Her hands gripped the plate beneath the soapy water as she glanced at Tim over her shoulder. *Here it comes*, she thought.

Then, her eyes widened as his grim features brightened. His dark curls hung over his damp brow and the fresh scent of grass and rich soil clung to the farmer as he halted behind her.

He smiled at Reyna, the girl busily drying dishes, and then turned to Jill. "Miss Jill, the land is perfect. Rich black earth just waiting to be planted. The soil is right, and tomorrow I will begin to plant the trees."

Jill's eyebrows knitted together. "But what about what we were told at Fort Kearny, that this land is not suitable for farming?"

Tim shrugged. "The fools were talking about fields of crops, not trees. I don't need large, flat places for trees. I can put them anywhere. There are plenty of spots, including some meadows for cutting hay."

Jill tilted her head, stunned by Tim's positive assessment. Could this be true? Could they live here after all?

Accepting a bowl of soup from Reyna and a cup of water, Tim settled on a chair. "I'll easily be able to plant my trees on the land that is already cleared. We'll need the hay for the horses come winter and possibly for protection of the young saplings. The barn is infested with mice. Probably some grain was left behind, but I saw a dozen of the little varmints when I inspected the building. Whoever built this place, built to stay. The buildings are sound, solid. I wonder why Murphy left after going to such trouble to get this place."

Tim gulped his water, his tanned neck working as he swallowed. Jill looked away, pretending not to notice his broad shoulders. When he wiped his mouth with the back of his hand, Jill shot him a disapproving look as he motioned to Reyna for a refill.

"Well, the water is good. Much better than that filthy river water in town. The land is very hilly with deep gullies and ravines, and a few open meadows. None of which are too big. But I discovered a road on the north end of the property that seems like a pass through the hills running east to west. It must be the gap the blacksmith told me about. A branch of it runs through the hills to this house. I don't know what Murphy saw in locating this farm, because he didn't intend to farm, but the soil is rich and there's water near at hand—perfect for a tree farm. These hills just to the north of us will provide excellent wind break from the winter storms."

Reyna took Tim's empty dishes and brought him a steaming cup of coffee. Jill glanced at her, amazed at the girl's willingness to serve. Reyna never acted like it bothered her. On the contrary, it seemed to please Reyna to help people. Jill had observed the same attitude in Samuel. She wondered at their similarity.

"I would like to help you dig holes for your planting, Tim," Samuel interjected, hobbling to the table. "I'm a first-rate hole digger," he added with a grin.

"I'll take you up on your offer, Samuel, but first let me help around here." Tim turned to Jill. "I can give you one day of help before I must plant the trees. I want them to root well before first frost."

She considered a moment before saying, "If you will, help Samuel clear the chimney and make the barn usable. Perhaps you can check the well and the pump too, make sure all is right. Reyna and I can do everything else around here. You need to get into the fields, and I would not interfere."

NEBRASKA HAVEN

She reached for a dish towel and dried her hands, peering intently at each of her companions in turn, the tension she'd felt all day starting to slip away. She felt blessed. The satisfied sensation surprised her after so much worry and turmoil. Jill smiled as her gaze rested finally on Tim. "I'm very pleased to hear the land meets with your expectations and approval. Thank you again, Mr. Hunter, for bringing me here."

Tim frowned. "Miss Jill, stop calling me Mr. Hunter. Call me Tim."

Jill was not entirely comfortable with the informal title but chose not to argue further at this time. After all, they would be living in close quarters for some time. Might as well relent and make the best of a temporary situation.

She nodded. "Very well, I will, Mist—Tim, I mean, if you will simply call me Jill."

"Done." He slapped his knee, settling the matter. "Samuel, we have some light left if we hurry. Would you like to inspect the barn before it grows too dark?"

Samuel rose quickly. "Let's go. You can show me how you like the horses stabled."

Jill stood beside the cold fireplace, peering into the darkening front yard. Shadows stretched from the house to the barn and beyond, the trees along the river appearing thick and foreboding in the fading light. Paths through the weeds in the yard reminded her she'd need to cut them down. She glanced up through the tall window, watching the last pinks and oranges of the day reflected in a pair of hovering clouds.

An unexpected sense of joy and thanksgiving enveloped her. She had arrived at the property in Nebraska. All her fears had been for nothing. She breathed deeply, the fresh air filling her lungs. A desire to thank God came over her, and she nodded, watching the pair of colorful clouds.

"Thank you, Lord," she whispered, wondering if this was how Reyna or Samuel would do it. They both seemed so much better at talking to God, so much more comfortable.

A commotion across the yard drew her gaze, and she saw the two men stride from the barn, a halo of artificial light illuminating their way. Samuel's shifting gait was apparent, even in the dim glow of the swinging lantern Tim carried.

The dirty pair of men seated themselves wearily on the porch, just beyond Jill's position in the house. Behind her, Reyna bustled around the kitchen, pots and pans clanging as the Irish girl continued to clean.

"Thank you, Lord," Jill went on, not wanting to conclude her unfamiliar connection with God. "You've led me here, haven't you? Samuel said you were with me, guiding me, yet I can't believe the unexpected ways you worked to maneuver me to Nebraska."

Jill's whispered prayer grew even softer as she shifted, feeling emotion swell and overtake her. Tears streamed down her cheeks. "Perhaps you do have a plan for me."

As if a dam had burst, her grief and fears bubbling over like a boiled pot of water, she quietly sobbed. She'd arrived in Nebraska with Samuel. Tim and Reyna would stay on, helping her settle. Jill was not alone. All her anxieties slipped away, and she realized she'd been holding her emotions in check, not sure what would happen to her. But now she felt safe, safe to let her guard down and soak in God's provision.

As she sagged against the wall beside the window, Jill tried to regain her composure. "You are with me, Lord. Thank you for Samuel, Reyna, and Tim." She glanced around the large room, now shrouded in shadows as the final rays of the disappearing sun vanished. "Thank you for this haven, a safe refuge."

NEBRASKA HAVEN

Too exhausted to pray further, she nodded, trusting God knew the depth of her gratitude. She wiped her sleeve across her face, thankful also for the gloomy lighting as she summoned Reyna to join her on the porch with the men.

The hum of insects droned around them. The soft summer twilight felt pleasant, Jill thought as she basked in the relaxation of the first evening at the stone house. A gentle breeze brought cooler air up from the nearby river. Perhaps this place would grow on her.

"Well, the barn is good," Tim said, leaning against the stone house. "I didn't expect to begin cleaning it tonight, but when we got there, we started in. We also filled a couple of barrels with water. They promptly leaked, but I think the wood will swell and they'll hold water. I can use them to take water to the trees when I get them in the ground."

He paused, accepting a cup of fresh coffee from his niece. He sipped from the hot mug before continuing.

"After we clear the chimney, I'm going to cut some hay for the stalls. Samuel will start digging holes. I can join him later." Tim took another sip. "We want to work while the weather is fine. Folks say the weather changes here mighty quick, and we need to be ready."

Jill barely heard him. She studied his mannerisms, the way he held his cup, the way he lifted his mug, the way he smiled at Reyna. The breeze ruffled his damp hair and she found herself liking the look of him, his strong profile in the dim light from the lantern near his boots. Even his beard appealed to her.

With a jolt, Jill straightened and glanced nervously around the small group. Had anyone noticed her studying Tim? How embarrassing. She leaned against the rock wall again, sinking into the shadows just beyond the circle of lantern halo. What had made her think of Tim? Her interests leaned toward refined men of culture, men of bearing, not scruffy farmers. She must be really tired. A low chuckle rose from her throat, dismissive and flippant.

Reyna turned to her. "What are you laughing at, Jill?"

Jill smiled into the darkness. "Oh, nothing. Nothing at all."

CHAPTER 24

The next day, Jill and Reyna started a blaze in the large open stone fireplace after the men completed their chimney inspection. Afterward, Tim hurried to hitch the wagon, eager to cut hay so they could attend next to the trees while the hay dried. Plus, they'd need the wagon—still loaded with trees—to move the dried hay.

For the next few days, they toiled before sunrise to well after sunset. Tim fussed over the newly planted saplings, making sure each were watered every day. When the trees were planted, Tim and Samuel returned to the hay and not a moment too soon. As they loaded the wagon, Reyna pointed to dark clouds forming on the horizon.

Jill frowned. She'd hoped there would be time to go to Fort Kearny and place an order for additional supplies, including a new window. It could take months for the glass to arrive.

Thunder rumbled, heralding the summer rainstorm, the air growing heavy. Jill felt her hair tingle, stiffening in the stifling thick air. Lightning flashed across the hilltops, and the ringing peals of thunder clapped low and long before a single drop of rain fell. Finally, the rain came with a gentle spattering, then a heavier downpour accompanied the thunder rolls.

Tim stabled the team and ran to the house just as the torrent let loose. Laughing, he raced up the front steps to stop in the open doorway and watch the rain soaking the dirt yard, the tall weeds having been cleared away. "This is just what the trees needed," he exclaimed. "Perfect timing."

"God's timing is always perfect, Uncle Tim. You should know that by now," Reyna chided from the kitchen. The Irish girl reached for a bucket and moved toward the back door, the water bucket swinging as she glanced at the rain before dashing through the open door.

Tim growled, his smile disappearing as he turned to watch his niece. Jill dumped another cup of flour into a bowl and cringed, wondering if an argument brewed. She'd learned quickly Tim wasn't interested in spiritual matters, yet Reyna persisted.

He glanced at the back door where Reyna disappeared before sidling closer to Jill, peering into her mixing bowl. "Does that God talk irritate you like it does me? I get so tired of hearing Reyna go on and on," Tim complained, keeping his voice low as he rolled his eyes.

Jill chewed her lip, considering. "No." She shook her head, surprised but pleased with her answer as she lifted her chin. "No, I am not irritated. Samuel has helped me understand many things about God. I never gave spiritual things much thought before I met him. I've even begun to read the Bible."

Tim stared at her, a look of disbelief clouding his face. "So? They got to you too? Well, believe what you want. I don't care. Just don't start giving me any of their Bible nonsense. I won't stand for it."

Tim marched from the kitchen and crossed the living room, leaving Jill standing alone. She peered out the window and observed the widening puddles forming across the dirt yard. Overhead, dark, steel-gray clouds sagged. Yet, despite the drab day, Jill warmed within, vividly aware of a sudden inner joy she had not expected. With her rebuttal to Tim's query, Jill realized she enjoyed hearing the connection between everyday events and God's loving, involved hand. Reyna and Samuel had led her to understand and experience God's participation in all of life. Jill felt invigorated, growing in her newfound faith.

She shivered then, a tingle racing down her back. It was true. She had been pondering some of the hard truths Samuel shared with her on the way west, and those truths had sunk in. She was starting to believe. The simple truths that Samuel explained, and she'd found in Scripture, made so much sense to her now. Especially in light of her difficult circumstances. God was reaching out to her, trying to teach her something. As if he was using her struggles to draw her to him.

Jill smiled, watching the rain come down. This was her farm. God had brought her here. Why? Samuel said it was an adventure, for a purpose that God would reveal in time. Now, she must be patient and have faith.

Still, she must not get too comfortable here, Jill reminded herself. A job waited for her back east, she hoped. Soon, she would hear from Mr. Hopkins about a posting or perhaps the letters she intended to write would discover a teaching position. Either way, this farm was not forever.

The storm raged that night and the next day as well. Even Reyna's preaching could not dampen Tim's joy at the sight of the saturating earth, soaking in the rain like a sponge. "This will help the trees better than any watering I will do," he said, watching the shower from the protection of the sitting room. He sat on one of the three chairs they had found, a cup of hot coffee in one hand.

"We've all been working so hard and for so long, it's good to be forced to rest," Jill commented. She sat with

Tim, her own hands busy mending a sock. Outside, the rain on the porch roof sounded pleasant. Even more pleasant was the fact they had not discovered any leaks in the roof.

"We did a good job cutting that hay. A lot is stored in the barn now. We'll have to cut more before winter. Lots more. But it's a good start." Tim uncrossed his legs, stretching them out before him.

Jill noticed how long his legs were, how tall he was. Her gaze shifted hurriedly, hoping Tim hadn't seen her measuring his height. In the kitchen, Reyna leaned on the counter, a pencil scratching, adding items to a list. Jill welcomed her unexpected call.

"Uncle Tim? Jill? What other things do you want to add to this list? As soon as the rain clears, I would like to run into town, if you can spare the wagon."

Jill narrowed her eyes, a finger drumming her chin as she thought. What else did they need? They brought supplies with them for a month. She could think of nothing else.

Then she tilted her head, her eyes widening. Things had become so much simpler. In Kentucky, at the girl's college, she had always been concerned with her appearance. Did she have the right clothes for the right occasion? The stress of making sure she dressed appropriately for every event kept her constantly on the lookout for the proper apparel and accessories. Also, the proper social connections seemed of the upmost importance. It had worried her a great deal if she didn't receive invitations to certain events.

But out here, Jill felt content to have meals at the table, in a clean kitchen, in a simple house. She tilted her head, surprised at not missing the hustle and bustle of city life.

"Well, I have a number of items to add," Tim suggested, gesturing for Reyna to bring him the list. "I'll see if the wagon can be spared for a run to town. Samuel and I need it most days."

Watching the young Irish girl come to her uncle, Jill considered Reyna. Only fourteen years old, she seemed far more mature than anyone Jill remembered. Certainly, more spiritually mature. Perhaps she'd endured more than her share of challenges, forcing her to grow up before her years, especially after her missionary parents died. The girl seemed to have an innate ability to see God's hand in any situation.

Reyna handed the paper and pencil to Tim, watching over his shoulder as he leaned into the chair once more. He scanned the short list, squinting as he read. "More flour, sugar, and coffee. Maybe more bacon too. If we get stuck in the house for any length of time, we'll need supplies."

"It's mid-summer," Reyna protested. "We will not be getting trapped in this big house for quite a spell, I'm thinking."

"This is not Ireland, and it certainly is not Africa, so you have no idea what you're talking about, do you?" Tim glowered at Reyna over his shoulder.

Jill's needle poked her finger, and she winced at Tim's sharp words.

Instead of being cross at her uncle's severe tone, Reyna laughed. "Uncle Tim, I have no more been to Ireland than you have, as you well know. And as for Africa," Reyna sighed heavily. "I dearly wish to see that beautiful land again one day."

Tim's relaxed, outstretched frame recoiled like the teeth of a triggered trap. His boots thumped loudly on the hardwood floor. "Reyna Maguire, how can you say such a thing? That evil land took my sister, your parents. I would never have you go to Africa again."

She shook her head. "No, Uncle Tim, it wasn't Africa that took my parents. It was the good Lord who decided it was time to bring those two sweet souls home. God is sovereign.

Nothing happens that he doesn't allow or arrange. God uses every situation for his glory. Some good will come from every bad thing that happens. It is a promise of his. God will work all things for our good and his glory."

"Nonsense, girl!" Tim roared as he leaped to his feet and faced the young girl, his dark hair standing like a mane. "What good can come from your mother's death?" Tim glared at his niece, demanding an answer.

The young Irish girl smiled patiently. "That's an easy one. Because of my parents passing, I have come to live with you." She grinned as her blue eyes twinkled. "And you know my purpose with you."

Tim stared, too flummoxed to speak, but Reyna's boldness concerned Jill. She glanced to see how Tim received the young girl's brave comment. Finally, he found his voice.

"Yes, I believe you have come to torment me. You are like a mosquito, buzzing around my ear, refusing to leave me alone," Tim whispered, his eyes large and penetrating. "My days of peace are over."

The tall tree farmer stalked out the open front door and into the pouring rain, trudging slowly toward the barn, heedless of the pelting deluge.

That evening, the rain moved away to the east, and a bright sun broke from behind gray clouds before finally dropping behind the western horizon. Tim and Samuel dodged the puddles dotting the yard to feed and water the team.

Dinner was more subdued than usual that evening. Tim would not make eye contact with Reyna, and he seemed testy and preoccupied. Soon, all headed to bed. Jill lowered the wick on the lantern after lighting her candle, conserving the precious lamp oil. She glanced at Reyna as she placed the candle on the upturned crate between their beds.

"Tim was quiet during dinner," Jill began, watching the young girl. Reyna snorted and punched her pillow before pulling the covers back and slipping between the sheets.

"He's giving me the silent treatment," she announced. "He's done it before when we argue. I'm used to it."

Jill grinned and crawled into her own bed. "Well, you are a bold one. Does it bother you? I mean, how does it work? Does he eventually apologize?"

Reyna giggled, her eyes glowing, and Jill thought of the times in college when girls had shared secrets about boys late at night in their dorm rooms, the other girls listening attentively. Some of those girls giggled like Reyna did now.

A kindred connection united them, like old friends. Jill snuggled deeper into her bed, grateful for the company of this new friend.

"It doesn't really bother me," Reyna explained, her head resting on her pillow. "Like I said, I'm used to it. But sometimes I feel like the adult, like maybe he should apologize for his behavior rather than me always trying hard to stay out of his way. I am the guest, you know. When Mother died, I was sent to live with Uncle Tim. Some mix up with the mail, and he didn't know I was coming. I told him about his dead sister and I was moving in with him, all in the same breath."

Jill scowled, suddenly pitying Tim. "That's awful," she whispered.

A smile tugged at the corner of Reyna's lips. "I know. I try and remember that when he gets angry at me—that I am the unexpected guest, not a cherished loved one. I try to not annoy him."

"But he does love you. I can see it in him," Jill said, propping herself on one elbow.

Reyna wrinkled her nose and shrugged, doubt swimming in her blue eyes. "I think he loves me. But he was planning on leaving his land and escaping the war. His rented farm was in the thick of things, then I came along. Yet, we are kin."

"Then maybe don't annoy him so with your spiritual discussions. He's not ready for them like I am. He doesn't want to hear about Jesus."

Reyna nodded. "I know. But if you believe you hold the secret to life, you hold the greatest gift a person could have, would you want to share with others, especially those you love?"

"Well, of course," Jill agreed, stretching beneath the covers and pulling them to her throat.

"Then I'm doing my best to share Jesus with Uncle Tim," Reyna explained. "I'd hate to get to heaven one day and not find him there."

Jill was about to reply, to somehow comfort Reyna, to reassure her she was cherished, when the moment was interrupted by the sound of an approaching wagon, the wheels creaking outside in the still night.

CHAPTER 25

Jill heard the wagon rolling from the trail through the northern hills. With a rush, both girls leaped from bed and scurried into dresses. Jill heard Tim's door open just before she stepped into the entry and followed him to the sitting room, brushing shoulders as they peered out the window.

"What is it?" Jill whispered.

"A stagecoach, I think," he muttered as he turned toward the entry. "Samuel, bring the lantern." Tim sat to pull on his boots. Samuel quickly joined them, the circle of lantern light revealing the axe in his hand.

"You won't be needing that," Tim called over his shoulder as he hurried to the front door.

Jill ran to her room for a coat. Reyna sat on the edge of her bed, praying. "Jill? What is that noise? Is it a wagon?"

"Tim thinks it's a stagecoach." Jill pulled the coat from a peg and hurried outside, joining Samuel on the porch. She glanced at the axe he still held low, the other hand gripping the raised lantern. A large silhouette loomed before the house, and Jill heard the stamp of horse's hooves. One of the animals snorted and then another whinnied. Voices sounded in the front yard.

Samuel limped from the porch and lifted the lantern higher, the range of light extending toward the clamor. Jill watched as a group of passengers descended from a stagecoach, the vehicle rocking as weight shifted. Tim talked to the driver who'd already clambered down from his high seat and opened the stage door.

"We're coming from Fort Laramie. The storm rained out the usual ford across the Platte. I knew of this one, but I surely didn't know anyone was living here. I thought we would have to keep going all night. Thank God you folks are here. We're about to drop."

Reyna appeared at Jill's elbow and then rushed forward to greet the weary travelers. "Come right in, folks. I'll put some coffee on, and you can have cornbread. It'll cheer you up."

A businessman dressed in a rumpled suit, a soldier, and a dour looking older woman followed Reyna silently into the kitchen. Jill's gaze followed the passengers inside where she saw the glow of a few candles appear on the table.

"Let me help you unhitch the teams," Tim offered. Samuel moved quickly to lend a hand.

Jill retreated into the house as the lantern was carried to the teams of exhausted horses. Reyna had already put water on to boil. Jill swiftly sliced leftover cornbread onto plates and served the hungry travelers. The businessman and the sour faced woman's heads drooped in the dim candlelight. The soldier seemed friendly and talkative.

"First the rain. It poured all night and most of today. That's what really slowed us down. We'd be at Fort Kearny by now if it hadn't been for the storm," the blue uniformed man explained.

Jill scowled as she remembered the Yankee soldiers on the docks at Paducah. Pushing the memory from her mind, she handed him another thick piece of the yellow bread.

The soldier nodded his thanks. "Henry," he gestured out into the night, "the stage driver, said he knew of another ford. That's what brought us here. The old trail is washed away completely. The bank is now too steep for a wagon. We were surprised how easy the trail was through these hills. Deceptive, they are. It looks like you can't get through them, and then that gap in the hills leads you right here."

Behind her, Jill heard the front door open, and the three men entered.

Henry, the stage driver, slapped his leg with his hat. "I tell you it makes me laugh. Old Murphy swore this was a better route for the stagecoach. Better road, better ford. He tried for almost a year to get the stage contract and become a station, but it never went through. This house is even big enough to accommodate travelers, which is what Hazlett intended in the first place. Hoped to get the contract to feed passengers and put them up for the night. But the lieutenant over at Fort Kearny said if it ain't broke, don't fix it. Besides, he didn't like the way Murphy got the place from the meat hunter who built it. He wouldn't alter the stage road to come through Murphy's place. It sure made Murphy sore." The driver accepted a cup of coffee from Reyna with a nod. "He hated living out here alone. It was him who threw a bottle into his own front window. He said he was so mad, he broke his own glass window and left the place. It's been empty ever since. That was back in March."

After the group finished eating, Reyna settled everyone upstairs. Although there were no actual beds upstairs, each person had their own room with some blankets. Jill wondered how they would sleep without proper bedding, but the next morning, all the travelers except the older woman assured Jill they'd slept well.

For breakfast, Reyna made potatoes, pancakes, and bacon served hot out of the skillet. It took two pots of coffee to satisfy the talkative group.

Tim helped Henry hitch the teams to the stage. Then the travelers shuffled from the house, appearing almost reluctant to leave. They climbed into the wagon for the short journey to Fort Kearny.

The taciturn woman mumbled her thanks, and the businessman echoed her appreciation. The soldier, however, was loud in his acclaim. "I'll sure be telling the lieutenant about this place. Watch for Indians, though. They scared Murphy something fierce." He turned and followed his companions into the waiting stagecoach.

Henry climbed to his perch and took up the long leather reins before touching his hat brim to Jill and smiling. "Thank you, miss. I'll tell them at Fort Kearny about your hospitality. 'Bye for now."

With a flick of the reins and a clatter of hooves, the wagon lurched into motion. Tim joined Jill on the porch, watching the coach vanish into the trail through the thick foliage along the river.

"Well, Jill, if I were a Christian man, I would say God started something big here last night."

She frowned and crossed her arms over her chest. "What does that mean?"

Tim scratched his ear. "According to Henry, the stage rolls through here a couple times a week. It needs a ford to cross the river. This one here is the only one for miles. You'll have stages stopping here soon enough, I think."

He strode to the barn as Jill squinted toward the river. Could he be right? How could this information help Peach Tree Farm? She drummed her fingers on the railing and glanced at the barn, just catching a glimpse of Tim before he disappeared into the low stone building. She pursed her lips, considering.

Three days later, Tim's predication came true as a stage entered the clearing from the river and stopped long enough for the passengers to stretch their legs and eat something while the horses were watered. Hurriedly then,

NEBRASKA HAVEN

the stage reloaded and departed, a cloud of dust following them as they disappeared into the northern hills toward the emigrant trail.

The next day, Tim balked at Jill's request to take the wagon for a trip to Fort Kearny.

"I have a lot to do around here. And I need the wagon."

"I need to check and see if a letter has arrived for me. And I need to mail these too." She waved a few envelopes at Tim from where she stood on the porch waiting for Samuel. "Besides, I have to replace the food the travelers consumed."

Begrudgingly, Tim agreed but said, "Hurry back."

Jill and Samuel moved quickly to leave before Tim could change his mind. Reyna chose to stay at home, welcoming the opportunity to get caught up on laundry and other chores.

As Samuel guided the team through the avenue between the trees to the ford of the Platte River and down into the bumpy, shallow river, Jill gripped her seat and recalled her old dreams in Missouri. She thrilled anew at the prospect of the journey she now found herself entangled. What was God doing? Clearly, he had brought her to this frontier, even if temporarily.

She suspected the Lord knew she would come here long before she'd even considered the idea. Jill enjoyed the Christian adventure, trusting God was in control even when things appeared so chaotic. Samuel had been right. Patience and faith were all that was required to see the Lord's providing hand.

Fort Kearny lay sleepy and still in the late morning. Bright sun blazed across the dirt parade ground, the young trees brought from the river offering small pools of inviting shade. Pulling the team to a halt beneath the tallest tree, Samuel scrambled to the ground while Jill leaped from the wagon. She straightened her dress and hurriedly glanced around, hoping no one had seen her indecent landing. She felt so independent since coming west.

"Samuel, stay with the wagon. I'll not be long," Jill instructed.

A hammer rang against an anvil from the blacksmith shop as she walked the short distance to the general store. Despite last week's rain, dust clouds puffed around every step she took.

The storekeeper greeted Jill with eagerness. "I've heard of you, Miss Foster. I'm Mr. Billings and am glad to finally meet you. We don't have lots of settlers around here, but there are a few."

"It's good to meet you as well." She courteously extended her hand to the only professional she'd met in the region. Certainly, her father had been a professional as well, although only a storekeeper. Surely this desolate frontier could boast of nothing more prestigious, as there could be no proper gentleman all the way out here.

Jill allowed her gaze to roam the crowded shelves, concealing her surprise at the quantity of goods the store contained. "I am expecting an important letter from the east. Please inform me immediately when it arrives." She handed him her mail.

"Of course, miss, I will." Mr. Billings took her letters and dropped them into a canvas bag. He paused, licked his lips, and then touched the tip of the pencil tucked into his apron before he went on. "The lieutenant told me that if you came to town, I was to ask if you would go see him. He wants to talk to you."

Jill smiled as her eyebrows arched, feeling honored. It was appropriate for a lady to be received by the leader of the community's social order, even if he was only a Yankee. She wondered what the lieutenant was like as familiar butterflies of anticipation swirled inside her. She always felt a little nervous before an event. She completed her shopping and promised to return soon for the goods.

Jill followed Mr. Billings's directions to the headquarters building that bordered the parade ground, passing Samuel on her way.

"The lieutenant wants to see me," she told him, unable to keep a note of excitement from her voice. "I'll be right back."

Jill sensed the sharp scrutiny of a few soldiers as she neared the building. *Ignore them,* she thought as she kept her poise, regretting not taking the time to consider her appearance before leaving the farm. But who could've guessed she'd be meeting a gentleman?

The soldiers eyed her intently, making Jill feel uneasy as she smoothed her plain dress. There could be only a few women in the territory.

Stepping lightly onto the wide porch, she touched her hair, making certain no rebellious strands peeked from beneath her bonnet. Lifting her chin, she spoke to the waiting sentry on duty. "I am Jill Foster. I am to see the lieutenant."

The young soldier led Jill into the inner office. The room was cool and dark after the bright sunlight of the quiet fort.

The young soldier knocked on a plank door. He waited, trying to look Jill over without seeming to, his gaze roving around her and the small office. A bark sounded from within, and he opened the door. A uniformed man stood and greeted her, coming around his desk to shake her hand. Jill did not miss his appraising glance, her brow puckering at all these inappropriate Yankee stares. Did the blue devils have no sense of decency? Oh, how she yearned for the refinements of Southern culture.

The officer released her hand and gestured to a seat opposite his desk. She pushed her bonnet back and lowered herself, but not before noticing his proper haircut and neatly trimmed moustache. Brass buttons gleamed on his pressed, dark blue uniform, and she couldn't help but notice the clean-shaven cheeks, so different from Tim's dark whiskers.

Her gaze roved the room as the officer moved around his desk to sit down. The sparsely furnished room was small with only the scarred desk and two chairs. A battered file cabinet stood against one wall, beside a neat row of rifles. A narrow window allowed light from outside.

"I am Lieutenant Alcott. It's a pleasure to meet you, Miss Foster," he began, his confident voice sounding crisp as he shuffled papers on his desk. "Henry Bromberg reported to me regarding the situation of the washed-out trail, and the provided meals. The tavern here at the post is such a disreputable place, dirty and poorly managed." He leaned forward, as if sharing a secret. "The food is the worst."

The young officer placed the papers to one side and rested his elbows on the edge of the desk. He clasped his hands together, peering over them at Jill.

"I wanted to thank you personally for your service to the stagecoach passengers. The army is charged with protecting the stage route across the frontier and, of course, the emigrant trail along the Platte. I would like to protect them from that horrible tavern here at Fort Kearny." He grinned suddenly, his eyes shining, and Jill knew he was teasing. Yankee or not, he had style and was enjoyable to look at. The dark blue uniform lent him a regal flair. She smiled politely at his hint of humor.

"When Murphy mustered out of the army and acquired that big stone house to the south of the pass, we all laughed and thought he was crazy. He tried to explain what his

NEBRASKA HAVEN

intentions were, but I confess I did not listen. Perhaps it was because of his drinking habit or maybe because of his never-ending, get-rich-quick schemes."

Lieutenant Alcott paused and frowned before he went on. "He won the property in a card game, taking the property from the hunter who provided meat to the post. Whatever the reason, I didn't bother to take him seriously when Murphy petitioned for the stage to go through his place. According to Henry Bromberg, the trail and the ford is better at your farm."

Jill stared at him, tilting her head as he rambled. The information he shared was so dull. Yet, she had learned in college that men could be so difficult if you wounded their pride, so she nodded occasionally, feigning interest. Better to appear attentive, as if what he said was actually fascinating. Still, she wondered at his intent. Why tell her all this?

Finally, the lieutenant smiled, his monologue concluded, and she stifled the urge to heave a sigh of relief.

"I guess what I'm trying to say is that the army would appreciate it if you allowed travelers to lodge at your house. Cook meals for them. We would pay for the service. Also, we will furnish you with supplies and lumber for beds or any other furniture that might be required. Mr. Billings has a shed full of discarded furniture from west bound emigrants. Perhaps he has something you could use. Tell him I sent you. In the meantime, I will do my best to secure the stage contract for you as a stage station."

A dark scowl crossed his features as he went on. "Of course, there is no telling when I would receive confirmation, what with the war and all. The conflict demands all the army's focus. We get very little attention out here, even in regard to replacements. Why, I've heard rumors that captured rebel prisoners will be allowed to serve on the frontier if they take an oath to the Union."

Jill narrowed her eyes. Stage contract? What did that mean? She had no intention of opening a business in her home, but they would need an income while she waited for word from Mr. Hopkins. She pursed her lips, squirming in her seat. Tim had suggested this might happen, but things were falling almost too neatly into place. Concerned, Jill leaned back, her elbows on the armrests as she pressed her fingertips together in a steeple. For months now, everything that could go wrong had. Now, it seemed like things were going her way.

She mentally chastised herself. Why was she surprised when good things happened to her? Irritated, she clenched her stomach muscles and tried to smile to show the lieutenant she was not startled by good fortune coming her way once more.

She wondered if God were involved somehow. Hadn't Samuel taught her to look for the Lord's guiding hand? Was this it? Somehow, Jill had believed good things were for other people, not for her anymore.

The uniformed man shifted, his chair creaking as he cleared his throat. Jill's gaze found his, embarrassed she'd forgotten his presence. "Is there something wrong, Miss Foster?" She could tell he was surprised his news had not affected her favorably.

Jill's smile broadened. "I'm sorry, Lieutenant. I had not intended to seek a stage contract, but I do need the business. Who would've guessed this land, Peach Tree Farm, would be a stage station?"

The tall soldier smiled in return and a thrill ran down Jill's back, alerting her to the splendid figure the soldier made. He scribbled out a note and handed the slip to her. "Give this to Billings at the store."

She nodded and stood quickly, holding out her hand. "Thank you, Lieutenant Alcott. I look forward to hearing from you soon."

He rose gracefully and shook her outstretched hand, gripping her fingers a moment longer than necessary, his broad shoulders stretching the uniform. "Indeed, you will, Miss Foster. And I hope to see you even sooner. Look for me at Peach Tree Farm. I intend to check in on you."

"I will hold you to your word, sir." Jill felt the heat creep up her neck as she turned and hurried from the office. She hoped he didn't see the affect his promise had on her. He was only a Yankee army officer, but so far he stood head and shoulders above the other men in the region. The first gentleman she'd discovered in Nebraska.

Jill pulled her bonnet up and grinned as she passed the young corporal stationed by the door. Her thoughts drifted to the lieutenant and his vow to visit her soon. Had she been too bold when she shook his hand? His smile had shone in his eyes when they parted.

She glanced back once on her way to the store. The military officer stood at his door, still watching her.

CHAPTER 26

Jill brought Samuel to the store to introduce him to the shopkeeper. Mr. Billings shook hands with Samuel, to Jill's surprise.

"I'm from Lawrence, Kansas," he told the former slave. "I was friends with John Brown, God rest his soul. You are always welcome here, Samuel."

Jill stared, her breath caught in her throat as she studied the abolitionist. The shopkeeper's views were like her father's, and Jill glanced over her shoulder, searching the empty store for anyone who might have heard Mr. Billings.

But no one else was present, and Jill felt her breath leak out, her shoulders relaxing. Did people not have to be so guarded out here on the frontier? Would people in Nebraska respect others' opinions?

Mr. Billings read the note from the lieutenant and quickly filled the order with more flour, sugar, and coffee than Jill expected.

Jill added blankets to the pile and then asked about glass for the broken window.

The shopkeeper shook his head doubtfully. "Windows are hard to come by. It usually takes weeks to order them from Omaha. We'll see what we can do."

"Lieutenant Alcott mentioned you had some discarded furniture I could look through too."

Mr. Billings hooked a thumb over his shoulder and nodded. "The sawmill is located near the blacksmith shop if you need lumber for building. If you choose, you can have furniture from the open barn out back." He shook his head. "It's sad to see what people discard when they realize their stock cannot pull such heavy wagons all the way to Oregon ... or California if they're going for the gold."

Jill nodded. "I'll tell Mr. Hunter of your kind offer." She left Samuel to load the supplies as she left the store again to introduce herself to the blacksmith.

"I only operate the sawmill when I need to," the burly blacksmith explained, wiping his leather apron with huge hands. Jill noticed the burns on his leather apron and the dirt beneath his broken fingernails. Then a wide grin creased his sweaty face. "Henry said you served the best cornbread he ever tasted. I have high expectations, miss."

Jill bobbed her head slowly, liking the man's earnest manner. She blushed then, realizing she'd unjustly judged this book by its cover. The man seemed polite and respectful, in a rough sort of way.

"Call me Big John, miss. Everyone does. And if you can't find the furniture you need in Mr. Billings's stuff, I'll cut you all the lumber you want."

"Thank you, Big John," Jill said with a laugh, pleased to meet the friendly blacksmith. "And I hope you will visit for the cornbread."

Samuel held the reins taut as Jill climbed into the wagon, scrambling atop the front wheel to sit beside him. With a flick of his wrist, the team leaned into the harness, the wagon lumbering through the dusty street.

As they departed, Jill glanced at the small army outpost situated on the southern bank of the Platte River. A few stores, the old Pony Express office, a freighting business, the deplorable soddy that served as stage station, and the scattered buildings of the tiny fort were all there was. Tim had shared this settlement was an important stop along the Oregon Trail, but how important could this tiny town be? Jill's lips pursed into a thin line as she pondered, turning to face forward from the sunbaked hamlet. Certainly the village could not boast the culture or society of St. Louis, New Orleans, or even Paducah.

"How was the lieutenant?"

Samuel's unexpected question brought her back to the present, and Jill drew a deep breath, pushing away her desire to, once again, walk the shaded streets of the great Southern cities. She'd be back there soon enough.

She shifted on the hard wooden seat. "He was a gentleman, I think," she lied, trying not to recall the way the soldiers had all looked her over so brazenly. She bit her lip. "For a Yankee."

Samuel laughed. "Are Yankees less than other men?"

She frowned, unable to explain to a runaway slave that Yankees certainly were less than the educated and refined men of her desired social circle. But Lieutenant Alcott was the most influential man she'd met out here so far, and surely Samuel would look upon the blue devils with favor, so she deigned not to reply. However, she did recall how handsome the lieutenant appeared in his clean uniform.

She shot a glance at her companion from the corner of her eye. "Did you enjoy meeting Mr. Billings? Just your sort of people, I should think."

A scowl creased his features as he looked at her, one eyebrow arching. "My sort of people?"

She squirmed, not liking how she'd phrased her comment. "Well, you know, a Jayhawker. I remember reading about their mischief in the newspapers. The way they sneak across the Kansas border to torment the Missouri citizens. Murderers and thieves, I understand."

Samuel squinted at her. "Wasn't your father against slavery? Like the Jayhawkers?"

A lump rose in her throat, and Jill gripped the side of the seat, not wanting to think about her father. She'd been so busy since coming to Nebraska, she hadn't spent time pondering the catalyst that pushed her from the South. Samuel had said her grief would take time to process, but this was not that time. Her scowl deepened as she peered intently at Samuel. It was her father's dangerous ideas that had gotten her into this fix, and now she lived in a stone house on the Nebraska plains.

She shook her head, dispelling the disturbing thoughts.

"Besides," Samuel interjected, "I think you might have a bit of the Jayhawker in you, Miss Jill. After all, it was you who helped me escape."

His remark stunned her, and Jill gasped, seeing clearly that he was right. She *had* helped him escape. Was she changing, her Southern ideals slipping?

Her conversation about the stage station at Peach Tree Farm rang in her mind, and she seized it with both hands, like a life preserver tossed to a drowning man. She sighed, grateful to change the subject. "The army wants us to help travelers on the various routes across the plains, to feed them and let them stay over when they need to connect with other stages. Although I appreciate the small income this will produce, the increased traffic of people through the farm will alert folks of your presence. I confess I am worried for you if the stages continue to frequent our land. Perhaps word of your location will drift back to Kentucky."

Samuel jerked and his head turned, facing her. "Our land?"

Jill smiled. "Well, of course, your land. I would not be here if it were not for you. You know that. Peach Tree Farm is your home for as long as you wish."

NEBRASKA HAVEN

She thought she detected a shine in his eyes before his gaze turned to the horses, the clip clop of their hooves pounding softly on the dirt road. Suddenly, Samuel threw his head back and laughed.

"What's so funny?" Jill looked around, searching for the culprit of his outburst.

Samuel shook his head, a wide grin on his face. "I love it when God surprises me. It reminds me how weak my faith is, and how faithful he is."

"What are you talking about?"

He turned to her again, eyes gleaming in the afternoon sun. "I read this verse one Sunday when I was cleaning the church and sneaking some reading. 'Be joyful in hope, patient in affliction, and faithful in prayer.' I try so hard to believe God's Word, to really let it soak into my heart, to believe it is for me too, a slave—"

"An escaped slave. A free man," Jill corrected swiftly.

Samuel nodded. "A free man but still a servant of Christ. I love when he surprises me with good things."

She felt her brow wrinkle. "Does God have good things for me too?"

He chuckled. "Are you serious? Can't you see how he brought you out here, bringing me along? How Tim and Reyna have become part of our team? God is with you, Miss Jill, and he won't ever let you go. Be joyful in hope, patient in affliction, and faithful in prayer. God is for you. In his timing, he will show you his plan for you."

Jill sat back, watching the scenery without really seeing anything. Was God *really* with her? She had come to the farm safely. Samuel had helped her and escaped slavery. The farm would provide a small income while she waited for letters from the east. But what about the future? Would the Lord lead her back to the South she loved? Would a teaching position open for her?

Surely, the land in Nebraska had allowed a respite from the worries of which way to turn next. She felt safe here. Perhaps the Lord had provided Lieutenant Alcott too, the only gentleman within miles. Jill smiled, pondering.

Upon their return to the farm, Jill filled Tim in on what had happened with the lieutenant. She expected him to be happy for this development, but the tree farmer scowled at her instead.

"I can't go to town for furniture. We have to cut hay and pile it alongside the barn. We need to place manure around the saplings to hold in the moisture. I need Samuel and the wagon here. We need to be preparing for winter."

"Well, if you don't want real beds or chairs or dresser drawers, then all right," Jill huffed as she waved a dismissive hand. "I was only thinking of what's best for the travelers. Until I receive a letter from the east, we will need the income from the stage stop to keep us afloat."

He scowled at her for a moment longer and then mumbled, "I'll go. I'll go," as he received a steaming mug from Reyna and retreated to the porch.

Soon, the two a week stages became three and then four a week. They carried passengers west to Fort Laramie and South Pass City. South into Kansas to Fort Hays and Council Grove. East to Omaha and the routes beyond. Often Jill and Reyna entertained lodgers who stayed overnight. Jill was always surprised to have them pay her money for the service. She felt as if employment had come to her, like an unexpected job had landed in her lap.

Jill's gratitude grew as she realized the fantastic team she had in Reyna and Samuel. The young Irish girl could cook and clean like no one Jill knew. The guests always commented on the quality of the meals and accommodations. Jill enjoyed setting a tidy and well-organized table. Her experiences from the girl's college stood her in good stead here. Soldiers and businesspeople from Fort Kearny began to call for meals. Even Mr. Billings and the blacksmith, Big John, made an appearance. Jill thought it funny to be running a restaurant and hotel in the middle of Nebraska.

"Don't act so surprised," Reyna told her one day as they watched another stage depart. "The good Lord knew what he was doing when he brought you here. Your reputation has spread, and folks come from miles around to be fed. It's God's blessing on you, Jill."

Indeed, Jill felt blessed. Suddenly, everything seemed to be falling into place. Except Tim.

Tim worked hard every day and his exploration along the river's edge had netted him many blueberry bushes, which he and Samuel transplanted. Also, blackberries, gooseberries, and even some wild strawberries were soon added to the farm. Yet Tim seemed restless and moody. Reyna and Samuel's preaching bothered him, annoyed him really, and he often left the table before their evangelism could blossom. Where Jill found herself hungry for God's Word, Tim didn't like talking about spiritual things and avoided them at all cost.

Often after dinner, Reyna would open her Bible and read passages aloud. Jill looked forward to this time, as it gave her opportunities to ask questions and learn more about the history of the Bible. Also, she began to understand God's expectations for his people.

During these times, Tim would go to the barn, work on the ever-increasing pile of winter firewood, or retire early to bed, often muttering under his breath before leaving the room.

Reyna was always positive and patient. "Don't you worry about Uncle Tim," she would say in her Irish accent. "He's wrestling with the Almighty. The good Lord brought us out here where he can ponder truly important things."

Jill wished she could share the young girl's confidence. It bothered Jill that Tim was so antagonistic toward God.

One day while Tim was busy positioning an elm tree he had moved from the river to the front yard, Jill brought him a cup of water. He nodded as he accepted the cup and then tilted his head and drank.

He handed the empty cup back to Jill, smiling his thanks, but his gaze lingered on her, making her uneasy. She dropped her eyes to the newly planted tree.

"I'm glad to have shade trees placed around the yard."

"Give it a year or two and this tree will give plenty of shade." Tim gestured to the small tree before wiping his hands on his pants.

"Then you're pleased with the farm? This is where you will settle?" Jill hoped the question wasn't too forward. They had come to Nebraska out of desperation, him fleeing the war in the east and her not having other options. Peach Tree Farm had rewarded both of their searches and had proved a haven in the middle of life's storms. But it was none of her business where he would settle.

Tim's gaze drifted to the hills, his eyes softening as he inhaled deeply. "Yes, I'm pleased. I think I'm more pleased than you are, Jill. I've seen the letters you've written to the east." He turned to look at her. "You're still hoping to teach back there, aren't you?"

His words challenged her, and she bristled. "I'm a teacher," she reminded him, feeling suddenly defensive. "You knew when we came here I planned to move east once a position came available. I am a Southerner, I belong in the South. Why the surprise about my letters?"

NEBRASKA HAVEN

Jill wondered what was going through the farmer's mind. Over the past couple of months, they had grown comfortable with each other, even friendly. She enjoyed his company, his attention and playful words often warmed her.

Tim kicked at a dirt clod. "I was just wondering if the farm could ever become a permanent home to you." He glanced up at the stone house. "It's a nice house. You have a good business here. The land is good. I intend to stay, if you will allow it."

"You and Reyna will always be welcome here. I will never sell the farm. Samuel has found a home here, also, and I'm happy for him. This is a good place." Her eyes went to the hills, as his had earlier. The tops of small trees dotted each ridge, stretching to all the land she could see. She sighed. "Only, I know it's not for me."

She had always planned on returning to the east when a teaching post opened. She had not been secretive about her plans. But she also thought about how these people had become her new family and how this place felt like home.

Tim picked up his spade and walked to the barn without further comment. Jill watched him go, wanting to say something more, something helpful to relieve his concerns. She bit her lip as he vanished into the barn. As she turned to the house, she lifted her chin, Tim's empty cup dangling from her hand. He had his path to walk, and she had hers. He was a farmer, she a teacher.

"Your uncle is difficult to understand," Jill said when she noticed Reyna standing on the porch.

Reyna smiled, a twinkle in her blue eyes. "Not difficult for me to understand. I think his heart is troubled."

"His heart?" Jill wondered aloud. "What is wrong with his heart?"

Reyna's eyebrows arched as she looked at Jill, her smile widening. Without another word, she turned and walked into the house, leaving a perplexed Jill alone on the porch.

CHAPTER 27

After breakfast the next day, Reyna made bread, kneading the dough roughly while she softly sang hymns. Jill listened to Reyna's comforting hum as she washed dishes. She wiped her brow with the back of a wrist, shoving a rebellious strand of hair into place. Sweat trickled down her back, and she wished for a breeze from the river to cool the hot room.

A glance out the front window revealed nothing out of place, yet a gentle whir of sawing lumber drifted from the barn. Tim had allowed Samuel to convert one of the empty stalls into a workshop, and the former slave had lined the walls with tools.

Samuel worked there now, making a bed, cutting and shaping wood. Jill looked at Reyna again, grateful for the activity around her, the company of friends. The stone house was becoming a home.

"I'll need another egg." Reyna opened the oven door, the room filling with the smell of fresh baked goods. The four chickens purchased from Mr. Billings had been a positive addition to the stage station on Peach Tree Creek.

Jill nodded and dried her hands. Tossing the towel on the counter, she strode to the barn as the sun warmed her back.

The fragrant scent of fresh cut hay mingled with the sharp, pungent odor of horse manure and the more earthy scent of leather as she stepped into the shadows of the barn, the coolness surprising her like it always did when she visited here.

"Samuel, I don't want to interrupt your work, but Reyna has baked fresh muffins. Can I bring you one?"

The saw paused, quivering in the plank. Samuel glanced up and smiled at Jill. "Thank you, Miss Jill. That would be fine."

She moved further into the low roofed barn, scanning for signs of any of the hens from Fort Kearny. Jill and Reyna had made a journey into town only two weeks ago and were thrilled to return with not only the four hens, but also a kitten. Reyna was particularly pleased to have a pet.

Tim had frowned as Reyna petted the little, furry creature. He did not see the cat as a pet but as a necessary farm animal with important responsibilities. The barn had a serious mice infestation. Nonetheless, this didn't preclude Reyna from doting on the little calico kitten and even allowing it free admittance throughout the house despite Tim's protests. "The thing is probably full of fleas," he'd grumbled. But Reyna only laughed.

Jill saw something move in the shadows. Stepping closer, she jumped when the black, tan, and white cat pounced on her shoelaces. Jill smiled, relieved to identify the fluffy culprit. She'd discovered a few empty eggs lately, the oval surface pierced by two tiny holes.

As her search continued, the kitten followed, swatting at her shoelaces. Jill chuckled and reached for a grain sack. Peering behind the bag, something stirred, and she saw a rattler coil, its buttons singing a warning.

Without thinking, Jill grabbed a spade and speared the serpent in half, then decapitated the snake. Sometimes, the slithering creatures visited the barn, searching for eggs or the mice that enjoyed the grain intended for the horses.

She stared at the writhing thing as her eyes widened. Would she have killed a snake in Kentucky or Missouri? She shook her head and soon located a nest, gathering the lone egg as the hen cackled in protest.

Jill walked slowly back to the kitchen, depositing the egg on the counter. Reyna reached for it, glancing at Jill. "Are there any more?"

"I didn't look any farther. Do you need more now?"

Reyna studied the cooling pans of baked goods, tilting her head as she considered. "No, I guess not. I have enough for dinner. If no stages arrive today, we'll be all right." The young girl wiped her flour covered hands on her apron.

Jill picked up a muffin from the sideboard and returned to the barn. On this trip, she sighted two hens scratching in the dirt at the other end of the barn. "There you are," she murmured, calculating where their nests might be hidden. She would have to discover them for additional eggs.

She handed the promised muffin to Samuel along with a cup of water. He drained the brimming cup, gulping the cool water. Handing the empty mug back to Jill, he smiled and returned to his work. Jill watched him a moment as he fashioned another bed. They'd taken all the furniture Mr. Billings had to offer, but more items were needed at the station. Much of the discarded furniture at the general store had been unsuitable for their needs. Jill had seen two pianos, a heavy wooden trunk, countless books, and a smattering of discarded, broken wagons unable to make the arduous plains crossing. She'd even seen an assortment of small wooden toy horses, their features finely carved.

Dust puffed as her shoes trod the hard ground of the front yard. She recalled the wall of tall weeds that had greeted them when they arrived only a couple of months ago. Now the ground was bare of vegetation, pounded into fine dust by the numerous stages and passengers.

As her shoe touched the bottom step of the porch, she caught the sound of running horses and the faint yells of a frantic driver. Jill shielded her eyes, peering northward. Suddenly, Reyna stood beside her.

"What is it?" the young girl asked, lifting a hand to shield her own straining eyes.

"Sounds like a stage running hard," Jill muttered as the thudding of pounding hooves neared.

Samuel appeared in the doorway of the barn. "Sounds like they're being chased," he called to the girls on the porch.

A quartet of horses broke from between the hills, running all out, and stretched low. A driver stood atop the careening stage, pulling on the reins as the horses thundered into the yard. The animals reared and pranced as the wagon slowed and finally stopped before the house, a rolling cloud of dust obscuring the vehicle for a moment.

Jill recognized Jimmy Hartman, one of the stage drivers who frequented the station. Jimmy dropped to the high seat of the stagecoach, his face ashen and drawn. Hatless and his hair standing on end, his chest heaved with great gasps.

"Jimmy!" Jill called, her eyes scanning behind the wagon. She took a step from the porch, the dust still swirling. "Are you all right?"

The driver slumped wearily on the box and wiped his face with a dirty handkerchief. His hands shook. "We are now," he replied.

Samuel opened the door of the stage. Three men climbed out, their clothes covered with a fine layer of dust. They slapped their clothes and holstered pistols before they peered at Jill.

"Gentlemen, come right in. We have coffee and cornbread, and I'm sure we can make sandwiches." Jill glanced to Reyna for confirmation, but the Irish girl had already disappeared into the kitchen.

NEBRASKA HAVEN

Stepping aside of the passengers, Jill looked back at Jimmy. The driver sat still on the wagon, eyes closed, hands still griping the reins. Her breath caught as she noticed two feathered shafts protruding from the side of the coach.

Jill grasped one of the shafts and tried unsuccessfully to pull the arrow free.

"Don't worry about that, Miss Jill," Jimmy called down to her. "It'll look impressive when I roll into Kearny in a little while."

He chuckled at his own joke and swung down. His legs buckled, but he straightened with a grin. Jill felt pleased to see some color had returned to his pale cheeks.

"Are you all right, Jimmy?"

He nodded. "We're coming in from Laramie, and about six miles out, a bunch of bucks jumped us. They got a couple of arrows into the box, but no one was hit. They followed just out of firing range. We shot a lot of lead but didn't hit anything."

Samuel stiffened beside the coach, his eyes widening. He gaped at Jill. "I thought Henry Bromberg was joking when he mentioned Indians." He looked back to Jimmy. "Are there a lot of wild Indians around here?"

Jimmy winked discreetly to Jill before facing Samuel. "Well, you better believe it. Hundreds of wild redskins right over those hills." He gestured to the distant ridge. "Just waiting for a chance to come riding in here and scalp the lot of you." Then he slapped Samuel on the shoulder and stepped to the stage door. "Ma'am? You can come out now. The fighting is over."

Jill tilted her head as she studied the coach. She thought all the passengers had gone inside the house.

"Leave me alone," a familiar voice spoke from within the wagon. Jill stepped up and peered inside, trying to locate the speaker in the darkened space.

"Nan? Is that you?" Jill could feel her chest tighten, remembering those awful days with Earl and Nan.

Silence greeted Jill's search, and then a small figure, tucked into the farthest corner, sighed.

"Nan? Why are you here? Where is Earl?"

"I see you, Jill. And I see Samuel there. I know you didn't like Earl," Nan said with a note of bitterness. "But he was my man. I know he had faults, but I needed him. The trip was too hard for us, and Earl didn't make it to Laramie. I sold my gear and bought passage east. They call folks like me a turn back. I don't care. I'll live with a cousin I know in Illinois. She's a Yankee, but I can't afford to go all the way to my daughter in Oregon."

Jill pursed her lips, not knowing what to say, simply nodding at the rail-thin woman. "I'm sorry, Nan."

The old woman turned and stared out the window. Jill glanced at Jimmy and the driver shrugged before going inside. Jill's steps faltered as she walked to the porch and leaned heavily on the railing. This could've been her situation had not things turned out differently. Samuel had helped her, and Tim and Reyna. Where would Jill be now without God guiding her?

Samuel had disappeared into the house but now returned carrying a tin cup. He hobbled to the coach and passed the cup inside. A few minutes later, the stagecoach rolled from the yard, the passengers thanking Jill before boarding and departing.

Samuel frowned as he and Jill watched the wagon vanish into the wooded avenue toward the river. "That pair were mean folks, but I don't wish them any harm. Still, I wonder if anyone else will miss Earl."

Jill's eyebrows bunched as she wondered the same.

Samuel shifted beside her. "Do you think it's safe to live out on this prairie?" His gaze lifted, scanning the distant hills.

Jill shrugged, but she wondered too. "We've been safe so far," she said as Tim joined them. He'd been checking the trees and only arrived at the house when the stage left the yard.

"We had Indians in the hills of Tennessee where I'm from. They didn't seem to bother those who left them alone," Tim said with an assurance that calmed Jill.

From the corner of her eyes, she studied him. He didn't seem unduly alarmed by the nearby Indians. Although he wasn't a gentleman, she decided he was brave.

Later, during dinner, he continued the conversation. "We're actually on their land, you know." He leaned back from the table. "Sure, someone bought this land and got a title of ownership. However, maybe they don't appreciate how the land is being used. These Indians around here are not farmers."

Reyna moved quickly to clear Tim's empty plate and fetch him another cup of coffee. Again, Jill admired how the young girl worked so hard to make sure her uncle's needs were taken care of. Yet Tim didn't seem to notice.

Jill stood and glowered at Tim. "Let me lend you a hand, Reyna."

His eyes widened. "What'd I do?"

"Nothing," Jill snapped as she followed Reyna into the kitchen with a load of dishes.

CHAPTER 28

Two days later, breakfast was interrupted by the trample of approaching horses. The sound stilled outside the front door, and Tim craned his neck to identify the riders, bunched just out of sight. He and Jill exchanged glances. Slowly, everyone rose and moved to the large front glass window, peering out into the dirt yard.

Four half-naked Indians with feathers in their long hair sat astride wild, ragged ponies.

Tim and Samuel stood in front of the girls, Reyna and Jill hiding behind the men. The Indians stared at them through the clear window.

"What do they want?" Samuel asked in a whisper. No one replied. "What are we going to do?" Samuel shifted and glanced over his shoulder, his wide eyes locking with Jill's. She pursed her lips and tried to ignore the fear in his voice.

"I don't know," Tim finally muttered. "We don't even have any guns."

"No," Reyna agreed, untying her apron as she turned to the kitchen. "But we have apple pie."

She moved swiftly, and before Jill could comprehend what the girl intended, Reyna had flung open the front door and stepped onto the porch.

"No, Reyna," Tim called, following her out onto the porch.

The young Irish girl moved among the four Indians. Cutting thick slices with a knife, she handed them up to each brave in turn. Their dark eyes followed her, not trusting, yet wanting the golden treat in her hand. Soon, all four Indians were busy stuffing the apple pie into their mouths. They grunted with satisfaction, and one even laughed, pointing at Reyna and saying something in his native tongue.

Tim gripped the porch railing and watched as Reyna stepped between the ragged ponies and served the entire pie.

With the final morsel consumed, one of the braves spoke to his companions, and they all turned and rode from the yard.

Tim sagged against the porch post, the tension gone, and raised a trembling finger toward his niece. "You could've been killed. What were you thinking?" Jill noticed his pale face, his usual tan gone.

The young girl grinned, an amused look in her eye. "I was thinking what God's Word says about guests. Some have served angels when showing kindness to strangers. Hospitality is a gift. Also, Jesus says to serve one another." She shrugged and smiled at Jill. "I felt safe."

"Those were no angels," Tim blustered as he gestured toward the cleft in the hills where the Indians had disappeared.

"You don't know that," Reyna said simply.

Jill could see from Tim's disapproving look that he didn't believe the Indians should be served. Nonetheless, calamity had been avoided due to Reyna's fast thinking and kindness.

Later that morning, Tim entered the kitchen. "Reyna, do you have something I can put these in?"

Jill stared at the bundle of wildflowers wilting in Tim's grasp. Her mind whirled, wondering.

As if reading her mind, Reyna spoke as she handed Tim a jar filled with water. "Who are these for?"

His cheeks pinked before he glanced out the window. "Can't a man bring flowers to the table? I thought they'd brighten the room."

The girls exchanged a curious look as Tim placed the colorful bouquet on the table, then cleared his throat. "Jill, I'd like to discuss something with you, if you have time."

She blinked. "Now?"

He nodded, a warm look coming to his eyes. "Yes, now, if that works for you. I'd like to start by showing you the work I've done."

Her gaze shifted to Reyna once more as she untied her apron. The young girl's eyes were large, but a look of amusement filled her face.

Not sure whether she felt excited or dismayed, Jill grabbed her bonnet from its peg in the entry, speaking to Reyna as she moved. "I'll not be gone long. Finish the dishes and begin that new loaf of bread. Don't forget to cut the green beans too. A stage is due today."

Jill thought she detected a sly smile on the young girl's face before she turned away.

In silence, Jill and Tim trooped up the low hills west of the house and strode along the ridge. Down below, Samuel stood at the barn door and peered up at them, but Jill only waved as she trailed the quiet farmer.

The warm summer breeze caressed her cheeks and made her hair whip about her face as she climbed the protective hills, moving to the north of the stone house. She gripped the loose strands and tucked them beneath her bonnet, wondering what Tim wanted of her.

A smile creased her features as she realized how much she enjoyed being with the tree farmer, even though at present he seemed aloof or preoccupied. After a short trek, he pointed out a few of the young saplings, planted on flat spots behind the crest of the hills. Still quiet, he indicated one of his hay meadows and sighed, as if struggling with something. In the distance, far to the north, she could vaguely discern the path of the emigrant trail as the road wound through the pass at the end of her property. Jill grabbed Tim's arm when her chest heaved from the climb, halting him.

"What's wrong?"

Tim stared at her while she regained her breath, and then turned away, leading her along the ridge.

She followed, determined to not allow Tim's confusing mood to ruin her outing. A thrill ran through her as Jill surveyed her land, the horizon stretching endlessly in every direction. A perfect blue sky draped overhead, and Jill marveled anew at the peace she felt here, unexpected and satisfying. The wind kicked up briskly, and Jill gave in and pulled her bonnet off, allowing the breeze to ruffle her long hair. She wrestled the flying tresses.

At her laugh, Tim turned. "I love the wind in my hair," she explained to his questioning glance. He studied her, and Jill tensed at the look of longing in his gaze.

When she looked away, he cleared his throat. In the distance, she saw six buffalo grazing on the side of a hill.

"I asked you to come out here to show you what I've done," he began, stepping close to her. "If you look there," he pointed to where a small grove of trees stood in a narrow valley. "Those are my cherry trees."

Jill peered into the little valley and could see the thoughtfulness and care of each tree's placement. Protected from the wind, each sapling wore green leaves that shimmered brightly in the sunshine.

"There, I planted the peach and apple," Tim reported, his long arm pointing to various folds in the land.

The cry of a hawk made the pair look skyward. Jill shifted, an appreciation welling within her for the wild land she owned. How could she have guessed she'd come to love these grassy plains and vast distances?

"The original peach tree is over here." He pointed to a narrow ravine where the creek ran. "Fresh water pours from that limestone cave, giving your land the best water in the region."

He looked at her as a gust of wind buffeted, wrapping her dress tightly around her slender figure. With a blush, Tim looked quickly away.

"Other, non-fruit-bearing trees were planted up on top," he went on hurriedly. "Some elm, some oak, even an odd cottonwood. I just moved ones from the river that were not difficult to transplant. The oaks and hickory, I planted in special places so they will be sure to live. I know the hardwoods are valuable to furniture makers."

He grimaced, deep lines furrowing his brow. "Samuel wants to make a cross from oak." He paused, his lips thinning before he continued. "The nut trees are over here."

Jill studied the young saplings, so lovingly planted and cared for. The meticulousness revealed something about Tim and his character, but she wouldn't think on that now. She enjoyed the tour, the jaunt over her property, and her farm and the land soon took on a new meaning. This was a place to build, to shape, to live.

They tromped over much of the property, the knee-high grass lush in the brilliant sunshine. Wide patches of shorn grass indicated where the men had cut prairie hay for the winter. Jill appreciated where Tim had planted the berry bushes—in a protected draw not far from the fruit trees.

As they walked the rugged hills, she saw why no one believed the land could be farmed. Certainly, large scale crops could not be raised in such terrain. However, Tim had cleverly positioned the trees in such a way as to protect them from the brisk prairie winds and so they could still be watered by hand.

"Just until they develop good roots," he explained.

She observed the wagon track he'd created, bent grass showing the way he drove the wagon to deliver water to his trees.

"That's the emigrant trail," Tim said, pointing at the road through the northern hills. "It makes me wonder where I'd be now if Reyna and I had continued west."

A chill raced down her back. She didn't want to consider that possibility. She enjoyed her life here in Nebraska, more than she ever expected, and Tim and Reyna were a part of that now. She turned her gaze to the south, where she saw the Platte River with its timbered banks.

Jill drank in the wide, empty prairie around her. Odd that she, a city girl, should take so readily to this rural lifestyle. Yet, here she stood, and her heart swelled. The farm served her well while she waited for word from Mr. Hopkins or a response to her many letters.

"This is beautiful," Jill breathed, awestruck by the enormity and emptiness of the plains about her. "One would never guess there is a farm down there."

She turned to look at Tim, but his gaze was fixed on her. "Yes, beautiful," he murmured.

Jill shifted. "Well, I know you didn't bring me out here only to talk about the farm. What's on your mind?"

Tim bent and tugged a long stem of grass. Poking the blade between his teeth, he nodded. "Have you heard from the east? Any news about a teaching position?"

His unexpected question made her frown. Why did he have to spoil her pleasant day? She shook her head before studying her shoes. "Nothing yet. Perhaps this fall."

"Good," Tim mumbled. Then he glanced at Jill. "I mean, I wish you luck."

They stood quiet for a moment, before he drew in a deep breath. "The war doesn't frighten you? If you go east, won't you be thrown into that mess again? I lost my farm back there."

Was he worried about her? Or did he worry about her selling Peach Tree Farm? She reached for a stem of her own, and slipped the blade between her lips, enjoying the tangy taste. "I will not sell this farm, if that's what has you concerned."

His brows wrinkled and he tugged the long stem from his mouth, tossing the blade away. "I was thinking of Reyna's education. I know you're a teacher of young ladies, and I was wondering if you would take it upon yourself to teach her some of the finer points of being one." At Jill's obvious hesitancy, Tim continued. "You must have noticed by now how unladylike my niece is. My sister would want her to know how to conduct herself in proper society. Reyna is not going to live on this farm all her life. I would like her to have the opportunity to go east if she so chooses. She'll need to be ready for events and dinners and such."

Tim paused, frowning at Jill's silence. "What? You don't agree?"

Jill tossed her piece of grass aside. "It's just that I think Reyna is innocent. I don't want to spoil her with refinement. I enjoy her openness and honesty. It's so refreshing, so different from what society says is proper. Reyna is who she appears to be. Society demands a certain appearance, a false front of dignity, decorum, and breeding. Even if it's not real, it's what is expected. I just don't know if I think that's going to go over well with Reyna."

"You moved in such circles," he said, his words laced with an accusing tone.

"I was selfish, only thinking of myself," Jill snapped. "I would not wish that for Reyna."

His face pinched at her rebuff. "Selfish?"

"Yes," Jill confessed. "Until I knew Jesus better, I thought I was right in pursuing my own desires, regardless of anyone else. Now I realize the Lord wants me to think of others before myself."

"They got to you, didn't they?" His solemn, whispered query made her laugh, then she shrugged.

"I've always been a Christian, but I never took my faith seriously until I met Samuel. And Reyna is a positive example for me to follow. She lives her faith every day."

"Oh, no," Tim grumbled, but Jill nudged him with an elbow.

"I am pleased with what I've recently learned. My faith is developing, and I love spending time with God. More than that, I'm eager to see how my spiritual journey unfolds."

"Dare I ask?" Tim's eyes narrowed. "What is a spiritual journey?"

She laughed. "My life, my growth. I'm learning more about Jesus and how he moves in my life. I find it exciting."

"Really?" Tim tilted his head.

"When I only thought of myself, I didn't see God moving. Now, I see how he brought Samuel to help me come here. And ..." She hesitated, glancing away.

"What? You can't stop now. Tell me."

"Well, you and Reyna," Jill rushed to add. "You both have played a significant part in my journey." She paused a moment and then added, "I'm glad you're here."

Tim stared, speechless.

"As for Reyna, I don't want to change her."

"I don't want to change her," Tim agreed, shaking his head. "It's just that I want her to have the opportunities young women need to properly move in society. I don't want to neglect anything my sister would've done for her, that's all."

She squinted and peered at him from the corner of her eye. He was truly thinking of Reyna and what his sister might've wanted for her.

Tim had tried little but had done much to impress Jill these last months they'd known one another. He was strong and hardworking, she had to admit. His qualities showed clearly here where quality was important. That he wanted what was beneficial for his niece seemed clear.

Jill had embraced the changes she'd encountered, eager to become a woman of God. Was there hope for Tim, even though he protested loudly when Samuel and Reyna confronted him on his spiritual shortcomings?

"All right," Jill agreed. "I'll try and show her some basic good manners that will help her anywhere. She should feel comfortable in any society, not worrying about her upbringing or abilities. But I will not change her. Reyna has a charm I would greatly miss if it were replaced with one of snobby behavior and rude attitude. She is sweet, and I would have her stay that way."

Tim sighed with exaggeration and rolled his eyes. "That's all I'm asking for. Just help her have some manners."

Jill nodded, relenting.

"I want to check on the trees," Tim said as he gestured to the east end of the property.

"Great," Jill replied as she started for the house.

"Hey, Jill." At his call, she turned. "Thanks. I appreciate your help."

She nodded again and strode down the hill, the afternoon shadows stretching across the front yard of the clearing as a chicken cackled loudly from the barn.

As she walked down the narrow trail, she glanced over her shoulder. A thrill raced along her spine when she caught Tim watching her depart, an intensity in his dark scrutiny she couldn't identify.

CHAPTER 29

Two days later, Jill peered from the front window, listening once again to the pounding of hooves. She gritted her teeth as she spotted twin columns of blue uniforms, but then shook her head, remembering Lieutenant Alcott and the favorable impression he'd made on her. *Don't judge,* she reminded herself as she hurried to the front door.

"Who is it?" Tim called from the kitchen, pouring himself another cup of coffee before turning to follow Jill toward the door.

"Yankee soldiers," Jill replied without thinking. Memories of the recent visit from the four frightening Indians streaked across her mind, and then she shrugged, considering the diversity of the guests to Peach Tree Farm. She chuckled, surprised to find she enjoyed meeting such a variety of people.

As she stepped onto the porch, Jill saw Lieutenant Alcott leading the columns. She retreated swiftly to the entry, glancing toward the kitchen before peering at herself in the hall mirror. In the reflection, she saw Tim's eyes on her as she pushed a loose strand of chestnut hair into place and smoothed the folds of her dress. He frowned, his eyes narrowing, but she only smiled to herself as she stepped once more onto the porch, head held high.

Tim was a farmer, albeit a handsome one, but the lieutenant was the only man of social standing in hundreds of miles, and Jill knew where she belonged. If she never received an offer of employment from the east, it would be prudent to cultivate a relationship with the only gentleman in the region.

"Good afternoon, Captain," Jill called, waving as she gripped the railing. She heard Tim's step right behind her.

"Good afternoon, Miss Foster," the lieutenant greeted as he lifted a hand, signaling a halt. A cloud of dust rolled across the yard as the troopers halted their heaving horses. "We were on patrol and thought we'd stop here to water our mounts before returning to Fort Kearny." Alcott dismounted with the ease of a career military man and faced Jill, then strode forward to take her hand. A thrill raced through her when she noticed Tim's frown deepen as the officer kissed her hand, not sure which she enjoyed the more.

Jill allowed the tall soldier to hold her hand for an instant longer than decorum required, her other hand reaching for her throat. Jill glanced toward Tim in time to see the farmer roll his eyes.

"Also, Miss Foster, I am only a lieutenant," the tall officer corrected, smiling broadly.

"Only a lieutenant? Well, I declare, I could've sworn you were a captain," Jill replied, fluttering her eyelashes. Tim shifted beside her, sputtering into his coffee mug before breaking into a coughing fit. Jill shot him a disapproving look.

"Oh, Lieutenant, it is so seldom we get any visitors way out here," Jill lamented, releasing the soldier's hand. "Other than the stages that come through, we are so in need of friends and decent society. Thank you for stopping by. I will have refreshments served to your men immediately."

Jill peered over her shoulder, ignoring Tim's darkening countenance, and called through the open door. "Reyna, please bring that plate of cookies out here for our guests."

NEBRASKA HAVEN

The other soldiers of the detachment had dismounted and were leading their dusty horses to the water trough near the barn. Samuel appeared with a bucket and a dipper, moving among the thirsty men.

"Why, Captain, I mean Lieutenant, what is that trooper carrying?" Jill pointed to a soldier with a bundle tucked in his arms, wrapped in a soiled shirt.

Alcott scowled. "Well, it's a young Indian boy. A toddler, really. He must've gotten separated from his people during the buffalo hunt going on over here to the west. We found him wandering lost on the prairie. He was dehydrated and starving. We also found an Indian camp trampled by stampeding buffalo. They probably ran through camp and caused this youngster to stray from his family. His people possibly believe this little one dead."

Jill's gaze shifted from the officer to Reyna, who served cookies with a cheerful nod to each man. The young girl held the plate with one hand, her other arm tucked neatly behind her back. She looked older now, her red pigtails replaced with a stylish coiffure Jill remembered from school. Reyna's auburn tresses gleamed in the morning sunshine.

Jill faced Alcott again but watched the young girl from the corner of her eye, making sure Reyna carried herself as Jill had instructed.

"Excuse me, sir." Jill stepped from the porch and approached the Indian toddler, his dark hair peeking from the soldier's blue shirt. She tugged the shirt lower and studied the small boy. Large black eyes stared back at Jill, his little round face smudged with dirt.

"He's little more than a baby," she whispered, not wanting to frighten the child. She put a tentative hand out to smooth his hair from his forehead, but the boy shifted, leaning away from Jill.

"Yes," Lieutenant Alcott put in, "We'll take him to the fort and hope his people will come looking for him there. I will say, however, it will be difficult for a bunch of cavalrymen to tend to the little fellow." He glanced toward his milling men. "Few of us has any experience with children."

Jill faced Alcott. "Then you must leave him here, with us. It only makes sense that a couple of women can take care of a child better than a bunch of soldiers, isn't that right, Reyna?"

The young Irish girl stopped near the cowering infant and raised a corner of a cookie to the boy. The frightened lad reached for the piece hesitantly, but eventually took the morsel from Reyna's hand. He pushed the cookie eagerly into his mouth, chewing the tasty treat with haste, his eyes brightening. They all laughed.

"See? He likes Reyna. You should leave him here, Lieutenant," Jill persisted.

"The little man likes the cookie, that's for sure." The officer chuckled, then dropped his gaze, running an admiring glance over Jill's figure as she turned back to the small boy. She noticed the brazen look in the officer's eyes and felt heat color her cheeks. She wondered if anyone else had seen the bold appraisal. Tim stepped between her and Alcott, turning his back on the officer. He peered at Jill, his dark eyes searching.

"Miss Jill," Tim said. "That's kind of you to offer to look after this little fellow, but what if he's never claimed? What if the Indians believe him dead and abandon him? You might be stuck for all time with a child you did not expect nor want."

Reyna froze in her tracks, staring at Tim as he spoke. She pursed her lips, her eyes brimming with sudden tears. "So, that's how it is, is it? Stuck with an unwanted child, are you now?"

NEBRASKA HAVEN

Thrusting the plate into Jill's hands, Reyna fled for the house, her shoulders shaking with sobs.

Jill glared at Tim. "That was harsh, don't you think?"

Tim watched his niece flee, then turned to Jill with a scowl. "What? I wasn't talking about Reyna, I was referring to the Indian boy. You must make her understand. I wasn't talking about her."

She thrust the platter of treats into Tim's hands and reached for the little boy, taking the toddler from the soldier, Jill spoke over her shoulder as she moved toward the house. "I will see what I can do, Mr. Hunter, but I would encourage you to speak with more thoughtfulness in the future."

As she stepped into the entry, their bedroom door slammed. *Better give her some alone time*, Jill thought and leaned against the wall, cuddling the Indian boy. She heard the sergeant order the men to mount their horses, and Lieutenant Alcott spoke. "Don't let it bother you, Hunter. It's hard sometimes to know what to say to women."

Tim's boots thudded on the porch as the army patrol rode from the yard. She pushed herself from the wall and scurried to the sitting room, not wanting to see Tim right now.

However, she heard him approach the stone fireplace as she lowered herself to the buffalo hide-covered couch. Jill turned her back to him and lifted a cup to the small boy's mouth.

"Where's Reyna?" Tim growled, looking past Jill to the kitchen beyond.

Jill studied the toddler, refusing to meet Tim's eyes. "She's in her room, crying, no doubt, at your insensitive words." Jill glanced up, unable to retreat from battle. "You should be more sensitive to your young niece. She is a wonderful girl and a real help around here. You might consider telling her that some time."

247

Tim sank onto a chair Samuel had built from spare lumber, his features taut. "I don't know how to talk to a young girl," he confessed, staring out the window. "She was dumped on me with no warning. I don't know how to take care of a girl. I've tried my best, but I know it isn't right." Tim paused, turning to watch Jill and the little Indian boy.

"You seem to have some ability with children," he observed, one eyebrow arching. "Perhaps you could help me with Reyna."

The child grasped Jill's finger in his own chubby grip. She smiled and cooed to the youngster, watching him play with her hand. "I *have* been helping you, Mr. Hunter. You don't seem to understand we have all been helping each other. Even Samuel relates better to Reyna than you do. You might try and find a way to connect with your niece. She is very special."

Tim scowled, shifting nervously on the blanketed chair. "I never wanted another person to be responsible for. When Kathleen went away on her silly mission to Africa, I knew it would only result in tragedy. Why stick your neck out for other folks? I told her that, and do you know what she said to me?"

Jill shook her head, finally facing Tim.

"She said it was not all about me. That God had a bigger plan in mind. Well, you see where that way of thinking got her. She's dead, and I'm trying my best to raise her daughter."

Jill winced at the unexpected connection, a sense of understanding welling within her. Only recently, she'd thought the same way. What had happened to make her change her selfish thinking?

Jill realized what it was immediately. Or whom—God. The Lord brought Samuel into her life to know more about God and his greater goal. The nice things in life, the education, and the parties, were not of utmost importance to Jesus. Rather, relationships were his priority. Jesus was in the business of helping people. Jill saw clearly how she had grown in these last few months. The concept of thinking of others before yourself had been hard for Jill to process. Clearly, it was for Tim as well.

Love one another, pray for one another, and serve one another. These familiar Scripture verses spoke to her now, challenged her. Jesus was working in her soul, and she knew it, welcomed it. She had so much to learn. Maybe Tim did too.

A faint smile tugged at her lips. "Tim, you can't see what God is doing because you are so fixed on what you think is good for you. You are so selfish that you cannot see God has brought that wonderful young woman into your life to teach you about God. You need Jesus," Jill determined, her grin broadening at the shocked farmer before her.

"All you were interested in before Reyna entered your life was yourself, your trees, your farm. Now you're having to think beyond yourself, and it's driving you crazy. Stop fighting it, go with it, and learn what God is trying to teach you through your niece."

"But it's ridiculous," Tim blustered, spreading wide his hands in a helpless gesture. He stood and began to pace. "I believe in what I can see, not what I can't. This God stuff is made up, not real, for people who can't handle reality." He stopped abruptly and glared at her, his eyes imploring Jill to see reason.

She laughed outright, the little boy peering curiously up at her. "That's ridiculous. You're a farmer. You have faith that a seed planted will produce a crop. You have faith that the sun will rise each day. You can't see what happens underground to that seed, but you have faith that something is happening."

Jill paused, allowing her words to sink in. The little Indian boy played with her fingers, making sounds.

"That's different," Tim protested. "That's the natural order of things. Seeds grow, the sun rises." He shrugged a shoulder. "That's not anything exceptional."

"You're right, that is how God made those things to work. Just like he made people to be social. It's in our nature to be in relationship with one another. The most important relationship is with God."

Tim rolled his eyes and grinned at her words, causing Jill to bristle. She shifted the toddler, holding him close as she tried to ignore Tim's condescending smile.

"You're a great one to lecture me, Jill. I know this thinking is new to you too. It seems to me that Samuel has filled your head with all these silly notions. What made you finally accept his teaching? Are you a Christian now too?" Tim challenged, leaning forward eagerly to study her reply.

Jill pondered the question. Was she a Christian? She would have answered in the affirmative not long ago when she thought it meant something different than she now understood.

In her circle of acquaintances, everyone went to church regularly, revered the Bible without ever actually reading it, and believed that if you tried occasionally to be good, then you were saved ... a Christian. When you died, it was assumed you would go to heaven because you didn't murder or do awful things like those people. God would accept you because there were others so much worse than you.

Jill smiled suddenly, remembering what she'd learned these past few months. It did not matter what you thought or how good you were. What mattered to God was that you have a humble heart, want to serve others, and love and obey God's laws and teachings written in Holy Scripture. To be a Christian meant to accept God's forgiveness for your sins and live your life for his glory, not your comfort. Everyone's a sinner, and the murderer is no worse than anyone else. All have sinned and fallen short of the glory of God.

Jill drew a deep breath. "Tim, I am a Christian, thank God. I was selfish, like you. But now I've come to realize life is a journey. Not a contest to see who gets the most stuff, but a journey to develop you as a person. To learn how to serve without worrying about yourself. To love God with your whole heart and soul. To trust in his plan, despite the pain. To have faith that he has your best interests at heart."

She paused and remembered Samuel's words. "Be joyful in hope, patient in affliction, and faithful in prayer. I want to know God's plan for me, and I'm willing to wait on the Lord."

Tim stared at Jill, his mouth gaping. "I can't believe what I'm hearing. You lost your job, your parents, and now you're preaching about God's love. Do you hear what you're saying?"

"Yes, you're right." Jill nodded. "Two absolute truths I've come to accept is that God loves me, and he allows suffering. The Lord uses pain to draw people to him. Through my pain, I realize I need his comfort. I must believe God brought Samuel to open my heart to God. I had everything stripped from me that I valued. Now, I feel uncertain about the future, not sure what God is doing with me, and yet I embrace the uncertainty." She looked down at the now quiet child in her arms and then back to Tim. "The lack of control, the not knowing, excites me like I have never known excitement before. God promises in the Bible to always be with us, to never forsake us. He is shaping me into the woman of God he desires, in his way, in his timing. I hope he molds me into the person he sees I *can* be, not the person I see in the mirror."

Tim dropped into the chair once more as if his knees buckled. He leaned back and scowled at her, a dejected look in his eyes. Jill lifted her chin, wondering if he was as surprised as she was at the account she had given of her new-found faith.

The small boy sighed contentedly in Jill's arms, and Tim glanced at the sleeping child. Jill narrowed her eyes, watching him. Was he preparing for another go around? Was he finally willing to dialogue about spiritual matters? Jill hoped so. His honesty felt refreshing.

When Tim sighed and his shoulders sagged, Jill knew this battle had gone her way. Her heart warmed as a thrill raced through her. She had stood for what she believed.

"A soldier at the fort told me an old Cheyenne saying. Stay and fight and you might die. Ride away, and you will surely live to fight another day." He rose slowly to his feet and squinted down at her. "This fight isn't over," he added softly before marching stiff-backed to the front door.

Jill patted the sleeping boy and tilted her head. Who were the Cheyenne?

CHAPTER 30

"What are you going to name the little boy?" Samuel asked one night at dinner.

For three days, Reyna and Jill had taken turns taking care of the Indian boy. Now, the small child sat on Reyna's lap and ate the pieces of bread she handed him. He ate heartily, especially the sweet baked goods Reyna provided.

He'd come with no clothes, so they'd wrapped him in spare shirts and fitted them the best they could. He seemed content in their home, enjoying all the attention. For hours a day, the small boy would chase and pet the calico cat. He even chased mice in the barn, helping the furry mouser.

"You'd better give him a name if he's to live here with us," Tim added, his chair creaking as he shifted and glanced at his niece. "Better to make him comfortable and let him know he's loved."

Reyna refused to meet his searching gaze. Although she'd been quick to forgive in the past, she seemed aloof toward her uncle. Clearly, she knew now how Tim felt about her, and it'd created a rift between the two once more.

"I'm not going to name him," Jill said, her eyes on the little hands reaching for the morsels of bread from Reyna. "I'm still praying for his safe return to his family."

Tim pressed his lips into a tight line as he shrugged but said nothing.

The next morning, an unexpected chill lingered in the air, and Jill draped her shawl around her shoulders as she reached for the door handle. As she walked to the barn in search of eggs, she considered the hot summer would soon come to an end.

A sudden drumming of running horses' hooves halted her in the middle of the yard. She glanced north to where the trail opened into the hills.

With whoops and shouts, a band of Indians descended upon her, their wild-eyed ponies kicking dust as they reined before the stone house.

She quickly scanned the hills, searching for signs of Tim, but knew he was out watering the trees. Squaring her shoulders, she turned to the Indians, unafraid. The previous visit had taken the fear from her. Now, only curiosity remained as she studied their dress and how they wore their hair.

Five braves fanned out, facing her, their faces and chests painted with black streaks. A long scar decorated the cheek of one brave. Jill recognized him from the earlier visit. The Indians stared at Jill for a long minute before the one with the scar spoke.

"We look for baby."

His accent made it hard to decipher his words, but Jill understood. They searched for the child.

"Yes." Jill nodded. "Yes, the boy is here."

The front door opened behind them, and the braves turned swiftly in their saddles as Samuel stepped onto the porch. The small band began to murmur and point as Samuel froze in his tracks, glancing from Jill to the staring, painted riders. His dark face wore a mask of anxiety.

The brave with the scar slid from his horse, and with one hesitant glance toward his companions, moved with slow steps toward the porch. Finally, with a leap, he stood before Samuel. The runaway slave shot Jill another worried glance and then straightened, a look of resignation coming over hm. Jill held her breath as the Indian with the scar stretched a hand to touch Samuel's face, gently rubbing his cheek. Then, the brave lifted and examined Samuel's hand. With a grunt, he rubbed it as if scrubbing a stubborn stain.

Turning to the quartet of mounted braves, the Indian shouted something. Visibly, his companions relaxed and nodded to each other, sharing grunts of satisfaction and obvious pleasure. Jill, having been temporarily forgotten, now became the center of the scarred brave's focus once more. He left the porch and strode to her, weaving among the horses. Hooking a thumb over his shoulder, he indicated Samuel. "Black man. Special. Holy man?"

Jill glanced at Samuel, not sure she comprehended the brave's meaning.

Samuel chuckled, then stopped when the Indians turned to stare at him. "They think I'm a priest or something like," he said, scratching the side of his head.

The Indians' eyes widened, and once again they murmured among themselves.

Reyna appeared, the small boy in her arms. At sight of the five braves, the boy squealed and held out his arms.

One of the Indians slipped from his horse and retrieved the toddler from Reyna's hold, smiling briefly at the young Irish girl before claiming the boy, hugging him to his chest. He handed the boy to one of his comrades and mounted again. The scarred brave mounted too, nodding to Jill before tugging on the leather reins.

The five braves turned their horses and rode from the yard, Reyna, Jill, and Samuel watching them go without a word.

The clatter of hooves came from behind Jill, and she turned to see Tim lashing the team, their wagon bouncing over the uneven ground as the vehicle raced into the front yard. He dragged on the reins as the last rider disappeared from view, a thick cloud of dust settling over the trio of onlookers.

Tim leaped from the wagon, glanced at Reyna, then stared at Jill, fixing her with an anxious gaze that startled her. She didn't recognize the emotion in his eyes, but she stiffened at the sudden attention.

"She's all right, Uncle Tim," Reyna said softly. "We're all right."

Tim nodded and looked away. He removed his hat and ran a hand through his unruly hair. "Did they come for the boy?"

Jill sighed. "I didn't think I'd get that attached to him so quickly. I'll miss him."

Samuel snorted. "You'll be having children of your own one day, if I don't miss my guess. I saw the way that Yankee officer looks at you."

Jill felt the heat leap to her cheeks, but she frowned when she saw the anger in Tim's eyes.

Three days passed before they were once again visited by guests—an army patrol led by Sergeant Thornton, one of the soldiers from Fort Kearny. Jill noticed the bright yellow stripes sewn neatly on his blue jacket, as if only recently placed there. They'd stopped at Peach Tree Farm to water their horses and present gifts. When Jill seemed surprised by their offerings, the sergeant explained.

"Well, miss, the gifts are not from us. It's like this," Thornton began, his untrimmed beard dancing on his sun-browned face. "A number of Indian tribes have gathered west of here to hunt this big herd of buffalo for their winter meat. Part of the herd stampeded a week ago and trampled one of the Arapahoe camps. They lost a little boy in the confusion. They told us they found their boy with the tree growers where the black holy man lives." He glanced at Samuel. "They believe the Great Spirit protected their small one, and they present gifts to show their gratitude."

The troopers handed Tim two finely tanned buffalo robes and a haunch of buffalo meat.

The sergeant added, "Those Indians also said they'd be bringing a special gift soon, when the fall hunt was completed." The sergeant scratched his jaw and frowned. "They said they wanted the sweet food they received before. Does that make sense to you, miss?"

Reyna laughed, her eyes twinkling. "It means, Sergeant, that I'll be baking a couple of pies."

Jill smiled, recalling the frightening visit from the Arapahoe braves when Reyna had served apple pie.

Sergeant Thornton's gaze swept over the huge stone house and the hard packed dirt yard. A smile formed, and he nodded. "I remember when Hazlett built this place. Murphy tricked him out of the land and later went east." He glanced at Jill and cleared his throat. "Miss? The lieutenant told me to give you his regrets. He's busy with another matter at present but hopes to visit you soon."

Jill nodded, embarrassed, yet suddenly pleased to be remembered by the only gentleman in the area.

CHAPTER 31

After Jill's bold declaration of faith to Tim, she threw herself wholeheartedly into the relationship—her relationship with Christ. While she waited for word from Mr. Hopkins, she vowed to learn all she could from her more spiritually mature companions. Samuel and Reyna proved ready teachers, eager to share Bible study insights with their willing pupil.

Jill drank in her growing faith with desire, realizing for the first time in her life that the Christian walk was a journey filled with love, challenges, and satisfaction. God loved her in ways she struggled to comprehend. Every tear she'd shed, every ache of her heart was known by the Lord. He knew everything about her and still cherished her. Despite her selfish heart, which had craved only her own benefit, God had launched Jill on an adventure of faith, designed to develop her in ways she longed for. To become a better person, one who loved Jesus more than anything else.

As the threesome gathered after supper each evening—when the duties of the stage station allowed—Jill sensed Tim watching her, testing her resolve and commitment. Yet, she suspected he listened to their discussions with a personal interest too.

Evening devotions and Bible study with Reyna and Samuel, including the history surrounding the events and writings of the Scriptures, were followed by prayer time and reflection. Jill felt astounded at how much she didn't know.

Though she always considered herself an educated and good Christian, now she realized what the title meant. The term, "a new creation in Christ," truly now applied to her. Not only in head knowledge, but in change of heart as well. The Bible—God's Word—had come alive to her and spoke to her as she explored the mysteries of life.

An increase of recent stage movements had kept the Peach Tree Creek stage station bustling. People from all over the west seemed to want to make final travels before winter limited movement on the plains. Seldom was the house empty from guests. The four upstairs rooms constantly held passengers transferring to other stage routes. Rarely did a holdover at the farm have to wait more than three days before the connecting stage arrived to carry travelers onto their final destinations.

Due to the increase in travelers, Jill and Reyna made frequent trips to Fort Kearny for supplies. Tim grumbled about each trip, claiming the interruptions interfered with his use of the wagon. On more than one occasion, Jill and Tim had argued over whose need for the wagon seemed greater. Then, just yesterday, two Arapahoe braves had presented Tim with a pony. With simple words and gestures, they indicated the pony was a gift for helping and protecting the small boy while in their care.

This morning at breakfast, Samuel had held his companions' attention as he explained how best to train the pony.

"Master Carter had many interests," Samuel said, accepting another short stack of pancakes from Reyna. "Some of his people did brick work in Paducah, a few hands he rented out to other farmers, his tobacco fields, and to the docks, where I was. He also had a few horses he trained. I worked with the trainer for a summer before they decided the work was more than I could do with my bad foot. I couldn't keep up with the animals."

Tim narrowed his eyes. "You harness-trained horses? Well, if you could train the Indian pony and we had another wagon, it would surely make things simpler around here." He shot a meaningful glance at Jill.

Reyna poured coffee for a pair of travelers at the big table where the guests were served. She replaced the coffeepot on the stove and glanced at the trio seated around the smaller table against the wall, avoiding eye contact with her uncle. Despite her forgiveness for his harsh comment a fortnight ago, a lingering tension hovered, as if some business were unfinished.

"I don't know if this is a help or not, but I saw a broken wagon behind Mr. Billings's store the last time I was in Fort Kearny. Perhaps Samuel could repair it." Reyna moved away before anyone could reply.

Jill glared at Tim. Reyna still harbored ill feelings from her uncle's hurtful words a few weeks ago.

"I could kick you," she whispered when Reyna moved out of earshot.

"Me?" Time's eyebrows arched as he lifted his coffee mug. "What'd I do?"

Samuel glanced away, pretending not to pay attention as Jill continued her tirade. "You know you hurt her feelings. You need to patch things up. She's your only family."

Tim shook his head and mumbled beneath his breath. She watched as he glanced at his niece and then looked out the front window. Early morning shadows retreated across the yard, promising to bring another hot day. He looked back at Jill, suddenly catching her eyes upon him.

Jill dropped her gaze, embarrassed to be found studying him. Despite the rift between him and Reyna, the young girl had agreed to cut Tim's hair. Although his beard required a good trim, the farmer now appeared more handsome than ever.

Jill felt the heat stain her cheeks, but she refused to meet his searching gaze, ignoring Tim's stare.

The room fell silent for a long moment before Tim finally spoke. "Samuel, can you spare a couple of hours for a quick ride to town to see this wagon behind Mr. Billings's store? If you could break the pony to harness, maybe we could have another little wagon for town trips."

Jill kept her attention on her mug, afraid to discover where Tim might be looking. She sipped her coffee, her jaw tightening. Of course, he was taking a jab at her with his pointed comment about town trips, but the errands she and Reyna ran to town were to keep the stage station operating smoothly. She bristled at the thought that she worried about his feelings or his interests. After all, Jill surmised, the stage station was currently their only source of income. Sometimes, sudden trips to town could not be avoided.

Tim's chair scraped as he stood, and Jill glanced up.

"Besides," he added, looking directly at Jill. "Soon I will be cutting winter hay, and Samuel and I will need the wagon every day, no exceptions."

"Well, make sure you get the broken wagon for a good price. Even with the pay the station brings in, it's barely enough to make ends meet. I'm almost out of funds," Jill snapped, turning her back on Tim. With a lunge, she leaped to help Reyna clear the dishes and begin preparing dough for the baking.

The two men departed, and Reyna worked by the sink as Jill arranged ingredients on the scoured clean table. Soon, the passengers also left, and the room quieted.

Jill glanced out the window in time to see Samuel and Tim leave for town, the heavy farm wagon vanishing into the avenue between the trees bordering the nearby river. She eyed the baking supplies and reached for the flour, wishing they had a cow. Milk would certainly be appreciated. A farm should have its own milk cow, she thought as she measured the proper amount of flour into a bowl.

Adding the yeast from its tin container she kept in the ground box, she began forcefully kneading the large pile of dough. Flour soon covered her hands and reached above her wrists.

She smiled to herself, wondering why she should care about her fights with Tim. In the spring, there would surely be a letter from Mr. Hopkins about a school position, if not sooner. The war could not go on forever, and the latest reports indicated that a turn in favor of the Union had recently occurred. With the Battle of Antietam Creek, President Lincoln declared the stalemate a Union victory. However, she knew the Confederacy wouldn't give up that easily.

Although the farm had worked out better than she could have ever hoped, it produced nothing. However, the stage stop was a gift she could not deny. God was good. She certainly had never expected anything as lucrative as this. Besides, the farm had only been a temporary refuge as she awaited a teaching position. Once the war ended, Jill would have no reason to stay in Nebraska.

Yet, she wondered, could there be another purpose for her here—something more to this safe haven? The farm had proven to be a harbor from the storms of life or, at least, the life she used to know. Life had become full again. Her friends meant everything to her. Jesus lived in her heart, and she pursued a deepening faith. All these things happened here, unexpected, and yet so fulfilling. Was God telling her something?

Jill rolled the heavy dough, bending the blob over upon itself, punching the mound with a flour-covered fist. True, a milk cow would be appreciated, but not necessary, she figured. The others would get on without a cow as they had thus far. The newly tinned condensed milk, however, seemed a poor substitute for fresh milk.

Her hands stilled, and she felt a shiver race down her spine. They didn't need a milk cow, and they didn't need ... her. Jill could be replaced. The farm didn't need her. She could take a position in the east and move on. That had been her plan all along, right?

Jill glanced around the kitchen and spacious sitting room. A pang of unexpected regret filled her at the thought of leaving. This had become home to her. Samuel, Reyna, and Tim had become more than friends. Did she really want to leave Peach Tree Farm?

"Jill?"

Reyna's call brought her back to reality. She looked at Reyna, worried she'd been discovered in her reverie. The young girl wasn't even looking at her.

"Do you think we'll have rain? I want to hang laundry later."

Jill sighed, grateful her daydream went unnoticed. She glanced outside, observing the clear sky. "Doesn't look like rain to me. Ask Samuel. He always seems to know what the weather will do."

Reyna nodded, not lifting her gaze from the dishes she washed.

Jill punched the dough and thought again of leaving the farm. Of course, she did want to leave, she argued with herself. Soon, Jill hoped, she would hear about a teaching position back east, and she would be on her way.

And Tim? Jill wondered at the tight squeeze on her heart at the thought of the handsome young farmer. Handsome? Yes ... handsome. And strong. She liked to watch him work and the way his dark eyes gleamed when he talked of the farm and his plans for the land. He loved this land. Could he ever love anything else?

Jill squinted at the dough, rolling the lump once more, dismayed at the startling idea. Well, that was certainly none of her business. She loved teaching, God, and her life back in Kentucky.

Yet, she admitted, Nebraska had surprised her. Jill dreamed of a Southern gentleman, rushing in with gallantry, sweeping her off her feet. Despite her obvious distaste of Yankees, she'd considered Lieutenant Alcott. Perhaps her tastes had altered more than she allowed.

She punched the thick dough again and again, wondering why she was so unsure of herself. She was a teacher, not a stage operator, wasn't she? Then why was she so upset at the thought of leaving?

Yet, while she stayed, she could not deny the lieutenant's obvious interest in her. And he was a gentleman.

CHAPTER 32

The wagon rocked and creaked noisily on its way toward the ford. The wild, native trees that lined the Platte River never ceased to attract Tim's ever-searching eye. Today, he noticed the changing colors of the forest as they sped past on the empty wagon, the fading leaves fluttering in the morning breeze. Tim saw the elm, cottonwood, and occasional hickory trees with their golden leaves only barely visible among the dusky green of other foliage. He remembered with satisfaction the two black walnut saplings Reyna had discovered for him near Fort Kearny. Tim treasured them and spent extra time transplanting them, ensuring their survival.

Tim reflected on this with an unexpected sadness. Usually, the thought of trees made him happy and excited, but recalling the strain on his relationship with Reyna put a damper on this normal sense of joy.

He slowed the horses as they approached the low bank of the river, the team walking forward with tentative steps. He allowed them to find their footing as they traversed the shallow, muddy water. A white crane lifted from a nearby sandbar, wings flapping gracefully. Tim admired the foresight of the man who'd constructed the stone house. The builder had located the perfect place along the river.

The banks of the Platte were covered in dense undergrowth and trees, some of which were of considerable size. Tim believed Murphy—or was it the other man he'd cheated with cards—had found this site while on patrol with the troopers and returned numerous times to clear a path to the water's edge. Only the army used the ford until the other, more widely known, ford had been rendered unusable by the storms.

Vaguely, he wondered if the Oregon Trail traffic would continue its westward tide on this very ford when the spring migration resumed. What effect would that have on the stage station at Peach Tree Farm?

Honking geese called overhead, and Tim glanced up, marveling at the perfect wedges of birds as thousands of them flew south. He chewed his lip at the reminder of imminent hay cutting. Winter would be upon them soon.

The horses lunged up the rutted bank, water streaming from their legs as they pulled the bouncing wagon behind them. The trees on this side of the river often captured Tim's attention, and he'd pointed to particular trees, noting certain characteristics or size. However, this was not the case today. Tim gripped the reins tightly, casting an eye to his companion. Did Samuel notice the absence of Tim's usual lessons on the foliage of the river bottom? Did Samuel even care?

"What's bothering you, Tim?" Samuel asked, breaking the silence. "I saw the way Reyna snubbed you."

Tim clucked to the team, increasing their speed on the flatter ground. "I can't get her to forget what she thought I meant when we had that Indian boy at the farm. She thinks I don't want her." He flicked the reins as he felt his irritation swirl.

Samuel nodded. "Do you want her?"

"Of course, I do," Tim sputtered as he shot an angry glance at his companion.

"Well, your actions don't show it."

Tim could feel his brows furrowing. "I've always provided for Reyna. She's my older sister's kid, and I've never shirked my responsibility."

"No, you haven't," Samuel agreed. "But you also have never gone out of your way to welcome her, either. You've been harsh with her when she shares her faith or tells you things that interest her."

"It's annoying," Tim grumbled. "I can't stand to hear her tell me what God wants from me, or how a particular prayer was answered. I just want to be left alone with my own beliefs. I don't mean to criticize her ideas, but I have my own, and they're not the same as hers."

The two men rode in silence. After a few moments, Tim shot Samuel another sidelong glance. Samuel watched the clouds, his lips barely moving. Tim could feel his eyebrows arch as his palms began to sweat. Was Samuel *praying*?

He clenched his teeth. These religious people were really making him angry. And now they'd recruited Jill, sweeping her into their fantasy world. He wanted to spit.

"Tim?" Samuel's voice interrupted his thoughts, and he tugged gently on the reins, realizing they were going faster than necessary.

"I have to confess I didn't know you had beliefs of your own. I'd be eager to hear what they are," Samuel finally said.

Tim chewed the inside of his cheek, suddenly worried. Maybe he shouldn't have said he had his own beliefs. Now he would have to explain what they were, and he wasn't too sure about them himself.

"Well," he began, sweat starting to bead his forehead. "They're not like Reyna's beliefs."

"All right," Samuel encouraged. "What exactly are they?"

Tim scowled. "Don't push me. Let me think and put it into words."

He fidgeted on the seat, letting the long reins dangle between his fingers. Then he nodded. "My god allows me to be who I am. He doesn't expect me to change or fix things others might think are wrong with me."

Tim glanced at Samuel from the corner of his eye, watching what impact his words might have on this Christian. Samuel merely watched the countryside, listening attentively. Tim continued.

"My god doesn't make me ask for forgiveness when I hurt someone. Nor do I have to forgive someone who offends me. It's just life, it happens. My god doesn't make me be thoughtful of others, my life is my own. I'm not bound to serve people if I don't want to. It's too much work. Let everyone alone, I say. My god agrees with me," Tim concluded, pleased with his response.

Samuel remained silent. Ahead, Fort Kearny showed through the trees that bordered the parade ground, and neither man took up the conversation as they neared town. Tim smiled, satisfied at how he'd defended his beliefs. They were *his* beliefs, and no one could tell him he was wrong.

His smile broadened as he tugged on the reins and halted the team in front of Mr. Billings's store. Suddenly, the day seemed brighter. Tim wrapped the reins around the brake handle and the two men climbed down from the tall wagon.

Mr. Billings greeted them warmly when they entered, the bell ringing as they stepped through the door.

"Tim, Samuel, how are you?" he called, coming around the long counter which sat heavily loaded with stacks of dry goods. He shook hands with both men. "Now, what can I do for you?"

"My niece told me you had a broken wagon about here somewhere," Tim said.

NEBRASKA HAVEN

"It's not much," Mr. Billings allowed, turning to lead the men through the crowded store to the back door. "A man from Indiana left it here on his way west. One wheel had already broken, and the poor horse pulling it looked like he was about to drop. It's too small for carrying much, only a little bigger than a cart, and too narrow for two horses to pull. You can tell whoever built it didn't have any idea what he was doing."

Mr. Billings stopped on the rear stoop and pointed at the leaning wagon. Samuel moved forward, inspecting the slim vehicle with a knowing eye. The wagon listed precariously to one side. One wheel was broken, another missing.

Tim tilted his head, a skeptical look on his face, then grunted. "I'll be honest, Mr. Billings, I'd hoped it'd be in a little better shape. It's already missing one wheel." The two men stared at the ruined wagon as Samuel walked around it.

"Well, Mr. Billings, I won't take up any more of your time," Tim announced, turning to enter the store again.

"Wait, wait," the storekeeper said hurriedly and grasped Tim's arm. "Don't be too hasty. I'll bet you could fix this wagon real nice, a handy fellow like yourself. And I've heard of the furniture Samuel's made at Peach Tree Station." He gestured to the leaning wagon. "It doesn't need much. The box is real solid. I'll let you have it cheap."

Tim saw Samuel motion to him just as the front doorbell jangled and a sudden call from within drew their attention. Mr. Billings hesitated, and then turned to go. "Think it over, Tim. I'll be right back," he called over his shoulder as he disappeared inside.

Tim stepped off the stoop and kicked the sideways vehicle. "Come on, Samuel. We're wasting our time here. I need to get back to the farm."

Samuel stole a quick glance at the store before he spoke, lowering his voice. "Tim, this is perfect. I can make this a one-horse dray. If you can get it cheap, this will do."

Tim squinted, peering at Samuel through slits. "Are you crazy? This is a piece of junk. It'll never work again. Only the wheels have value now. Mr. Billings was right. Too narrow for two horses to pull, too long and heavy for one."

"That's just it, I agree," Samuel whispered. "Trust me. See how cheap he'll go. I can make this a good rig for us."

The screen door slammed, and both men looked up to see Mr. Billings join them. "What do you say, gentlemen? It has potential, right? A little work and it'll be good as new." He rubbed his hands together.

Tim frowned and squeezed the back of his neck. "Well," he began, "It might be used for scraps." He kicked the wagon again. "How much do you want for this pile of used lumber?"

"Now, Tim, that's the wrong attitude. This wagon still has a lot of life left in her. I have faith in your abilities. This rig is solid." Mr. Billings scanned the vehicle with a shrewd eye, as if locating hidden value. "I would have to have thirty dollars for this fine wagon," the storekeeper said, his gaze fixed on the vehicle.

Tim laughed. "Come on, Samuel. Let's head home."

The two men moved to leave.

"Tim, Tim." Mr. Billings's hand shot out, grasping the farmer's arm. "Hear me out. I paid good money for this rig last year, and I've only sold one wheel off it. I need to get my investment back. I can let you have this rig for twenty-two dollars, no less."

Tim hesitated, looking over his shoulder at the broken wagon. He turned slowly, eyeing the vehicle with disdain, then shook his head. "No, Mr. Billings, I think I'll pass. Thanks for your time, but this rig isn't what we're looking for. I think we'll wait for another wagon."

"There might not be another wagon until spring, perhaps never," Mr. Billings protested. "It would be foolish to let a good deal like this get away." The storekeeper dropped his hand and nodded. "Make me an offer."

"Mr. Billings, you and I both know this is not a good deal." Tim turned to leave again, speaking over his shoulder as he moved away. "It's worth about twelve dollars to me." He gripped the door handle and paused as the storekeeper laughed.

"Tim, I can sell the wheels alone for ten dollars apiece."

Tim faced Mr. Billings. "Maybe. But that could take two or three or four years. You never know when a man will buy a wheel from you. By then, these wheels might be rotted. They need to be kept wet so they don't dry out and the spindles slip from the hub. They'll be worthless then. You know what they say about a bird in hand." Tim shook his head as he glanced at the wagon again, his nose wrinkling. "No, I won't give any more than twelve dollars."

Mr. Billings's face pinched, as if he'd eaten a sour pickle. He scratched the side of his head and shifted. "I'll take fifteen, Tim, and I'm giving you the better end of this deal."

Tim glanced at Samuel and the runaway nodded slightly. "I'll give you fourteen, and not a dollar more," Tim declared in a doubtful tone, as if he didn't want the broken wagon even at that price.

Mr. Billings beamed as he shook hands quickly before Tim could change his mind. "Deal. Pay me when you pick it up."

The bell rang again from within the store, and Mr. Billings moved to return inside. "Have a good day, gentlemen."

Tim glanced at Samuel, one eyebrow arching. "I hope you know what you're talking about," he growled as they mounted their wagon.

"Don't worry. I have a plan, and it'll look great when I'm done," Samuel promised.

CHAPTER 33

The next morning, Tim entered the spacious front room, shaking his head. He accepted a steaming mug from Reyna before saying, "I need to pay attention to those saplings on the north ridge." He blew on the liquid in the hot mug as everyone faced him.

"What about the wagon at Mr. Billings's store? I thought you'd pay him today," Samuel asked as he pulled back a chair and seated himself at the kitchen table.

Tim nodded. "Yeah, I know. But the trees are more important than a wagon for the girls."

Jill stepped forward from the kitchen where she'd been helping Reyna prepare breakfast and pointed her wooden spoon at Tim. "We're new to this country and need to honor our promises. Our word counts for something. Perhaps you should've paid for it yesterday and brought it home then, not wasting the trip."

Tim waved a hand. "I didn't think of it. Besides, it only has three wheels. Couldn't bring it home if we wanted to."

Jill arched an eyebrow, but Samuel grinned. "We'll get it today."

"Then take the money in to Mr. Billings. The trees can wait a few hours."

Reyna shoveled a stack of pancakes onto Tim's plate as he joined Samuel. "Nope. The trees are for the future of this place." He gestured to Samuel with his fork. "Samuel can take the money to town and work on the wagon, if he's a mind to. But the weather is perfect for cutting hay and it shouldn't rain. I cannot be absent from the farm today."

Jill glared at Tim. "This isn't because the wagon is for me and Reyna, is it?"

Tim frowned before he placed his fork on the table and leaned back in his chair. "Listen. This is not a conspiracy to keep you and Reyna from running errands to town. But I need to stay here and work." He dug into his pocket and pulled out a few crumpled bills, spreading them carefully on the table before Samuel's plate. "There. You can take care of this, okay?"

Samuel's eyes widened as he stared at the wrinkled money. He glanced once at Jill and then nodded, his lips pursing. His anxious look was not lost on Tim.

"Look, Samuel. If you can't do this, tell me now. I'm already losing one of the team for your trip to town. I don't want to lose the whole day of work." He reached for his fork once more. "It's time to cut hay. I felt frost in the air, and we need to hurry if we plan on stacking enough for the winter."

Jill reached for the money, and leaning over Samuel's shoulder, stuffed the bills into his shirt pocket. "Samuel can do it, Tim. Don't be so grumpy."

Tim ignored her and jabbed at the flapjacks. She tilted her head and squinted at him from behind. Something was eating at him, and she wanted to know what it was. She decided she would accompany Samuel to town and see if he had any clues about Tim's sour mood. Besides, she needed to see if a letter had arrived from the east. The prospect didn't excite her, but she pushed the nagging thought away.

Tim peered at her sharply, scowling as he shoved another fork of pancakes into his mouth. Samuel looked up with an apprehensive glance, but Jill gave him an encouraging nod.

"I'll go with Samuel. I need to pick up a few things anyway. Maybe a letter has arrived from Mr. Hopkins."

Samuel quickly pulled the money from his pocket and held the wad out to Jill. She shook her head. "Tim gave it to you."

Tim's chair scraped as he abruptly pushed back from the table, as if something Jill said irritated him. "Hurry back, Samuel. You'll only need one horse to retrieve the wagon from town. When you return, hitch the team, and meet me in the hay fields. I'll start cutting hay after I tend to the trees."

Samuel watched him go.

"Hey," Jill said, drawing Samuel's attention. "Don't let Tim's cantankerous mood bother you." She chuckled, a wide grin spreading a bit before turning serious, the smile fleeing. "Are you sure this broken wagon was worth fourteen dollars? I'm running out of the money my father had in his box, and the stage station makes only enough to pay for supplies. We could use another town rig, but I don't want to waste the little money I have."

Samuel stood and faced her. "Don't you worry, Miss Jill. I'll fix this wagon in a jiffy."

Jill's smile returned. "Thanks, Samuel. I trust you. Fetch a horse, and I'll meet you on the porch."

He led the horse from the barn, the saw and hammer tucked beneath his arm. Shuffling to the long porch, he was joined by Jill. She watched as he held up pieces of harness for her inspection. She untied her apron and tossed it over the railing as he draped the harness over the horse. "I'll be back soon, Reyna," she called as she followed Samuel down the dirt road toward the ford.

"Do you need to ride?" she asked the former slave, eyeing his hobbling gait.

He shuddered and grinned. "I'm all right, Miss Jill. I don't like to ride horseback."

As the pair disappeared into the thick foliage bordering the Platte River, Samuel broke the short silence. "Miss Jill, if you want to carry the money, I don't mind."

Jill shook her head and repeated, "Tim gave it to you."

Samuel scowled and then lifted his head. "I've never been given money to carry. Master Carter would make a deal when he rented me out for work, but I never handled the money."

Jill smiled. "Then it's high time. Things are different in Nebraska."

They halted before the wide river, the muddy water lapping the low bank where they stood. Samuel groaned. "How're we going to get across this river without getting muddy? I surely didn't think this out right." His gaze surveyed the ford and the rippling, dirty water.

Jill frowned, studying the river's course, and then glanced at the horse before laughing. "I suppose we can ride double across the river. Come on, lift me up." She'd never ridden a horse double, and the thought made her laugh even more, a sense of freedom assailing her. She would never have imagined such a thing in Kentucky.

Samuel took a step backward. "Miss Jill, that ain't fitting. Nebraska or not, we cannot ride double."

Jill chuckled again, but Samuel shook his head and took another step backward. "No, miss. It's not right."

She hesitated, then glanced around, finally locating a log sticking out of the muddy bank. She led the horse beside the sun-bleached driftwood and used the improvised step to scramble atop the horse, arranging the loose harness pieces around her. Gripping the reins, she kicked the horse and walked once more to the river's edge.

"There. Ready?"

Samuel nodded and she kicked the horse into action. Water sprayed as horse and rider descended into the shallow river. A glance over her shoulder revealed Samuel following, the dirty water rising to his knees as he trailed the walking horse across the Platte, her father's old shoes dangling by their laces around his neck.

While Jill trooped in a straight course, Samuel took a devious route, avoiding deep channels and using various sandbars and brush-covered islands. Finally, with a lunge, Jill and the horse stood on the opposite bank, water streaming from the horse's legs as she watched Samuel trudge the rest of the way. With a smile, he dropped to the sandy bank and shoved his feet into the shoes.

After he stood and wiped the sand from his pants, he gestured at the road to town and started walking.

"You sure you don't want to ride?" she called after him, noting his shuffling stride.

"I'd rather walk," he replied cheerfully, not bothering to look at her.

Jill trotted alongside Samuel a few paces before slipping from the horse's back. With the reins gripped in one hand, she walked beside him.

"Nice day for a walk," she remarked as she slowed her pace to his.

"A beautiful day," he agreed.

Jill nodded and then frowned. "Tim was sure surly at breakfast."

Samuel chuckled. "It's the Spirit working on him. We talked about Reyna when we came to town yesterday."

"Oh?" she said softly. "You spend a great deal of time with Tim. What's he like? Is he easy to work with?"

Samuel shrugged. "That's funny you ask. He was asking me about you just last week."

"He did?" She felt her eyes widen. "Why would he ask about me?"

Samuel shrugged again. "No telling."

Jill looked toward town, the buildings of the frontier outpost not in sight yet. From the trees along the nearby river, birds whistled and chirped. The horse clomped slowly behind them as the pair made their way down the road, the sun warming their shoulders. Abruptly, Jill nudged Samuel with an elbow.

"Hey, we've come a long way, you and me."

Samuel chuckled. "A long way. Kentucky and Missouri seems like a long time ago now."

"Want to know a secret?" She leaned toward him and smiled. "I love Nebraska. I never thought I'd love a place not in the South. Things are very different out here from what I'm used to."

"That's all right, though." He shot her an anxious look. "I mean, change is good. The Lord is always keeping us on our toes, making sure we don't get lazy."

Laughter bubbled up within her as she caught sight of the distant outbuildings of Fort Kearny. "No chance of getting lazy at Peach Tree Farm."

"No," Samuel agreed. "God uses new situations to stretch our faith, to grow us. Like trees, we can produce fruit for Jesus only when we mature."

She stared at him, startled at his insight. "You're right. I have so much to learn." She paused, considering his words. "You didn't learn that from Tim."

"Tim doesn't see God working on the farm, the planning and the growing, the rain and the harvest. But God's hand is in everything. You should see that by now."

Jill nodded, pleased how eagerly her heart leaned toward spiritual wisdom. The Lord worked within her, and she felt exhilarated. She glanced at Samuel. "I do see God's hand in things more than I used to."

"Keep looking. There's always more going on than you know."

She tilted her head at his cryptic words. "Do you sense something I'm not aware of?" Did the Spirit guide Samuel in other spiritual matters, or did he know something particular about Tim?

"Wait on the Lord," Samuel advised sagely. "His timing is perfect. You will see things clearly when the time is right."

Jill grinned. "I'm grateful for you. We've become good friends."

"Good friends," he agreed.

They walked in silence for a distance. When they passed the military grounds, Jill glanced at the officer's building. She wondered at her disappointment at not seeing Lieutenant Alcott.

Mr. Billings stepped from the front door when he saw them approach. "I thought Tim was fetching the money into town?"

Jill nodded at Samuel, and he hurriedly presented the folded bills to the storekeeper. Samuel shot her a relieved look as Mr. Billings jerked a thumb around back. "It's all yours."

Jill's heart sank when she saw the wrecked wagon, but Samuel only grinned. "Don't worry," he told her as he rolled up his sleeves.

After tying the horse to a hitching post, she found a bench in the shade of the store and watched as Samuel began to work.

CHAPTER 34

Samuel stood, studying the wrecked wagon for almost a minute before moving. First, he removed the one good rear wheel. Placing the sphere near at hand, he pulled the retaining pin from the axle of the broken front wheel. Pushing the wagon up with his great strength, he pulled the broken wheel from the axle, letting it fall at his feet. Still holding the heavy wagon with one hand, he reached for the good wheel he'd taken from the rear, and rolling it into position, shoved the wheel onto the axle.

Slipping the retaining pin into place, Samuel stood back to survey his work. The wagon balanced easily on the front wheels now, the rear of the wagon slanting to the ground.

Jill clapped and called from the shade, "Bravo."

Samuel grinned at her and wiped the sweat from his brow with the back of his hand. "Well, I don't know what that means, but I'll take it as a kind word."

Eyeing the exact place where he would begin sawing, he used a bent nail and marked a straight line from side to side. He studied the wagon again from another angle before lifting the saw. He glanced at Jill. "Measure twice, cut once." Squinting, he lined the saw with the mark and began cutting the wagon in two.

Leaving Samuel to his work, Jill rose and walked into the store. Mr. Billings busied himself with another customer, a man in a suit, and she didn't intend to intrude on his business. Rather, she strode to the front of the store and stood on the stoop, covertly watching the headquarters building.

Was Samuel right about Lieutenant Alcott when he'd reported the military officer looked at her with interest? A warm glow started in her belly and worked its way into her chest at the thought. Alcott was, after all, a Yankee. But he was also a gentleman, a man of class and position.

A bird called from the distant river, and Jill peered that way, searching for the creature among the leaves. The greenery had already begun to change colors, heralding the approaching winter. A bitter smile played on her lips, remembering last spring and the closing of the ladies college. So much had happened since then.

The screen door slammed behind her, and the man in a suit tipped his hat to her as he hurried down the steps. Her gaze followed him a short distance until the line of squat trees and thick foliage along the river arrested her attention again. She had dreamed of this river and the open prairies beyond. Now here she was. Was she to stay? What if she never received a letter from the east, requesting her to return?

She tilted her head, studying her surroundings. The river was nothing to write home about, but the wide sky was spectacular. So big, immense. She loved to watch the occasional cloud skitter across the blue canopy. Honking geese sounded above her, and she scanned the sky, finding the V-shaped wedge as the Canadian geese migrated south for the winter.

Her gaze strayed back to the river, a thin ribbon of water shimmering through the undergrowth that choked the banks. She frowned and wrinkled her nose. Something about that ugly river taunted her, and she felt drawn to it for reasons she couldn't fathom. It certainly couldn't compete with the mighty Ohio or the magnificent, powerful Mississippi. Even the Missouri carried more charm. The Platte was plain ugly. Dirty, shallow, filled with shoals and tiny islands, yet she admitted the waterway had a charm of its own. It made her smile.

"How's he doing?"

Mr. Billings's unexpected question made her jump, and Jill's hand flew to her throat. "You startled me, Mr. Billings. I was thinking about ... uh, thinking of the river and the people out here."

The storekeeper chuckled, gesturing to the nearby waterway. "Well, that river is vital to this land. The water is essential, no doubt, but it supports a trail to the west too. The Oregon Trail, numerous stage routes, water, and wood for the Indians. I've even heard rumors that one day a railroad will follow this old river."

Jill laughed, wondering at the foolish talk of idle men. "Oh no, surely a railroad will never be built out here. Why consider it? There is not the population to support such an endeavor."

Mr. Billings shrugged. "Not now, but maybe one day. The land is good for farms, good soil. With Mr. John Deere's steel plow, this prairie can be cultivated. Plenty of room for towns. And the train will connect the east to California. They say there's gold out there, beautiful farmland, and two growing seasons a year."

Jill smiled courteously, allowing the storekeeper his irrational remarks. Captain Bridgett's similar prediction came to her, and she stopped herself from rolling her eyes. A train out here and two growing seasons in California? What men would not think up to attempt to fool or tease women?

"I'd better check on Samuel." She hurried away, irritated the storekeeper had intruded on her reverie with his ridiculous claims. She made her way around back, spying a sweaty Samuel still working on cutting the narrow wagon. Jill paused, searching for a shady spot to wait, reluctant to return to her initial place near the store. Her eye was drawn to the open-sided barn, cast off furniture stacked haphazardly under the protective roof.

Jill glanced again at Samuel before moving to the shaded barn. A meadowlark called, and a hawk cried from the woods near the river. At the edge of the covered building, various cupboards and wardrobes stood, concealing most of the interior pieces. Moving past these, Jill saw couches and overstuffed chairs strewn across her path. Forced to weave among the furniture, she eyed them for significance to the stage station. They'd already taken advantage of Mr. Billings's charity, borrowing a few beds and a table along with two dresser drawers. An oak chest lay at the foot of her bed, containing the winter clothes Mr. Stanton had sent to her from St. Louis.

She kept looking. A grandfather clock held no appeal for her. Stacks of discarded books lay in piles between other pieces.

Then she saw a larger piece, and her heart beat more slowly, almost reverently. One of the pianos she'd noticed when they'd first come to town stood beside a walnut wardrobe, a pink cushioned bench sat before the musical device. Jill hesitated and then crept toward the instrument. When was the last time she'd played?

Her fingers stretched over the keys as she took her seat, her feet searching for the pedals. Lightly, she caressed the ivory keys, the touch reminding her of former days of parties, recitals, and courses on proper social behavior. She began to play, the music wafting around her, taking her back to a time when war wasn't an issue, when runaway slaves weren't a consideration ... when her parents still lived, sending her small amounts of money to support her selfish lifestyle.

The piano dearly needed tuning, yet Jill didn't mind the rough chords as a tear slipped down her cheek. Ignoring the ache in her heart, she plunged into the moment with the melody of the music as her fingers darted across the keys. She had never been an excellent pianist, not willing to give the time that title demanded. But here, with the silent, discarded furniture around her, she played for herself, immersing herself into her memories, wondering where the Lord wanted her to go. Was this place in Nebraska for her? Did Lieutenant Alcott have any hold on her heart? Or was she to stick to the plan and take her God-given teaching talents to the east?

Her heart swelled, her chest throbbing as she cried, tears streaming unchecked. Samuel had said she would grieve when the time was right. Now, she grieved. For her parents, for her career, for her future. She thought she had loved the South, the refinement, the social maneuvering. Yet, now that she was away from the tumultuous merry-go-round, she realized she loved Nebraska even more. The vast beauty and solitude of the prairie called to her, calmed her, refreshed her weary soul. Here she had friends, real friends, a living. And her relationship with the Lord had deepened, flourishing in ways she'd never considered.

"What do you want from me, Father? Am I to go back or stay here? You know my heart. I will do whatever you say. Your will be done," she prayed as she played, but no answer came to her.

God had brought her here, using Samuel and an unknown piece of land to guide her steps to Nebraska. To a new family and a beautiful home, yet a restlessness still filled her. Was she to return east? The stage station did not provide enough income to sustain the farm. And now she loved Jesus more than life itself. Wouldn't he guide her?

As she neared the finale, she closed her eyes, forgetting the late summer heat pressing upon her and the smell of rain clouds building on the horizon. Samuel had predicted rain later.

Instead, Jill thought of the river, the rippling waters that lapped the low islands and the wooded banks. The Platte River called to her, like it had in St. Louis, but now Jill sensed the pull more acutely. Her heart yearned to call this place home. She wanted to settle down, enjoy her friends, and build the farm and the stage station. She wanted a life in Nebraska. The glimmer of fine chandeliers lighting social events with finely dressed people had grown dim in her mind. The luster of the South no longer held any desire for her. She'd come to love the prairies in deep ways.

But her faith was deeper still, deeper than her love of Nebraska. Hadn't Jill learned anything from her selfish lifestyle of before? Now was not the time to think of herself, her desires. She would follow the Lord, his guidance, his will.

Yes, Jill thought as the final notes trailed off, she would submit and obey God. With slow, somber moves, she struck the last chords, her wrists resting on the edge of the tray as she bowed her head, the final note drifting away on the stuffy air.

Thunderous applause descended around her, cascading like a waterfall, and Jill opened her eyes. Big John beamed at her, dressed in his leather apron, and Mr. Billings clapped enthusiastically. Samuel was there too, smiling proudly at her. A few soldiers in blue clustered just beyond, clapping politely. And near the Yankee blue coats, Lieutenant Alcott stood, smiling, his eyes shining as he stared at her.

Her heart lurched at sight of the regal officer. Was this a sign? Would God speak so quickly after her fervent prayer?

Jill dabbed at her damp eyes and smiled, embarrassed at her unexpected audience, yet her heart warmed. Had she ever received such an ovation before?

CHAPTER 35

More than two hours passed before Samuel finished cutting the wagon in half. He stopped often to check his work, making sure his saw cut straight. With a final groan, the last plank snapped, severed in two. Jill eyed the short wagon with a critical eye, then shrugged, pleased at how it balanced on only two wheels.

Samuel hitched the horse into place. Stooping, he gathered pieces of the severed section of wagon that might prove useful. "I'll fashion a tailgate from these pieces at home."

Home? Jill climbed into the dray, shifting as the little wagon leaned. Was Peach Tree Farm her home? Certainly, it was for now, but something Samuel said made her search the pair of clouds gliding above her.

"Am I home, Lord?" she whispered. She glanced over her shoulder, watching Samuel pick up loose boards, then studied the clouds once more. "You know what I'm thinking. I'm a teacher. Surely you want me to go east to teach again. But ..." She hesitated, frowning at the sky. "But if you have other plans for me, show me. I want to give you my heart, my future, my dreams. Guide me."

Samuel loaded the spare planks in back and scrambled beside her, taking the reins. He grinned at Jill as he rolled his sleeves down once more. With a wipe of his arm across his brow, he called to the horse and jiggled the leather reins. The horse moved off, the wagon lurching as it left the grassy place behind the store and glided onto the dusty road. Jill glanced over her shoulder, a somber smile tugging at her lips as she watched the open-air barn disappear from view.

Samuel clucked to the horse. "I'm impressed how smoothly the wagon rolls." He indicated the trotting horse. "Look, he likes how light it feels, probably much different than the heavy farm wagon he's used to."

Jill grinned in return, the wind whipping her honey-colored hair as she gripped the side of the seat. With a flick of his wrist, Samuel urged the horse faster. Jill squealed, then laughed as she abruptly realized she'd forgotten to ask Mr. Billings about any letters for her from the east. She patted the wagon. "It's wonderful, Samuel."

As the little wagon passed the empty parade ground, Samuel glanced toward the military buildings before he spoke. "I saw that Yankee officer speaking with you after you played the piano."

His observation held a note of accusation, as if she'd done something wrong, and Jill shifted on the seat. "Lieutenant Alcott said he enjoyed hearing me play. Said he intends to visit soon."

Samuel said nothing to this, but Jill recalled the officer's praise and surprising presence. As if by magic, he'd appeared while she prayed, begging for answers. Was God speaking to her?

As they left Fort Kearny behind, the cart rolled straight. "I'm pleased," Samuel said, gesturing to the half wagon beneath them.

Jill smiled and wondered if her fortunes had indeed shifted. Perhaps she would stay in Nebraska.

With a shout of pleasure, Samuel leaned his head back and started to sing. At first, he sang low and deep, then his voice gained strength, and Jill joined in, the hymn belted out in full measure.

When they finished that song, Samuel led with another, the pair singing as loud as they could. Jill felt her chest tighten as the worship song touched her heart, unexpected emotions cascading over her in a wave. Tears stung at her eyes for the second time today, the wind whistling past them, the little wagon bouncing merrily as the horse trotted swiftly from Fort Kearny along the southern bank of the meandering river. The first time, she'd cried for the daunting circumstances that overwhelmed her. Now, she cried for the Lord's tender hand upon her, his restoration, his endless love. Through her struggles, Jesus walked with her, holding her close. His provision of the last few months were abundantly clear, and she praised him. She wanted to shout, but her throat tightened, and she pressed her eyes shut, listening to Samuel continue singing as her heart swelled with joy.

God had brought her here. A variety of horrible events had befallen her, challenging her, yet growing her faith too. Her words to Tim resurfaced, and she nodded to herself. *God loves me and he allows suffering.* She loved God more than she thought possible. He had saved her, not only from financial ruin, but from loneliness and sorrow. She would always miss her parents, but now she was surrounded by a new family, one that shared her daily struggles. What had she done to deserve such love and happiness?

She pried her eyes open to peer down the road, Samuel singing beside her, apparently oblivious of her sudden silence. Ahead, she spied the ford.

She studied him from the corner of her eye as the wagon slowed, preparing to enter the path to the river. Jill watched the trees surround them as the dray turned into the narrow avenue carved through the foliage.

Samuel gripped the reins securely and looked ahead, unaware Jill studied him. He seemed so calm, so strong, so steadfast in his faith. She silently thanked God for Samuel and turned to watch the horse as Samuel encouraged the farm animal to move on, stepping bravely into the swirling, muddy water of the Platte River.

The little dray lurched and swayed as the wagon was pulled across the shallow river. Jill surveyed the water rushing around them, the mud sucking under the turning wheels. *Life was like this*, she thought suddenly, peering eagerly to the opposite bank. *You're thrown into the mud, and only the Lord can drag you out, but the bank might be a long way off. I must wait on the Lord. God will bring me through, in his timing.*

Jill laughed as they emerged from the river, water dripping from the lone horse as it trotted easily through the tree-lined avenue to the clearing before the stone house. She glanced once more to the blue sky overhead, narrowing her eyes and nodding. The Lord had spoken to her. This man beside her was a reminder of God's provision. God would answer her. She was not alone, and she could be patient and wait on the Lord. He would tell her which way to go. Perhaps he already had.

As the pair approached the house, Jill saw Tim close the door behind him, halting on the porch. Although Samuel chuckled with pleasure as he drew up in front of him, Tim's eyes locked on her. Jill cringed beneath his piercing stare.

"Have you been crying?"

She turned away and wiped her eyes quickly, not replying. But Tim stepped from the porch, coming closer to the dray. "Jill? Are you all right?"

"We've been singing praise songs," Samuel explained. "Must've touched her deep."

Tim snorted, still staring.

"I'm fine," Jill sniffled, facing Tim. His anxious gaze unnerved her, but she lifted her chin. "Actually, I've had a wonderful time in town."

The farmer tilted his head, a questioning look on his face she couldn't ignore. But again, Samuel interjected.

"While I sawed the wagon, Miss Jill played a piano in the furniture shed. Everyone came to watch, even that Yankee officer."

"Lieutenant Alcott?" Tim's eyes blazed.

Jill sniffled again. "He was very kind," she said softly.

A pained look came into Tim's eyes she couldn't understand, but Jill nodded, recalling the impromptu recital, her prayers, and the appreciative crowd. Again, she wondered if the Lord had spoken to her.

"I can build a tailgate from this spare lumber I took off the rear of the wagon." Samuel indicated the pile of scrap lumber in the short bed behind the seat. Tim nodded absently as he stepped closer, pretending to scrutinize the little wagon. But Jill caught his eye, and hurriedly turned away.

"How do you like her?" Samuel asked, still grinning with pride as he indicated the short wagon.

Tim nodded again "She's beautiful. Looks great." He paused and shifted his boots before peering at the cart once more. "If you can train that little horse to pull, this rig is certainly light enough for even the mare to handle."

Jill leaped from the wagon and Reyna joined the trio in the yard to inspect Samuel's handiwork.

"Samuel," Reyna breathed, her eyes bright. "I'll be able to fly to town in this little rig."

Tim glanced at Reyna and narrowed his eyes. "Reyna, I'll make you a comfortable seat cushion from that ripped blanket the last stage left behind. This rig will be for your special use."

His sudden and encouraging words to Reyna made everyone stare.

The young girl regarded her uncle for a long moment. Then, she nodded once. "That would be grand, Uncle Tim. The good Lord would have us serve one another." Turning, she marched into the house, her back stiff as a board.

CHAPTER 36

Samuel swung the heavy, curved reaper, mowing rows of grass, the stems falling under the sharpened blade of the farm implement. For the last two weeks, Samuel and Tim had worked from sunup to sundown, cutting and stacking hay for the coming winter. The pile of cut prairie grass rose gradually as they added to the haystack each day.

The mound grew steadily, purposefully placed on the south side of the small barn to protect the stack of hay from the northern winds of the prairie winter. The barn contained only a few stalls and was too small for storing the large supply of winter feed.

Nearby, Tim gathered the cutting. As large beads of sweat flew from Samuel's face and arms, he worked on and on, outperforming Tim's best efforts.

Retrieving a bucket of water, Tim called for a break. Samuel stopped the reaper and then mopped his brow as Tim handed him the dipper. He drank thirstily, water sliding down his neck as he drained the tin dipper.

"Ahhhh," Samuel said at last, handing the ladle back to Tim. "Thanks. I needed that."

Tim took the scoop and pointed it at the dark bank of clouds on the horizon.

Samuel nodded. "I saw it too."

The farmer crossed his arms over his chest, staring at the thunderclouds. "When?"

Samuel glanced once more at the coming storm and positioned the reaper, taking a fresh hold on the handle as Tim moved a safe distance away. "Tonight, I reckon, if we're lucky. I think today is our last day."

Samuel's prediction proved correct. By late afternoon, the wind increased, and early darkness descended. The clouds scurried across the sky, worrying Tim as he hurried to gather all the hay he could.

They pulled the heavily laden wagon alongside the barn just as a heavy drop struck Tim's arm. He glanced up, studying the gloomy sky that had surrounded them all afternoon. The first drop of rain was quickly followed by a second and then came in a rush, the deluge soaking the two men before they could empty the wagon.

Samuel grabbed the pitchfork and tossed the hay onto the heap next to the barn as Tim unhitched the team. He led the weary animals into the snug barn, the small Indian pony nickering at the company from her own stall. Chickens cackled loudly, wings flapping as they leaped from his path. Tim drew the team into their stalls and spent a few moments rubbing the heated animals down with a handful of hay before rushing back into the rain to help Samuel.

Together, the sodden men ran through the downpour. Laughing, they stopped briefly on the front porch to shake the cold drops from their hair.

Jill had watched for the men from the window near the big fireplace in the sitting room. When she saw them run for the porch, she quickly poured two mugs of coffee and placed them on the small table by the couch.

They rarely used the fireplace in the sitting room, but today's sudden cold storm warranted the roaring blaze now filling the hearth.

Jill glanced once again at the cheerful fire and the steaming cups on the table before she walked to the entry. Something made her glance swiftly at her reflection in the mirror, and she tucked a rebellious chestnut strand behind her ear. Frowning at her unexpected impulse, she opened the front door.

"Get in here before you catch a cold," she called to the two men. "Don't you have sense enough to come in out of the rain?"

With wide grins, the two wet men stomped their shoes before entering the house. Reyna appeared in the entry and handed each man a small kitchen towel. Drying their faces and necks, they retrieved the hot mugs and stepped eagerly to the fireplace, their backs to the roaring blaze.

"Well, haying is done for this season," Tim declared, sipping his drink. "I have to say I think we did a great job. Of course, I don't know what a real winter looks like on this prairie, but if we were in Tennessee, I could guarantee we have enough winter hay for three horses."

"So, is this winter, then?" Reyna asked, seating herself on the empty couch. The calico kitten quickly leaped onto her lap and curled contentedly.

Jill handed Tim a cookie. He popped the treat into his mouth whole, not bothering to take small bites. Her heart lurched in her chest when he smiled his thanks. Startled at her reaction, she studied the wet farmer for a moment before looking away.

"Well," Tim said, "This is the first winter I don't have a hundred things to accomplish before the storms arrive."

"What do you mean?" Jill seated herself on the couch beside Reyna.

The rain slapped against the windowpanes, and Jill wondered if they should light the lamp. The room seemed dark and chilly, despite the ruddy glow of the fire. A hiss came from the blaze as the occasional raindrop fell down the chimney.

"Usually I need to cut hay, gather crops from the garden, and pull the final fruit from trees. Apple season just ended. I'd have apples in the press by now, making cider."

Samuel nodded in agreement. "That's true enough. With the trees being so young, no harvest this year. Also, we got here too late in the season to plant a garden." He paused, sipping his hot drink. "It'll be a different story next year."

"True," Tim agreed. "But the winter is soon upon us. We can repair tools, finish that tailgate on the half wagon, work on breaking the pony to harness, and relax for a while."

Jill appraised the blanket that covered the broken windowpane. A dark dampness spread across the material, despite being under the protection of the porch. It would be soaked through soon enough, if the storm continued to rage, the rain blown by the wind. Mr. Billings had said he could not promise when the requested pane might arrive. Supplies from Omaha could come at any time.

"I wish we could get glass before snow flies."

All eyes turned to the blanket, its red color darkening from rain. The cover billowed suddenly from another gust of wind.

"I'll ride to Fort Kearny when the storm breaks," Tim promised. "Maybe by then the new window will have arrived. If not, we'll nail boards from the broken wagon across the window for the winter."

CHAPTER 37

Two days passed where the rain barely let up, its cold becoming more and more intense with each hour until the storm raged itself out, leaving sporadic sprinkles and dull sunlight streaming between dark clouds.

On the third day, Tim decided he'd ride to town.

"Reyna, why don't you come with me," he said as he shrugged into his coat.

A stunned look swept quickly over the young girl's face before she just as swiftly agreed to go along.

Jill sidled close to Reyna. "Are you all right, going to town with Tim?"

Reyna nodded, eyes wide.

"Perhaps he'll finally apologize."

A scowl creased the young girl's features, and Reyna shook her head. "He told Samuel he doesn't believe in apologizing. But I've been praying, and I trust the Lord will use this time wisely."

Jill frowned at her confident remark, and then watched as the pair departed for the barn. A few minutes later, Tim waved to Jill and Samuel as the half wagon sped toward the ford.

As the dray moved toward the avenue, Tim glanced at the woods where trees stood like sentinels. He waved to Jill and Samuel, then pursed his lips. He couldn't blame Jill for the anxiety he'd read in her eyes. He felt it too, knowing he'd hurt Reyna with his insensitive words about being stuck with someone he didn't want. He'd been encouraged when Reyna allowed him to build a seat cushion for the half wagon, a kind of truce struck between them. But how could he tell her he didn't feel burdened by her anymore? Reyna could be annoying with all of her God talk, but she was family ... the only family he had left.

Tim gripped the reins as the dray dropped into the shaded avenue that led to the river. A scattering of bright yellow and orange leaves surrounded him, few remaining, and clinging tenaciously to the almost bare limbs. The season was far advanced, and Tim wondered when they'd see the first snow. Not only winter approached, but he wondered what this trip with his niece might bring.

The little cart moved more rapidly than the heavy, cumbersome farm wagon. The lone horse pulling the two-wheeled vehicle seemed unsure of such an easy load. The gelding leaned into the traces, but Tim pulled on the reins, not wanting this trip to pass too swiftly.

Tim smiled to himself, pleased. Samuel had been right. This light rig would make town trips easy and quick. But today, he wanted time with Reyna.

He gripped the reins tighter now as he studied Reyna from the corner of his eye. Tim nudged her, smiling with a feigned cheerfulness he hoped would set a cheerful mood. He needed to speak soon and hoped he had practiced the right words.

Crisp air greeted them as they neared the river, and Tim wished he'd brought his gloves. The rutted, muddy road was hard packed now, frozen from last night's chill. The road would thaw during the warm day, as he hoped Reyna would, and forgive him. He'd have to be careful.

He felt reluctant to begin the conversation, but enough time had passed, and he knew the moment had come to address the issue between him and Reyna. He glanced into the dull brown and gray woods beside the path.

Despite the latest rainstorm, the river was at its lowest point since their arrival at Peach Tree Farm. The snow melt of the Rockies to the west had ended in mid-summer. Now only a shallow sheet of water covered the sandy bottom of the river. Large, brush-covered islands peeped through the slowly gliding brown water.

Tim cleared his throat and glanced at Reyna before facing forward once more. "You know," he began, attempting to break the frigid silence. "There's a German settlement just east of the fort. About forty miles, I think. Called Grand Island." He leaned closer to Reyna, hoping she'd say something. He scowled when she didn't respond.

With a tug on the reins, Tim slowed the dray even more as the horse stiff-legged gingerly to the water's edge. Water splashed, and the horse snorted as the little wagon careened across the low river.

They crossed without incident, the wheels threatening to stick in the mud, but Tim felt his anxiety grow as they scrambled up the opposite bank and moved into the cover of the leaning trees that guarded the path through the thick foliage. The horse turned knowingly into the road that followed the river, and Tim could feel his stomach knot, the time growing near when he would have to explain why he'd asked Reyna to join him on this cold and dreary day. Fort Kearny was not far away.

A few more awkward minutes passed before Tim tried again. "That big buffalo herd the Arapahoe were following has moved to the south. The soldiers told me so."

Again, no response.

He shifted, feeling the tension hunch his shoulders. "They say there were Pawnee, Cheyenne, some Sioux, and of course the Arapahoe, all hunting the huge herd. The Indians don't all get along, you know."

Reyna said nothing to this.

Tim fumed and narrowed his eyes, his bushy brows bunching in consternation. Just as he was about to make another attempt, Reyna spoke up.

"I'm glad we have this time to talk, Uncle Tim," she said abruptly.

A sense of peace filled Tim, and he sensed the rift had slackened between them. He smiled, pleased he'd weathered this storm with his niece. His face fell as she continued.

"Samuel told me about your god," she said in an accusing tone, her thick Irish accent stressing the final word.

For a second, Tim scowled into the distance, trying to comprehend what she meant. Then he remembered his offhand conversation with Samuel a few weeks ago. He shifted again on the seat and his smile returned, recalling the words he'd used to describe his idea of the perfect deity. Perhaps this day would not be as difficult as he'd feared.

"Reyna, I was just teasing," he said, hoping his grin would persuade her. He felt happy to be talking again with his stubborn niece, no matter the topic, but he knew how notional she could be. Especially when it came to spiritual discussions.

"Teasing?" she snapped. "You told him I annoyed you with all my spiritual talk. Was that teasing?"

He squirmed. "Maybe Samuel talks too much," he growled. "Reyna, you know you get me riled when you go on about Jesus all the time. I was talking foolishness with Samuel, that's all."

"Is this your way of apologizing? Samuel said your god doesn't care if you ask for forgiveness when you offend someone." Her crisp words tripped over one another, her thick accent making it difficult for him to follow.

Then he huffed, his scowl deepening as he looked at her. He glanced hurriedly to the forest, searching for particular trees. Yet even this favorite pastime couldn't calm his raw nerves.

He drew in a deep breath as his eyes darted back to the road. "Reyna, I took you in after Kathleen died, and I'm glad I did. You're my kin. I love you as my sister's kid. But sometimes your Bible talk wears on me. It gets annoying."

"I know it annoys you. Samuel told me so." Reyna nodded, crossing her arms over her chest.

They rode on in a tense silence, and Tim wondered how he could avoid an argument. This wasn't how this ride to town was supposed to go.

"I have been praying," Reyna continued after the short break. "God has told me what to do."

Afraid of her possible answer, Tim squared his shoulders and took the bait. "What did the Almighty God of the universe reveal to you?" He didn't attempt to conceal the sarcasm, but Reyna ignored his tone.

"He has told me it is not my job to make you a Christian. The Bible says that's the job of the Holy Spirit. It is only my job to share my faith. My conscience is clear. I have done what the Lord would have me do."

Tim glanced at his now-quiet niece, wondering if she would say more. He flicked the reins again, the trotting horse's hooves beating a rhythmic pattern on the dirt road. He had intended on making a half-hearted apology and clearing the air with Reyna. Now, he saw his mistake in allowing her to trap him alone on the wagon. He peered ahead to see if the buildings of Fort Kearny were visible yet. Nothing. He shifted uneasily on the thick seat cushion.

Tim turned on her. "Look, I asked you to ride to town with me so we can work out our problems. I'm not looking for an argument. I just want things to be like they were before."

Reyna shrugged, not looking at him. "That's fine, Uncle Tim. We can act like this never happened. Your eternal resting place is on your head, not mine. I have done what I should do as a Christian. Let's enjoy the ride." She stared stern-faced down the road.

Tim felt himself go cold as he watched her lips moving silently. A chill ran down his spine, and he knew she was praying. Praying for him?

Tim ground his teeth, then licked his lips. "Eternal resting place?" He repeated the words slowly, his head tilting.

"Yes." Reyna smirked at him. "Doesn't your god allow you into some kind of heaven after you die? Surely you didn't think you'd go to the heaven described in the Bible, the one reserved for those who love the God of the Bible. You couldn't want to go there." It was her turn to be sarcastic, and it rankled him.

Tim squirmed even more. The thick blanket did little to cushion the hard seat beneath him. "Well, I thought—"

"I know exactly what you thought," Reyna interrupted, waving a dismissive hand. "You thought you could live any way you want, selfish and self-absorbed, disobey God and all of his guidance, and still go to heaven with all the people who chose to love God and try to obey his wise boundaries."

Her words struck him like a splash of icy water, and his eyes widened. That was precisely what he thought. Tim wanted to go to heaven, but he didn't want to listen to God's words. He didn't want to hear about the need for repentance. He didn't want to change himself or his beliefs.

He shook his head and squeezed the reins, his gaze fixed on the horse's ears. "I always imagined I would go to heaven where my folks and Kathleen are," Tim admitted in a low voice.

"Why would you believe you go to the heaven God talks about in the Bible when you don't believe in it or him or anything he has to say? Or maybe your god has his own heaven, different from the one where Christians go when they die."

Tim slapped the reins sharply, making the horse pick up his pace. He didn't like Reyna's tone or implication. "I'm not such a bad fellow," Tim said defensively.

Reyna arched an eyebrow. "According to who?"

Tim shifted in his seat to look directly at his niece. "I'm better than most. I work hard, I don't get drunk, and I've never killed anyone." His self-analysis pleased him, and he nodded as he turned back toward the road.

"That is your assessment of your goodness, not God's. According to his standards, we have all fallen short of his glory. Our best is not good enough for him."

His forehead furrowed with Reyna's critical response. "That's ridiculous. Then who can go to heaven?"

Reyna moved closer, and Tim felt their shoulders touch. "Well, no one is good enough to go to heaven, not on their own merits," Reyna explained. "Only by accepting the sacrifice Jesus made for us on the cross can someone be allowed to enter heaven." She paused and then quoted, "'I am the way, the truth, and the life. No one comes to the Father except through me.'"

He recognized the Scripture from previous debates. "Sounds like a trick. A person has to accept Jesus, or they can't go to heaven. Why can't we just try and be good? Sounds fair to me," Tim persisted. This God stuff was too much work. Thank goodness he'd caught sight of Fort

Kearny on the horizon. He flicked the reins, making the horse quicken once more. Town would put a stop to this nonsense, he hoped.

"It is no trick," Reyna said in a soft voice. "It's God's grace. A free gift to us we don't deserve. It is love."

Tim snorted loudly. "Love? How is that love, if God sends people to hell?"

"It's their choice," Reyna went on. "'God so loved the world that he gave his one and only Son, that whoever believes in him shall not perish but have eternal life.' If they choose not to, then they choose eternity away from God. Their choice, not his."

Tim scowled and pressed his lips tightly shut. He vowed not to speak, not to respond to Reyna's taunting words. The little snippet seemed to have a ready reply to any of his arguments, arguments he'd based his life on without much deep thought, he admitted to himself.

He felt angry now, angry at himself and angry at being bested by a young girl. His flippant, shallow replies had gotten him nowhere. He narrowed his eyes, realizing the discussion had not gone as he'd intended. Tim barely gave the ring of trees around the parade ground a second glance as he tugged on the reins and halted the half wagon before Mr. Billings's store.

Leaping down before Reyna could add more, Tim marched toward the store. As he mounted the steps, he glanced again at his silent niece, his anger burning even hotter when he saw her still on the wagon seat, eyes closed, lips moving.

Not fifteen minutes passed before Tim reappeared with the heavy windowpane. Moving gently, he loaded the narrow window in the small bed of the cart. "Reyna, you'll have to hold this upright as we move. You cannot allow it to fall. We'd never get another window before spring."

Scrambling over the back of the seat, Reyna sat facing backward, pinning the windowpane between her knees.

Tim remounted and turned the horse around, slowly walking down the hard-packed street, past the blacksmith shop and the parade ground, and out of town. The return trip would force them to take their time, allowing Reyna to resume the previous debate over whose God was greater. Tim suddenly regretted his desire to share some time with his chatty niece.

He jumped when Reyna reached over the seat and patted his arm. "It's all right, Uncle Tim. We don't have to continue discussing your god. There is only one God, and he is the Almighty. Other gods have tried to fight against him, but to no avail."

Tim's ears pricked at this information. "Other gods? What other gods fought your God?"

He could feel Reyna's stare on the back of his head. She had his interest again, and he cursed himself for a fool. Couldn't he just keep his mouth shut? He frowned, hoping she wouldn't answer hm.

"In the Book of First Kings, God's prophet, Elijah, duels with the four hundred prophets of Baal. They are all destroyed, and Baal is made to look ridiculous and weak. There is only one real God, the others are imposters, made up by people who don't want to obey and love their Creator." Here she paused, letting her words sink in. Tim shifted, guiding the walking horse around a deep rut in the road.

"Just like your god. It can't really *do* anything. You can't even go to heaven following your god. Only the true God, and his only Son, Jesus, can promise things and deliver you from your sins."

Tim half turned at this declaration. "So, your God can promise things? Like what?"

Without hesitation, Reyna answered. "God the Father promises us that he will never leave us or forsake us. He promises to always help us and strengthen us. He also promises that if we accept Jesus as his Son and the sacrifice he made on the cross, we will have eternal life with him in heaven."

Tim didn't say anything to this, but hung his head, pondering her words. Only the constant wind and the sound of the wheels sloshing through the puddles in the trail broke the heavy silence.

Tim continued to drive the half wagon slowly along the rutted road, making sure to keep the vehicle from the deep puddles and deeper ravines. It bothered him he could not push the nagging ideas Reyna had introduced from his mind. Previously, he'd always discounted them as the ranting of a missionary's child. For some unknown reason he could not fathom, the ideas now persisted, and he could not shake the feeling they were somehow supremely important to his life.

CHAPTER 38

Since Tim and Reyna had returned from Fort Kearny, Tim seemed more argumentative and sarcastic with Jill and her fellow Christians. One by one, the verbally combative tree farmer drove them further away. Jill had hoped the pair would solve their differences, and Tim would see the light. However, he seemed still uninterested in hearing about Jesus and did not wish to be subjected to Bible lessons while he worked with his housemates. Instead, he took every opportunity to show where his "faith" was stronger and more reliable than a joy based on a man who'd died on a cross.

"He seems so agitated," Jill whispered to Reyna after an explosive argument one day after breakfast when Tim had slammed his hat on his head and stomped from the house.

Reyna nodded, watching through the new window as Tim entered the barn. "He's stewing, pondering the deep things of God. The Spirit is working."

Stagecoaches rolled less frequently now into the yard—cold weather slowing traffic on the plains. Only a few courageous travelers braved the frigid trails and increasing danger of crossing the prairie in winter.

Samuel spent long, patient hours working with the smaller Indian pony that Reyna had named Lila. Though not as large as the other horses on the farm—it would be impossible for her to work in tandem with the bigger, stronger team—Lila did possess the necessary strength to pull the dray.

Jill now peered out into the desolate yard as a few curled leaves skittered across the hard-packed dirt clearing. Out beyond the barn, she could see where Reyna watched Samuel working with Lila. Jill shivered, grateful to be indoors on such a chilly day.

Her gaze shifted to the new window she stood before. Additional light filtered into this room now, despite the gloomy weather that often inflicted the land these days. She stared out of the clear pane, studying the gray, dismal day that greeted her, not completely unlike the dreary winter days she remembered from Missouri.

Jill chewed her bottom lip, arms crossed over her chest, as she pondered her predicament. Wrinkles furrowed her brow as she thought of how much had happened to her in such a short span of time.

The fireplace at the front of the house and the stove along the back wall made this long room the most comfortable space in the house. She was safe and warm, thanks to the hard work of her three companions, none of whom she'd known a year ago.

The back door burst open, and Jill turned, watching Tim stagger in under a load of firewood. He kicked the door shut, muting the howling wind outside. Jill hurried to pour a hot cup of coffee.

Wood tumbled into the firebox, and Tim straightened, brushing bark from his hands. As he turned, his eyes widened when Jill held out the steaming mug. For a brief moment, she thought he'd refuse, then he reached for the mug, his eyebrows bunching as he blew on the cup.

"So? I haven't scared you off with my sour mood? I appreciate the coffee, but I don't want to talk about Bible things," he growled.

"Truce," Jill promised, smiling at Tim.

He gestured with his mug toward the window where she'd stood. "Were you watching Samuel work with Lila, or waiting for the army? I hate when they visit, but you seem to enjoy their invasions."

Jill laughed, happy to be speaking civilly with Tim once more. She nodded. "I do enjoy their visit. Breaks up the day and gives us something to talk about. I appreciate any news of the east. The war won't let up, and I'm worried for myself, my future, but more importantly, I'm worried for this country. What will happen, Tim?"

The farmer made his way to the blazing fire and turned his back to the heat before replying. "I'm not sure. I wanted only to escape the coming conflict, to save my trees. I didn't care about the country."

Jill frowned, shocked by his selfish motivation. Then she recalled her own indifference toward the war ... at least until the intrusion had upset her way of life. Her plans had gone awry, but the Lord had something else in mind.

Jill smiled as her gaze swept the large room. Everything had changed for her. Much had been taken away, yet she'd gained much too. "Well, I guess saving the trees was important to you."

Tim took a sip of coffee, watching Jill over the rim of his mug. "That's what I told myself. Trees last and produce good things. But I really fled with the other refugees to avoid the difficulty. Then I met you and Samuel." Tim paused, taking another drink. "The two of you seemed so brave. You were helping him escape slavery, and after meeting Samuel, I realized how little I had considered the lives of slaves. Reyna is right. I am selfish."

Jill stared, astonished by his honesty. "Then you're aware of your ... your—"

He held up a hand. "Don't say it. I already admitted I'm selfish. But then I met you and Samuel. Don't tell Reyna this, but even her preaching has shown me how self-centered I am."

He glanced out the window, and Jill wondered if his gaze searched for his niece. He lowered his voice as he continued.

"It's as if I was led here to learn about myself, and I don't like what I've discovered."

Jill tilted her head, impressed by his candor. "Then you've enjoyed the conversations with Reyna and Samuel?"

Tim looked at her, a lopsided grin on his bearded face. "Absolutely not. Learning is followed by change. Growing pains hurt. Action is required when we learn something new, something better, but it's rarely easy. Now that I know I'm selfish, I know I need to change, but I was comfortable with my old self. I only had to think about me. Now, I have to think about Reyna. And Samuel makes me want to be a better person. And you, well, you make me think things I've never considered."

"Like what?" she whispered.

Tim shrugged. "Like staying in Nebraska. When I fled Tennessee, I had no idea where I'd end up. Now I can't imagine living anywhere else."

Jill bit her lip and turned away, hoping he couldn't see the blush that heated her cheeks. So, he felt the pull of this special place too. She longed to stay here, but she needed to consider the welfare of her friends more than herself. Perhaps if she married well … If she married Lieutenant Alcott, perhaps she could support the farm. With the income from the stage contract, perhaps they could hang on until the farm could produce its own harvest. Surely, the trees would mature in the next few years. Without the necessary money, only a teaching position back east would provide the needed funds to keep the farm afloat until then.

She nodded thoughtfully. Yes, Tim made her think about things too. Like staying in Nebraska, but also serving her new friends. Jill's previous selfish heart had gotten her into a dilemma she never wished to face again. She vowed to think of others first and see what the Lord would do with her.

She fixed her gaze on the crackling blaze in the stone fireplace. "Do you have plans now? I mean, what will you do with these new thoughts that assail you?"

Tim didn't reply immediately, and Jill turned to him, studying his piercing eyes as they bore into her.

"It means I've never thought of love or home or family like I do now. It means I have begun to dream, to allow myself to consider things beyond my personal goals for myself. It means I'm thinking of others for the first time in my life, and I like it. My thoughts have deepened, my dreams have developed. I want things that I never thought possible a few short months ago. That's what I mean, Jill Foster."

Tim's unexpected and honest speech made her turn away again, unable to face him with her own truth. Her thoughts swirled in a confusing tangle, but his loud sigh made her look at him once more.

"But I see the way you look at the lieutenant. I don't know what you see in him, except a pompous Yankee in a blue uniform. But he's on the right side, I see that now. I cursed the day the Union troops swept into Tennessee, but now I understand about the struggles it takes to bring about change. Without this war and those blue-suited devils, slavery would never end. Now I wish them luck. No matter the size of struggle, change is difficult."

Jill smiled, pleased at his personal growth. He'd come a long way since they first met. But a still, small voice whispered to her, reminding her that her friends were more important than her own desires. Her selfish heart had created a nightmare she would not soon forget. Her blossoming relationship with Jesus demanded she consider beyond herself.

A pounding of hooves interrupted her musings, and Jill looked to the northern hills, watching the twin columns of troopers ride into the clearing.

CHAPTER 39

"What do you think of that, Miss Foster?" Lieutenant Alcott asked.

Jill jumped, hoping no one had seen her stealing glances at Tim. She tilted her head as she looked away, pretending to contemplate deep things as she placed her cup on the low table before the couch. Her gaze fixed on the crackling fire, and she considered making excuses. She couldn't very well say she had been watching the tiny curl of Tim's hair dance above his creased brow.

She blushed, embarrassed to be caught inattentive. At least, inattentive to the lieutenant. A lady must always pay attention to a gentleman, even if they're boring.

She lifted her chin and looked at Lieutenant Alcott, smiling her most beautiful smile so he wouldn't realize she hadn't been listening.

"I'm sorry, Lieutenant. What was your question?" Jill fluttered her eyelashes.

The officer smiled. "I asked if you planned on staying on the frontier, or whether this was only a brief stopover? Many people come out here only to determine the life is too difficult. Certainly, a lady of quality such as yourself has noticed our lack of refinement."

If only he knew that she'd pondered this very question many times. How could she say she was waiting to see what God had to say on the topic?

"Time will tell," she replied, attempting to keep her doubts concealed. "Only God knows what the future holds for me."

She felt Tim's eyes upon her. He'd not spoken since the lieutenant arrived, the army patrol taking a break beside the barn as the officer visited inside the comfortable stone house. Now he shifted, his chair creaking loudly as he gaped at her.

"You really don't know? Are you still open to offers from the east? I thought with the stage station doing well, and the farm prepared for future harvest, you wouldn't be able to leave what you've worked so hard to build."

Jill tensed, not wanting to tell him her plans might well depend on the Yankee officer sitting beside her and not opportunities from the east. She smiled broadly. "Well, I have options, I guess. Of course, I hope to hear from Mr. Hopkins, my former headmaster. Perhaps a teaching position will come through soon. Or ..." She paused, batting her eyelids once more at the army officer. "Maybe something else will keep me in the west."

Tim tilted his head, his eyes narrowing. "I know that," he snapped. "But I thought, well, I thought—"

Jill laughed uneasily, cutting him off. "Besides, you mean what you three have built," she said, gesturing to Samuel and Reyna. "I only supplied the land. It is you three who have labored so hard to create this wilderness oasis."

Tim stared at her, his dark eyes piercing, but Jill looked away.

"So, if you were to receive a job offer, you'd return east?" he pressed, leaning forward.

Alcott cleared his throat. "Well, rightly speaking, the east might not be the place for a lady right now. The war has strangled the South. Many towns and farms have been destroyed."

Ignoring the lieutenant, Jill glanced at Tim and shrugged. She wished he could see how the conflict warred within her. She didn't know which way to go, which way she *should* go. Oh, why didn't God send her a telegram, or knock at the door, and simply tell her what to do? She so desperately wanted to do the right thing.

She drew a deep breath and prayed for peace. Go or stay, she would serve the Lord. Could God see her submissive heart? Jill hoped so.

"We will do everything in our power to make you stay," the confident lieutenant interjected with a grin. "This land needs women, strong women, and mothers. Women who come west should stay to help build a new civilization. Look at the social skills and arts of a lady you are imparting to Reyna. All women should possess such qualities. I'm sure it'll only be a matter of time before other ladies of refinement also venture west. You will not be alone out here long, Miss Foster. I can guarantee it."

Alcott paused and then added, "Perhaps, in time, you could open a school out here for pioneer children."

Jill nodded appreciatively at the officer's kind encouragement, but her gaze drifted back to Tim. He stared at Lieutenant Alcott, his eyes blazing.

Alcott put down his cup and reached for his hat as he stood. "I'll not take any more of your time, Miss Foster. The patrol needs to return to the fort. Thank you for the coffee."

"You've had three cups," Tim grumbled under his breath as Jill rose to accompany her visitor to the door. They stepped through to the entry where Alcott shrugged into his thick coat and then tugged his hat low. Samuel held the officer's horse as Alcott signaled for his men to form into columns as he mounted and then tipped his hat to Jill.

"Thank you again, Miss Foster. Until next time."

Jill stood on the porch, her shawl draped tightly around her. She could see her breath in the frigid air and wanted to hurry back into the warmth of the sitting room, but she waved courteously to the troopers as the column left the yard.

As she turned to follow Samuel indoors, she glanced at the sky, noting the darkening clouds hanging low on the horizon. She wrapped her shawl tighter around her.

Walking back into the entry, Jill closed the door behind her. She didn't check her reflection in the hallway mirror before she opened the door into the sitting room, a welcome blast of heat drawing her in.

Tim paced before the roaring fireplace as he spoke. "I find him self-important and arrogant. I don't even know why he bothers to come out here. It's not like any of us enjoy his company."

"I do, immensely," Reyna said as Samuel strode from the kitchen, coffeepot in hand.

"No, you don't," Tim barked, continuing to pace. "I wish he'd stay at Fort Kearny or patrolling the Oregon Trail. Doesn't he have some military duty or obligation that should better occupy him?"

"I think it's obvious why he bothers to visit," Samuel put in as he circled, filling cups.

Tim stopped and looked at him. Jill approached with slow steps, surprised she might be afraid at what Samuel might say. Surely he knew she welcomed the lieutenant's attention. She nodded as she accepted her filled cup from him.

Samuel did not speak for a long minute, returning the pot to the kitchen while Tim glared at him, waiting impatiently.

"Well?" he demanded as Samuel finally took a seat near Reyna. Samuel sipped his steaming mug. "Why do you think he visits?" Tim pressed, unwilling to wait longer for a reply.

NEBRASKA HAVEN

Samuel blew gently on his cup and glanced at the fire before he spoke. "I think the man is taken with Miss Jill."

Jill felt the heat creep up her neck to her cheeks. So, others suspected what she did herself. Lieutenant Alcott *was* interested in her. That was her intention, right? The gentleman would provide the security she needed to help support the farm. And her friends.

Jill bit the inside of her cheek. And why not? Hadn't she encouraged it with her initial interest? He'd been the only man in the region on a social level of a gentleman. She squinted and watched Tim from the corner of her eye, suddenly eager to see his reaction.

Tim's eyes bulged in his red face as he sputtered. "That blue Yankee has no business around this farm. I think I'll tell him to stay away—his presence here is not wanted."

"But how do you know that, Uncle Tim?" Reyna asked, a note of mischief in her voice as she winked at Jill. "Perhaps Jill enjoys the lieutenant's attention. He certainly is dashing, and he's so handsome in his uniform."

Tim's retort choked in his throat. He struggled to regain his composure and then frowned, his gaze turning slowly upon Jill. She read something in his eyes she didn't recognize. Hurt? Anguish? Frustration?

Jill shook her head, clearing her muddled thoughts. She must think of what was best for her friends. The farm had provided the safe haven they all required, and she promised to do everything she could to see they remain on her land, a refuge from the tumultuous events they'd all suffered. A runaway slave, an orphaned girl, and a landless farmer. They needed her, and Jill gloried in the ability she possessed to give them a place to belong. The lessons she'd learned about her self-absorbed ways would serve her well now. God had worked in her, and Jill felt excited that she could do something for those who'd done so much for her.

Jill sipped her coffee as she peered into the flames, pretending to watch the fire dance, as if she hadn't heard the conversation around her. She could feel Tim's gaze on her, but Jill ignored him, grateful a situation had arisen where she could serve them. If the lieutenant was to be her solution to her current crisis, she would accept him gratefully. He was, after all, a gentleman. She could do much worse.

Without another word, Tim left the room, the door slamming behind him. Jill cringed at the racket.

"The poor man seems miserable," Samuel observed as the trio watched through the window as Tim disappeared into the barn.

"He does seem very upset," Reyna agreed, her eyes on Jill.

Jill nodded. "We spoke earlier, before the lieutenant's visit. Tim knows he needs to change, but he's having a hard time. He said change is not easy."

"No, but he has the makings." Reyna patted the kitten on her lap as Jill tilted her head.

"You think he'll come around?" She studied the confident young girl.

Reyna nodded again. "I've seen good things in Uncle Tim," she declared with a note of pride in her voice. "Down deep, he wants to do the right thing."

"How can you be so sure?" Jill drained her cup and glanced at the fire. The blaze settled, and soon someone would have to toss more fuel on the flames.

"Because he took me in," Reyna explained in a soft voice. "He didn't have to, yet he did. Right now, the Spirit has convicted him. In the end, I believe the Lord will call his name."

CHAPTER 40

For the next two days, Jill moved through her routine with a sense of purpose she hadn't experienced before. Now, she wasn't just washing dishes or scrubbing laundry, she was praying while she worked, an important responsibility had been placed on her shoulders. A mission, a focus, drove her. Either she would go or stay, but either way, she would save the farm, thus securing a place for Samuel, Reyna, and Tim. Where Jill had prayed only at specific times of the day—before meals and at bedtime—now she prayed unceasingly. Her faith grew.

"Let me serve my friends, Lord," she whispered as her hands moved through the soapy water. "My heart is for you, to bring you joy. As I learn to love you more, let me show that love to others."

With a lightness in her step, she went from task to task, realizing the significance of her efforts. Lives were changed by prayer. She spent the entire day with God, not just stolen moments.

The dark clouds Jill observed the day Lieutenant Alcott departed proved the prelude to the season's first snow. The ever-present wind buffeted the northern side of the house, screaming wildly as the zephyr rounded corners and whistled under eaves. Driving sleet heralded thicker flakes, quickly turning to a flurry of white, making the barn invisible from the house. The extreme cold soon forced everyone to seek protection from the raging storm.

Tim had continued to evade the nightly prayer meetings held in the comfort of the sitting room, working outside as long as he could. Cutting wood allowed him to keep warm, the swing of the axe making his blood heated as the others enjoyed the warmth of the heated house. He worked long hours in the barn, fixing tools or preparing the runners he and Samuel were shaping for the wagon. Soon the wheels would be replaced by the sled runners for snow travel.

However, the fierce wind and bitter cold finally drove the reluctant Tim into the warm house, where the others gathered before the blazing fireplace, holding Bible study after the day's chores were completed.

He hesitated at the open door as Samuel read the Scripture, his deep voice raised to be heard above the whipping wind. Jill watched Tim from the corner of her eye, an unaccountable curiosity making her observe the farmer covertly, as if she were doing something she shouldn't.

Tim frowned and glanced over his shoulder toward the barn, as if debating whether the solitude and cold of the barn might be preferable. In the end, he closed the door behind him, the heated room winning out.

Slowly, with a deep scowl on his chilled face, he approached the fireplace, as if he were approaching a coiled rattlesnake.

"So, we know that even Jesus felt anguish as he prayed in the Garden of Gethsemane," Samuel pointed out.

"Yes," Reyna agreed, her auburn hair bouncing as she nodded. "The Lord has experienced every human emotion we have, yet he never sinned. He sympathizes with our struggles because he has struggled too."

"That's because Jesus was just a man," Tim interjected from where he stood beside the fireplace, his hands held to the flames. All heads turned in unison at his unexpected intrusion.

He shifted and then lifted his chin. "Jesus was a human, like you or me. Why do you believe he was God?"

Jill shivered with anticipation as she turned to look expectantly at Reyna and Samuel. Surely, one of them would have a good answer. She gripped her mother's Bible tightly, wondering if the Lord had anything to do with driving Tim indoors with the extreme cold.

Before Samuel had returned Mrs. Foster's Bible to Jill, he'd retrieved a replacement from the piles of books at Mr. Billings's store. Jill had never known the significance of owning her own, and the family Bible now felt comforting in her hands.

"The Old Testament teaches that there are a number of prophesies about the coming Christ. Signs to watch for that would indicate the coming Messiah. Jesus fulfilled these prophesies," Reyna explained.

"Really?" Jill tilted her head. Why had she not been taught this in church? "You mean there were signs to watch for that the Jews didn't realize?"

"Oh, they realized these signs would show the Christ, but they refused to see them," Reyna added, her eyebrows arching. "The Jews were expecting a warrior king, someone to free Israel from Roman domination, but Jesus came in peace. He was not what they expected for a Messiah."

"What signs were given about the Christ?" Tim wanted to know, a note of curiosity in his voice Jill had not heard before. He reached for a chair and dragged it closer to the fire.

Jill could feel her jaw drop as Tim leaned forward, waiting. He'd never shown interest in spiritual matters before.

"The Messiah would be from the line of King David, from the tribe of Judah. He would be born in the city of

Bethlehem, he would ride into Jerusalem on a donkey, the sign of a king coming in peace. The Christ would be born of a virgin. He would be betrayed for thirty pieces of silver. He would be hung on a tree, none of his bones broken. His coming would be heralded by one calling out in the desert. That was John the Baptist."

Jill listened in awe as Reyna listed the prophecies about the Christ and the credentials of Jesus as he satisfied each requirement.

"Those are just some of the signs my parents taught me. Besides these prophecies and the miracles he performed, Jesus showed he was the Son of God, the Christ sent to save men from their sins." Reyna narrowed her eyes as she studied Tim. "Only through a relationship with Jesus can a person be saved from their sins. Only with salvation can a person enter heaven."

"Well," Tim mumbled as he leaned back in his chair and ran a hand over his face, "How can someone be saved from their sins? Everyone sins, even you Christians. So how can you go to heaven?"

He straightened his shoulders, as if achieving a great victory, and grinned at his audience, triumphant.

Reyna smiled at her uncle. "I thought you'd never ask. Only through believing in the sacrifice Jesus made for you on the cross can you receive eternal life. Jesus paid the penalty for our sins. He died in our place so we can know God. The Father wants you to have a relationship with him. We are created to worship him, but he is a holy God and cannot look upon sin. Jesus takes that sin away and now we can know the Father."

Jill held her breath, sensing something significant while Reyna hesitated before glancing at the ceiling, a serious look on her face. Then she stared directly at Tim. "Accept Jesus into your heart, Uncle Tim, and know the Father's forgiveness. He loves you dearly and is calling to you."

Slowly, Jill let out her breath as she stared at Tim. Only the whirling wind outside intruded on the silent living room. Would Tim ask to become a Christian? Would Reyna lead her uncle in the sinner's prayer of forgiveness, accepting Christ's sacrifice?

Tim's chair creaked loudly as he shifted his weight, but he said nothing more. Yet Jill read the turmoil behind his eyes.

An awkward silence followed until Samuel spoke, clearing his throat. "That was wonderful, Reyna. I always love hearing about what the Savior did for me on the cross. Let's close in prayer."

Wind howled outside, and Jill saw Tim stalk to the kitchen as Reyna closed the meeting with a prayer. Jill couldn't take her eyes from him. Had he refused to accept God into his heart? Dearly, she hoped he might come to know the joy Jill felt in knowing the Lord.

Jill bit her lip and rose to toss another log on the fire as she organized her thoughts. Would God ever speak to her? What was she to do? She knew God would answer in his timing, but Jill grew impatient, worrying over her future.

As if sensing her distress, Samuel stepped to the mantel, rested an arm on the roughhewn timber, and smiled.

"I can tell your heart is troubled. But don't worry, Miss Jill. You are a child of God. He has a plan for you, a plan that will be right. Be confident that he who began a good work in you will see it to completion. Stay the course and walk with Jesus."

Jill felt her shoulders sag, a sense of relief flooding over her at Samuel's encouraging words. She wasn't alone.

She smiled at him and placed a hand on his arm. "You've been a good friend. Thank you."

"Friends, remember?" He nodded and moved away, leaving her with her own thoughts. She would trust in the

Lord. She would wait and be patient. God knew what was best for her—what was best for her friends—and she could trust God.

That night, the sun seemed to set early, as if eager to depart the extreme cold of the Nebraska plains. Jill knelt before the banked fire, stretching her candle toward the low flames while taking a final glance out the window. Although dark outside, she faintly discerned snow swirling angrily against the clear pane. Winter had finally come, and it would be here for a long time. Jill wondered if there would be other such conversations this season like the one today.

Her candlewick sizzled and caught, and she rose to follow Reyna to their bedroom, a heated brick wrapped in burlap tucked under her arm. Would Tim become a Christian? Would he ever submit his stubborn heart to the Creator?

"Goodnight, Tim," she called as she passed the men's room. "Goodnight, Samuel."

"Goodnight, Jill," a muffled voice called from within, but she couldn't recognize the voice with the wind battering the house.

The door closed softly behind her, and Jill dropped the warmed brick on her bed as she placed the candle on the shelf. Reyna scurried beneath her blankets, kicking her brick into position as she curled into a ball, watching Jill prepare for bed. The young girl's long auburn hair coiled in a thick braid atop her pillow.

"Well, what do you think?" Jill shoved her brick beneath the covers and kicked off her shoes before sliding between the sheets. She shivered violently as she searched for the warm brick with her toes.

"I think the Holy Spirit guided that conversation," Reyna said, her teeth chattering as she shivered.

Jill nodded. "I hope Tim's heart is ready for Jesus."

Reyna stared at Jill for a long moment. "Uncle Tim's heart has already been busy. He's been wrestling other matters."

Jill frowned. "What other matters?"

Reyna bit her lip. "Never mind," she said as she blew out the candle.

That night in their room, Samuel and Tim prepared for bed. Laying work clothes aside and slipping into night shirts, the pair leaped under their own blankets, a bed on either side of the room. Heated stones lay at their feet, and Tim blew out the single candle, plunging the room into total darkness.

Samuel lay shivering for a few minutes before his body warmed enough to relax. He yawned, thinking of Lila and the half wagon, the next step in her training. Would tomorrow's weather cooperate? His thoughts revolved around the harness and commands he planned to use. He thought of the war too, wondering if Lincoln's Yankees would whip the rebels. Samuel knew well how tough the Southern men were. It would not be an easy victory, he mused. The war had lasted far longer than anyone could've guessed.

"Samuel?" Tim's voice stilled his wandering thoughts. Samuel looked up, staring at the unseen second story floorboards above him. "When you became a Christian, did you pray that prayer Reyna spoke about today?"

Suddenly, Samuel was not tired anymore, and his eyes widened. He gripped his blankets and shot a quick prayer toward the invisible ceiling. "Yes, Tim. I prayed when I gave my life to Lord Jesus."

There was a pause before Tim continued. "I know I'm a sinner. I've always been selfish and wanted things my way. Reyna coming to me has opened my eyes to my shortcomings. I see I'm not a good person." There was a longer pause before he spoke again. "I guess I need a Savior," he whispered.

Samuel said nothing but silently prayed fervently for the Holy Spirit to touch Tim's heart, to lead him to Christ's redemptive love.

"Samuel?" Tim continued quietly. "Could you help me pray that prayer of forgiveness?"

With the freezing cold and howling wind outside, Samuel led Tim in the sinner's prayer. Tim confessed his sin, and his need of a Savior. He asked Jesus for forgiveness and welcomed him into his heart, to lead Tim all the days of his life.

Tears stung Samuel's cheeks as he prayed with Tim.

CHAPTER 41

Winter descended with a vengeance, and stage travel slowed even more, but the extra time gave Tim the chance to explore his newfound faith. He hungered for truth and spent hours a day searching the Scriptures. He flooded his housemates with questions regarding Jesus's ministry, and his talks with Reyna helped them each to develop a new relationship between uncle and niece. Instead of bickering, they now became kindred spirits as children of God.

This would be the first year Jill and Tim celebrated the true meaning of Christmas, and both felt excited. The Savior's birth had lacked significance before.

On clear days, Tim and Jill would wander the hills together until the cold sent them home again. One of their favorite destinations was the old peach tree at the head of Peach Tree Creek, its bare branches twisted and gnarled in the bitter winds that roared from the north.

Today, as they stood on the brink of the small stream, they watched the gurgling water course through rocks that had tumbled from the limestone bluff. From a crack in the stone wall, the rivulet poured, meandering across Jill's land on its way to the Platte River.

On the opposite bank, the ancient peach tree leaned, protected from winter's wildest winds in this secluded nook. The tree bent with age, the thick trunk scarred and weathered.

Tim gestured at the crooked tree. "Peach Tree Creek. Best water in the region. I believe the trees will do well on your land." He paused and drew a deep breath of the crisp air. "I can see myself living here forever." He leaped lightly across steppingstones to the other side of the creek where he intently studied the old fruit tree.

"And why not?" Jill watched him examine the ancient tree trunk. "You've developed the farm. In time, the harvest will provide the funds necessary to maintain the land." She looked away hurriedly, worried she'd said too much.

Tim turned from his inspection, his eyes clouded. "But the stage income surely allows a living, right?"

A frown creased Jill's features as she faced Tim. She shook her head. "Not really. We did well in the summer when travel peaked. But we make nothing when stage travel falls off." She shrugged. "We get by. And things will get busy again, come spring."

Tim straightened. "You mean we are barely hanging on."

Jill smiled, wanting to allay the concerned look in his eyes. "If I get a teaching position back east, I will make enough to keep the farm operating until harvest."

"That could take years," Tim said in a quiet voice. "I don't want to see you leave."

"Perhaps there is another way." Jill glanced at the skittering clouds in the steel gray sky. Wind moaned across the hills, reminding her winter gripped the prairies in an icy hand. She shivered, concentrating on the cold around her, attempting to ease her anxieties.

"Another way?" Tim squinted at her.

Jill shrugged again and tried to grin, not wanting to think of Lieutenant Alcott while she spent time with Tim. They'd become good friends, especially now that his defensive walls had crumbled after accepting Christ. She didn't want to think of the Yankee officer in his blue uniform and inappropriate glances. True, Lieutenant Alcott was handsome, but so was Tim. She'd even come to appreciate his beard.

As if struck by lightning, Jill felt her eyes bulge. What was she thinking? She and Tim were merely good friends. She shook her head hurriedly, but the observant farmer across the stream titled his head.

"Another way?" he persisted, demanding a response.

But Jill didn't want to think any more about the lieutenant. With a shout, she leaped for the rocks in the middle of the current, teetering precariously on one foot as her other shoe swayed in the air, seeking balance. Giggling nervously, she put out her arms to steady her footing, but she felt her dangerous position waver.

"Jump," Tim encouraged from the other bank. He'd stepped to the edge of the stream and held a hand to her. "Jump," he urged with a laugh.

Her shifty plan with Lieutenant Alcott forgotten, Jill giggled again as she sprang for the opposite bank. She squealed when Tim grasped her hand and pulled her to safety. But she stopped laughing when she stumbled and crashed into Tim, his strong arms encircling her slim waist as he held her close.

For a moment, they looked at one another, their faces only inches apart. A gleam shone in his eyes she'd seen before but couldn't identify. When butterflies swarmed in her stomach, she glanced away, blinking as she straightened.

Tim mumbled an apology under his breath while Jill smoothed her dress. A gust of bitter cold wind blustered around the secluded cove, and Tim leaped back across the stream, seeming to want distance between them.

Eyes downcast, she followed, this time stepping easily across the stones to the other side. Walking in silence, the pair hurried back to the warmth of the big house.

"There's something funny about Tim lately," Jill whispered as she and Reyna watched the farmer retreat to the barn. Steam wafted from the mug of coffee he carried across the yard. When he vanished into the squat structure, Jill turned to Reyna. "I know you know," Jill accused. "Tell me."

Reyna shrugged and sipped her coffee, her gaze darting to the empty kitchen.

"You taunt me but won't explain," Jill pouted, begging Reyna once more to spill the beans. Sometimes, Tim seemed so far away, deep in thought. Other times, he showed her such attention, drinking in their friendship, and making Jill feel relaxed and special in his company.

Reyna shook her head. "The Spirit is working. God's timing is perfect. Wait on the Lord," she cautioned.

Jill narrowed her eyes at the young girl. "So cryptic." She tilted her head. "What do you know?" But Reyna only shrugged again.

Yet, not comprehending Tim's clandestine behavior didn't keep her from spending all the time together they could find. Their friendship grew as the short winter days passed. Gathering firewood now seemed fun instead of a chore as the pair tramped the frozen woods along the river, chasing one another with snowballs. The duo endured trips to town in the bitter wind, bundled into the sled and covered with the buffalo robes the Arapahoe had given them as the team plowed through snowdrifts. Inclement weather could not dampen Tim and Jill's high spirits.

With an unfamiliar joy in his company, Jill realized Tim had become her best friend.

"Today, I'll hitch Lila," he announced one day in early March. Winter refused to release hold on the frozen plains, and spring was still far off. "We don't need the sled to go to town. Most of the snow has melted." Tim winked at Jill before he left the living room to trudge to the barn, kicking at the tenacious, low snow ridges that ribbed the front yard like creamy butter.

Reyna watched him go before turning to Jill. "He's a good man. I met Uncle Tim less than a year ago, after I left Africa and came to the States, but I've come to appreciate him the more I get to know him."

Jill nodded, a slow grin creasing her face. "I know what you mean. He's good company. I've never had a friend like him."

Reyna smiled, her blue eyes twinkling as she sipped her coffee. "Patience and prayer, me mother always said. God's timing is perfect."

Jill scowled at the young girl's puzzling words as she shrugged into her coat and joined Tim.

As they rolled across the frozen Platte, the shallow water solid as stone, Jill studied the path through the woods. Bare branches pointed at her as Lila tugged the small cart up the opposite bank, the forest enveloping them once more, cutting off the biting wind. She wondered again about the man who'd carved this trail in the woods, the man who had traded the land deed to her father for travel supplies. Her father had come to believe he'd been taken in by a smooth talking, scheming customer, but Jill knew God had masterfully maneuvered this land to her. Her heart threatened to burst with joy as she looked at Tim, laughing at his chilled cheeks and red nose. Then she recalled her constant dilemma, and she stilled, her thoughts swirling with possibilities, none of which appealed to her anymore.

"Why so quiet?" Tim glanced at her as the half wagon left the woods behind and followed the road to Fort Kearny.

"Just thinking," Jill confessed softly.

"A penny for your thoughts," Tim pressed, but Jill shook her head, suddenly too upset to speak.

She realized she needed answers. What was God doing? Jill wished she knew his plan for her. Would a letter come from Mr. Hopkins soon, or would she be forced to speak with Lieutenant Alcott? Either way, the security and safety of her friends seemed paramount, and she wanted to protect their place on the farm. They deserved everything she could do for them, no matter the price. Jill would not think about herself. She was through being selfish.

Tim allowed Jill to muddle silently with her worries, and soon the outbuildings of town loomed on the bleak landscape. Jill averted her gaze when they passed the military buildings, the wagon slowing as they approached the general store.

Mr. Billings greeted them as the bell rang over the door. "Tim, how are you?" The storekeeper's eyes widened when he saw the little half wagon through the window. "Samuel sure did a good job on that contraption. Every time I see it, I tell folks what condition it was in when you bought it." He turned to his guests. "Miss Foster, you're looking lovely on this winter day."

While the pair huddled near the potbellied stove, Mr. Billings gathered the needed supplies from the shelves, piling them on the counter.

"Better order seeds soon, if you plan on a garden this year," the storekeeper advised as he bustled to fill their order. "Better beat the rush, you don't want to come up short." He chuckled to himself and reached for a sack of flour, then hesitated. Mr. Billings scratched his bald head as he faced Jill. "Oh, Miss Foster, I almost forgot. A letter arrived a few days ago for you. I almost gave it to Lieutenant Alcott to deliver as I know he is always ready for an excuse to visit Peach Tree Farm." Mr. Billings's eyebrows arched as he grinned at Jill.

She glanced sheepishly at the bearded farmer beside her. Tim glowered and shoved his hands into his pockets.

NEBRASKA HAVEN

Ignoring the storekeeper's insinuation, Jill accepted the envelope from Mr. Billings, her hand trembling. She could feel her stomach knot as she turned the letter over and studied the address, written in a strong hand. Her breath caught in her throat when she read Mr. Hopkins's name.

Mr. Billings turned to Tim and continued. "I must admit, I've been knocked off my pins by this war news going around, I've had a hard time keeping things straight. I plumb forgot about your letter until I saw you."

Tim stepped forward. "War news?"

Jill glanced nervously at Tim and then thrust the unopened letter into her pocket as Mr. Billings nodded. "Yes, sir. As you know, I'm a Jayhawker from Kansas, never had any use for those slave holders across the border. Well, Mr. Lincoln announced the worst kind of news for them. Made me smile, it did. I tell you, I'll bet those Johnny Rebs will think twice about pushing this war further. There's no reason to keep fighting now."

Tim frowned at Jill and then tilted his head. "Mr. Billings, what are you talking about?"

"Oh, see what I mean? I can't keep anything straight. The president signed a new law, the Emancipation Proclamation he calls it. It says all the slaves are free, except the ones in the Border States and the Southern states already conquered by the Union army. He says if the Confederacy thinks they have the right to leave the Union, he has the right to end slavery."

Jill caught Tim's arm and squeezed as her heart swelled with excitement. "What about Samuel? Is slavery really over?"

Tim scowled and shook his head. "This will actually do nothing to end slavery. Do you think the Confederates will simply release their slaves because Lincoln says they're free? He has to win the war first before he can proclaim anything."

Jill felt a shiver run down her arms, making her hands tingle. Dark spots swam before her eyes, and she leaned against the counter as she looked from Tim to Mr. Billings and back again, desperately wanting to hear good news. Was it real? Had slavery ended? How did this unexpected news affect her plans for the farm? Previously, she never considered slavery, but with her father's final wish and Samuel's friendship, she now hoped the wicked institution were over.

Mr. Billings scratched his head again. "Well, Tim, I don't rightly know. You could be right. Perhaps the president must win the war to make this stick. But I hear England is not pleased with the turn of events. There's talk they will no longer support the South, despite their need for cotton."

Jill couldn't breathe. She steeled herself and forced a deep breath, trying to fill her lungs. Was slavery over? Was God answering her prayers? Perhaps she could stay in Nebraska with her friends. She certainly had no desire now to return to the South, although she would do what it took to help Tim, Reyna, and Samuel.

She pressed the letter in her pocket, realizing she might even now possess some of the answers she sought. But then, out the window, she saw Lieutenant Alcott, striding toward the general store. His hands were tucked deeply into his dark blue overcoat as he hurried across the barren parade ground toward her.

"I need some air," Jill whispered to Tim as she hastened to meet the Yankee officer on the front porch.

CHAPTER 42

Jill closed the door behind her and tugged her collar higher as she watched Lieutenant Alcott approach. She'd hoped to have a more opportune moment alone with the officer, to clarify his intentions, but there was no time to waste. She needed answers now. Things were progressing faster than she'd expected. Perhaps Mr. Hopkins's letter in her pocket would give her direction, but she viewed the lieutenant's abrupt appearance as a sign from above, and she wouldn't let the opportunity slip away.

"Lieutenant Alcott." Jill waved to the Yankee. He looked up and smiled, quickening his pace. With a chuckle, he ascended the few steps to stand before her.

She studied his strong profile as he glanced over his shoulder to the military buildings behind him. He *was* handsome, but she detected something in his manner that bothered her, and she needed to wheedle it to the surface now, before it was too late.

"Good morning, Miss Foster," he greeted warmly, taking her hand in his and pressing firmly. "It is good to see you in town today. I saw you pass headquarters and wanted to inform you I'd be leading a patrol to Peach Tree Farm later this afternoon. What could induce you to brave these frigid winds this morning?"

A brisk wind did sweep from the north, and Jill snuggled deeper into her coat. But the weather was the least of her concerns just now.

Jill shifted, wondering how to begin. "Lieutenant, I believe spring is on the horizon. Surely this bitter winter cannot last forever. And I wonder about your plans."

He arched his eyebrows. "Plans? What do you mean?"

"Well, you know the army is gathering promising young officers for the fight back east. I wondered if you'd heard any rumors."

Alcott stroked his chin with a gloved hand. "Yes, yes, I see what you mean." He glanced over his shoulder once more before leaning closer to Jill and lowering his voice. "Well, I suspect a well-positioned officer could not help but be noticed." He stared at her shrewdly, nodding. "I think we understand each other perfectly, Miss Foster, or should I say Jill?"

Her brows bunched at his forward use of her name, but she was in no position to stand on ceremony now. She recalled with distaste the inappropriate glances she'd endured from this Yankee, but he was from the north, and little proper behavior could be expected from such a man. Yet he was of the gentleman class, the only one in the region, and she was a lady. Their connection seemed obvious.

"What do you mean?" She wanted to hear him say something gallant or romantic, but her shoulders sagged when she remembered he was just a Yankee.

Alcott licked his chapped lips, his moustache dancing. Jill could not ignore the gleam in his eyes as he studied her. "I mean to ask permission to court you," he said as he smiled broadly. He gestured around the small stoop in front of the general store. "This was not the place I intended to reveal my desires, yet the time seems right."

He straightened, standing at attention as he continued. "I am an officer and a gentleman. You are a lady. We are a perfect match. I always wanted to marry a beautiful woman who would help bolster my career. With you by my side, I have no doubts Regimental Command would take notice. With luck, I could be posted on the battlefields by summer, where I intend on distinguishing myself with bravery and gallantry." He paused, then grinned. "If we hurry."

Jill shook her head, dismayed at his improper proposal. But what had she expected? They would make a dashing couple. Yet Lieutenant Alcott lacked everything Jill wanted in a mate. She'd never examined those particular qualities until now, but when she imagined a husband—her husband—she pictured someone like ... well, someone like Tim.

As if a curtain had been torn away to reveal the truth, as if scales dropped from her eyes, Jill saw clearly she wanted Tim. He'd become more than her best friend, and she suddenly wanted more than friendship with him.

Staring at the lieutenant, lips parted, Jill shook her head again. "I'm sorry," she stammered. "Forgive me if I gave you the wrong impression, but I do not want to marry you. I, uh, I do not wish you to pursue me, sir. I have ever only wanted a cordial relationship with you and all the soldiers at Fort Kearny. Forgive me. Have a good day."

Not waiting for a reply, she hurried back into the store. Jill peered furtively out the window to see if the officer followed, but Alcott scowled at the closed door and then turned, making his way slowly back toward the military buildings strewn around the parade ground.

"What are you looking at?" Tim's unexpected query made her jump.

Jill spun to face him, but she was unable to reply as her gaze roamed his bearded face, his strong jaw, his high cheekbones. His broad shoulders had always impressed her, but now she saw why, and she smiled, seeing the handsome farmer in a new light.

"I—I—" Jill faltered, staring into his piercing eyes as if she'd never seen him before.

Mr. Billings handed Tim a package and peered at Jill. "Like I was telling Tim, I'll wager 1863 will be an exciting year for the North. Yes, sir, I see great things for the Union," Mr. Billings predicted as he ushered them to the front door.

He waved as Tim helped Jill to the dray. She blushed furiously as he tucked the robes around her, his nearness making her feel sensations she'd never realized. Now, as if everything had fallen into clarity, she saw Tim for who he was.

How could she have been so naïve? So blind? All his subtle attentions now seemed obvious, as if she couldn't see them before.

Her gaze followed him as he walked around the mare and jumped into the cart. With a slap of the reins, Tim clucked to Lila, and the pony leaned into the harness. A cold wind blew from the north, a brisk gust threatening to work loose Jill's hair. She pressed a hand to her bonnet while secretly wishing the frigid air would cool her heated cheeks.

She glanced at Tim from the corner of her eye, realizing she'd felt something deep for him for weeks. Unnamed and unfamiliar, she now saw it plainly, and she trembled.

As the dray passed the parade ground, Jill glanced over to the headquarters building. Lieutenant Alcott stood at the railing, talking with a pair of suited strangers and other soldiers. Jill's cheeks heated even more, and she looked away, not wanting to see the army officer again.

"He didn't even wave," Tim mumbled.

"He must be busy," Jill suggested, then chided herself for defending the officer's lack of courtesy.

They followed the road along the river, the frozen Platte concealed behind a thick stand of woods, small ridges of snow straddling the skeletal arms of the trees. Jill gazed at the bleak forest, her thoughts whirling, as Tim guided the horse.

"I know you like him."

Tim's muttered comment made Jill focus, drawing herself from her chaotic thoughts. She stared at him, seeing him as now she thought of him, the man she loved.

How had this happened? For so long, for months now, she'd seen his thoughtfulness, his concern and protectiveness, but never considered he'd impact her heart as he'd done. She saw clearly now that Tim Hunter—although no gentleman—was the man for her.

She glanced at him. "Excuse me?"

Tim waved. "That army officer, Alcott. I see the way you look at him. And I sure see the way he looks at you."

His bitter words made Jill cringe. "No, Tim, you are mistaken. There is nothing between the lieutenant and me. However ..." She paused and looked away. "He did ask to court me today."

Tim flicked the reins over Lila's back, making the pony quicken. "I knew it," he muttered. "That blue devil has had his eye on you for months." He peered at Jill where she sat gripping the buffalo robe, her gaze fixed on Lila. "What'd you tell him?"

Jill nodded. "Like I said, there's nothing between us. I told him no."

Tim chuckled and pulled on the reins, slowing the pony once more. "Served him right, the pompous fool. He's no man for you, Jill."

She glanced at Tim once more. *You're right*, she thought, *because you are the man for me.* Why hadn't she seen it before? Why had God kept this realization from her as their friendship grew? Jill pursed her lips.

She recalled Samuel's words. The Lord knew what he was doing. Had God brought her all the way out here, to these desolate prairies, to reveal her shallow character? Was she here to learn the depths of her lack of wisdom? Alcott, the man she supposed to be a gentleman and the man for her, paled now in comparison to this hardworking farmer who sat beside her. How could she be such a fool?

"Did you hear what Mr. Billings said?" Tim tugged his gloves on snugger.

Jill tried to concentrate, wanting to ponder her new awareness but needing to be alone in her room for that. She exhaled slowly, recalling the storekeeper's comments. Then she narrowed her eyes, remembering. "Is it true? What do you make of it?"

Tim's brow puckered. "I heard about this last fall. I thought it was an idle threat. Last September, Lincoln said that if the Confederacy didn't return to the Union by January, he'd free their slaves. But Jill, it doesn't apply to Kentucky or even Missouri. Samuel is still an escaped slave, hiding from bounty hunters."

Jill clenched her teeth. "But Samuel *is* free in Nebraska. Surely no one will come way out here for him, right? Maybe the war will end soon."

"The North has successfully bottled the Confederacy, with only an occasional blockade runner slipping through the Union Navy, but the South has proven themselves tough soldiers. If the Union can hold out, they might choke off the South, starve them from both food and military supplies. Especially if England decides to withdraw their support."

He glanced at her. "I don't know how this will affect Samuel. Total abolition is a lofty ideal."

When he saw Jill's concern, he patted her arm. "He's probably safe on the farm." He grunted and slowed the wagon to a halt.

Jill looked at him, confused at the stop. "What's wrong?"

Tim wrapped the reins around the brake handle and tugged off his gloves. "You got a letter from back east today, didn't you?"

Jill nodded, eyes widening.

He gestured at her unseen pocket beneath the buffalo robe. "Well, let's see what it says."

CHAPTER 43

Lila pounded an impatient hoof on the frozen turf, wanting to get home and sensing the barn's nearness. But Tim and Jill didn't move. Jill knew the letter from Mr. Hopkins probably told of a teaching position back east. Why else would the headmaster write?

She could feel her heart pound slowly, like a funeral dirge. With a deep breath, she finally reached under the robe and retrieved the letter. She stared at the envelope, her hands quivering, until Tim broke the awkward silence.

"Is it from him?"

Jill nodded, still gripping the letter. Suddenly, she was filled with terror. Today, she'd realized she loved this godly farmer. Today, she'd refused the attentions of Lieutenant Alcott. And now, today, she'd received a letter from Mr. Hopkins. Why were things moving so quickly? What was the Lord doing?

"Open it," Tim urged, nudging her with an elbow.

Jill drew another deep breath and tore the letter open. Scanning quickly, she read the enclosed note, solidifying her fears. The hoped for, longed for information did not provide the peace she'd expected. If only she'd received this letter yesterday, before she knew her heart's desire.

She looked at Tim, a tear sliding down her chilled cheek. "I can't. I can't, Tim. I thought I could go back and work, but not now."

He narrowed his eyes. "Does he have a job for you?"

Jill nodded. "Yes. In New York. A college for young ladies."

Tim shrugged. "Well, they need manners more than most."

Jill laughed, still crying, and punched his shoulder. "I'm being serious here. My heart is breaking, and you're making jokes."

He took her hands in his and stared into her eyes. "Tell me what you're thinking."

She shuddered, but not from the cold of the frozen day. She trembled from the touch of his hands, the warmth of his nearness, and the kindness in his eyes.

"We need money," she blurted. "There's none left. The stage contract helps, but it's not enough for four people. And the farm won't produce a harvest for years. I even wondered if I could marry the lieutenant to save the farm, but I can't. I thought if I got a teaching job, perhaps I could send money back here, to Nebraska."

She dropped her head, unable to go on. But Tim put a finger under her chin and lifted her face once more. His encouraging grin allowed her to continue.

"I want my friends to stay and be safe," she whispered. "I want to do the unselfish thing and serve my friends."

Slowly, he cupped her face with his bare hands, his smile broadening. "You're the sweetest, kindest person I know, Jill Foster." Then he kissed her.

Their lips molded softly, gently caressing as Jill leaned into him. She loved this man. His beard tickled, but she refused to pull away, enjoying the sensation as he pressed against her. His hands slid around her waist and embraced her in a tight hold as she wrapped her arms around his neck.

After a long moment, she withdrew, embarrassed at her boldness. She'd kissed Tim Hunter, the farmer. He wasn't a gentleman in the strictest definition of the word, but he was truly a gentleman in his soul. Caring and kind, a man who pursued the Lord. Jill could ask for nothing more.

She peered up at him and touched her fingertips to her still warm lips. "I love you," she whispered.

"I love you," Tim said softly.

Her eyes widened, and then she smiled, remembering Reyna's covert hints. "How long have you known?"

Tim shifted and tugged the buffalo robe higher. "I've known for months. I suspect Reyna knew too. She'd give me a look when she caught me staring at you." He paused, and then went on. "When did you realize your feelings for me?"

"Today, at the creek." She shook her head. "No, after that, at the store." When she read the confusion in his eyes, Jill laughed. "I mean I felt something tug at my heart at the creek when you helped me across the water, but at the store, I knew I loved you."

He arched an eyebrow. "At the store?"

Jill nodded, not wanting to explain the lieutenant had been responsible for her discovery. "But now I don't know what to do," she murmured. "I want so desperately to stay here, with you, with Samuel and Reyna. But I've prayed so earnestly for the Lord to provide a way for me to make the necessary money for the farm."

Jill glanced at the surrounding prairie, covered in scant patches of snow with withered grass stems peeking through the occasional drifts. Bleak, barren, and majestic, she'd come to cherish this land. The Lord had brought her to Nebraska, and she didn't want to leave. But she didn't want to be selfish either. To stay might spell disaster for all of them.

"I don't want to go, but I want to honor the Lord. I've prayed for so long." She waved the letter in the air. "This is the answer to that prayer. I must accept this position in New York."

Jill expected some heated argument about her perception of God's provision, but she figured wrong. Tim studied her seriously, then nodded, a grim look on his face.

"You're right," he said at last.

Jill tilted her head. "I am?"

Tim shrugged. "Well, I'm new at this, but I say trust Jesus. If you think this is his answer to your prayer, go with it. I won't allow my personal feelings to interfere. Something else will come up if he wants you to reconsider. But I say obedience brings joy to God."

Jill pursed her lips and then nodded. "Submit to his will. If I'm wrong, he'll show me."

"Or ...," Tim added, "he is observing your obedience and wants to do something unexpected, something you'd never think of. Either way, obey and please the Lord."

Jill pondered as Tim tugged his gloves back on. He leaned suddenly and kissed her cheek, then chuckled. "I could do that forever."

She beamed, feeling radiant after sharing the magic moment with Tim. But her heart felt like a stone in her chest as the dilemma weighed heavily on her. Then she calmed, resolved to do what she thought was best. For her, for her friends, for God. If she was mistaken, the Lord would show her.

"Please, Father, show me in a way I can understand. Let me be sensitive to the Holy Spirit. If I am to go away, I will. But speak clearly, and let my heart discern wisely and correctly. I want to please you. Your will be done," she whispered to herself.

With a cluck of his tongue, Tim allowed the cold horse to continue. The dray lurched as Jill stared straight ahead, submissive, willing to obey whatever the Lord determined.

If she had to accept the teaching position back east, she would obey and do her best. She smiled when she thought of Reyna. "Work unto the Lord," the young girl would say. And Jill promised she would.

CHAPTER 44

After crossing the frozen river, the little dray rolled through the leafless forest until they burst into the clearing. Jill and Tim exchanged worried glances when they saw a military patrol lounging around the barn, a cluster of men standing on the front porch.

"Oh, no," Jill groaned.

"What is it?" Tim narrowed his eyes as they approached the waiting men.

"Lieutenant Alcott told me in town he would lead a patrol out here this afternoon. I forgot until now."

"What does he want?" Tim growled as they pulled up to the porch.

Lila heaved, clouds of steam rising from her muzzle as Jill hurried from the half wagon. She shot Tim a conspirator's grin when she thought of the kiss they'd shared in the little cart, then she scowled as she faced the lieutenant. Their last meeting had not gone so well.

The lieutenant glared at Tim. But Jill was stony-faced as she stepped to the army officer. "Lieutenant Alcott, I didn't see you pass us on the road. How did you get here before us?"

Alcott continued to watch Tim from sight as the farmer drove the dray to the barn. "With the river frozen, we were able to use the ford nearer the fort," he explained. Jill noticed he refused to meet her eyes. "But we have business with you." He gestured to the two suited strangers beside him. They were the same men Jill had seen at the fort when they'd left town. "May we come in?"

"Of course," Jill replied, only too eager to get inside and near the fire. She led the way through the entry to the spacious living room where a blaze roared in the huge stone fireplace. Jill shivered as she stepped to the flames, turned her back, and faced her guests.

"I'm sorry to rush to the fire, gentleman, before proper introductions, but I'm half frozen," Jill chuckled as the three other men moved into the room. "Now, sir, who are your companions?"

The two suited men stepped forward to shake hands as Alcott spoke from behind them. "This is Mr. Clark and Mr. Manning. I have the privilege of guiding these surveyors over their chosen route, and we have come to discuss some important matters with you."

Jill gestured to the chairs, indicating the men should take seats while Reyna served coffee. Tim entered quietly, catching Jill's eye before accepting a steaming mug from his niece. He moved to a seat at the kitchen table, near enough to hear everything without intruding. His presence calmed her, and Jill thrilled at sight of him, thankful for his nearness.

"Important matters?" Jill echoed as she shrugged out of her coat. "With me?"

Alcott nodded and pointed to Mr. Manning, the younger of the two, who smiled agreeably as he tasted his coffee and then brushed at something unseen on his coat before tasting one of Reyna's baked goods.

"Cakes," he exclaimed, shaking his head. "Who would've believed this wild frontier would allow for such delicacies?"

NEBRASKA HAVEN

"Or for such lovely ladies," Clark added, his eyes on Jill. "We had no idea women of quality were this far west, Miss Foster."

"Gentlemen, as you can see, Peach Tree Farm holds many surprises," Jill said, smiling warmly, then squinted, studying the businessmen. Alcott said they were surveyors. Out here? Probably something to do with the stage line. If so, she would do everything in her power to impress them.

She nodded discreetly at Reyna, a secret message passing between the two women. Reyna nodded in return, as if she understood Jill's meaning. The young girl completed her rounds with the platter of treats and retreated to the kitchen, her auburn hair bunched stylishly above the nape of her neck. Jill smiled when she saw Reyna stop beside her uncle.

Lieutenant Alcott turned to his companions. "Didn't I say you would be pleasantly surprised with Peach Tree Station? It boasts the best food west of St. Louis." He shot Jill a searching glance, as if to ask her to reconsider his offer. She narrowed her eyes, apparently unmoved. Alcott cleared his throat and lowered his gaze.

Jill draped her coat around a chair and seated herself near the open fireplace, facing her guests with Tim in her line of view. She lifted the cup Reyna had served her, watching the visitors over the rim of the mug as she sipped the hot drink.

"Tell me, gentlemen, to what do I owe this honor? What brings you to our little corner of Nebraska Territory?" She shot Tim a quick glance. He crossed his arms over his chest and watched the intruders with a skeptical eye.

Mr. Manning rubbed crumbs from his fingers and leaned forward. "Miss Foster, we are commissioned by the United States Army to survey a route across the plains for a railroad."

"A railroad?" Jill echoed, her head tilting. Mr. Billings had said something similar, and she'd all but laughed at his confident speech. The wagon master, Bridgett, had said something about trains crossing the plains one day too. Could it be true?

"Yes, a railroad," Mr. Clark spoke up, casting an annoyed look at his younger partner. Manning dropped his gaze, a sheepish look on his face.

"We've been surveying a route from Omaha west," Mr. Clark continued. "And we have discovered a ridge of hills running north to south, blocking our path. Amazingly, the lieutenant showed us a gap through these hills, a gap that is on your property."

He paused to sip his coffee. When he had swallowed the hot brew, he continued. "Currently, the emigrant trail uses the pass. We were unaware that anyone owned this prairie land, but the lieutenant assured us you do indeed hold title to this parcel of land that includes this pass through the hills."

Jill nodded, not understanding the significance of her land ownership and the gap that allowed westward traffic to parallel the river. Railroads? Surveyors? What did this have to do with her?

The younger surveyor, Manning, leaned forward again, ignoring Clark's glare as he spoke. "Miss Foster, in plain language, we are interested in purchasing the right of way on your land. The government is prepared to pay handsomely for the pass through the hills that the emigrant trail already follows. It would save a tremendous amount of construction if we could avoid having to demolition a route through those hills or go all the way 'round. In short, if you are willing to sell a portion of your land, you will become a wealthy woman."

Jill sat back in her seat, stunned. Her gaze sought Tim, watched him, studied him for a clue. What should she do?

Tim rose slowly to his feet and stood directly behind Lieutenant Alcott. His eyes gleamed, a triumphant grin on his bearded face Jill couldn't comprehend. What was he smiling at?

"Of course, we will need to see the deed," Clark said, shifting beside the lieutenant.

Jill stood, eager to comply with an easy request. With a trembling smile, she cast Tim a glance before entering the unheated hallway. The chill enveloped her immediately, but she ignored the cold, not even bothering to steal a peek at her reflection in the mirror before pushing her bedroom door open. The rumpled land deed rested on a shelf above the small desk. She held the wrinkled paper, glancing at its familiar writing without really seeing the document.

She imagined her father taking the worthless land in trade for supplies over a year ago, a soldier from Fort Kearny probably believing he'd hoodwinked the naïve shopkeeper. A faint grin tugged at the corner of her lips. Perhaps her father was no fool after all.

Tears stung her eyes at his memory and Jill blinked, clearing her vision as she stared at the document that had launched her across the prairie to this lonely farm. Lonely? Her grin widened. No, not lonely. She'd found friends along the way. And love.

Despite the frigid air, a warm glow sparked in her chest, and she sensed an unseen presence. Quivering with excitement, she looked up at the ceiling. "Lord, what are you doing? As if this day couldn't get stranger. You have shown me how I love Tim, Lieutenant Alcott is a man I could never marry, and Mr. Hopkins has offered me a position in New York," she whispered, trying to calm her racing mind.

Her gaze darted around the Spartan room, searching, seeking. Then, unbidden, images flashed across her mind. The closing of the ladies school in Paducah. Samuel. Her parents' funeral. The trek from Missouri. Finally, the wide, shallow river with its brown water and wooded banks, unimpressive and yet incredibly significant.

"You brought me here," she said softly, nodding in recognition. "You are with me, aren't you, Jesus?"

Her thoughts darted to Tim. Unimpressive like the river, until she got to know him. She smiled with realization. "Is everything a lesson to teach me? Tim is not the gentleman I sought, and yet he is so much more. Back in Paducah, you knew I needed a change before I did. My life was moving in the wrong direction. Through disappointment, sorrow, and unexpected joy, you've worked to bring me to Nebraska, to develop my faith. And now you've blessed me more than I can comprehend. I'm so happy. Teach me, Lord. Shape my heart with your hands. Give me patience and trust to wait on you, to watch you work. Grow me into the person I should be. For you."

A tear slid down her cheek, and Jill swiped at the drop with the back of her hand. Her emotions seemed to be running away with her today. She lifted her chin when she recalled she was sent to retrieve the land deed she now held. Surely her guests waited on her. Her trembles subsided as she returned to the living room, her feelings in check once more.

"Well, gentlemen," Jill said as she presented the land title to Mr. Clark. "This is very unexpected news indeed. I would like a little time to pray about this matter. Perhaps I could provide a definitive decision in a day or two."

Mr. Clark scanned the document before handing the paper back to her. With a grunt, he stood. "Of course, Miss Foster. Take a week to think about our offer. We'll come back this way by then. But not too much time," he warned, smiling. "The railroad will not be put off for long. If you will not sell, a new route will have to be located or possible sites for demolition will be scouted."

Mr. Manning rose hastily, thanking Jill for her hospitality before following his colleague from the room. With a dour glance at Jill, Alcott accompanied them.

Tim and Samuel walked with the visitors as they stepped onto the porch, a cold wind whistling outside as the door closed behind them. Through the window, Jill watched the men mount their horses.

"Well?" Reyna stood at Jill's elbow, a curious glint in her blue eyes.

Jill quirked an eyebrow. "Well, what?"

Reyna nudged her. "Come on. You can't fool me. Something happened in town. Uncle Tim can't keep his eyes off you."

Emotion swelled anew, and Jill gripped Reyna's hands. "He said he loves me."

Reyna squealed. "Well, it's about time. But patience is prudent."

"What's that mean?" Jill studied the young girl thoughtfully.

"Do not awaken love before its time," Reyna quoted from the Scriptures. "It means the Lord brought you together, but faith and spiritual maturity need time to grow. The Lord promises to complete every good work he has begun." She tilted her head. "What did you tell Uncle Tim?"

Jill's smile broadened, her heart expanding in her chest. "I love him so much, Reyna. I didn't know how much, until today." She squinted at the Irish girl. "Tim thinks you knew about his love before he did, certainly before I did."

Reyna laughed as she moved about the room, gathering empty cups. "All in God's timing."

"His perfect timing," Jill agreed softly.

Hooves clattered on the frozen ground as the visitors rode from the clearing. Tim and Samuel entered the room, hurrying to the fireplace to warm themselves.

Tim rubbed his hands, his gaze fixed on Jill. "Well, you cannot deny the Lord's provision. With the sale of that northern piece of land, you'll have plenty of money to refuse Mr. Hopkins's offer. The farm is saved." His eyes glowed. "You don't have to leave. You can stay here, with me."

At Reyna's and Samuel's blank looks, Jill stepped to Tim's side. No one seemed surprised when the farmer slipped a hand around her slim waist. "I received a letter from Mr. Hopkins today," she explained, feeling the heat creep to her cheeks, nonetheless. "Offering me a position at a school in New York."

"You mean you considered moving back east?" Samuel's eyes were large as he stared at Jill.

She shrugged. "I have you to thank for such considerations. You have taught me much of selfless action. I was a spoiled, selfish girl when we met. Now, because of your influence"—her eyes darted to Reyna—"and Reyna's, I wanted to be more like Christ. I wanted to serve my friends above my own desires."

"So now we can stay here, in Nebraska, all of us together?" Samuel's gaze rested on each of his companions in turn.

"Yes." Tim laughed when he saw the bright color in Jill's cheeks. Smiling, he bent to kiss her heated skin. "For now, we will focus on what's best. For the farm, for our future, and ..." he paused, peering into her startled eyes. "And for us."

Samuel tossed another log on the fire and straightened, drawing in a deep breath. "I love this place. Nebraska has become my home."

Jill nodded, blinking against the tears that brimmed her eyes. She glanced up at Tim and nodded again. "I never thought this land would become my permanent home. Now I cannot think of a better place than our Nebraska haven.

God's ways have certainly surprised me, in more ways than one. Here, we will build our future."

"The Lord has answered our prayers, Jill," Reyna said as she moved to the kitchen to retrieve the coffeepot and clean mugs.

"Well, for now, the stage will continue," Tim said as he accepted a steaming cup from his niece. "In time, this new railroad will replace the stage. Change is inevitable." He glanced at Samuel. "But folks will always need produce. This farm will provide a good living."

Jill rested a hand on Samuel's arm. "For all of us."

He grinned as he looked at Jill. "Did you ever think this was possible, Miss Jill, when we were in St. Louis? The Lord has brought us a long way."

No longer able to stem the flow of emotion, tears cascaded from her stinging eyes, spilling down her cheeks. Joy swept over her in a wave. God had performed mighty works in her life this past year. Not only in her heart but in those around her. For the first time in many years, she was surrounded by friends who loved her for who she was, not for her social standing or her acquaintances.

Jill sighed deeply, content. God had encircled her with love and support she never expected. Life rarely turned out the way she planned but had a way of being better when following the Lord's plan, allowing him to lead.

She sniffled and blinked again. "I guess all things are possible with God."

Her breath caught in her throat when Tim pulled her into a tight embrace, and she peered up at the bearded farmer. A small giggle escaped her as she studied the man the Lord had brought to her, better than any gentleman.

"I love you, Tim," she whispered for the second time that day. Jill giggled again with nervous anticipation as Tim pressed his lips to hers.

ABOUT THE AUTHOR

Andrew Roth served in the U.S. Army before attending California State University, Bakersfield. He taught American History for twenty-two years at the middle school level before launching his literary career. Married for over thirty years to his wife, Laurie, Andrew has two married adult children and is a proud grandfather. A native of Kansas, he was raised with a deep love and appreciation for history, particularly the Old West. Andrew's hope is to glorify God and encourage readers through his writing.

Made in the USA
Coppell, TX
27 April 2023

16146641R00203